A HERO WILL RISE!

THE

MOUSE THAT ROARED

NOVEL BY

DWAYNE MURRAY, SR.

FR
(9)

MAY 2011

Published By

Madbo Enterprises
1444 East Gunhill Road, Suite #32
Bronx, New York 10469
Telephone: (917) 682-3693
Website: WWW.MADBOENTERPRISES.COM
Email Address: DEE64MAN@AOL.COM

Warning!
This is a novel of fiction. All the characters, incidents and dialogue are products of the Author's imagination and are not real. Any references or similarities to actual events, people, living or dead, or to locales are intended to give the story a sense of reality. Similarities in names, characters, entities, places and incidents are purely coincidental.

Cover Design/Graphics/Photography: Marion Designs
Email Address: MARIONDESIGNS@BELLSOUTH.NET

Model: Heather Johns

Printing Company: Latonya Pegues of Technical Communication Services.

Dedication

I dedicate this work to my loving wife Angie who stood by me, encouraged me, supported me and loved me from the first to the last letter. I love you and I am truly blessed to have you in my corner. Thank you for loving me.

Acknowledgements

First and foremost, I want to thank my **Savior Jesus Christ** for giving me the strength to complete this endeavor. It was His Grace that made this all possible.

To my wife **Angie**, "Baby, You know the deal and nothing more needs to be said."

To my son **Dwayne Jr.,** while I sat at that computer hour after hour, day after day, "Thanks!" for keeping me updated on all the games I was not able to watch on television. You were my personal "ESPN" newscaster.

To my son **Daniel**, who had no mercy and played hard with me in basketball in the backyard. It was much needed leisure time to unwind after writing. Just one thing, "Danny, have mercy on your old man!"

To my mom **Christine**, who always believed in me and encouraged me to pursue my writing. "Thanks Ma!"

To my belated grandmother **Esther**, who would be so proud of me. I know if she was still with us, she would call me 3-4 times a day to see if I was finish with the book. "I miss you grandma."

To my niece **Evelyn**, who spent her whole Saturday reading my book before I sent it to the printer. Thanks for your time, your willingness, your constructive criticism and honesty pertaining to the book. Your input was imperative and I really appreciate your help.

A special thanks to all my extended *family* and *friends* for your love and support. I recognize the importance of each and every one of you and I am blessed to have you all in my life.

Chapter One
The Apple Doesn't Fall Far From Its Tree

It is the summer in the Gunner's muggy Bronx apartment and a nine-year-old, chubby-cheeked boy named Doug is quietly looking through his parent's slightly opened bedroom door. His father is aggressively moving up and down on someone who is not his mother. As Doug continues to look at the moaning individuals under the blue sheets, Fred Gunner quickly turns around catching Doug with his mouth wide open.

"Doug, I'm gonna bust your ass! Get the hell away from this door!" Fred yells.

"I was just looking for mommy to tell her something," responds Doug. Fred, who stands six feet, three inches tall and weighs about one hundred and ninety pounds, jumps out of his bed while dragging a naked Diana Cruz the Gunner's next door neighbor with him. Quickly walking over and opening the blue painted door, Fred reveals a shocked and frightened Doug who has now urinated on himself.

"This look like your momma?" Fred yells. Not getting an answer, Fred reaches down yanking Doug by his gray t-shirt lifting him off the ground and directly in the face of a nervous Diana. "Is this your momma?"

Shaking and sweating with his feet dangling in the air, Doug manages to swallow and answer "No sir" Fred slowly lets his son down as Diana watches in silence.

"Well that means she is not here, so get your ass in your room until I tell you to come out," says Fred. As Doug turns and runs to his room, Fred smacks Diana on her naked backside and directs her back to the bed.

Doug's bedroom; painted with a flat red paint is beginning to chip away in certain areas on the walls. Clothes are all over Doug's dirty floor and white curtains adorn two dirty windows. On Doug's wall is a giant poster of a basketball player. A nineteen-inch television with a metal coat hanger substituting as an antenna shows Tom & Jerry. Quickly removing his wet pants and underwear, Doug scrounges his room for dry ones.

Sitting in a corner of his bedroom at an old wooden desk Doug plays with his 1001 electronic set. As he lights up the small bulbs and makes the bells ring, Fred Gunner violently pushes the bedroom door open, scaring Doug and causing him to jump out of his seat. Fred, relishing this sight, let's a huge grin come across his face.

"You want some ice-cream, boy?" Doug, standing at attention like an army soldier, nod's his head. "What the fuck does that mean?" Fred asks.

Doug's lips begins to quiver before responding, "Yes, sir." Fred, moving to the right side of the door, stares at Doug.

"Bring your ass on then." As the timid Doug walks towards his door, Fred quickly grabs him by the collar, pulling his head towards his face. "What you saw today better stay away from your momma cause if she ever finds out it would kill her and I would kill you."

* * *

It's Friday evening, Margaret Gunner and Doug are sitting on their red velvet couch watching a drunken Fred hold a brush in his hand, pretending as if it was a microphone trying to sing "Ain't Nobody." Reaching into his black dungaree jacket, Fred pulls out a pint of Bacardi rum. Taking a long swig from the bottle, Fred motions to his wife to join him for a dance. Giving her husband a half smile, Margaret jokingly shoos him away. Looking at his wife with a startled look, Fred reaching down to the couch pulls his wife by the wrist towards him causing her to thrash her neck.

"Bitch, when your man tells you to dance, you dance." Squeezing her small wrist tightly, Fred grabs Margaret by the hair and dips her to the floor.

"Fred please, you're hurting me!" She cries. Using her right hand, Margaret is now trying to free herself from his grip.

"Give me some tongue, baby," a sweaty and smelling Fred asks. With pain on her face and her wrist now sporting a bad bruise Margaret pleads with her husband,

"Fred, please...let's go to our bedroom."

With one quick motion, Fred shoves his wife onto the couch and begins to unzip his pants. A now crying Margaret looks at her son standing by the living room entrance in a daze. "Baby, go to your room right now", Margaret says. Looking at his drunken father force himself between his mother's legs, Doug retreats to his bedroom. Putting his ear to his bedroom door, Doug can hear his father's wild moans over the music.

* * *

Saturday afternoon finds Doug dribbling his Spalding basketball on the concrete pavement after leaving the park. Doug waves to some of the neighborhood kids. Most of the children are wearing brand name sneakers like "Puma," "Adidas" and "Converse." One kid in particular named Elvis points at Doug's old worn out "skips." "Hey Doug, tell your drunken ass father to get off his lazy ass and get a job so he can buy your poor ass some new sneakers." As Doug begins to pick up his pace, the kids point at his sneakers and begin to laugh.

* * *

Doug entering his apartment finds his father standing by the door waiting. "Dumb ass, where the hell you been?" asks Fred. Doug, looking past his father into the kitchen at his mother, notices her rubbing her cheek. Fred, getting impatient, snatches his son by the arm, pulling him closer.

A teary-eyed Doug mumbles in a low voice, "I was at the park playing basketball." Fred, still staring at his son, releases and pushes him to the floor.

"Leave him alone, goddammit!" Margaret yells.

A shocked and surprised Fred stares at his wife and asks, "Bitch, you lost your mind?" Margaret who is shaking moves herself in front of her son, shielding him from Fred. Now red-faced, Fred stares down Margaret and Doug, pointing his finger at the both of them saying, "Bitch you ain't shit, that punk ass boy ain't shit and your never gonna be shit, you know why? Cause I ain't shit. If I am going to hell, then your two are going with me." As Fred angrily storms out of his apartment Margaret turns and kneels down to her son

"Doug I will not mince words; I don't know how much I have left in me to take this. You are going to have to learn how to make choices in your life picking and choosing who you follow. Do you understand?"

"Yes I do," says Doug. Margaret could tell by the confusion in her son's eyes that he did not.

* * *

It is Sunday, and the sun is sending down hot summer rays into the crowded park on Valentine Avenue. Basketballs are making clanging sounds off the rim. Men and teenagers alike are yelling for the basketball so they can take the shot. Doug, holding his basketball under his arm wearing his "Magic Johnson" jersey, hopes someone will choose him to play. Looking far-off to the park entrance, Doug can see his secret idol "Dollar Bill" conducting business with his many clients. Doug cannot take his eyes off Dollar Bill's clean, crisp clothes and his always-fresh sneakers, and he always wears a new pair every day. In a dream-like state, Doug drops his basketball and begins to walk towards his icon.

Standing at the top of the steps, Doug is about fifteen feet away from Dollar Bill. He can clearly see the exchange of money for aluminum foil between the clients and Dollar Bill. Taking a deep breath, Doug slowly walks towards Dollar Bill when a huge, dark-skinned brother named "Bucky" grabs Doug by his arm, scaring the living daylights out of him. "What do you want shorty?" asks Bucky.

A wide-eyed Doug barely whispers, "Just to say hello to Dollar Bill." Bucky, who is twenty years old, stands six feet – three inches tall, and weighs about two hundred and forty pounds, looks at his boss for confirmation. Dollar Bill, staring at the young Doug, smiles then, nods to

Bucky, who in turn lets Doug through. As Doug walks toward Dollar Bill, the little boy's hero sticks his hand out grabbing him by the arm, pulling him violently towards him feeling for a weapon or police wire. Not finding anything, Dollar Bill rubs Doug on his head in a playful but serious manner, turning him around to face him. "Shorty, I have six eyes behind my head and I have noticed you have been watching me for the past three weeks, what's up?" asks Dollar Bill.

Doug, mustering up valor, answers as cool as possible: "I just think your dope." Dollar Bill looks at Doug, then at Bucky and then at Doug again, who is now starting to perspire and lets out a colossal laugh that draws some attention from some people sitting on the benches. Dollar Bill hugs a now smiling but still edgy Doug around the neck and pulls him close to his chiseled chest.

"Shorty, do you know what I do in these streets?" asks Dollar Bill.

Doug who is feeling a little more comfortable answers, "You're a businessman." Reaching into his pocket with a smile on his face Dollar Bill pulls out a twenty and places it in the palm of Doug's hand. Staring at the new crisp bill, Doug looks up at Dollar Bill and says, "Thank you."

Dollar Bill pointing across the street points to his new Pontiac Grand Prix and looks back at Doug, "Shorty, tomorrow at noon I expect that car to be shining and looking good, cool?"

Doug, still holding his twenty, joyfully answers "Yes, sir."

Dollar Bill is now focusing his attention on a skinny brother named Jackie, who is standing on the corner lighting a cigarette. With his smile gone, Dollar Bill motions to Bucky to look across the street. On the spot, the two young men take off after an unsuspecting Jackie, leaving a now nervous Doug where he stands. From a distance, Doug watches as Bucky runs up behind Jackie, punching him in the back of the head and knocking him to the ground. Dollar Bill is now standing over Jackie kicking him all over his entire body.

As people begin to look from the park and their apartment windows, Doug slowly begins to exit the park but not before catching Dollar Bill's eyes. "Noon tomorrow, Shorty. Don't forget me!" shouts Dollar Bill. As Doug starts to jog home, he stops to go back for his basketball but does not. Instead, he looks back across the street and now can no longer recognize a beaten and bloodied Jackie. Running down Valentine Avenue, Doug repeats to himself, "Noon tomorrow, noon tomorrow."

*   *   *

Six cruel winters later, a 15-year-old Doug stares at himself in the mirror putting on his beige sheepskin coat while concealing his handgun in the waistband of his pants. Walking inside his living room, he stares at his father who sleeps on the couch, cradling a quart of Jack Daniels in his arm. Looking down at his father for about thirty seconds, Doug walks to the door. Before unlocking his front door, Doug looks up at the picture of his mother that hangs above and says, "I miss you; I hope you're proud of me and please forgive me."

* * *

The Tiger Lounge is packed and the stereo is blasting the hit by Erik B and Rakim "Follow the Leader" A well-groomed Doug walks inside, greeted by men and women almost twice his age. Looking around the club, Doug spots his mentor, Dollar Bill, who is sitting at his private table flanked by three sexy women. Dollar Bill spots Doug and waves him over to his table.

"My son, what's up?" asks a high Dollar Bill.

Smiling from ear to ear, Doug answers, "Just chillin, what about you?"

Dollar Bill, pulling one of his girls close to him and giving her a long, wet kiss, looks up at Doug with a smile and says, "This is what I am up to baby."

Reaching out with his hand, Doug gives Dollar Bill a pound and asks, "Do you think we can talk outside for a minute?"

Taking a long taste of his Remy Martin, Dollar Bill stares at Doug then answers, "Shit it's freezing outside, but hey, anything for my son."

* * *

Sitting inside Dollar Bill's red Bronco, the two of them share a joint together.

"Shorty, I can remember when you were just a snot-nose bastard that washed my car. Now look at you holding meetings in shit. So, what's up?" asks Dollar Bill.

Doug, never taking his eyes off Dollar Bill, lets out a calm laugh.

"Yeah, I always looked up to you and I still do" says Doug. As they pass the joint to each other, a crawling Jackie, on his hands and knees holding a 12-gauge pump shotgun, makes his way around to Dollar Bill's side of the Bronco. Dollar Bill, looking straight into Doug's eyes, tells him, "I love you, Shorty, like a son." Doug reaching over gives Dollar Bill an embrace and then shoves Dollar Bill towards the driver's side window. Dollar Bill, looking at Doug with shock and confusion, notices Doug diving down on to the truck floor.

As a nice beat plays from Dollar Bill's car stereo, Jackie pops up on the driver's side of the truck pointing the shotgun. Pumping his shotgun once, Jackie yells, "Payback motherfucker!" As Dollar Bill turns his head towards his window, a big blast of light shatters the darkness of the night and the sound of breaking glass is heard from the store to the flower shop. Doug, who is covering his face from the flying glass, looks at his pants and sees Dollar Bill's brains and skull all over him. Wiping glass and blood away from his coat, Doug reaches for his automatic weapon. Jackie's face turns to dreadfulness as he notices the barrel of Doug's gun.

"Oh shit, Shorty. What's up?!" Without hesitation, Doug lets off four rounds, hitting Jackie three times in the head killing him instantly. Hordes of people are running from the club, looking at the scene of the incident. Some women are screaming and crying while some men get closer to the car and peep inside. Before Doug crawls out of the Bronco, he grabs three packages of cocaine that Dollar Bill had under his seat.

Bucky, out of the crowd, grabs Doug by the shirt and pulls him up to his feet. "What the fuck happened?!" yells Bucky. A blood soaked Doug points to the driver's side of the Bronco. Bucky runs over to the driver's side and comes upon a dead Jackie and a half-headed Dollar Bill. Holding his head and falling to his knees, Bucky starts to cry.

Looking on, Doug says, "I killed him Bucky, but I could not save Dollar Bill."

With the sounds of police sirens getting closer, Bucky tries to gather himself and tells Doug, "Run shorty, get the fuck out of here!" With the speed of a gazelle, Doug takes off down Webster Avenue. Feeling for the bags of cocaine in his shirt, Doug wears a huge grin.

Chapter Two
Meet Sandra Lyte

The summer finds Richmond, Virginia baking like hot peach cobbler. Scanning the country side, we come upon a large piece of land that is perfectly landscaped and manicured. Sitting atop this land is an egg-colored, four-thousand-square-foot, plantation-like home like the one seen in the movie *Gone with the Wind.* Looking through an open window, we come into the bedroom of twenty-one-year-old Sandra Lyte, who is posing in front of a full-length mirror, wearing a scarlet red, two-piece bathing suit. As Sandra smiles, twisting, turning and admiring her thick, hourglass figure, her mother, Anna Lyte, sits on the edge of Sandra's bed, nervously looking at her wristwatch.

"Mama, there is no way I am not going to win Miss. Richmond. This is my pageant" said Sandra. Anna, shaking her head with total doubt written on her face, looks at her watch again.

"Your father is going to hit the roof Sandra, when he finds out you are defying his wishes," says Anna.

Sandra, looking at her mother, walks over to her closet and removes a very expensive gown adorned with rhinestones. "I am a twenty-one-year-old college graduate; I am not his little girl anymore, and he cannot scare me with 'If Jesus was here' speeches anymore" Sandra answers.

Anna, hearing her dog Sheba bark, jumps off the bed and looks at Sandra with a worried expression on her face: "Ok, we agreed last month we would tell him on the day before the pageant so he would have no time to fuss, so hurry and put this stuff up," says Anna.

Sandra, rolling her eyes slowly, hides her things, watching her mother ruffle her dress and hurry down the steps to greet her husband. Sandra grabbing two decks of cards from off her table begins to shuffle and spread them all across her bedroom floor. One by one, Sandra begins flipping over cards until gradually she starts to not only match them by numbers but by the exact same suit. Within two minutes, Sandra has fifty-two pair of cards that are the same. Looking at her neatly stacked piles of cards, Sandra blows her knuckles and wipes her chest with braggers bravado.

Walking down the steps into her gigantic living room that contains beautiful artwork and sculptures, Sandra walks over to her father, Minister James Lyte, and kisses him on his cheek.

"Good evening minister," says Sandra.

Looking at his daughter from under his bifocals, James responds "When do you plan to get those ghetto braids removed from your hair?"

Looking at her father with an astonished look Sandra replies, "Minister, these are not ghetto braids; they signify my African heritage." Standing up slowly from his chair, Minister James rolls his eyes in disgust at his daughter and exits the living room. Showing the same frustration, Sandra returns to her room. Anna, looking up at the ceiling, just holds her head.

*   *   *

A cool summer breeze has come upon Sandra and her best friend, twenty-year-old Karen Robinson. The two young women sit under a large tree listening to a "Luther" CD. Sipping on some lemonade, they sing along to "Superstar." Looking from his window is Minister Lyte, who has a look of not only anger towards his daughter but also of hatred. Pulling a plastic bag from her handbag, Karen shows Sandra the many pictures that she snapped while on her vacation to New York City. "My goodness Karen; New York looks so big." Karen, smiling and giggling, begins to describe each snapshot to Sandra, who is totally focused and somewhat hypnotized by the pictures. "What's it like there, Karen?" asks Sandra.

Taking a deep breathe, Karen begins, "First of all, the men are fine girl. I could not take my eyes off of them."

Sandra interjects, "What about the job opportunities? Is there room for another news anchor?"

Karen, rolling her eyes, looks at Sandra likes she is stupid. "Sandra, I was not looking for any damn job, girl. I was club-hopping my ass off." The two women laugh as they sip on lemonade.

"I have to get out of Virginia, Karen. If I can win this pageant, it just adds to my accomplishments, showing that I have charisma and talent to sit in front of millions of people."

Karen reaches out and grabs Sandra to give her hug. "That is why I have always admired you, girl; you go for what you want," says Karen.

Looking away from Karen, Sandra takes notice of her father sitting on his porch reading his bible. Sandra helps Karen to her feet and takes her a few yards away to the lake. Holding Karen by the shoulders, Sandra looks her in the eyes and announces, "I know he hates me; he always has. My mother told me when I was born that he stood three feet away from the delivery room window." Turning away from Karen, Sandra, looking down at the reflection of the moon on the water, continues: "I have to take my chance. I get no support from my mother, who is so damn submissive to him."

Karen turns Sandra around and notices the tears on her face. "New York is nice, Sandra, but I have to be honest about something. While I enjoyed the clubs and people, I also saw some very shady people who will try to take advantage if you are not careful." Rubbing away her tears, Sandra gives Karen a smile and says, "I realize the risk I am taking, but sometimes when you want something really bad, you have to be willing to stick your hands into the fire and grab it."

Walking Karen to her car, Sandra gives her a hug and kiss on the cheek.

Before entering, Karen asks, "Have you mentioned the pageant to your father yet?"

Looking back at her home, Sandra answers, "No, not yet, but in due time, I will."

Watching Karen drive away, Sandra walks up the steps leading to the front door of her home where her father sits reading his bible. "Good night Minister," says Sandra.

With his eyes focused on his bible, Minister Lyte never looks up at his daughter but does manage to get a few words directed towards her before she enters her home: "Peter denied his master three times before the rooster crowed."

*   *   *

It is Sunday morning and the deacons are standing at the top of the church steps greeting the many families attending morning service. Inside the ministers' quarters, we find Minister Lyte looking through his bible as his wife steams his suit jacket. Standing off in the corner reading a journalist textbook is Sandra, who is wearing an all black pants suit. Anna, helping her husband put on his jacket and robe, kisses him on the cheek. Grabbing his bible with his wife and daughter by his side, the Lytes walk to the pulpit.

*   *   *

The organist is playing "Rough Side of the Mountain" as the church choir and the worshipers sing and clap along. Sitting in the first pew is Sandra, who is clapping way off chorus and has an emotionless expression on her face. As the singing and clapping end, everyone takes their seat as Minister Lyte walks to the podium greeting the congregation, "Good morning brothers and sisters." As the crowd greets him, the minister opens his bible and clears his throat. "My God tells me that inwardly beauty is his joy not outwardly adornments, such as jewelry and fancy braided hair."

As the crowd nods and voices in agreement, Sandra's eyes are burning a hole through her father as Anna slowly looks at her daughter, quickly turning her attention back to her husband.

Minister Lyte continues, "My God tells me that our bodies are temples and should not be polluted by the evil worldly products and messages of this world." The crowd is now agreeing with the minister a little louder as some are standing on their feet. The organist glides his fingers across the organ to symbolize his agreement. "Look at all the sex videos that our precious little children are being forced to watch by the so-called entertaining rappers and singers," shouts the minister. Sandra, biting her lip, does not take her eyes off her father. The minister continues, "Brothers and sisters, I want to bring to your attention one of these so-called entertaining events being shoved down our throats in the next two weeks." Walking away from the pulpit, Minister Lyte wipes his brow as he grips his microphone tightly. "Our beautiful town of Richmond has allowed a so-called car magazine to sponsor an exploitive, show, not a beauty pageant, to take advantage of our young women."

Karen, who is sitting in the middle pew of the church, stares at an emotionless Sandra. The minister, who now has his congregation fired up on all cylinders, takes a sip of bottled water and continues, "I will not hold my tongue, brothers and sisters. This pageant exploits not only our town and our church but most importantly our misguided daughters who are involved." The crowd is yelling for the minister to continue and is now standing. "I will not stand by and let them just walk into our blessed community and parade our young women around a bunch of immature men hoping and hollering like these girls are prostitutes, no not me!" The crowd is pumping their fists in the air as Sandra turns around and looks at the ruckus being raised by her father. "Brothers and sisters, I do not know about you, but when this magazine company arrives two Fridays from now, I will be standing at the gate waiting to protest in peace but also in the presence of my God!" People can barely hear themselves as the church is in pandemonium of agreement about the protest. "Within the next two weeks, the church and I will begin to organize our protest, and I know I can count on you brothers and sisters!"

As the crowd starts to sing the church hymn, Anna looks at her daughter and leans over to her ear, "If you do this, you are on your own," whispers Anna.

Sandra, turning to her mother, whispers in her ear, "This is my life and I will control my destiny." The two woman turn away from each other and focus on Minister Lyte.

*   *   *

It is Friday morning, the day of the Richmond pageant, and the Minister James Lyte's firestorm protest. Standing in her bedroom in front of her mirror, Sandra is wearing a grey panty and bra set jogging in place. Dripping with sweat, she holds two rubber, ten-pound dumbbells in her hands. Within every five seconds, Sandra lifts the weights over her head and lets out a deep breath. After running in place, it is now time for crunches, as Sandra does one hundred and fifty in three minutes. After that, Sandra does four hundred and fifty jumping jacks, three sets of one hundred and fifty to be exact. Once completed, Sandra stands in front of her mirror, admiring her thick but well toned body. Letting a smirk come across her face, Sandra proclaims, "The competition does not stand a chance."

Minister Lyte stands before twenty members of his congregation inside the Richmond Baptist church. There are large white cardboard signs nailed to two-by-fours denouncing the pageant. With his sleeves rolled up, the minister gathers the group in for prayer. "Dear Lord, we go to battle today not for recognition or for the spotlight, but we go to battle, Lord, because of what we believe to be right and true in your name and glory." The people in the prayer circle all praise in unison, as the minister continues, "We ask that you not only protect us in our journey, Lord, but we also ask that you free those behind this sinful act that they believe to be a pageant. We pray in your name, Amen." As everyone lifts their heads, the minister lays out his final instructions to the congregation: "Brothers and sisters, as I have said for the past two weeks, we will protest in peace and harmony, not anger. We will obey the laws of our police department and stay behind the barricades. Finally, we will not get into name calling or any physical confrontations with the sponsors or attendees of this event, but rest assured; they will hear our voices and our voices will echo our disapproval." As the members each line up to shake the minister's hand, two men gather the signs and bull horns taking them to the church van. The minister watches his flock exit the church one by one until he stands alone. Looking up at the church ceiling, the minister proclaims, "If I pull this off, it will surely glorify me."

*   *   *

It is now four hours away until the Richmond beauty pageant, and we see Sandra gathering up her personal cosmetics and clothes that she will be wearing, putting them inside her tan canvas suitcase. Looking at her new hair style in the mirror, Sandra hears a knock at the door. Turning around to see whom it is Sandra looks at her tearful mother Anna who enters her bedroom with hands out in a pleading manner.

"You have to reconsider, Sandra, just for me please?" asks a shaken Anna.

Sandra stares at her mother with disbelief. "Listen, everyone needs to get a grip on reality; it's just a pageant," answers Sandra.

Taking a seat on Sandra's bed, Anna grabs Sandra by the hand and makes one final plea before she leaves for the event. "I know we have not been the greatest parents Sandra, but please look at it from our perspective. We have built a reputation in this town for being an upright family and a God-fearing one at that."

Sandra, picking up her bags, looks at her mother before leaving and responds, "As long as I can remember, I have played the sweet little minister's daughter, very well I might add. However, Momma, do not stand before me and preach what is right according to God when it comes to this family. When you and minister know fully well what is in our little secret closet and why I do not have a little brother."

Anna's light-skinned face turns to tomato red after hearing Sandra's response, and in a fit of rage, she leaps off Sandra's bed and gets directly into her face so that each woman's nose is touching.

With Sandra's eyes blinking rapidly because of the closeness of her mother, she takes a step back, bumping into her dresser. An angry and fiery red Anna fires back, "Be very careful what you dig up, Sandra, because you know and I know this family can not handle repercussions very well. You being the weakest would surely crumble without us around, so be very fucking careful." As Sandra grabs her pageant belongings she turns and looks at her still red-faced mother, who is now biting on her bottom lip so hard blood slowly oozes from her mouth.

*   *   *

It is seven o'clock in the evening and the Richmond College auditorium is slowly filling up with ticket buyers who are mostly men. Sitting in the middle aisle in the first row are the pageant judges, which consist of three men and one woman. The stage is beautifully decorated, and the electrician is rotating different color beams of light onto the stage. The sponsors' banner for the pageant draped overhead reads "HOT RIDES MAGAZINE." A man dressed in blue jeans walks on stage and tests the microphone by tapping it with his hand. Slowly we hear the men in the audience begin to make wolf and barking noises.

Back stage is total chaos as women are running all over, helping the contestants with their dresses and make up. Inside the dressing room, Sandra is calmly putting the final touches to her hair and now begins to get into her black glittering dress. As three other woman walk in, they start to crowd Sandra in an attempt to share the mirror. With time getting near, an older looking woman enters the room and says, "Ladies, lets hurry; you have ten minutes before the curtain rises." All the contestants including Sandra begin to move faster.

*   *   *

Outside across the street from the auditorium, Minister Lyte stands with members of his church with signs in their hands and a bullhorn in the minister's hand. Forming their circle, the group begins to march as the minister announces, "Our women are God's gift, not the hot rods thrift!" As the members march in a circle, they repeat the ministers' proclamation loudly and proudly. As they march, a News Channel 21 television van pulls up to the curb. Exiting the van is anchorwoman Sheila Brown, who is being followed by her cameraman. Standing on the grass lawn with the Richmond auditorium as her background shot, Sheila gets the nod from her cameraman that they are now on the air. Showing her pearly whites, Sheila greets her audience. "Good evening, Richmond. I am Sheila Brown in here now the news. Tonight, in the midst of what seems to be a harmless beauty pageant, we have controversy brewing about ten feet away from me as protesters show disapproval led by a Minister James Lyte. If possible, we are going to try to get a word with Minister Lyte." Walking over to the protesters, Sheila approaches the minister with microphone near his face. "Minister Lyte, what is this protest about?"

Giving the newswoman a stern stare for about three seconds, the minister decides to answer, "It is about bringing to light what this is all about. Not some pageant as you may call it…no, this is nothing but an exploitation of young women of this town."

Looking at the minister, Sheila says, "Minister, some would say this protest is somewhat overblown simply because it is nothing more than a pageant for some talented young women."

With the minister holding a sign high in the air, he retorts, "You can call it what you like, Ms. Brown, but take a look at the sponsors' magazine promotion space in the back; they sponsor sex chat lines and escort services. So who knows what they have planned for some of these young women?"

Sheila, listening to the minister, pushes at her earphone to listen to a transmission. Looking at the minister with a concerned expression on her face Sheila turns to him with another question, "Minister Lyte, we at News Channel Twenty-One have a second crew inside the auditorium covering the event, and we would like to show you live footage if you would not mind, sir?"

Looking somewhat puzzled, the marching minister answers, "Why would I want to see that filth that is unfolding, Ms. Brown?"
Pointing to a live monitor that sits inside the news van, Sheila answers,

"Minister Lyte, is that your daughter Sandra Lyte on stage wearing a swimsuit?"
Focusing his attention on the monitor, Minister Lyte slowly opens his mouth in complete shock as the sign he is holding falls to the ground. As the other protesters gather around the news truck they witness a bikini-wearing Sandra walking from one end of the stage to the other. Some of the members are patting the minister on his back in a gesture of comfort.

A serious looking Sheila Brown ask the minister once again, "Minister Lyte, is that your daughter, sir?"

Without saying a word, the somber looking man slowly begins to walk to his car. Two women of his church try to escort him but are gently and firmly pushed away. Getting into his Lincoln town car, a camera operator trying to get a shot of the minister is pushed away by the deacons of the church.

Two hours have elapsed and Sandra stands on stage being crowned Miss Richmond as the other contestants give her hugs and kisses. The chief editor of "HOT RIDES" magazine gives Sandra her check for five thousand dollars and a two-foot trophy, crowning her as Miss Richmond. Walking off the stage, Sandra cannot help to notice that one of the many men in the audience is Deacon Frye, who leads the Tuckahoe Baptist Church. As the two stare at each other as if they were the only ones in the building, Deacon Frye slowly stands and exits the building. Two other pageant contestants are escorting a somewhat numb Sandra off the stage.

*   *   *

It is a little past midnight and the long white stretch limousine pulls up to the driveway that leads to the forty-foot walkway to Sandra's home. As the door opens, loud music and screaming comes from the car. Stacy and Patrice, two of the contestants, are standing on the car seat with half of their bodies hanging out of the moon roof. Both girls are holding bottles of champagne and are clearly drunk. Sandra putting a finger to her mouth, signifying for them to keep quiet, waves her Miss Richmond crown in the air with jubilation. Sandra wave's goodbye, as the limousine drives off with the girls still exposed from the moon roof. Sandra begins to walk towards the home that sits atop a dark, grassy hill. Walking with her crown and trophy in her hand, she can hear the sounds of crickets and frogs. With every step, she can feel the cool moisture of the grass on the bottom of her soles. Not taking her eyes off the home that is now twenty feet in front of her, Sandra flinches when the foyer lights illuminate from the glass entry door. Slowly walking up her porch steps, Sandra is two feet away from her door when it flings open and standing in front of her is an incensed Minister Lyte, who is wearing nothing but blue jeans and his always perfectly combed hair is in shambles. Sandra, looking up at her father, stares at him as if she was a deer looking into headlights of a car. Coming out of her trance, Sandra focuses enough to notice her mother Anna standing behind her husband. As Sandra starts to back away, her father, reacting with cat-like reflexes, snatches his daughter by her long braided hair, pulling her violently into their secluded home.

"You fucking bitch!" yells Minister Lyte, tossing Sandra against the foyer closet door. Sandra, smashing into the door, winces in pain as the doorknob jabs her in the back. Fighting the pain, Sandra quickly crawls for the front door but is blocked and then pushed back down by the foot of her mother Anna. Reaching down with both hands, a now crazed Minister Lyte grabs Sandra, who is in pain, by her left arm slinging her into the dining room where she smashes into one of the oak chairs.

"We are ruined, you dumb ass bitch" yells a psycho Anna. Walking over quickly to his now battered daughter, Minister Lyte grabs Sandra by her throat and drags her to the back entrance of the house, tossing her on top of four large garbage bags. Anna, who is right behind her husband, unlocks the door and proceeds to throw the garbage bags out on to the lawn.

Sandra, who somehow still clutches her purse, is grabbed by her legs and is dragged down the steps by her father. As her back hits each step, she screams in pain. "Why, oh please why?" yells Sandra. Anna, now standing over her daughter, begins slapping and scratching her across her face. Sandra, calling on strength from deep inside her, stunningly makes it to her feet. Holding her ribs, Sandra stumbles and runs towards the road. Minister Lyte, in a fit of rage, grabs the Miss Richmond crown and violently throws it at Sandra, barely missing her face. Reaching down, Sandra grabs the crown and hurries towards the road. Anna, who is now holding her husband back by his blue jeans, yells at her daughter, who is now fading into the wooded path leading to the road: "Don't you ever come back here! Do you hear me, Sandra? Don't you ever come back here!"

As the old, red Dodge pick-up truck pulls into the Greyhound bus station, an old white man runs to the passenger side door and opens it. Reaching inside, he gently helps Sandra out of the vehicle. The old man, wearing a black Pepsi Cola hat, stares at Sandra's, beaten and scratched face.

"Young lady, are you sure I can't get you to a hospital?"

Sandra, somehow putting a smile on her face, answers gently, "No sir, you have done so much for me tonight, thank you." As the old man stands back he watches as Sandra exits and limps towards the terminal.

As Sandra walks slowly towards the ticket booth, she can feel the few people who are inside the terminal staring at her. Still wearing her torn and dirty pageant dress, Sandra walks up to the ticket window with purse and crown in tow. "Sir when is the next one way to New York leaving?"

The ticket clerk, trying not to stare, looks at the bus schedule and answers, "The next bus leaving is in about thirty five minutes."

Sandra, digging into her purse, pulls out a credit card sliding it under the glass towards the clerk saying, "Please print me that ticket."

Listening to the printer spit out the ticket, Sandra looks around for a bathroom. Taking her ticket, Sandra walks to the bathroom to clean herself up.

*   *   *

Sitting on the bus, which is practically empty, Sandra listens for the bus driver to announce their destination. Leaning her head back on the headrest of her seat, Sandra reaches into her purse and takes out a Hershey candy bar with almonds and a photograph of New York that her friend Karen had given her a few nights ago. As the bus slowly pulls out of the depot, Sandra lets out a sigh of relief and declares, "I am free."

Chapter Three
Welcome To the Big Apple

Sandra slowly opens her hazel eyes and begins to focus as she looks out of her window aboard the Greyhound bus. As the bus travels across I-95, she can see the great New York skyline approaching. Feeling inside her purse, she finds the disposable camera she purchased along with her new clothes in Washington D.C. a few hours ago. Allowing a smile to come across her face, Sandra notices that her hands are getting wet and clammy. "Welcome all to New York City," stated the bus driver as he announces they will be pulling into the Port Authority bus depot shortly. Sandra reaches under her seat and grabs onto her duffel bag, which contains toiletries and her cell phone. As the bus pulls into the terminal, Sandra stands with the rest of the passengers and exits the bus.

"Excuse me sir, I was told that an information booth was nearby," Sandra declares to the bus driver.

Checking his bus schedule, the driver responds, "Up those escalators, and if you look straight ahead, you cannot miss it." Sandra smiles and walks away.

Grabbing all of the information guides that she can hold, including subway maps, bus maps, the five boroughs street maps and a miniature yellow page book. Sandra sits on a bench inside the terminal; looking for the different locations that her friend Karen gave her over the phone the previous night while riding the bus. On a piece of paper is a name of a cheap priced hotel where Karen and her parents stayed. Gathering her things, Sandra starts her ascent up the escalator, which takes her to a hot and muggy Manhattan street. Standing by a pharmacy store, Sandra is totally shocked by the crowd of people and cars. Sandra is almost too frightened to step in the middle of the sidewalk, afraid of being run over. Taking a deep breath, she gets the courage to approach an Indian man with her paper in her hand. "Excuse me sir?" asks Sandra. The man looks right through her and quickly walks by. Trying not to get discouraged, Sandra waits a few moments and approaches a Caucasian woman dressed in an expensive suit talking on a cell phone. Sandra politely asks, "Ma'am can you please tell me…" Once again, Sandra is brushed off as the woman walks around her. Looking frustrated and tired, Sandra looks up at the tall buildings across the street when she hears someone calling. "Miss, are you lost?" Sandra, turning towards the voice, spots a street corner frankfurter stand vendor who is waving at her. Cautiously walking over to the Old Italian man, Sandra gives him a smile. "You look lost, what are you looking for?" asks the man. Sandra, pointing to the hotel written on her paper, shows the man. "Oh ok, young lady, the hotel international is three blocks down that way. If you walk straight three blocks, it will be on your left," says the old man.

Sandra smiles and responds, "Thank you very much." Sandra proceeds to walk in the direction of where the nice old man showed her.

*   *   *

Unlocking her door, Sandra walks into her hotel room that looks a little dingy to be in the heart of Manhattan. Sandra brushes it off and lets the excitement of freedom take over her mind. Closing the door behind her, Sandra sits her belongings on a twin size bed that is covered with flowered linens her grandmother had back in Virginia. Looking around the room, Sandra notices cracks running up the beige painted wall and ceiling, and there is a 19-inch television that sits on an old wooden stand. Walking into the bathroom, Sandra looks at the white terrycloth towels that sit on the toilet bowl and miniature bars of soap that lay on the sink. Walking back to the sleeping area, Sandra sits at a small round table that has two dinette chairs. Removing her cell phone, credit card, notepad and her five thousand dollar check from her bag, Sandra reaches for the remote control turning on the television. Hearing the sound before seeing a picture, Sandra looks puzzled as she can hear moaning coming from the set. As the picture comes into focus, it is now clear that a porno flick is on. Looking with some slight curiosity, Sandra quickly turns the channel and watches the news. With her mouth half open, she looks without blinking an eye as the black newswoman reports the stories for the day. Coming out of her trance, Sandra slaps her thighs and stands up walking to her window draped with dingy white curtains and a slightly torn shade, saying to herself, "I will make it, I have to make it." Grabbing her room keys, purse and check, Sandra heads out the door and onto the Manhattan Street.

*   *   *

Walking down the street, Sandra passes the hustling people of the city when she comes upon a pizzeria. Upon entering, Sandra takes a deep breath and smiles at the smell of cheese and sausage. Walking over to the counter, Sandra orders a slice of pizza and a soda when a tall, light-skinned, handsome brother walks up beside her. Looking from the corner of his eye, the man looks Sandra up and down, admiring her nice, plump backside. Sandra, trying not to pay attention, gets her order and pays the Italian owner. "How you doing lovely?" ask the young man.

Sandra, giving him a half smile, responds, "I am fine, and you?"

Looking at Sandra and flashing a sly grin, he asks, "What is your name, baby?" Sandra, looking down at his feet, gets a puzzled look on her face as she notices the brother has no shoes or socks on and his feet are filthy.

Trying to act as if she does not notice Sandra responds, "Sir, I just want to eat my meal please." Stepping back from Sandra, the young man's smile turns to a smirk.

"Oh, so you gonna be like my bitch wife and brush me off, too?" Sandra, now obviously frightened, stands and tries to walk away when the young man steps inches away from her face, exposing a seven-inch piece of lumber. "Bitch, where the fuck do you think you are going?" The pizza, owner turning around and noticing the situation, grabs a bat from under the counter. Exiting the bathroom is the owners' son Mario, who stands six feet tall and weighs about two hundred and fifty pounds. Like a gazelle, Mario leaps over the counter and hits Sandra's tormenter with a rolling pin in the arm, causing him to yell in pain while dropping the piece of lumber.

"Get the fuck out of here you sick bastard. I am tired of you harassing our customers!" holding his arm, the brother quickly runs out of the pizzeria. Sandra, who is holding her chest trying to gain control of her heavy breathing, is standing against the wall. The pizzeria owner walks over to her to offer some comfort,

"Miss, we are so sorry. I run a respectable business, and I meant you none of this. Please take your money back." Taking deep breathes Sandra motions with her hands "No". Finally able to speak, Sandra responds,

"Thank you for your help and your offer. I just need to get some fresh air and find the nearest bank." Mario, taking Sandra by the hand, escorts her out of the pizza shop and points diagonally across the street to a Manhattan bank.

"We are so sorry, miss, our deepest apologies, and if you ever come back, the slice is on us. "A smiling Sandra walks across the street towards the bank. Before crossing the street, she looks carefully, for the no-shoes-having, light-skinned brother.

*   *   *

Inside the bank, Sandra marvels at its size compared to the First National bank in Richmond. Looking around for some help, a security guard taps Sandra on the shoulder, making her flinch a little. "Didn't mean to startle you, miss. I saw you looking around and figured you needed some help" Sandra, wiping a braid from in front of her face, gives the guard a smile.

"That's ok I have had a long day. Could you point out someone that can help me with opening an account with this bank?" The guard, looking towards customer service, gestures to Sandra to follow him. Walking over to the desk, Sandra stands and waits. "Next please," says the customer representative. Walking over, Sandra takes out her check and her Richmond driver's license. "Yes, I am here to open an account and deposit this check." The short Spanish woman whose nametag reads Ida Martinez looks at Sandra's check and then at her driver's license and then back at Sandra.

"Is there any reason why you cannot deposit this check in your home town?" Sandra, letting a distraught expression come across her face, explains to Ida,

"Ma'am, due to some unforeseen circumstances, I no longer reside in Virginia and have just arrived in New York today." Ida, shaking her head up and down then asks her,

"Well do you have a permanent place of residence?" Sandra, fidgeting with the chain pen on the counter, responds,

"No, I do not. Right now I am staying in a hotel a few blocks away until I find my apartment." Ida, looking at the check, looks up at Sandra and tells her,

"Well, Miss Lyte, this check has a sixty-day grace period until it expires, so I suggest you find a place that you can call home and establish an account with Con Edison. Then bring the check back to us, and we will be glad to have you as a customer. However, right now, our bank policies will not allow us to cash your check. I am really sorry." Ms. Martinez gently and slowly slides the check back to Sandra.

Putting her check and driver's license back in her purse, Sandra says, "Well, thank you very much for your help and hopefully you will see me again soon." A huge lump fills Sandra throat as she walks out of the bank.

*   *   *

Walking in the hotel lobby towards the elevator, Sandra stops at the front desk and asks the hotel manager, Jeffery, a white man in his forties, "Is there somewhere I could get something not too expensive to eat nearby?" Jeffery, whose hair is dyed black and has a tooth pick in his ear, looks at Sandra in silence for a few seconds before answering,

"There is a Chinese restaurant two doors down...the food ain't bad."

Turning around to walk back out the door Sandra responds, "Thank you very much."

*   *   *

Sitting on a radiator looking out of the restaurant window, Sandra takes her cell phone out of her purse and looks through her directory. Scrolling down, she comes upon her best friend Karen's number and is ready to dial but decides not to. "Once I get settled, girlfriend, I will call you so you can come up and visit. I miss you already." Sandra says quietly to herself.

"Miss, chicken wings and shrimp fried rice," yells the Chinese man. Sandra, getting up from her makeshift chair, walks over to pay for her food.

"Eight nineteen for you, pretty lady" says the old man. Looking in her purse, Sandra pulls out a twenty-dollar bill and hands it to the man. Waiting for her change, she takes stock of her money and counts one hundred and twenty four dollars. Speaking quietly to herself, Sandra declares, "I have to cash this check; I cannot keep charging my card." Taking her change and food, Sandra exits the restaurant. From the corner of her eye, Sandra notices a large cat jump on the counter. Looking at her bag of food, she says to herself, "That is just an old wives tale; get it out of your head."

*   *   *

Once again stopping at the hotel desk, Sandra stops and rings the bell. Coming from a room in the back is Jeffery, who has an erection from playing with his penis; walks up to the desk with a smile on his face. Sandra, trying not to notice, sits her food on top of the counter and asks, "Jeffery, I wanted to ask you a quick question. I have a check that the bank could not cash for me, and I wanted to know if you knew of anyplace that could help me?"

Jeffery, who is looking through some mail, peeps up through his black bifocals and answers, "How much is the check worth?"

Sandra, grabbing her bag of food, answers "Five thousand dollars." Rubbing his fingers through his hair, Jeffery tells Sandra,

"I need to see the check." Slowly pulling it out of her purse, she hands it to Jeffrey, who examines it for a few seconds.

"This is an out-of-state check. I can cash it, but it is going to cost you three hundred dollars. My bank frowns on out-of-state checks." Looking at the clock on the wall behind the desk, Sandra quietly answers,

"Ok, no problem. Three hundred dollars is the charge." Jeffrey, looking at Sandra, hands her back the check and tells her,

"Come back down and sees me in an hour. I will cash it then. Oh, by the way, if you do not check out by noon tomorrow, the room is sixty dollars for another twenty four hours." Sandra nods her head and responds, "No problem, and thanks for helping me out." As Sandra walks to the elevator, Jeffrey rubs his penis while looking at Sandra's large firm backside.

*   *   *

A smiling and obviously happy Sandra is sitting in her hotel room at her tiny table counting the forty seven hundred dollars that she got from Jeffrey the pervert. Still full from the large order of Chinese food, she pushes the remaining cuisine to the side. Pulling out her newly bought notebook, pencils and calculator, Sandra begins to add things up. On her pad she writes down that two thousand dollars should find her an apartment in Manhattan near the broadcast companies. Unknowingly to her though is that two grand in Manhattan will get you two days in a cardboard box in a subway station. She also writes five hundred dollars should get her a week worth of clothing until she receives her first paycheck. The remaining money, she writes, will be used on old furniture and miscellaneous things. Speaking to herself in a low tone, she says, "It will be a little rough in the beginning, but I will accomplish what I set out to do."

Feeling giddy and energetic, Sandra decides to play her memory game. Not having her usual deck of cards, she turns the forty seven one hundred dollar bills over so that the face of Benjamin Franklin is staring back at her. Concentrating on the first two letters and the first three numbers of the bills, Sandra scans her eyes up and down the different rows for about one minute. Now turning the bills over face down, one by one, she begins touching each bill and calling out the first five serials of each bill individually. After announcing each bill, Sandra turns it over and with very little doubt in her photogenic memory; Sandra gets all forty-seven bills correct. Blowing on her knuckles and then rubbing her chest, Sandra heads to the bathroom to take a nice warm shower.

* * *

Sandra lies in her bed wearing a pair of nylon jogging pants and a grey tee shirt. Looking at the window, she hears a few horns and engines of a few passing cars. Looking at her watch that reads 2:37a.m., she tells herself, "Sandra, take your ass to sleep; you have a big day tomorrow." Rubbing her ears, Sandra lifts her head up and listens to the couple next door having hot and heavy sex. As the bed rocks faster, it begins to pound on Sandra's wall, which in turn makes her bed vibrate a little. With a smile on her face, Sandra listens as the woman next door tells her man to "pump it harder." For a moment, Sandra thought she felt herself rub her breast but puts it out of her mind. Within a few minutes, Sandra can now hear the man start to moan as the bed moves faster until the couple together both let out a yell of ecstasy, and then all goes quiet. Sandra, trying not to laugh, says to herself, "I think I will call him speedy."

* * *

It has been an hour now and Sandra hears a sound coming from the table. Not able to tell if she is dreaming or awake, Sandra tries to ignore the sound but cannot now because she hears the box of her half-eaten Chinese rice hit the floor. Now fully awake, she sits up quietly and listens to the scrambling that comes from the table. Easing herself out of the bed, Sandra reaches on the night stand and slowly clicks on the bedroom light. To her horror and disbelief, Sandra is face to face with two New York City rats that have to be at least seven inches long. She tries to scare them away by shooing, but one of the rats' stands on his two back legs and sniffs at Sandra. "Oh, hell no!" she says as she grabs her sneakers off the floor and proceeds to put them on while standing in the bed. Not taking her eyes off her unwanted visitors who are now climbing into the food container, Sandra hears about three sets of footsteps walking towards her door. Listening to the door as her food container magically makes its way to her bathroom; there is a knock at the door. "Yes, who is it?" asks Sandra.

"Open the door, give me my money," the voice answers back. Sandra, who now has her sneakers on, can hear whispering in the midst of at least three people. Turning her head quickly to the door, Sandra sees the knob slowly turning.

"Who is that?" Sandra asks with a slight quiver in her voice. With a heavy jolt, the hotel door is ferociously shaken, making Sandra scream.

"Open this fucking door now, bitch, and give me my money from your bogus fucking check!" demands a heavy voice that sounds Spanish.

"What are you talking about?" replies Sandra.

In a low tone the Spanish man demands, "Jeff, open this goddamn door. I am going to kill her then you for fucking with my money."

Sandra, now hearing the jingling of keys, grabs her purse that contains all of her belongings, and she jumps off the bed. Running over to the table, she grabs a chair and sticks it under the door knob, jamming the door. Frantically looking around the room, Sandra looks at the window, which leads to the fire escape. Pulling the window up, Sandra climbs out onto the fire escape.

Cautiously climbing down the steps of the fire escape as quickly as possible, Sandra makes it to the next floor when she hears three popping noises. Looking up while holding on to the rail, to her dismay, she sees Jeffrey fall backwards out the window and land on the fire escape. Sandra, almost slipping on the now rain-soaked metal steps, is at the second floor when she hears, "Your next, bitch. I am coming for you!"

Breathing fast while crying, Sandra is at the first floor but still ten feet above the ground. Hearing running feet from the hallway staircase, Sandra climbs over the rail and lets herself hang over a metal dumpster filled with looks like pig slop and cow manure mixed together. Closing her eyes, Sandra lets go, and what seems forever finally lands dead center in the garbage slop. Ignoring the pain of her now sprained ankle and the stench, Sandra is able to grab her purse, climb out of the dumpster and run out of the alley. With no clue of where she is, Sandra runs in the direction of a light straight in front of her. As she gets closer, she recognizes the red, white, and blue neon sign for the drug store. Exiting the alley, Sandra looks both ways when she notices two figures, both tall and dark, looking up the other direction of the block. Quickly Sandra darts between two cars crawling to the other side on her hands and knees. Cautiously looking from behind a parked car Sandra spots and waves at a yellow cab, that has its off-duty, sign on. Holding her hands up and a begging gesture, the cab driver looks at Sandra and motions to her to come. Running to the cab, Sandra gets in, slams the door and proceeds to lie on the floor of the cab.

"Please take me to the place where I can catch the different buses please!" begs Sandra.

The cab driver, turning his meter on, answers "Ok, lady. I'll take you to the bus terminal." As the cab takes off, Sandra announces to herself, "I want to go home."

*   *   *

Sitting under a staircase in the Port Authority Bus Terminal, Sandra holds her head in her hands as she sobs uncontrollably. Her clothes are filthy and her ankle throbs with pain. Clutching her purse like a running back clutches a football; Sandra opens it in stares at her forty-seven hundred dollars, a pack of juicy fruit gum and her cell phone, which has one bar left on the battery indicator. Sandra lifts herself up and limps over to a closed Taco Bell. Walking over, Sandra takes notice to the many derelicts and homeless teenagers sleeping on floors and benches. With no police officer present in her sight, Sandra walks to the ticket booth area. Her phone now beeping, Sandra stops and pulls it out of her purse and stares around the large bus terminal. Wiping away her tears and clearing her throat, Sandra dials home. Sandra's heart is pounding as she swallows the large lump down her throat.

On the fourth ring, Anna Lyte, who was asleep, answers, "Hello, who is this?"

Taking a deep breathe, a nervous Sandra answers, "Momma, it is me, Sandra." There is complete silence for a few seconds when Sandra's phone indicates "low battery." "Momma, I'm lost in New York City. Can I please come home?" As the phone beeps, again Sandra hears a click and a violent voice.

"Don't you dare call here again. You have no home here anymore!" answers Minister Lyte.

A crying Sandra begs her father, "Daddy, I am so sorry. Please, can I come home?"

"No you cannot, and do not call me Daddy again, you little tramp. Do you know how you ruined my name and my church?"

Sandra, looking up at the sky, responds, "Daddy, I have been assaulted and chased by angry men claiming that my check for the contest was not real. Daddy, please can I come home?"

With no sympathy, the minister gives his final answer: "Hell no! You made your bed; now you lay in it. As far as I'm concerned, I never had a daughter!"

Before Sandra can respond, her phone sounds one final beep and goes dead. "Hello! Hello daddy!" a crying Sandra yells. Dropping her phone to the floor and falling to her knees, Sandra is crying hysterically when she feels a tap on her shoulder. Slowly turning around, Sandra is face-to-face with Brenda Taylor, a tall, slim black woman. Brenda, reaching out to Sandra, gives her a sandwich and a small container of orange juice.

"Here sweetheart...take this. You look like you had a long night." Sandra, looking watchfully at the woman, slowly reaches out and takes the food and drink. "My name is Brenda and I work for Project Outreach for the homeless and if you like, I have a van outside with a few young people like you. We can offer you a bed for the night, and in the morning we can sort some things out for you. How do you feel about that? Looking at Brenda for a while, Sandra nods her in agreement. Brenda puts her arm around Sandra and walks her outside to a waiting blue van where inside four young girls are sitting.

Chapter Four
Decisions Are Made

This particular winter is a brutal one in the Bronx. There is about
thirteen inches of snow still on the ground from the previous snowstorm.
Inside Doug's large three-bedroom apartment, Fred Gunner lays on an
Italian leather couch wearing silk pajamas and smoking a Cuban cigar.
On the 50-inch, big screen television, Fred is watching a porno film. As
Doug enters the living room decked out in an alligator two-piece suit with
alligator shoes to match, his father inquires, "Damn boy, where you going
looking like you just got back from Africa?"

Doug, who now at the age of twenty-three stands six feet-two
inches tall and weighs two hundred thirty pounds, stares at his father for a
moment before answering, "I told you last night I had an important
meeting to attend."

Sucking his teeth, Fred stares at his son from the corner of his eye
and says, "Just remember to bring home those steaks I like."

Doug, putting on his leather coat and grabbing his car keys, tells
his father, "If I make it home."

A now half-laughing Fred responds, "Confidence son, confidence."
Walking past his father Doug exits his apartment.

*   *   *

Forty five minutes later at his meeting place Doug holds his arms
in the air, as two large brothers both weighing over three hundred pounds
seize Doug's coat, cell phone and his 9mm handgun. Opening his shirt,
Doug reveals to the two men that he is not wearing a wire. Escorted up a
white flight of stairs, Doug is now standing in front of a door that has no
door knob or peephole. Within ten seconds, a buzzer goes off, and the
door slowly opens to reveal an all white room that consists of two white
chairs, four very large bullmastiffs and a standing Mario Chavez.

"Doug, my new friend or enemy…that will depend on you, please
come in!" yells Mario with laughter.

A wary Doug steps into the room leaving the large brothers
outside, while the door slowly closes. With a smile on his face Mario
points to the chair, "Sit, my man; let's get acquainted."

As Doug takes a seat, another door opens and out walks two Cuban women who are in their twenties, wearing nothing but black thongs. They are in perfect shape with not one ounce of body fat on them and not one wrinkle or blemish on their faces. The women carry champagne and caviar to Doug, pouring him a glass while offering him caviar on a cracker. Entering the room from the same door is another Cuban woman who totes an all white poodle on a leash. She gestures for the dog to heal, and the poodle lies at Doug's feet. Mystified by the whole scenario, Doug sips on his champagne while Mario nods his head and watches all three women leave the room. "Babies, make Doug comfortable for daddy," commands Mario as all four bullmastiffs form a square around a now curious Doug. Taking a seat, Mario says, "Doug, long meetings aggravate me because most meetings are ninety percent bullshit. We do not need to bullshit; all we need to do is become good communicators."

Doug, looking at the dogs, nods his head slowly with agreement. "I have many associates in your part of town who tell me you are an up-and-comer who enjoys hard work." Mario says.

"I have been fighting for this opportunity for eight years now, Mr. Chavez. I have no problem putting in long hours and spending the majority of my days away from home," responds Doug.

"I like that--a man not afraid to get dirty. Good for you, Doug." Reaching into his jacket pocket Mario pulls out a two pound bag of cocaine that is wrapped in plastic and tape. Mario tosses it to Doug who, catches it and reads the package which says "Baby Powder" in red letters. "Uncut and uncensored straight from Columbia, I have no competition and no equal," says Mario.

Doug sticks his pinky fingernail in the bag and puts the product on his tongue. After ten seconds, Doug is rubbing his mouth and staring at the cocaine and then at Mario with an astounded look on his face. Mario busts out in laughter as he stands from his chair. "This is worth fifty thousand dollars to me, Doug. However, I promise you; out there, it is worth two hundred thousand. They will pay for my pleasure; that I guarantee."

In an instant Mario's expression turns stone-cold as he stares at Doug, whose smile has left his face also. "I welcome you into my home and treat you with love and respect, right Doug?"

Staring at Mario, he answers, "Yes you have." With his head facing the white floor, Mario says, "I hope I can trust you, Doug. Because you understand that between love and rage is a razor-thin line, yes?"

Doug shakes his head up and down and agrees, "You can trust me, Mr. Chavez, and yes, it is thin."

Mario, whose eyes are ice cold, looks at Doug without blinking an eye yells, "RAGE!" At that moment, the four bullmastiffs are up on their feet and proceed to rip the defenseless white poodle apart. Doug, who is now on his feet, leaves his chair and hurries to the side where Mario stands. The floor that was once white is now covered with the poodle's blood and what body parts can still be identified. The dogs are now covered in blood and sit side-by-side staring at their master. Mario, who is now smiling again, puts his arms around Doug and asks, "One week from today, we make two hundred, yes?"

Doug, looking at the large package in his hand, looks up at Mario and answers, "No doubt."

*   *   *

Inside a cold and damp basement, standing at a table are Doug, Troy, Buster and Fish, who are all childhood friends. Troy, a light-skinned brother who is a college graduate, possesses the brain of an accountant. Buster, a muscular, dark-skinned brother with a long ugly scar on his face, is not much for words and will carve a man like a turkey at the drop of a hat. Finally, there is Fish, the elder of the crew, who knows any and everyone when it comes to the game of hustle. On an old wooden table lies the package of "Baby Powder" that has the four of them in a trance.

Clearing his throat, Doug speaks, "My brothers, today is the day when we will no longer be looked upon as small-timers. In one week, we will separate ourselves from the others."

Troy, looking at Doug, asks, "We only have one week to move this?"

Fish, reaching down to rub his hand across the product, says, "One week is a lifetime if this shit is as potent as your contact makes it out to be.

Doug who is smiling looks across at Buster proclaims, "We have to carve out a niche my brothers. Take what is ours."

Buster proclaims, "I have been waiting all my life to get paid like this. I'll carve our names into the other brother's faces so that they know a new product and merchant is on the street."

Doug, who is holding a large duffel bag, reaches in and pulls out four portable cell phones, handing each man one. "It took me a little while, but I have rigged these to last only two days after the initial time we use them. So when the time runs out, just throw them in the trash and meet up at the spot for another." Removing from the bag Doug takes out four electronic hotel room keys. "There are Baker Motels in the five boroughs. I got the hook-up through someone who owed me a huge favor. Each one of these keys will open room twenty-one at each motel. When I give you the word, we will meet to settle up for that night's work."

Troy, who is smiling ear-to-ear, asks, "Do you have any idea where we can go to start moving this?"

Fish looks up at Troy and answers, "We put a little out there and watch them come looking for us."

Doug, shaking his head in agreement, responds, "Tomorrow morning, Buster, you will gather your forces together, seeing who is hungry and wants to put in work for us. Fish, tonight you start putting the word out to your partygoers about the new brew in town. Troy, you and I will meet up at my place in the afternoon to prepare the powder for distribution." Doug motions for his men to get close to one another. As they huddle close, Doug declares, "This is our time, right now."

* * *

Friday morning at 6:00am, Doug and Troy are sitting inside a spare bedroom in Doug's apartment, packaging their new product. On a large brown table sits scales, sifters, a large plate of glass, ten playing cards, a box of at least one thousand miniature Ziploc bags, a box of baking powder, a large amount of cocaine and both men are sweating while they put together their supply. As Doug begins to package, he stops suddenly, paying attention to a knock at the door.

"Doug are you in there? What are you doing up so early?" asks Fred Gunner.

Looking at Troy, Doug motions to him to keep on going. "Yeah, its me…now go back to sleep" Doug, walking over to the door, cracks it open a few inches and passes a bottle of Johnny Walker black and two hundred dollars to his father. Closing the door quickly, Doug demands, "Please Pop, go back to bed." Walking back over to the table, Doug and Troy continue bundling the product.

* * *

Later that afternoon, Fish is sitting at the bar surrounded by numerous associates he deals with on a regular basis. The men are all drinking Remy Martin and Courvoisier. All eyes are on Fish as he stands and takes center stage. "My brothers, we have been dealing with each other for some time now. I have always been forthright with every one of you, and I have handed out numerous favors to you."

There are nine men who form a circle around Fish that are shaking their heads in agreement. One of the men named Jay Black owns "Class Barbershop" speaks out: "What you say is true Fish. Any way I can help, while at the same time making a little dough, I am with that."

Fish pats Jay on the back and smiles. "That's good to hear and know because what I am about to propose is an excellent opportunity for all involved." Fish pulls out his laptop computer and reveals a graph of how much product they are to sell from their establishments and how much they will profit. As the men sit and listen to Fish, everyone has a smile on his face except a heavy-set brother named Willie, who owns a meat market.

With his face twisted with anger, Willie quickly stands and pushes his chair to the ground, causing a loud bang and bringing complete silence to the room. "Fish, how is this shit fair? I have worked hard to create my business; now you want me to sell this product and risk my shit? I want double!"

Fish, never taking his eyes off Willie, continues to smile as he responds, "Brother Willie, I love you, baby. I would never cheat you out of anything, but when you could not afford to pay for your meat, who got it for you at almost half the price? C'mon I know that the money does not look long now, but you have my word; within the next few months, everyone will be satisfied."

Willie who is breathing hard shoots back, "Fuck that Fish, I am out."

Fish, still with a smile on his face, says, "No problem, Willie. I am sorry we could not do this. I truly understand how you feel." With that the room is so silent that Willie can be heard breathing through his nostrils. Putting on his coat, Willie grabs his briefcase and exits the bar. Fish, watching the bar door close, continues with the meeting.

* * *

Willie is driving a red Chevy blazer down the Grand Concourse when he stops at the red light. Coming up on the side of him is a black suburban with all tinted windows. The front passenger window rolls down and the horn is honked, gaining Willie's attention. Looking at the still red light, Willie asks, "What do you want?"

Buster, who is wearing all black, asks, "You got a light?"

Looking very pissed off, Willie snaps, "No, the hell I do not." "Then what the fuck are you good for?" asks Buster pulling up from his lap a sawed off shotgun that he fires at Willie, blowing his head off his shoulders. Willie's body spasms, while the blazer crashes into a tree. In an instant, the suburban speeds off. Buster, putting the shotgun under his seat, announces to his driver, "We will not be denied."

* * *

The summer is here and the east side of the Bronx belongs to Doug and his small but efficient family. Doug, sitting in his brand new Acura watches his corners bring in the cash. It could not get any better or easier because while his workers handled the corners, Buster made sure they stayed protected by the forces. Troy had a girl he was dealing with who owned a string of check-cashing spots in the Bronx. Through these businesses, Doug laundered his money. Meanwhile, Fish kept his promise to his associates that if they allowed the product to be sold in their establishments, they in turn would see under-the-counter cash and protection.

Mario Chavez is ecstatic for a few reasons. For one, Doug was always on time and never missed a payment deadline. Secondly, Mario liked the fact that Doug never revealed to anyone who his contact was because the less people knew about him, the better. Finally, Mario's product sold all over fresh territory he had yet to tap. As for the cops, Doug had that under control to an extent. He became quite physical with a female rookie cop over the winter. Through romance and dining, Doug was able to purchase "get-out-of-jail-free" cards and "free-to-sell" permits while obtaining information about the "Dirty 24" of the neighborhood precinct. The dirty twenty-four are a drug-and-gun unit whose main task is to freeze up drug trafficking. Through this female cop, Doug found out that the salary being paid to these men was peanuts, so through a meeting, Doug made the commanding officer of the unit a little offer for the exchange for his corners and the freedom for his sellers. Doug was now rolling in milk and honey, and everyone involved seemed to be happy.

Dialing on his phone while watching his masterpiece unfold, Doug waits for his father to answer. Clearing his throat, Doug announces, "Hello, Dad. Please be ready; I'm on my way to pick you up. Ok I will see you soon." Starting his car up Doug begins to pull off when a Ford pulls up next to him.

"What's up Doug, my man?"

Doug, looking at the driver of the vehicle, smiles and responds, "Detective Tommy Davis, how are you today?"

Reaching for his car visor, Doug pulls a yellow envelope from under it and passes it to Davis.

"My man, good looking out," replies the detective.

Doug, starting his car, tells the officer before pulling off, "Look forward to seeing you fellows at my party palace this Friday." With both men shaking their heads in agreement Doug drives off. Before turning on his music, Doug says to himself "Sorry, Pop."

*   *   *

As the sun begins to set riding up a paved road, Fred Gunner looks at the tall trees that line the roadway on both sides. With complete silence engulfing the car, Fred clutches his traveling bag as he now can see the very large brown Westchester residence: The Shadybrook Retirement Home. The building has to be at least a city block wide and seven stories high. Doug drives through an iron gate and parks in the visitor's parking lot. Doug, exiting his car, looks at Fred as he walks to the passenger side. Opening the door, Doug helps his father out of the vehicle and begins to walk him to the main entrance.

"You motherfucker, you think I do not know what this place is?" asks Fred.

Doug, stopping at the front entrance, looks his father in the eyes and responds, "I can not be home with you all the time and this place has everything you will need to keep you busy and healthy."

Fred, still clutching his travel bag, says, "Fuck you Doug I knew you planned to get rid of me from the get go!"

Doug, looking at his father, answers, "That is not true Pops. I am just too busy to care for you anymore. My life is going in a different direction and you are getting in the way."

From out of left field, Fred hauls off, slaps the shit out of Doug and says, "Boy, who the hell do you think you are talking to? Did you forget who spit your ass inside your dead mother? I know what you are doing and I know you are making money and if I do not like this fucking place, you will find me another. You understand you little bastard?"

Still standing at the entrance of the residence, Doug felt belittled and embarrassed by the way his father was speaking to him. Not knowing how to respond, he hands a bottle of Jack Daniels to his father.

Looking at the bottle of whiskey, Fred looks at his son and proceeds to throw the bottle on the ground right at Doug's feet destroying his $800 alligator shoes. "Fuck you boy, I do not need you to walk me in.

Chapter Five
A Friend Named Pamela Brown

Inside a small bathroom colored with baby blue paint, is Pamela Brown, an athletically built, dark-skin sister with beautiful long silky hair, giving her four-year-old son Derrick a bath before bed. Sitting on the toilet bowl, Pamela watches as the curly haired tot splashes his toy wrestling men along with his pet dinosaur in the sudsy, warm water.

"Wash behind those big ears for Mommy" says Pamela.

Little Derrick, revealing his baby white teeth, grabs his washcloth and does a masterful job. "Look mommy, like this?" he asks.

Pamela, now getting on her knees, leans towards the tub to give him a big kiss but cannot because of the vodka bottle that encases her. Smiling at his mother, Derrick stands up in the tub and waves goodbye to his mother. Pamela, who is now crying hysterically inside the large vodka bottle, motions to her son to sit down in the tub. As Derrick slips on the bar of soap that lies at the bottom of the tub, he falls backwards landing on his delicate head and submerging in the tub of water. Pamela using all of her strength to save her son but she cannot, as her bloodied fists hammer on her unbreakable glass prison.

"Mommy, help me!" Derrick cries from under the water.

Still on her knees, a sobbing Pamela screams, "Oh God, no! I am so sorry baby! Please God, no!"

Sitting up quickly in her bed, Pamela soaking from sweat holds her chest. Looking out towards her window, she can see the full moon in all its glory.

"I miss you so much baby, I miss you so much" sobs Pamela. Getting out of bed, she walks to her dresser where there is a picture of little Derrick smiling ear-to-ear. Staring at the picture for a moment, Pamela lights a candle and announces to her son, "Mommy has been doing so well; I hope you can forgive me."

*   *   *

The afternoon finds Pamela sitting amongst twenty people, standing and announcing, "Hi, my name is Pamela Brown, and I am an alcoholic.

"Hello, Pamela," the group responds.

Sitting down, Pamela says, "It's been two years and one month since my last drink." The people in the room break out in applause. She continues, "It has been three years to the day that my son has been gone, and he helps me so much as does my Higher Power."

The director, a white woman named Ms. Clarke, asks, "How has Derrick helped you, Pamela?"

Wiping a tear away from her eye, Pamela responds, "I talk and listen to him every night before I go to bed and there is no barrier between us. He tells me as long as there is no barrier, he will always be there to help me through this. Reaching from her right side, a Spanish man named Pablo rubs her shoulder for support.

*   *   *

Walking to the train station, Pamela puts on her sunglasses to fight the glare of the beaming sun when a little boy, about six years old and carrying a baseball bat walks up to her asking, "Excuse me Ms. Lady, can you tie my sneaker please?"

Pamela looks down on him with a smile on her face and responds, "Sure, sweetheart." Grabbing onto his laces she quickly ties his sneaker and rises back up.

"Thank you," says the little boy.

As Pamela begins to walk away, a heavy-set woman quickly runs to the side of the boy and yells, "What the hell did I tell you about talking to strangers?"

Pamela, looking at the boy's smiling face turn to a frown, responds to the woman, "It's alright, he just asked me to help him with his shoes."

Looking at Pamela with suspicion, she yells at the little tyke, "Derrick, you bring your ass on, and you better not do that again!"

As the mother walks down the street, pulling the boy by his arm, Pamela says softly to herself, "Bye, Derrick." Pulling out money from her pocket, Pamela walks down the steps of the subway.

*   *   *

It is a rainy evening in the Hunts Point section of the Bronx, where the warehouse is smelly and damp. The conveyer belt rolls out "no frills" boxed and canned foods. Wearing her earplugs and goggles, Pamela feels a tap on her shoulder. Turning around, she is face-to-face with a huge Spanish woman named Gladys, who looks about fifty years old and has huge bumps on her face. Looking up at the supervisor's office, Gladys points Pamela in that direction. Taking notice to the poorly lit office, Pamela sees her boss, Tyrone Jones, who motions to her with his index finger to come upstairs. Removing her protective gear, Pamela begins her ascent.

"Close the door behind you, Pamela," says Tyrone. Sitting at his desk with his huge, pot-belly sticking out, Tyrone lights up his cigar. "Sit down, baby" Tyrone says.

Pamela, not sitting, coldly says, "I will stand and I am not your baby."

Letting out a loud, ugly laugh, Tyrone blows smoke in Pamela's direction and says, "Baby, you owe me a whole lot of money because of your many cash advances and I am growing impatient with your twenty-five-dollar-a-week repayments. So let's stop playing games and clear this debt up the right way."

Pamela, looking down to the floor, can see a few of the female workers sneaking a peek up at the office. "You better take that twenty-five dollars I pay every week Tyrone and go meet one of your women on the 'Point' because that is all your getting from me."

Tyrone's smile is gone as he spits tobacco residue at her feet and responds, "I control many aspects of your life Pamela, like bills getting paid and food going into your stomach, so you should show me some respect."

Shaking her head up and down with a smirk on her face, Pamela says, "Fire me. I will have you bought up on charges with the union and keep talking; I will file sexual harassment charges too. But know this, Tyrone; I will never in a fucking lifetime give you anything but your twenty-five dollars and like I said, that should get you a lot from some girls on the point." As the two stare at each other, Pamela makes the first move and exits the office.

*   *   *

Walking from her job in a horrendous rainstorm with her three-dollar umbrella destroyed, Pamela hurries to the train station, four blocks away. Wiping her face with her free hand, she begins to jog towards the train station, which is now a block and a half away as she can see the green light that sits upon the subway entrance. Deciding that her umbrella has taken enough of a beating, Pamela throws it in a nearby trash bin. With her newly done hair getting drenched, she reaches into her pocket for some money to get on the train, when Pamela suddenly grabbed by her arm, violently thrown to the ground, is dragged to an abandoned building's alleyway. Kicking and thrashing her legs, Pamela can hear her assailant's deep breathing. Trying to get her hands on the assailants face, Pamela is thrown into some garbage cans, causing some major bruising to her ribs.

"Help me! Help me!" screams a battered Pamela. Struggling to make it to her feet, she feels a cold, hard smack across her face that releases blood in her mouth. Now grabbing a garbage can lid and swinging wildly, she connects to the predator's head, causing him to stumble backwards. Making it to her feet, Pamela stumbles to keep her balance.

"Somebody please! Help me!" she continues to scream. Looking down the dark alleyway, Pamela notices her assailant making it to its feet. Looking frantically on the ground, Pamela locates a piece of broken brick that she quickly picks up. Seeing the only thing standing between her and the alleyway entrance is her assailant, Pamela makes her move. With her arm cocked halfway up in the air, she runs down the alley towards the tall figure. With all the strength in her body, she smashes the rock across his face while, at the same time, pushing him into the garbage cans. As both of them fall to the ground, Pamela can hear his screams come from behind his hands as he holds his face. Using her assailant as support, she is able to push herself up to her feet. Feeling her swollen lip, Pamela unmercifully kicks the man in his balls and spits her blood on him as she stumbles out of the alley.

Holding her bruised ribs and drenched from the rain, Pamela sees a town car cab sitting at a red light. Gathering herself, she runs to the cab frantically knocking on the back passenger window. Hearing the door locks pop up, Pamela quickly swings open the door and jumps in. The Spanish cabdriver turning around and looking at her, asks, "Where you going?"

An exhausted Pamela responds, "Get me to Lincoln Hospital." As the cab takes off, she lays her head back and lets her tears flow softly, "Thank you God."

*   *   *

Removing her keys for her building, Pamela gingerly walks to the staircase leading to her fourth floor apartment. Gritting her teeth, she begins to climb one-step at a time, barely finding the strength to continue to the next step. Holding a cold compress she received from the hospital for her swollen lower lip, she pays no attention to the commotion coming from the various apartments on each floor she passes. Painfully making it to her floor, Pamela begins to unlock her door when very stealth-like; her next-door neighbor taps her on the shoulder, causing Pamela to jump out of her skin.

"Oh shit," yells a frightened Pamela, who quickly turns around, ignoring the pain coming from her sore rib cage. "Damn Doug! Don't sneak up on me like that; say something."

Doug, who is wearing a silk black shirt with slacks to match, smiles at Pamela as if she was the last piece of apple pie in the world. "Baby, what happened to my luscious lips," asks Doug.

Trying to ignore him, she continues to unlock her door and enter her apartment when Doug puts his hand in front of her in an attempt to stop Pamela from entering.

"Come on Doug. Please, I need to go inside."

Turning her head away from Doug, who has been drinking, Pamela continues to hold her ribs while at the same time sucking her teeth in frustration.

"Let me ask you something. When you first moved into this motherfucking apartment, I was the only person to show you some respect and now all you do when I try to talk to you is act all bitchy, like your shit does not stink!" yells Doug.

Pamela, not saying a word, jingles her keys in her hand, looking at the white ceramic tiles that decorate the hallway floor. A frustrated Doug continues, "You better start to realize, Ms. Bitch, that it would be to your advantage to accept me as a friend than to have me as an enemy." With a few seconds of silence, Doug slowly removes his hand and steps away allowing Pamela to enter her apartment. However, before doing so he makes one final statement to Pamela "Sooner or later, I will have you baby, so you should make it sooner."

With that Pamela violently slams her door so hard it sounds as if an M-80 firecracker has exploded in the hallway.

Standing inside her apartment with her back to the door, Pamela can hear Doug laughing loudly in the hallway. Removing her shoes from her swollen and sore feet, Pamela slowly walks to her dark bedroom. Feeling for her light switch, she turns on her light and a beautiful smile comes across her face as she looks straight ahead at her personal shrine of Derrick. Mesmerized by his radiant smile, Pamela holds her ribs as she walks over to her dresser where her son awaits. Looking at her battered face, she never lets her smile leave as she lights the vanilla scented candle that she dedicated to her son, a lover of all things vanilla. As the flame from the candle flickers, Pamela tells her boy, "I am here baby. We made it through another one." Bowing her head, Pamela closes her eyes and meditates to her Higher Power.

Chapter Six
A Rose is Still a Rose

The stands are jammed packed at Dade High School in Miami, Florida. Some of the fastest track and field boys and girls are competing in the three-day event.

Nine girls are lining up at the starting line for the 100-meter dash. Representing Dade High is a 14-year-old freshman named Rose Garden. With long corn braids that extend down her back, the very dark-skinned Rose has a body that is slim and tight, rippling with muscles. Wearing an orange mesh suit, Rose loosens her legs as she removes her warm-up suit. Hearing the judge over the loud speaker, all nine girls slowly walk up to the starting line. As the young women wedge onto their starting blocks, they all arch their backs while remaining on their knees. As the judge announces, "runners set," the women rise and wait until they hear...Bang!

Like greyhounds chasing a rabbit, the girls are off and running. Rose is currently in fourth place and pumping her legs hard. The crowd is roaring as a light-skinned junior from Pensacola High named Tammy Johnson is in the lead with about 50 meters to go. Finding another gear within her, Rose makes a move and passes two girls on each side of her, now neck-and-neck with Tammy. With the crowd in a frenzied state and other competitors looking on, Rose and Tammy separate from the pack with about 20 meters to go. Tammy gains a fraction of an advantage on Rose, who now bites her lower lip and asks her slender powerful legs for more and they respond by gaining back the deficit, taking the lead with 10 meters to go. Rose, seeing the yellow tape in front of her, sucks in a quick gulp of air, explodes towards the tape while Tammy, giving it everything she has, is unable to respond to Rose's challenge, fights for second place. Sticking her chest out, the fourteen-year-old Rose breaks the yellow tape and causes the 6,000 spectators that fill the stands to cheer in unison.

As the other runners cross the finish line, Rose grabbed gently by her arm by Tammy who whispers, "Your ass better stay ready because you may be Miami's pride and joy but we will be meeting again at the

Olympic trials."

    Breathing hard Rose says, "Thanks and looking forward to it."

          *   *   *

    Standing on the center podium, Rose bends her head down and receives her gold medal. Waving to the crowd, Rose looks around for her track coach, Eddie Wright. Spotting him on the side of the field with her other teammates, Rose runs off the podium and into his waiting, open arms. As Rose's teammates pick her up, she can see her father Butch Rose slowly clapping his hands together in the stands. As Coach Wright lets her down, Rose has no idea that the smile once on her face a second ago is gone. Her teammates notice it, but have no idea why. Rose, grabbing her coach by the neck, forces him down to her level and asks, "Coach Wright, do you think I could catch a ride home with you?" Smiling down at Rose, he responds, "Sure, sweetheart, no problem."

    Rose, looking at her father, motions with her hands in a steering motion points to her coach.

    Butch smiles and gives Rose the ok sign then whispers, "Daddy will see you when you get home." Putting on his straw fedora, Butch exits the stands and heads to his car.

          *   *   *

    As Coach Wright pulls up to Rose's small but modest looking Miami home, all five of the female members from the team hug and kiss Rose as she grabs her duffel bag and begins to exit her coach's van. Before exiting, Coach Wright tells her, "Young lady, we are all so proud of you, and you deserve all of the credit for getting us into first place. You be sure you tell your Dad I said hello and you make sure you study tonight." Reaching over to the middle row of the van, the coach pats Rose on her head and motions to her to get out.

    "Good night everyone, see you in class tomorrow" says Rose. Getting out of the van, Rose stares at the van carrying her teammates and friends down the dirt road. Turning to look at her home, Rose goes inside.

          *   *   *

    Rose, entering her room, looks around at the small but neat pink, painted area that has a canopy bed, a 19-inch television, a computer, a printer, and a couple of wooden dressers. Setting her bag down, Rose removes her gold medal from her neck and smiles. In the center of the wall is a picture that hangs in a beautiful oak frame. The picture is of a stunning, dark-skinned woman with the smoothest skin you have ever seen. Her eyes are hazel, her lips are plump and she has skin without blemish. Surrounding the picture are at least 100 medals from track and field competitions throughout the country. Newspaper clippings are pasted all over the wall as well. Dangling from the corner of the picture frame is a pair of ruby red track shoes. Rose, walking slowly to the shoes, lifts them off the frame and turns them over reading what is on the bottom of the sole: "Baby girl, I give you these wings so that you my fly wherever you want, love Mommy." Holding the shoes close to her chest, Rose hangs her gold medal on a new nail she put in the wall. Staring at her mother's picture, Rose proclaims, "This is for you, Mommy." Rose kisses the picture and admires her mother's beauty.

"Get your ass downstairs and cook our supper!" demands a six-foot-two-inch, two hundred and seventy-five pound Butch. Dropping her track shoes to the ground, a terrified Rose quickly spins around to face her bare-chested father.

"Yes Daddy I am coming down now," a quivering Rose answers.

Glaring at his daughter, Butch orders, "Now goddammit! I am hungry!"

Walking towards her door, Rose stands with her head bent towards the floor, not to dare look at her father. Smirking, Butch slowly moves to one side so Rose can go to the kitchen.

*　*　*

Getting out of the shower later that evening, Butch begins to dry off and now splashes cheap cologne on his body. Taking out his comb, he runs it through his nappy beard, causing popping sounds. Walking into his bedroom, he puts on a two-piece pajama suit that looks like the uniforms orderlies wear in hospitals. Turning on his radio, Butch grunts as he slowly lies across the bed, smiling and looking up at his chipped plastered ceiling.

Rose, preparing herself for bed, is wearing her mother's favorite blue pajamas and a pair of pink cotton socks. Gathering her books for school, Rose puts them inside her schoolbag. Looking over at her chair, she looks at the school outfit she has prepared. Finally, Rose looks over to her mother's picture and says, "I miss you, and I will always love you." Grabbing her small brown bible off her dresser, Rose opens it to Psalm 23, laying it at the foot of her bed. Getting on her knees, Rose asks, "Heavenly Father, thank you for all of the blessings you have given me and for taking care of my momma. I do not know if you will be angry with me for asking this, but could you please bring me to my mother tonight? I just want to feel safe again. Please maybe tonight bring me to my Momma. Amen." Getting up from her knees, Rose sits her bible back on her dresser, gets into bed, turns off her lamp and waits.

*　*　*

One hour has passed and Rose, feeling a calm come over her room, begins to close her eyes when she hears the heavy footsteps. Closer and closer they stop in front of her door. Looking towards the bottom of her door, Rose can see the black shadow, and now she can hear the turning of the door knob. As the door slowly opens the smell of the cheap cologne penetrates her nostrils. Tears now running down both sides of her cheeks, Rose can see the dark and hairy monster standing over her.

"Move over for Daddy," Butch requests in a firm voice.

A crying and shaking Rose pleads, "You said no more after the last time. This is not right, Daddy, please." The bed now makes a loud creaking sound as the hulking Butch lies on top and engulfs a defenseless Rose.

From outside of the bedroom door the moans of Butch Garden and the creaking of the white canopy bed travels throughout the house.

*　*　*

The ultimate violation is over and Rose feeling dirty clicks on the light in her bathroom, barely able to look at herself.

"You will not take me God because I am dirty, right? Well I did not make myself this way; he did." Removing her pajamas, Rose examines her body in the full-length mirror and gently rubs the bruises between her sleek athletic thighs. Bowing her head down in self-pity, she turns on the water in an attempt to cleanse herself in the shower. Stepping in, Rose lets the hot pulsating streams of water hit and penetrate her skin. Not paying attention to the scolding damage to her beautiful skin, Rose begins to build up her threshold for the pain.

"You refuse to take me, so I guess I will send him to you. You refuse to protect me, so I will protect myself," proclaims Rose. Turning off the shower and dropping her face cloth to the tub floor, Rose steps out of the shower into a steamy, sauna-like bathroom. Barely seeing what is in front of her; she wipes the fogged mirror and stares at her welted body. "I will hurt no more."

*　*　*

Looking at the clock that hangs crooked on the hallway wall, Rose reads that it is 3:45 in the morning. Setting her duffel bag and her red track shoes on the hallway floor, Rose puts her ear to her father's bedroom door and can hear his loud disgusting snores. Gently turning the door knob, she slowly and quietly pushes the door open. Sticking her head into the slightly opened door, Rose can smell the repulsive mixture of Old Spice cologne and Jack Daniels whisky. Sure, that he would sleep forever she steps into the unclean bedroom lit by a small nightlight.

Rose looks at Butch sprawled face up naked in his bed. Walking directly to his closet with the missing door, Rose reaches for the brown shoe box at the bottom of the closet and removes the cover. Staring at its contents for a few seconds, she reaches in and removes the black .38 special. Feeling the weight of the gun, Rose can barely level the gun straight with two hands. Walking slowly over to the comatose Butch, Rose trembles as tears begin to fall from her eyes. Using all of her strength, she takes two more steps forward, raising the gun when she kicks an unseen green metal case the size of a sneaker box.

While Rose holds her breath and remains, the sound of the box causes Butch to shift his naked body in the bed and change his snoring pattern. Staring at the scene, Rose is as still as a boulder. Seeing her father fall back into a deep sleep, Rose gently bends down and sits on the dirty wooden floor. Sitting the pistol in her lap, Rose gently lifts the box off the floor and sets it in front of her. Seeing that the box is not locked, she slowly lifts the cover and looks inside. Not sure of what she has found,

Rose removes a handful of white plastic cards that resemble postcards. Evening them out in her hand, Rose turns them over to see if the other side makes sense. Slowly bringing it to her eyes, Rose grabs her mouth and holds her breath, trying not to scream. What is in her hands are Polaroid pictures of little boys and girls not more than seven years old engaged in horrific and graphic sexual acts with grown men.

Not able to hold her dinner, Rose crawls over to a corner as quietly as she can and vomits. Still looking at the pictures, Rose looks at the innocent little one's with frowns on their faces and black bags under their eyes. The children are black, white and oriental. They look as if they suffer from malnutrition. The men who look like businessmen from corporations have smiles on their faces. Walking over to her father, Rose steps over the loaded gun and stands directly over him. Wiping away her tears, Rose gently spreads the pictures around his body and on his bed. Looking at her father, Rose announces, "I will be back you fucking sick pervert."

*   *   *

Reentering her father's room, Rose has a red metal can in one hand and a book of matches in the other. Not paying attention to her still snoring father, whose leg and arm are now hanging off the bed, Rose screws the cap off the can and begins to spread the kerosene fluid throughout the bedroom. Making sure not to get any fluid on Butch's face, Rose soaks his bed and the pictures with kerosene. Looking down at the snoring monster, Rose removes a set of pantyhose from her jacket pocket and proceeds to tie Butch's dangling foot to the bottom post of the bed. Making sure her knots are tight, Rose soaks the rest of the bedroom leading to the door.

Standing in the doorway of her father's bedroom Rose removes the car keys to her father's truck from her pocket, grabbing her bag and track shoes. Using the book of matches, Rose calmly lights the entire book, tosses it on the bedroom floor, closes the door and exits the house with her belongings.

*   *   *

Sitting in the black truck, Rose can see from the rearview mirror her father's bedroom going up in flames. Starting the truck, a crying Rose clutches her gold medal that sits around her neck and says, "I am sorry coach Wright," as she drives off down the highway towards the Trailways bus depot. From the back of the truck and through the trees, the Garden's house is going up in flames.

*   *   *

While sitting on the bus, Rose sees that the sun is beginning to rise, and she listens to the engine start up and the door close. The bus is three-quarters full and pulling out of the depot when the bus driver, over the loud speaker, announces, "This is the six fifteen to New York City; our arrival time is twenty two hours." Looking at the bottom of her track shoes, Rose reads her mother's quote: "You may fly wherever you want." Closing her eyes, Rose falls asleep.

Chapter Seven
Let's Be Friends

It is Friday evening and Doug is wearing a two-piece Hugo Boss suit as he prepares for his party at his Bronx Co-op that none of his partners knew he owned. Inside the large living room, there is a large Italian leather sectional and a marble coffee table. In one corner of the living room sits, a 50-inch rear projection television hooked up to a state of the art Bose home theater system. On the other side of the room, there is a large table with heated pans of lobster tails, imported Alaskan crab legs, filet mignon, baked salmon, pasta with Alf redo sauce and five different types of vegetables. On ice sits forty-eight bottles of Dom Perignon and forty bottles of imported beer. Admiring his set-up, Doug slowly rubs his hands together and walks to his three bedrooms.

Walking down the long hallway, Doug stops and opens a door that is to his left. Stepping inside, Doug inhales the smell of jasmine that fills the room. The room is large and is lit by scented candles that sit atop oak armoires and oak night stands. Equally spaced apart are three full-size beds that are covered by Egyptian bed spreads and sheets. Sitting on each bed is a beautiful woman wearing Victoria Secret lingerie. There is a thick Asian woman named Kim, an hour-glassed-shaped Spanish woman named Maria and a dark sister named Moesha.

Doug, looking at each of them, smiles and asks, "Ladies, you do understand how important this is to me, right?"

The three women smiling at Doug answer "Yes, Daddy."

Taking one last look at the women, Doug smiles and closes the door behind him. Two steps to his right, Doug opens another door that has the same set-up as the first except for two differences. One, the room has the smell of cinnamon, and on each bed sits three Russian woman named Abir, Helena, and Tabitha. All three women are wearing identical one-piece leopard print teddies and are listening to classical music. Walking into the room, Doug kisses them all on the cheek and asks, "Will you ladies screw their brains out tonight?

Smiling at Doug, they all respond, "All night long," in their native accent. Exiting the room, Doug makes his final stop to the last bedroom, which is at the end of the hallway directly in front of him. Before entering the room, Doug stops and stares at the door, shaking his head slowly. As Doug grabs on to the door knob and enters the room, his eyes widen as he looks at the 300-pound German woman named Mabel. Wearing an all-black, leather get-up, Mabel slowly stands to her feet as the fat from her pale body overlaps from the various openings on her outfit.

Wearing fire-truck-red lipstick and black eye mascara, the silent woman says nothing but smacks a black leather whip on her right hand. Wearing a black leather motorcycle cap and boots to match, she finally asks, "Where is my fucking man?"

Doug, still staring, snaps out of his temporary trance and answers, "Easy, big girl; your man is on his way."

Closing the door slowly and looking at Mabel, Doug says, "Whatever turns you on partner."

*   *   *

Sitting in his living room, Doug hears the doorbell and gets up to answer it. Looking through the peephole, a smiling Doug opens his door and greets his guest, "Detective Davis what is going on?"

As a tall blonde-haired, well-built Tommy Davis enters the apartment with eight other police officers; they greet Doug with a handshake and a pat on the back. "Doug my brother from another mother…where the party at?" asks the detective.

Doug, laughing aloud with the rest of the officers, closes and locks the door behind him and answers, "Right here, my brother, right here."

Inside the living room, Doug observes the nine high-ranking officers from three different precincts chow down on his spread and drink beer and champagne. Detective Tommy Davis, Detective Sam Daniels, a sixteen-year African American veteran, Detective Joseph McCarthy, a thirty-year old Irish American who heads the Bronx drug task force and Detective Tony Harris of homicide are sitting on the couch admiring Doug's apartment.

"Hey Doug, you have to give me the number of your accountant so I can be like you," jokes Davis as the three detectives bust out in laughter, continuing to enjoy their meals.

*   *   *

An hour later walking down his hallway, Doug can clearly hear the moaning and groaning coming from each room where six officers are having their own little orgy. Walking straight ahead, Doug covers his mouth from letting his laugh be heard as he can hear the sound of the whip being smacked on detective Tony Harris by the three hundred pound Mabel. Before returning to the living room, Doug removing a remote control the size of a credit card, points it towards a light fixture that sits atop the ceiling. Looking carefully at the light, Doug can see a small glowing red light come on. With a devilish smile on his face, Doug enters his bathroom.

Closing and locking the bathroom door behind him, Doug bends down to his vanity under his sink and opens the locked door. Moving toilet paper and cleaning products to one side, Doug slides open a small door and smiles at six VCRs that are recording everything going on in every room of his apartment. On the VCRs are labels that read "Living room," "Bedroom #1," "Bedroom #2," "Bedroom #3," "Kitchen" and "Outside front door." Sliding the door closed and locking it, Doug puts the cleaning products and toilet paper back where they were and says softly to himself, "Just in case motherfucker's , just in case." Standing back up and brushing himself off, Doug returns to the living room.

Doug returns to the living room with three brown, thick envelopes in his hand. The detectives stop their conversation amongst themselves and focus on what is in Doug's hand.

"You really want to make an impression on us now, don't you?" asks Sam Daniels.

"Business is business," responds Doug, who hands each officer an envelope. As each man removes five thousand dollars, Doug looks over at his grandfather clock and winks at the pinhead camera that sits in the screw that holds the hour and minute hands together. All three officers stand by Doug, who then turns his attention to Detective Tommy Davis.

"Doug, as long as you stick to the agreement, you will have our loyalty and protection. We will see to it that you will have your corners with no hassle," says Davis.

Nodding his head up and down, Doug focuses on Detective McCarthy, who adds, "I will always give you a heads up when my department is ready to conduct a sweep of your district. That way you can give your men a rest while the competition gets caught up in the web."

As the six officers who were having sex return to the living room, they all walk over and begin to fix a plate of food. One of the officers, Sergeant Carlos Ortiz, sits on Doug's couch, putting his feet on the marble coffee table.

Doug, looking agitated, asks, "Brother that is a three thousand dollar table; can you please remove your feet?"

Looking at the Doug from the corner of his eye, Ortiz ignores him. Taking control of the situation, Detective McCarthy orders, "Hey, Ortiz, respect our friend's home and take your fucking feet off his table."

A somewhat embarrassed Ortiz does and responds, "I apologize." Doug, who is steaming responds, "Yeah, no problem."

The three detectives remove their coats and Detective Sam Daniels tells Doug, "Ok, partner; we are ready to get deep into some putang right about now." Putting his arm around the detective's shoulder, Doug says, "Right this way my friends."

* * *

It is 4:00 a.m. Saturday morning, and all nine police officers gather in the living room making one last plate of food to go. Doug is putting bottles of champagne in plastic bags and handing them out to all of the officers. Sneaking a peek up at his grandfather clock, Doug is aware that his camera is still on and recording the festivities of the long evening. As the men began putting on their jackets, Doug announces, "I want to thank you for this opportunity to establish, hopefully, a long and prosperous relationship with you all."

All the men hold up their champagne bottles as a sign of toasting, and all say, "Yes, yes!"

Doug, walking them to the apartment door, opens it and watches them leave one-by-one until he is face-to-face with Detective Tommy Davis, who tells Doug, "Just remember, partner. This can go two ways; we can have a good working thing where everybody wins, or you can fuck us and then in turn, I promise you we will bury your ass. But I believe you will do the right thing Doug."

Smacking Doug on his shoulder, Tommy exits with the rest of his comrades. Closing the door behind him, Doug says, "You motherfucker's are already buried; you just don't know it."

*   *   *

The women, all cleaned and dressed up, are getting two thousand dollars apiece from Doug as he shakes their hands. "Ladies, you hooked me up tonight. Every one of those men left with a smile on their face this morning, and I want to thank you all for helping me. I have everybody's' number, so when another event comes up, you will be the first I will call. There are three limos waiting for you downstairs, so please get your asses out of my place," he says. One-by-one, the women leave the apartment until all are gone.

Inside his living room, Doug pulls his laptop from underneath his couch. Turning it on, he puts in a disc and pulls up some private files on all nine officers. Smiling ear-to-ear, Doug says, "I guess that Coke-bottle-glasses-wearing Timothy is good for something. That book worm bastard was able to hack into the precincts computer system with no problem. That was the best fifteen hundred I spent in a while." Looking at the officer's files, Doug accesses their salary, family history, all the reports they have filed, and most importantly, all of the people they have busted. To top it off, Doug even has access to their past major purchases for the past two years.

Looking at Detective Davis's file, Doug says with a surprised tone, "This motherfucker has a Porsche and a Yukon? Yeah ok duly noted."

After a few minutes, Doug decides he needs a little sleep, but before lying down, he places a phone call to his partner Troy. Hearing a sleeping Troy answer his phone, Doug responds, "Yeah, boy gets your ass up and make some more dough for the baker man. Nah, I'm just fucking with you. Listen, tell Buster and Fish that we will all meet up at the club tonight for Dinner, dancing and sticking hood rats with big pieces of meat. I just might find my future ex-wife for the summer. Ok, partner, I will see you there."

Hanging up his phone, Doug pulls his remote control from his pocket shutting down cameras throughout his apartment. As the sun rises, Doug stares out of the window and says, "See Mama, Pop was wrong. I am doing well for myself. I know you are looking down on my black ass and I hope you are somewhat proud of me. I wish you could see me now." Walking slowly to his couch, Doug plops down on it and within twenty seconds, he was sound asleep.

Chapter Eight
What Have You Been Up to Girl?

It has been a little while since that rainy night at the bus terminal, but Sandra has come a long way since then. Sitting in her Harlem kitchenette that is located at 119th street and 5th Avenue, she looks over her cell phone and light bills.

Her kitchenette is tiny but very comfortable. Sitting at her small round table that can only seat two, Sandra walks over to her dresser and grabs her paycheck she has been receiving from American Temps. For the past three months, she has been working at small businesses in the Bronx and Brooklyn consisting of clerical work.

Not being able to afford anything out of Macy's department store, Sandra has decorated her place very nicely with second-hand goods. Her walls are covered with beautiful African art bought for three dollars from the local street vendors while her bed is covered with afro-centric colored throw pillows from the Saturday flea shop on Lenox Avenue. She has made a multi-colored bookshelf out of plastic milk crates she received from Alvin, the manager at the local grocery store, who has a thing for Sandra. In the crates are at least sixty books ranging from African history to how to make anything out of chicken broth. Her cooking area consists of a tiny stove and a very small refrigerator, but you can eat off her floor, and there is not a dirty dish in her sink.

The only thing she does hate about her place is the sharing of the bathroom with the three other tenants. The three women, Missy, Pearl and Anita, all seem to be nice, but Missy and Pearl are nasty when it comes to cleaning up after themselves. Anita, who is a party girl, was the first to welcome Sandra to the two-story brownstone and from time to time, they hang out. Sandra has even managed to put away about twelve hundred dollars from her pageant prize money she won in Virginia even though, Sandra found out the hard way, that the check was bogus.

The 19-inch television is not bad for something out of a pawnshop. Sandra keeps at her bedside a bible that she received from the woman who befriended her at the port authority; Brenda Taylor. Almost like a guardian angel Brenda, helped Sandra get her place, recommended her to the temporary agency and wrote her encouraging letters from time to time. The other book Sandra keeps at her bedside is the New York University masters' degree program directory she picked up from work a few weeks ago. Realizing how tough the job market is in the city, Sandra still holds on to her dream of becoming a news anchor but now knows it will take a little more education and a lot of hard work.

Walking over to her mirror, Sandra plays with her braids and puts a stick of gum in her mouth, getting ready to go to the bank when there is a knock at the door. Looking through her peephole, she sees that it is Anita. Opening the door, the two women embrace and sit at the dinette table. Anita, wearing tight, stoned-washed jeans and a blue wife beater, is light-skinned with an hourglass figure and an attitude to match. Wearing a white gold necklace and a titanium Movado watch, she looks at Sandra's check that is sitting on the table and asks, "Girl, how the hell do you make it on two hundred and thirty-six dollars a week?"

Smiling at Anita Sandra responds, "It is not that hard, I just have to budget, while not spending what I do not have."

Holding the check up to the sunlight shining through the window, Anita says, "Baby, when will you learn that you can have anything you want? You just have to go and take it. We have plenty of assets at our disposal; you just have to know who to use them on."

Sandra, looking down at her floor, says, "I was bought up to believe that hard work always pays off in the end. God says 'If one does not work then one does not eat,' so although my check may not be much, it helps me maintain until things get better."

Anita, letting out a high pitch laugh, looks at Sandra in her eyes and says, "Listen, baby, all that sounds good, but that shit does not pay for the things on my neck and wrist. There are a lot of motherfucker's out here with big dollars to spend, looking for a trophy to show off to their homies. I know I am fine as hell and can cook my ass off. My momma says there is one way to get what you want from a brother, walk in a room with a plate of food butt ass naked, and he will get you anything you desire. Why spend my shit when I can spend his."

Sandra, putting her check in her pocket, asks Anita, "I am going to the bank; you want to come?"

Staring at Sandra for a few seconds, Anita answers, "Yeah, sure, but only if you come with me to Macy's after."

Grabbing her apartment keys, Sandra answers, "Ok, no problem." The two young women exit the apartment into the sun-splashed streets of Harlem.

* * *

Sandra is in total awe of Macy's as she walks around the department store, looking at the clothes, smelling the fragrances and admiring the many appliances that she wishes she could have. Meanwhile, Anita is holding a coach bag, a Donna Karen suit and two pair of Tommy

Hilfiger jeans. Sandra, who allows a Spanish woman to spray her with a nice smelling perfume, turns her attention to Anita who is now making her way to the cash register. Sandra, walking from another direction, meets her before she gets to the register.

"Oh Anita, can I see what you have, please?" Sandra asks.

Letting Sandra look at her things, a stunned Sandra grabs and looks at the price tags on the merchandise. Adding everything up quickly in her head, Sandra asks, "How can you afford this Anita? I would have to work for three months to have this."

A grinning Anita, pulling out a credit card and a fifty-dollar bill, walks up to the cash register and hands her things to the white cashier, who is now ringing it up.

"Will you be paying cash or charge?" the cashier asks.

Anita hands the woman the credit card and watches her swipe it on the card reader. "Mr. Clarke, I will need some identification, please," requests the cashier.

Reaching across to the cashier, Anita hands her the fifty-dollar bill and asks, "Is that sufficient proof?

A smiling cashier answers, "Yes and I will need you to sign here, please."

Grabbing the pen, Anita does so as the cashier packs her bags. Taking her merchandise, Anita says, "Thank you very much."

Sandra, not saying a word, stares at the cashier, who just smiles and takes care of the next customer. Anita, putting on her sunglasses, exits the store with Sandra not too far behind.

* * *

As Sandra sits on the third step of the brownstone of her apartment, she watches Anita lean over into a red Cadillac driven by a dark-skinned brother, who could pass as an offensive tackle in the NFL. Anita reaches into her jeans pocket pulling out the credit card she used in Macys giving it to the brother. Meanwhile, Sandra can clearly see him with his hand down Anita's shirt, rubbing on her breast. A few moments pass when Sandra can see the dark-skinned brother attempting to stick his tongue in Anita's mouth. Before he can though, Anita waves her finger from side to side and walks away from the car. The smiling brother, who is wearing shades, slowly drives off. Anita returns to the stoop, smiling and says to Sandra, "Assets, baby. You got them too and if you stop acting so damn shy, I will show you how to use yours also."

* * *

It is 7:00 p.m. and Sandra is relaxing on her bed, eating Breyers strawberry ice cream and watching a rerun of the old game show "Concentration". With little effort, she picks the numbered blocks one by one, revealing the matching cubes that contain a prize or money. Getting frustrated with the two contestants, Sandra says, "Oh my goodness, what kind of memory malfunction are you people going through? Choose four, not nine. Oh, forget it you have no hope." Getting off the bed, Sandra removes her nylon jogging pants and t-shirt, lying back down with nothing on but her panties and bra. Tuning out the television, Sandra closes her eyes and thinks about the tall, dark-skinned brother who delivers packages to her temporary job site.

Thinking about his hands caressing her face and her thighs, Sandra slowly slides her hand into the front of her panties while at the same time lifting her bra and revealing her plump but firm breast. Rubbing her nipple, Sandra lets out a moan as she can almost feel the strong, dark brother grabbing and lifting her large but shapely thigh in the air while he slowly gives her soft wet kisses. Creating a rhythm while she caresses herself, Sandra slowly arches her back in the air as a cool summer breeze comes through her open window moving gently over her body. Looking up at her imaginary lover, who is strong and confident, Sandra slowly wraps her thighs around his wide back as he creates his rhythm to the sounds of The Isley Brothers "Between the Sheets". Letting out a louder and more intense moan, Sandra feels the eruption getting near and decides she can no longer wait for her lover and lets herself go: "Oh, shit yes!" she yells, drowning out the contestants on the Wheel of Fortune. Sweating and somewhat drained, Sandra lifts herself off the bed, looking at the blonde-haired man trying to figure out what letter to choose when she says, "Choose a vowel."

Slowly putting on her pants and t-shirt, there is a knock at the door. "Who is it?" asks Sandra.

From the other side of the door where she heard everything, Anita answers, "Girl, you are going to go blind doing that shit. Get your ass up so we can party tonight." Letting out a long sigh Sandra walks to the door letting Anita enter.

*   *   *

After spending, an hour or so getting ready Sandra is looking good in her short but not too scanky skirt with a sleeveless baby blue silk like shirt. Wearing a pair of Anita's black pumps, Sandra fixes her cornrows in a ball that sits on top of her head with a few braids coming across her face making her look very sexy and exotic. Sitting on the bed staring at Sandra is Anita, who is very pretty herself and is wearing the most expensive clothes and jewelry but cannot hold a candle to Sandra, who just has the look of someone with natural, pure beauty.

Turning to Anita, Sandra asks "How do I look?"

Letting a small grin come across her face, Anita answers, "You look nice with my bad-ass shoes on."

Looking down to the ground, Sandra responds, "Thanks, Anita." Picking up her cell phone, Anita dials a cab company and requests a cab. Hanging up her phone, Anita tells Sandra, "Ok, baby doll. We have ten minutes to get outside."

Looking hesitant, Sandra asks, "Where exactly are we going tonight? I really don't want to be out too late."

Anita, rolling her eyes up to the ceiling, says, "Oh, girl, please... shit. I found out about this hot new spot where the players hang out. It is called The Baby Powder Club, and its run by this guy named Doug or something." Hearing the horn blow outside the window, Anita grabs Sandra by the hand and pulls her towards the door as the two women head into the neon lights of Harlem.

Getting inside the cab, Anita tells the driver "One hundred and forty-fourth Street and Malcolm X Boulevard. As the cab takes off Sandra feels like she is part of the scene.

Chapter Nine
Blinded By the Light

The club jammed packed with the sounds of "The Fugees" being blasted through the sound system has Sandra in total awe of how well club "Baby Powder" is coordinated. The bar resembles an oval-shaped racetrack with over one hundred plush leather chairs and four bartenders mixing drinks. The dance floor is large and consists of polished, white-stained oak. Looking around, Sandra notices that all of the men are wearing designer two-piece suits and expensive shoes to match. The women also are dressed eloquently, which makes her feel a little out of place. Looking towards the back of the club, she notices beautiful tables with white linens and flowers for those who would like to eat.

"This is nothing like Richmond night clubs," says Sandra.

Anita grabs Sandra by the hand leading her to the bar where handsome and distinguished brothers are present.

Trying to keep her composure, a nervous Sandra fiddles with her hair, trying not to stare at anyone. "Girl relax and have some fun. This is a party and we are going to have a good time, shit," says Anita. As Sandra looks around the club, a light-skinned, tall and handsome brother approaches with a slight smile on his face, "Good evening ladies. My name is Greg. Can I buy you ladies a drink?"

Smiling at Greg, Anita is taking stock of him from head to toe gently answers, "No thank you Greg, but that was very nice of you."

Looking somewhat dejected but trying his best not to show it, Greg smiles and quietly walks away.

A puzzled Sandra stares at Anita and asks, "He seemed to be very nice and sincere; why did you turn him away?"

Giving Sandra a smirk, she answers, "Baby, if you want to survive in my world, you have got to pay better attention to the real players and pretenders. First, the brother was wearing shoes from Payless. Second of all, he was wearing a Timex watch. Finally and this shit tops the cake, three teeth missing from the back row of his damn mouth, which means more than likely no benefits, which probably means no job, which makes me ask how the hell did his ass get in here?"

Sandra, trying to look away, cannot help to bust laughing as Anita rolls her eyes from the direction of Greg. As Destiny's Child's "No, no, no" plays, Anita yells and announces to the club, "Damn, that's my song!" Anita grabs Sandra by the hand and pulls her off the bar stool as they quickly make it to the dance floor. Sandra, watching and trying to keep up with Anita, who obviously knows all the new dance moves, decides that she cannot so she creates her own moves. Slowly and seductively moving her body side to side, Sandra finally lets her hair down literally. With braids flinging from side to side, men who were once enjoying their drinks and private conversations are now focusing on the brown-skinned sister with the thick, tight body, letting it all hang out on the dance floor. As Anita and Sandra dance with each other, neither girl takes notice of the small circle that has been created around them.

Sitting in his owner's box that overlooks the club patrons and employees, Doug relaxes in a leather executive chair with a glass of champagne in his hand. The room is off-white with cherry oak wood molding around the ceiling and floor. The lights are soft and somewhat dimmed, giving off a mellow ambiance. Inside the room with Doug are his associates Fish and Troy. Everyone except Doug has two women sitting on each side of them nibbling on their ear and being fed lobster with butter sauce. Doug cannot take his eyes off the dance floor looking at the brown-skinned sister with the thunder thighs, firm breast, small hips and plump backside. However, it is not her body drawing Doug's attention; it is the innocence in her face. That look that says "I would never hurt a soul. If a puppy was in the street on a rainy night I would take him in." You see, Doug's experience in this game of making money and making enemies has taught him one thing: nobody can be trusted and loyalty is as definite as winning the lottery. Continuing with his fixation on Sandra, something felt right and pure about her. Still one of the lessons that Doug had learned from Dollar Bill, was never trust a woman totally because she would do and tell you anything to stay close to your stash. Sex them and treat them with the respect they earn, but never let them wake up in your kingdom. Doug knew Dollar Bill was right, but looking at Sandra brought a sense of calmness in the storm for which he lived in.

"Damn Doug, wake the hell up! What are staring at, boss?" asks Troy.

In a calm tone, Doug asks, "Troy, I need you to go down and give that woman with the baby blue blouse on dancing with the light-skinned female--a bottle of Moet and dinner on the club."

Troy, who is kissing on a Spanish woman while feeling on a light-skinned sister, answers, "Come on partner. I am a little busy as you can see."

Doug, cutting his eyes at Troy so hard it could cut a rock, demands, "Goddammit, man! Fuck these women. I asked you to do me a solid!" As Fish stares at an enraged Doug, Troy a little embarrassed gets up and does as told.

Sandra is sweating and smiling ear-to-ear as she watches Anita return to their table with two bottles of water. "Shit, this is nothing but faucet water, and they are charging me six dollars. The next time we'll just drink from the Johnny pump."

Sandra laughs so loud that a few women sitting in the vicinity stare at her. As the women sip on their water, a short Cuban man approaches their table with a large serving tray on his shoulder. Right behind the man is handsomely dressed Troy, who has a forced smile on his face. As the two puzzled women watch the waiter sit lobster and leg of lamb, two bottles of Moet and two dozen of pink roses at their table, Troy excuses the waiter and steps to the table introducing himself.

"Good evening ladies, I hope you are enjoying yourselves tonight. My name is Troy and this dinner along with the bouquet of flowers is a gift to you from the owner, Mr. Doug Gunner." Troy, pointing up to the owner's box, shows the women where Doug is sitting. As Anita picks up her bottle of champagne and waves it wildly in Doug's direction while Sandra shyly and slowly waves her hand up to Doug.

"Thank you Troy and please let Doug know we appreciate the hospitality," Anita says. Troy nods his head in acknowledgment and heads back up to the owner's booth. As Anita goes berserk on her dinner and champagne, Sandra says her grace and begins to eat her food. Chewing and savoring every bite, Sandra inconspicuously looks up at Doug, who is staring down back at her.

* * *

After refreshing themselves in the women's room, Sandra and Anita move slowly with the crowd towards the exit door. Still holding her flowers in her hand, Sandra is sticking close to Anita, who is making her own path to reach the summer night street. The sidewalk is jammed packed with people who are waiting for cabs and their cars to be retrieved by the club's valet attendants. As Anita looks to hail a cab, she feels a tap on her shoulder, when she turns around, Troy is standing behind her.

"Hi, pretty lady. I'm Troy; do you remember me?"

Smiling Anita answers, "Hi Troy, yes I remember you." Troy, pointing towards the corner a few feet down the block, brings to Anita's attention a white Cadillac limousine.

Looking at Troy with suspicion and disbelief, Anita asks, "Who is that for and where is it going?"

Rubbing Anita across her face gently, Troy answers, "It is for you. The driver has been ordered to take you wherever you like."

Anita, looking at a puzzled Sandra and then back at Troy, asks, "What about my girl? Can she ride also?"

Troy, pointing in the opposite direction answers, "Actually, that is for your friend."

Parked with a driver standing by the passenger side is a blue Mercedes Benz limousine. Anita, grabbing Sandra by the arm cautiously and curiously, walks slowly towards the shiny blue limousine. On the face of Anita is one of pure anticipation while Sandra has a look of confusion. As the two women stand near the car, the back tinted window slowly rolls down, revealing a well groomed and handsome Doug Gunner wearing an all white Giorgio Armani suit. Removing his black shades, Doug smiles at the women while tapping on his door with his finger. The driver, who is wearing a tuxedo, opens the door for Doug, who slowly steps out of his car, revealing his blue gators.

"Good evening ladies. I really hope you enjoyed yourselves tonight," says Doug.

Anita, taking a step forward, replies, "Yes we did and you have a classy club."

Never taking his eyes off Sandra, Doug says, "Thanks a lot. I have put much time into my place."

Sandra, with a girlish smile says, "Thank you for the flowers; they smell very nice."

Nodding his head and smiling like a kid at Christmas, Doug asks Sandra, "May I ask your name?"

Sandra replies, "My name is Sandra Lyte and this is my friend Anita Crane."

Doug reaches out, shakes Anita's hand, and smiles. Two cars that are driving by stop and honk at Doug, who in turn acknowledges them. Quickly turning back to Sandra with a sly grin on his face, Doug asks her, "Do you have any idea why I gave you those roses, Sandra?"

Thinking about it for a second, Sandra answers, "No Doug, I do not. Why don't you tell me?"

Rubbing his hands slowly together, he replies, "Because I wanted the roses to know what real beauty looked like."

Anita, who had a "you are full-of-shit" look on her face, is somewhat caught up in the moment. Then it happens; Sandra and Doug's eyes meet and lock, remaining that way for a few seconds. Doug, who stands six feet, three inches tall weighing two hundred and fifty-five pounds, with the physique of Adonis, is melting inside. Anita, watching the whole scene unfold, breaks the silence: "Well, it is getting late and it has been a long day."

Doug, shaking his head in agreement, asks Sandra, "Do you think you would like to spend your Sunday afternoon with me tomorrow, Ms. Lyte?"

Looking at Doug for a few seconds, Sandra answers, "Where did you have in mind, Doug?"

Twisting his shades between his fingers, Doug replies "Whatever pleases you is fine. You know, New York is a big place."

Looking at a smiling Anita, Sandra answers, "Ok, you have a date; noon will be fine."

Reaching into his pocket, Doug pulls out a calling card with his name and number. "Sandra, you call me when you are ready, ok?"

Studying the card while looking into Doug's eyes Sandra answers, "Ok, I will."

Doug, looking at his limo, says, "Well, I was hoping we could have gone for a ride tonight, but that is cool. So, why don't you and Anita take the Cadillac home?" As he shakes Anita and Sandra's hand, Doug, on the down low, slips a miniature box of Godiva chocolates into Sandra's hand. Smiling at Doug, Sandra slowly walks away and heads down the street with Anita to their waiting limo. Doug, who is still standing outside his vehicle, watches in a daze as he admires the perfect shape and proportion of Sandra's knockout figure.

Inside the Cadillac, there is complete silence as Anita opens Sandra's box of chocolate and begins to eat them. Savoring the sweet taste of the creamy chocolate, Anita glances at Sandra from the corner of her eyes and rolls them; mumbling to herself in a very low tone, "Bitch."

Sandra, who is playing with the radio, thinks she heard something and asks, "Anita, did you say something?"

A smiling Anita responds sweetly, "No boo. I did not say anything."

*   *   *

Doug, standing still outside the club, hears a horn coming from across the street and sees that it is Buster's black Suburban. Putting his shades in his jacket pocket, Doug makes it to the truck and is let in by one of Buster's soldiers. Inside the vehicle's backseat is Buster holding a meat cleaver on the wrist of a man named Dexter. His mouth is taped shut, with his hands bounded with plastic and duct tape.

"Yo, boss. I hate to disturb you on your get-out night, but this is the motherfucker that has been stealing from the Laundromat's cookie jar, and we have him on film," says Buster. Dexter is crying and shaking, trying to get a word out but cannot.

"Damn Dexter. When you were dirt ass poor, who gave you a job and paid your sister's rent? Who loved you like a son baby? Doug asks.

Sweat and tears are pouring down Dexter's face as he begins to shake uncontrollably. "You cannot pay me back, Dexter. You do not have shit that I need. But you know what, my man? I am going to show you what it feels like to come up short." Doug, stepping out of the truck, sticks his head in the window and nods at Buster, who raises the meat cleaver chopping down on the wrist of Dexter, who is going berserk while a soldier named Dave holds him. The plastic is filling up with blood, and Buster raises the cleaver again, landing with another swift blow that causes Dexter's hands to dangle by their skin.

Doug, showing no remorse, tells Buster, "Drop him off at Harlem Hospital and call me tomorrow; I need some rest."

Buster, smiling at Doug, punches a wailing Dexter in the jaw, knocking him out completely says, "I hear you boss. We will talk tomorrow."

Doug taps on the hood of the truck and walks towards his limousine. Looking at his driver, Doug says, "Home, my good man."

* * *

Sunday finds Sandra standing in front of a mirror nailed to her door, nervously doing some last final changes to her long, braided hair. Wearing a white blouse and a pair of new black slacks from The Avenue, Sandra looks at her black shoes and thinks if she should wear them. After a moment, Sandra decides that she will keep them on. Looking at her juicy lips, she reaches in her purse and puts some strawberry lip gloss on for good measure, deciding that most men like sisters with glossy, big lips. A horn blowing in front of her place causes Sandra to quickly turn her head and walk to her window. Peeping through her mini-blinds, Sandra sees a fantastic looking Doug dressed in a grey, two-piece Calvin Klein leisure suit. Looking at his clean shaven head, Sandra admires the elegance and style that Doug gives off. Watching Doug blow his horn again, Sandra exposes herself to him from the window with a smile and a wave. Doug, smitten with her beauty, waves back and walks to the other side of his brand new, shiny red Lexus that is not available to the public for another seven months. He opens the door motioning to Sandra, with his finger to get in. Trying not to rush, Sandra motions with her mouth "Ok" and exits her apartment.

Walking down her staircase, Sandra runs into Anita, who is walking up the stairs to her apartment. With a huge smile on her face, Sandra asks, "Girl I am so nervous! He looks so handsome, doesn't he?"

Anita, who is holding a bag of food she bought from the Chinese restaurant, reveals a half smile and responds, "Yeah, I saw him and the motherfucker did not even speak to me when I said hello. Just be careful with him."

Sandra, who has a puzzled look on her face, smiles and says as she walks towards the door, "I will let you know everything that happens when I get back"

As she walks out into the sun-splashed street, Anita says to herself, "Your dumb ass won't last two days with him."

Doug, who is admiring how the sun shines off Sandra's face and hair, says, "It is good to see you, my lovely sister. You look very nice, Sandra."

Trying to do everything not to blush, she responds, "Thank you very much. You look very nice yourself."

As Doug gently grabs her hand, Sandra allows him to lead her into his car. Putting on her seat belt, Sandra discreetly looks at the rear view mirror; watching and admiring the tall muscle-bound Doug enter next to her.

Looking deeply into Sandra's eyes, a smiling Doug, who has his car smelling like "Grey Flannel" cologne, asks her, "Are you ready to have a good time, Sandra?"

Looking back into his eyes, she responds, "Yes, I am." As the sound of smooth jazz plays through the car speakers, Doug and Sandra drive off down 5th Avenue.

* * *

As the two of them sit in Tavern on the Green, Doug is enjoying his swordfish as he watches Sandra eat her lobster and steak. Reaching across the table, Doug pours her some more red wine and does the same for him.

Holding his glass slightly in the air, he asks, "May I propose a toast?"

Holding her glass next to his, Sandra answers, "Yes you may."

Looking into her eyes from across the table, he says, "To a new and hopefully long, exquisite relationship between two people."

Sandra, not saying anything at first, responds, "I agree, same here." As they gently tap glasses, they both take sips of wine and continue to eat.

"Sandra, what part of New York was you born in?" asks Doug.

"I wasn't, Doug. I was born and raised in Richmond, Virginia."

Doug, looking puzzled, asks, "How long have you been here? And what made you come?"

With her looking a little down ridden, she replies, "Maybe once we get to know each other a little better, I can tell you my story."

Nodding his head slowly up and down, Doug replies, "I understand Sandra and I respect that." Smiling at each other, they finish their meal.

* * *

It is late in the afternoon, and Doug is leading Sandra out of the theater on Broadway where they have just finished seeing "Bring in Da Noise, Bring in Da Funk." Sandra, who is holding a t-shirt and a program from the show, is smiling ear-to-ear as she is in awe of the bright lights and excitement coming from the entertainment capital of the world.

"How did you like the show?" Doug asks.

Shaking her head back and fourth, she responds, "I have never seen anyone dance like that before. The show was great thank you."

Putting his arms around her shoulders, Doug turns her around to face him pulling two more tickets out of his pocket, "The night ain't over yet, baby." In Doug's hand are two tickets to Radio City Music Hall to see "Luther in concert"

Looking at the tickets, Sandra grabs her mouth and then around Doug's neck yelling, "Oh my goodness. Luther is my man! Thank you."

Doug, holding her by her thin waist, savors her sweet smelling perfume and says, "Come on; let's go see your man." Walking in the direction of Radio City, Sandra puts her head on Doug's massive arm and walks side-by-side with him.

* * *

As Doug, drives Sandra back to her place, the moon and stars on this warm summer night illuminate from the sky directly into the open moon roof of Doug's car. As "Cherish" by Kool and the Gang plays on the radio, Sandra rests her head sideways on the passenger seat, gazing at Doug. As they now drive across the F.D.R. Highway, Sandra admires the lighted skyline of the city.

"Doug, I just want you to know that this has been the best time I have ever had out with anyone and I want to thank you again," says Sandra.

Smiling at Sandra, Doug responds, "I had a nice time too and like I said, hopefully we will remain friends."

"Doug, if you do not mind me asking what is it that you do?"

Clearing his throat, Doug answers, "Sandra, I own my club and I also work in exporting for a good friend of mine, which earns me some extra cash.

Sitting straight up now in her seat, she says, "That's really interesting work; do you travel much?"

Coming towards their exit, Doug answers, "Every now and then, I have to leave town."

As they get closer to Sandra's place, Doug asks, "Do you need anything from the store before I let you off?"

Contemplating for a minute, Sandra answers, "No thank you Doug; I am fine."

Pulling up in front of her place, Doug puts the car in park and turns to Sandra saying, "I am throwing a birthday party for a good friend of mine this Friday, It would mean a lot to me if you joined me."

A smitten Sandra answers, "It would be my pleasure to join you." As the two of them stare into each others eyes, Doug moves in for a goodnight kiss and Sandra moves in also. As they slowly kiss and hold each other, they both began to moan.

Taking control of the situation Doug is able to slowly pull away and say, "You better go before something gets started."

Sandra letting out childish giggles, slowly opens the car door and gives Doug one more kiss before exiting.

"Sandra, I'll call you tomorrow when you get home from work," says Doug. Shaking her head in agreement, Sandra enters the brownstone as Doug watches. After a few moments Doug seeing her light come on starts his car and drives off.

While driving, Doug dials a number on his cell phone, "Mr. Chavez, this is Doug. How are you? Just wanted to confirm my pick up tomorrow morning? Ok, very well. I will see you then."

Throwing his phone on the passenger seat a smiling and happy Doug says to himself, "Time to go stick it deep into my Spanish mommy, Jasmine." Pressing his CD button on his dashboard, Doug nods his head to the jam "Gangsta Paradise" by Coolio as he drives to the Bronx for some wild sex.

It's Wednesday, Sandra has not been to work since Friday, but work is the last thing on her mind right now. She's holding Doug's hand as they walk into Tiffany & Company jewelry store on Fifth Avenue. Doug looks across the store spotting Cindy, a white salesperson who notices him and waves as she walks over. As Doug whispers something in Cindy's ear, he moves to the side watching as Cindy and another girl make a fuss over an overwhelmed Sandra.

As they leave the store, Sandra is in a trance-like state as she admires the diamond bracelet and the gold Movado watch that she now sports on each wrist. Walking briskly down Fifth Avenue, they stop inside Sachs Fifth Avenue to purchase Sandra some clothes. Before entering the store, Doug turns Sandra towards him and says, "I know this is fast and to the point, but I have to say this, so please just listen. You are my woman right now, as my woman; I have to be able to trust you. Loyalty and trust is more important than clothes, money or jewelry. Because if at any point and time things go bad, I have to know that you will be there for me and that you would never betray me. Do you understand?"

Sandra, who has a serious look on her face, responds, "I have never met anyone like you and yes I believe in the same things as you. So please believe me when I tell you I would never betray or hurt you in any way. I will always stick by you as long as you want me to. I would never do you dirty and for some reason right now I feel like I really love you, Doug."

Taking Sandra in his arms, they kiss in front of the store as people go around them. Hearing her phone start to ring, Sandra answers it.

"Hello, Ms. Jones. Yes, I am sorry. I have just been under the weather for the last couple of days, but I promise I will be in tomorrow."

Doug, reaching for Sandra's phone, gently takes it from her hand and says, "Hello Ms. Jones, I am Sandra's man and I am letting you know that at this moment she quits."

Hanging up the phone, Doug hands the phone back to Sandra and says, "You will no longer work for anyone. I am your man, so anything you need or desire, you come to me. Also, I want you to start looking for a real apartment tomorrow. I will take care of all the expenses. Now come, let's go shopping." Walking in front of her, Doug extends his hand backwards for Sandra, who reaches out and grabs hold to him.

*   *   *

Only candles light Doug's bedroom and the scent of cinnamon fills the air. Doug, sitting at the foot of the bed, looks up as the bedroom door slowly opens, revealing a luscious Sandra, who is wearing a purple, two-piece teddy. Walking over slowly to her man, Sandra stands between his large and strong legs gently rubbing his bald head. With his large hands, Doug slowly feels Sandra's thighs and her smooth behind as he pulls her close to him. Slowly pushing him on his back on the bed, Sandra sits atop of him slowly removing her top, showing her perfectly shaped breast. Rubbing her back, Doug reaches up and begins kissing her nipples softly.

Sandra, who is now moaning uncontrollably, slowly removes Doug's silk boxers, taking his large manhood into her hands. Squatting up slightly, Sandra helps Doug enter inside her. As the both of them moan and kiss with passion, Sandra swivels and grinds on top of her man with a fierce desire. As the candles flicker throughout the room, Doug and Sandra make slow, beautiful love throughout the night.

Chapter Ten
Diamonds Aren't Forever

The Manor ballroom in the Bronx is decorated with care and elegance for Troy's 30th birthday party. There is lobster, crab, fish, and steak for about fifty friends and family members. The hall is decorated with red and white balloons. Sitting in the middle of the floor is a large number thirty that is carved out of ice. The waiters are all dressed in black and white tuxedos. A professional disc jockey is in a booth playing music on state-of-the-art equipment. Bottles of champagne and wine sit atop a long table along with a five-layer birthday cake for Troy. As guests begin to take their seats, Troy arrives with his beautiful wife Beverly. Troy, who is wearing a white silk suit and white alligators to match, is smiling and waving at the guests, who clap and yell his name.

Looking at his wife, Troy asks, "Where is Doug? I see everyone but him. Damn, I thought this was my night."

Smiling at the people, Beverly whispers in Troy's ear, "Do not worry about where he is; you just enjoy your night with your friends and me."

Looking at his wife and admiring how beautiful she looks, Troy kisses her while walking around the hall to greet everyone in attendance. The first ones to hug him are Fish and Buster, who are sharing the same large, round table reserved for the crew. People are now looking towards the entrance of the hall where Doug and Sandra have just arrived. Doug, as usual, is decked out, wearing a tailored midnight blue, two-piece suit with a velour white hat and blue alligators to match. Doug is also sporting a diamond studded cane. On his finger is a 2-carat blue diamond ring and on his wrist is a diamond Rolex watch. Walking next to Doug holding his arm is Sandra, who is wearing a white silk gown with high splits on both sides, revealing her thick firm thighs. Her hair is corn rowed while her nails and toenails are painted red. Around her neck is a 3-carat diamond necklace, and on her wrist is a diamond Rolex watch that matches Doug's. As they walk to the center of the floor, Doug stops and proceeds to twirl Sandra around slowly so that everyone can admire her. Sandra, who looks a little embarrassed by the gesture, keeps her smile showing her pearly white teeth. Doug, looking towards the large round table, sees Troy, who is wearing a fake smile.

"What's up, baby!?" Doug yells at Troy. Walking towards the table with Sandra behind him, Doug grabs Troy giving him a hug, swinging him from side to side.

Smiling at Fish and Buster, Doug says, "My partners in crime; who loves you more than me?" Hugging both men, Doug now walks over and gives Beverly a quick kiss on the cheek.

Grabbing Sandra by the arm, Doug parades her to the side of the table and makes his introduction, "Everyone, I want all of you to meet my polished and unflawed diamond, my baby Sandra. Hey, ain't she the most beautiful rose in this room?" Everyone looking at Sandra smiles and waves, including Beverly, who is doing her best not to let her true feelings show.

"Good evening everyone. Nice to meet you all" says Sandra, who takes her seat next to Doug.

"Hi Sandra, this is my husband, Troy, for whom this occasion is for," says Beverly.

Sandra, looking at Troy with a smile on her face, says, "Happy birthday Troy and may you have many more."

Troy, who reaches for his wife's hand says, "Thank you Sandra, it is nice to see you again."

Doug, who is listening to every word at the table, sits in silence with his face twisted in a knot and his lips almost pouting.

On the sound speaker, the disc jockey announces, "Ladies and gentlemen, we at the Manor Ballroom want to thank you for taking the time to come out and share in the celebration of our good friend Troy Collins celebrating his thirtieth birthday. To start it off, I would like to spin this first record for the birthday boy."

As the crowd awaits the song, everyone yells "Happy Birthday" as the song of the same title plays. A smiling Troy stands and waves at the crowd as Beverly gets out of her seat, grabbing Troy's hand leading him to the dance floor. A smiling Sandra applauds them while Doug just looks on. The dance floor is flooded with people having fun and dancing. Some look good doing what they do, and others just look plain out of rhythm. But the one thing they all have in common is fun. They all have smiles on their faces, and they are having a ball. There are two people sitting out of fifty, they are Sandra and Doug.

With a small smile on her face, Sandra is clapping to the music and patting her feet when she asks Doug, "Sweetheart, come on and dance with me. I bet I could show you a step or two on the dance floor."

Looking straight ahead, he responds, "Listen, I'm not one for dancing. I am just here for my man, Troy. Besides, this disc jockey ain't playing anything I like."

Playing with her earrings, Sandra says, "Well, would it bother you if I took the floor by myself? I love to dance and I like the music."

Letting air exit from his mouth, Doug looks at Sandra calmly saying, "Sweet heart, if your man ain't on the dance floor, what makes you think I am going to allow you out there?"

Letting out a small chuckle, Sandra responds, "Allow me Doug?"

Turning to Sandra and looking at her with his dark, shark-like eyes, Doug tells her, "I am not going to speak on this matter anymore; I am done."

Turning her head away, Sandra erases her smile as the record fades away looking at Troy and his wife walk back to the table.

Holding his wife's hand, Troy asks Sandra, "So Sandra what do you do?"

Letting her radiant smile come to her face again, she answers, "Well Troy, I'm actually..."

Interrupting her, Doug answers, "She does nothing. My woman does not need to work for anything or anybody; that is my job to take care of her. The only person she needs to depend on his me."

Beverly, looking in the other direction, feels her sweaty forehead and says, "Baby, I will be right back; I want to freshen up. Sandra, you want to join me?"

Looking at herself in her pocket mirror, Sandra agrees, "You know what Beverly? I need to use the bathroom also; sure, I will join you."

As the ladies get up and excuse themselves, Doug tells Sandra, "Make sure you hurry back."

Not saying a word, Sandra acts if she doesn't hear Doug and laughs as she walks with Beverly.

Prompting Doug to ask a little louder, which draws eyes and attention from other nearby guests, "Sandra, did you hear me?"

Stopping and turning around, Sandra answers, "Yes Doug I heard you, damn."

As the women walk to the bathroom, Fish and Buster join Doug and Troy at the table.

"What's up partner? You ok tonight? You seem kind of edgy," Fish asserts.

Taking a long sip from his glass of champagne, Doug answers, "Yeah man I am cool. That meeting with my contact has me a little worn out, but I'm cool."

Buster, smacking Doug on his shoulder, says, "Come on Doug this night belongs to our partner, Troy. Let us show some love tonight man. No business tonight, just pleasure, ok?"

Doug, reaching across the table, hugs Troy and kisses him on the cheek. As Doug sees Sandra and Beverly making it back from the dance floor, a smiling Doug gets out of his seat and rushes over to a surprised Sandra. Grabbing her by the hand, he leads her to the dance floor where the disc jockey is spinning a song entitled "Don't wanna be a playa" by Big Pun.

As Doug dances like he is having an epileptic fit, Sandra is moving her hips smoothly from side to side as she takes Doug's hands, trying to get him to dance to the beat. As Doug's boys laugh and yell at him from their table, Sandra now puts her arms around his enormous shoulders and pulls him towards her to give him a huge kiss, for at this moment, all seems well between them.

*　　*　　*

Outside on the corner, diagonally across from the ballroom, sits a black Chevy suburban with tinted glass. Inside are seven brothers dressed in black jumpsuits that car mechanics wear in an auto garage. They do not say a word as they all inspect the weapons they carry. Four of them are holding Uzi submachine guns while the other three have .45 automatic handguns. They now put on black ski masks and black leather gloves as the man in the middle row of the vehicle taps the driver on the shoulder, who starts the truck up and drives it across the street into the ballroom's parking lot. Turning the engine and lights off, the driver says to the men inside, "On my word we go in and take those motherfucker's out." With that said, the men sit quietly and patiently with weapons in their laps.

*　　*　　*

As Doug and Sandra, along with everyone else at the table take their last bites of their dinner, Sandra takes a long swallow of club soda, which causes her to release a belch that has the sound of a passing tugboat in the night. Covering her mouth with embarrassment in her eyes, Sandra looks at everyone at the table, who in turn are staring at her. Within a couple of seconds, Beverly lets out a huge laugh followed by Fish then Buster. Now Troy is pointing at a smiling and giggling Sandra, who responds, "Excuse me everybody. I am sorry."

Everyone is laughing and patting Sandra on the arm in a gesture to show her that it is no big deal. Everyone except Doug, who is staring at Sandra as if she is the last person he wants to be around. From under the table Doug quickly kicks Sandra on her foot in disgust.

"Ouch! Doug what the hell is wrong with you?" Sandra asks.

Doug, wiping steak sauce away from his mouth, angrily responds, "What the fuck do you mean what is wrong with me?"

Getting up from his chair, he looks down on Sandra with anger in his eyes.

Sandra, who is now totally embarrassed, reaches into her bag to retrieve her cell phone and asks Beverly, "Can you give me a number for a cab company? I am going home."

"Doug, come on partner. She just burped' it's no real big deal man," says Troy, who is trying to soothe the situation. As tears start to roll down Sandra's face, Beverley walks to her side of the table to console her.

"Come on, baby let us go to the ladies room to freshen up." As the women begin to leave, they stop because of the yelling and commotion coming from outside the hall. Beverly looking towards the door holds her chest because at the ballroom entry are seven to eight masked men running into the room with guns drawn.

As people get up from their tables with fear on their faces, one gunman starts firing in the direction of the dance floor. It is sheer pandemonium as three women and a man hit the floor from bullet wounds. At Doug's table, Buster seeing the situation, reaches into his jacket and removes two automatic handguns firing at the masked men hitting one in the leg.

Troy, looking at his screaming wife holding Sandra yells, "Get down, Beverley! Get the fuck down!" People are crashing into each other as one man runs into the table holding Troy's birthday cake, knocking it to the floor. Sandra, who is holding her ears, is thrown to the floor by Fish who lies on top of her looking for his target.

The bullets are flying as the masked gunmen have now planted themselves behind tables and the disc jockey's booth. Troy, looking for his wife while he crawls on the floor, spots her screaming as one of the gunmen stands over her reloading his weapon and pointing it at her face. As he cocks the trigger, Doug holding a nickel-plated magnum comes from the gunmen's blind side and pumps one round into his head, removing half of his skull.

Buster, crouching behind a table, reaches out, grabs Beverley by her arm and drags her to safety behind a table. Fish can now see a shooter in the DJ booth squatting behind the turntables and decides to make his move. Rolling over Sandra, he fires at least twenty rounds from his two handguns, destroying the dj equipment and the masked gunmen, who screams before falling out of the booth onto the floor.

Doug, who now sees Sandra sprawled out on the open floor, rushes to her side, when twenty feet in front of him, two gunmen appear with guns aimed right at him. Raising his weapon, Doug fires, hitting one of them right between the eyes. Pointing at the other, Doug fires but is out of ammunition. With the masked man's finger on his trigger, he is ready to fire when an injured man named Harry, plunges a huge chunk of ice that was part of Troy's number thirty sculpted into the shooter's head, causing blood to splatter. Looking at Doug, Harry falls back to the ground and dies. Getting his thoughts together, Doug makes it to Sandra and drags her behind a wooden column.

"Are you hurt!" screams Doug. Not getting an answer, Doug looks into her eyes and can see that she is in shock. "Fish, how many of them are left?" Doug yells.

"How the fuck do I know!" responds Fish. Calm comes across the hall for a moment when Buster, who is still guarding Beverly, sees two masked men rushing for the door now beginning to shoot aimlessly in the air. Buster shoots, hitting one in the back of the head while the other makes it out of the door. Buster, looking at the scene, looks at the many injured and dead bodies lying throughout the dance floor.

"Doug, I think its all clear; we have got to get out of here man. The police will be here soon." A sweaty Doug is carrying Sandra in his arms as Troy consoles a crying Beverly.

Fish, who still has his weapon in his hand, says, "Everybody come on, there's an exit through the kitchen." Following Fish, everyone makes it to the kitchen by stepping over bodies and blood. As they walk through the kitchen, Troy notices cooks, waiters, and servers hiding behind two freezers.

"It's over…there are people out there hurt. One of you call an ambulance!" A waiter, trying to put on a brave face, reaches into his pocket and takes out his cell phone.

*   *   *

As everyone gets inside their vehicles, Doug says, "I have to get her to a hospital. I will call everyone tonight. Troy, is Beverly ok man?"

Troy, rubbing his wife's face, looks at Doug and answers, "No Doug. She was almost killed tonight, man!"

Doug looks in silence as an angry Troy puts his wife inside his car and begins to drive off. Hurrying while at the same time being gentle, Doug gets Sandra into the car and runs to the driver's side to get in when he pauses for a second to look at the scene of Troy's party. Hearing the sirens getting closer, Doug enters his car and speeds off to Albert Einstein Hospital.

Chapter Eleven
An Unwanted Blessing

As Doug sits in the waiting room, he observes the elderly and children who wait for medical care. Looking up at the monitor that sits high near the ceiling, he looks at the news report at the Manor Ballroom wondering who might have been behind it and how could they have known being that it was an exclusive party for Troy. The scene on the television shows pure havoc. Doug was not worried about the cops figuring out that he was there because all they had to do was look back on the reservation list. His only two concerns were making sure the murders would not link back to him exclusively and to make those who are responsible pay. Getting up from his chair, Doug walks to a secluded part of the floor and dials Fish on his cell phone.

"Fish, it's me. Is everybody alright? Good, what about Beverly and Troy? Listen, everybody's heat was untraceable, right? Ok, listen, everybody stay out of the club except Buster and me. I am going to have to smooth this shit over with the blue crew first. So whatever we put on the street will have to go through the back door for a minute…the doctors are looking at her now so let me get back. Remember what I said; tell Troy and Buster…ok talk to you later."

Hanging up his phone, Doug spots a doctor, who looks like he is searching for someone. Trotting down the hall, Doug runs up behind him and asks, "Excuse me doctor, my name Doug. I bought Sandra Lyte in about an hour and a half ago; are you looking for me?"

Dr. Meng, a short and stout Chinese man, holds his hand out for a handshake, which Doug obliges.

"Hello Doug I am Dr. Meng and yes, I was looking for you." The doctor, who is wearing a shirt and tie to go with his black pants, puts his hands on Doug's back and leads him to a small office.

"Please have a seat, Doug. There are some important things we need to discuss." Sitting in the chair, Doug looks around the room and observes the many charts on the body and all of the different equipment used to examine the body, which in a strange kind of way makes Doug a little skirmish.

"First off, your friend Sandra is going to be fine; she has just suffered a little rise in her heart rate because of the trauma she has gone through. By the way, what caused her heart rate to increase?"

Looking around the room, Doug takes a deep breath before answering, "Coming from a movie, two men attempted to rob us at gunpoint. Not having a gun drawn on her before, Sandra panicked and started losing her mind a little, which caused her to pass out. After giving them my money, they took off and that is when I bought her here."

Looking at Doug while shaking his head up and down, the doctor says, "Doug, do you know any reason why they did not take these from her?"

Reaching out his hand to Doug, Dr. Meng drops the very expensive jewelry that Sandra was wearing into his hand. Looking at the gems for a few seconds, Doug says, "When she started screaming and panicking, a few people started looking out of their windows and stopped to look out of their cars. This must have made the robbers nervous, so they took what they could from me and ran off, leaving her things alone."

Standing up and patting his feet on the floor while listening to Doug's story, the doctor, who seems a little skeptical about the whole thing, responds, "Well, I am here to tell you that Sandra is responding much better since she first arrived and her blood pressure is back to normal. Secondly and most importantly, I am also here to inform you that Sandra is in the very early stages of a pregnancy."

Doug's head is now spinning a thousand miles an hour as he stands up and remembers what Dollar Bill said, which somewhat feels like a hundred years ago: "Females are just mules who you hump; nothing more nothing less. Never let them set up base in your camp."

Dr. Meng, who is looking at Doug with some concern, asks, "Doug, are you going to be ok? By any chance, are you the father of this baby?

With his head buried in his hands, Doug lets out a long exasperating sigh and says, "I am not sure but I could be, doc."

Patting him on the shoulder, the doctor slowly helps Doug to the door. "Come, Doug let's go see if Sandra is up and able to talk. Walking down the corridor makes Doug feel as if he is being lead to a room where he will be given a lethal injection for all the shit he has done in his short but busy life.

Standing inside the room, the doctor pats him on the back and exits, leaving Doug alone with Sandra. Awake and after all, she has been through, Sandra still looks gorgeous. Doug, removing his jacket, takes a chair and sits next to Sandra's bed. The silence is deafening as Doug looks at the blue and almost too clean floor while Sandra still focuses on the smooth, white ceiling that is above her head. Doug staring at Sandra, who looks as if he is the last thing she wants to see, begins, "Sandra, how are you doing?"

Thinking how many coats it took to paint the ceiling, she answers in a low tone, "I am fine Doug."

Getting up and putting his chair closer to Sandra, Doug says, "Did the doctor tell you the news?"

"Yes. He told me I am pregnant."

"How do you feel about that, Sandra?"

"Doug, right now I don't know what I feel. I was just in a violent shootout at your friend's birthday party. Listen Doug, I know I am from some country town like Virginia, but my brain is not country. You told me you were an investor. What investors do you know carry big guns to a party and get involved in a gunfight? I am not stupid, Doug. Maybe a little behind in the times, but I am not stupid."

Looking at Sandra as if his pants are down in front of an audience, Doug gets up from his chair and takes a seat on the edge of Sandra's bed. As he slowly and gently grabs her hand, Doug holds it a little tighter, stopping her from pulling away. "Sandra, from the minute I laid my eyes on you, I knew you were someone I wanted to be with. I am a hustler Sandra and I am sorry I had to lie to you about that. Please try and dig where I am coming from; I just thought the less you knew about what I was doing the better it would be for the both of us. Besides, I know you are not stupid; sooner or later the shit would have hit the fan."

For the first time, Sandra looks at Doug and something inside her feels sorry for a man who surrounds himself with people but in all reality, is a lonely person.

"Doug listen to me, ok? This is really going to sound crazy, but you know what shocked me the most about you tonight? Not the violence, not your lack of respect for your friends, but more than anything, the way your mood swung from right to left in a matter of moments. I mean all I did was belch Doug and you almost crushed my foot. What did I do that was so bad? It does not change what kind of person I am. Can you answer that?"

Staring out of the hospital room window and looking at the lights from the surrounding buildings, Doug rises to his feet and faces Sandra. "Up until this day, life has always been tough for me. Nobody has ever given me anything. Not a piece of bread or a cup of water. My father never loved me and my mother died on me, so I never learned to trust anyone. So now, I finally meet someone who is pure as snow and admit I can act a little crazy Sandra, please try to understand. You are the best thing that has come into my life. Now the doctor is telling me you are pregnant. Please Sandra, forgive me and I promise you will see a new man."

Looking straight ahead, tears begin to fall from Sandra's eyes, as she cannot hold them back any longer. Trying to regain her composure, she sits up in the bed and reaches out for Doug's hand, which he grabs. "Doug, you said to me that all you wanted was loyalty and trust from your woman. I know it has not been that long between us, but have I given you any reason to doubt me?"

Realizing that this young woman from Richmond, Virginia is no dummy, Doug decides that he must be honest for once: "No Sandra you have not given me any reason to doubt you. That is why I am asking you to start over with me so I can show you that I am down for you as much as you are for me. I know what I am doing is not right, but it is all I know how to do. Please do not leave me as everyone else has in my life. Please Sandra I want to be a part of you and what is growing inside you."

Pulling Doug slowly towards her, Sandra puts his hand on her face, which he begins to caress softly. "Doug, I do not have anything in this city but you. You promised that you would look after me and I believed you, so please do not let me down. I have no place to go and no one to turn to except you."

Reaching in his pocket Doug takes out the diamond jewelry that Sandra wore at the party and sits it on her chest. Reaching down in front of her, Doug slowly kisses Sandra on the mouth and looks at her in her eyes: "I promise things well get better between you and me."

Pointing towards the chair and motioning for Doug to sit, Sandra says, "I am ready to come home tonight; can you get me out of here?"

Looking at the clock on the wall, Doug looks back at Sandra and responds, "The doctor said he wanted to take a few more tests in the morning. Besides, we have been through a lot tonight. I really think you should stay here and rest. I promise I will be here the first thing tomorrow to get you out of here, ok?"

Shaking her head in agreement, Sandra looks at Doug and smiles. Bending down and giving her one more kiss, Doug says, "If you need anything tonight, you tell them to charge it to me." Giving her one final hug, Doug exits the room and before shutting, Sandra's light off, he smiles and winks at her.

With the moonlight, shining through the window Sandra says softly, "I know I can change him."

*   *   *

Standing outside on the street, Doug's phone begins to ring. Looking at the caller ID, he looks up to the stars that illuminate in the sky saying, "Oh shit, I do not need this right now."

It is Detective Tommy Davis on the other end and Doug holds the phone away from his ear as Davis is screaming at the top of his lungs. "Listen to me, ok? Look at the book. It was a legitimate party for my best friend. I have no idea where they came from or who they were. All I know is that my guys did not fire back and no guns or ammo that will be found there can be traced back to us."

Staring up at the sky and shaking his head, Doug responds to the irate detective, "I understand that I have to lay low. What is it going to cost to keep me out of this? Ok let's meet at Echo Park on the Tremont

Avenue side tomorrow night, just you and me. We can make this work, talk to you later."

Hanging up the phone, Doug calls Fish, "Listen, tomorrow night I need some birds in the trees at Echo Park. I am setting up a payment that should clean this shit up. So get some birds ready just in case some shit jumps off. Ok, I will be in touch." Walking to his car, Doug looks up in the direction of the hospital and picks any window, assuming that Sandra is in there. "Just for humping and bumping, what the hell did I do?"

*   *   *

The next morning Doug is unlocking his apartment door, holding Sandra's belongings as he moves to the side so that she can enter. At that moment, Pamela Brown is leaving her apartment. Pamela sadly stares at Sandra then at Doug without uttering a word. Sandra walks in and stands in the long hallway decorated with nice looking artwork. Closing the door behind him, Doug says, "Please make yourself at home because it is your home also."

Showing Sandra around the large three-bedroom apartment that Doug has beautifully decorated himself, he sits Sandra down in the living room. "Sandra, in another nine months, we will become a family and our lives will change forever. Therefore, I think it is very important that from this point on, you should spend most of your time here at home. Also, you should find a private doctor that can see you on a one-to-one basis."

"Doug, I want to thank you for letting me stay here and I promise for as long as I can, I will try to help out around the house by making sure things stay clean."

"There's no need for you to do anything because I have a woman who works for a cleaning service come by once a week to clean the place up."

Touching her belly, Doug smiles at Sandra, saying, "From this point in our lives, things will be nice and peaceful."

Chapter Twelve
Seven-Year Sentence and Counting

What started out, as a promising beginning has been nothing but a relationship of lies, deceit and worst of all abuse on both the mental and physical level. Things have changed drastically in the lives of Sandra and Doug. The mood swings that Doug has are no longer there; that is because his mood is now simply nasty. With the rise in the usage of "crack" and "crystal meth," which is cheaper to produce and purchase then cocaine, Doug has seen his clientele drop dramatically. This meant a drop in sales and cash flow. On top of that, his large three-room apartment, which he considered his own private Idaho, is very crowded now with Sandra and the two most beautiful twins in the world, Chaka and Kareem. That is right, nine months after moving in with Doug; Sandra dropped a load on his ass weighing a grand total of 14 pounds and 9 ounces. As Sandra held and smiled at her two babies, a mystified Doug stood about four feet away from the visitors viewing window. While fathers rushed from work to see and hold their bundles of joy, Doug was too busy trying to find that new contact, which lead to the other reason for his bitterness.

You see, like a champion prizefighter, when you are on top, there is always someone waiting to knock you down and claim your throne. That was the case of Mario Chavez, who was the king of cocaine in most of the five boroughs. When the king got older, he did not have the sense to share the wealth and keep the young pups happy. He felt the need to be greedy which was not smart because those young pups became larger and hungrier. They formed a wolf pack attacking Mario until he could not fight anymore. After a few bloody battles in the Bronx, Doug's connection was no more and that left Doug scrambling for fresher product. Not being perceptive enough to change with the times, Doug fell off in the city. To his credit through, he learned to enhance what he was receiving from a new Italian cat named Johnny from Bensonhurst Brooklyn. It was not as good as Mario's was, but it kept his loyal customers returning to his club, which he still owned and maintained.

Doug's other problem was his buddies at the police department who still had their hands out every month and their zippers unfastened with penises hanging out ready to attend another orgy at Doug's expense. Eventually, something had to give; either Doug would have to cut them loose and risk losing everything he had left or he would have to cash in his chips putting them against the wall. The one thing Doug did not lose was his sense of security when it came down to covering his own ass. As time went by, Doug kept himself educated in the advancement of electronics when it involved the video tapes that he recorded of the cops' sexual escapades. Over the years, Doug bought new equipment, which allowed him to transfer all of that video onto DVD discs. What turned out to be four detectives and five regular police officers involved in sex parties included their indulgence in drug and alcohol use as well. Doug recorded everything in that co-op apartment that only he knew about. Doug has about ten discs that could blow a certain police department in the Bronx out of the water, creating the biggest scandal the city would ever see. So keeping this information a secret was no game; this was about life and death. This was Doug's life insurance policy against anything that came against him from the NYPD. He cherished those discs more than his own children.

Finally, if a person could withstand any more pressure, Doug was losing his grip on his crew. Fish, Troy and Buster became very fond of the life that Doug introduced them to and got a little cranky when they had to leave the club and hit the corners again to sell for Doug. This left them in a very dangerous situation because those young cats that started prowling the streets selling their product did not take kindly to some old-timers still trying to play the game. Doug knew this; he was not stupid and he knew it would be a matter of time before the boys wanted to come inside again even if that meant them setting up three against one.

Doug knew nothing was fair in the streets that is why he decided to go a little old school and look up an old friend of his when he was new to the game: his man Bucky. Even though he was forty-five years old, Bucky was sharp, in shape and loyal. Bucky loved Dollar Bill, Dollar Bill loved Doug and Doug knew this, so why not use it to his advantage? As long as Bucky never figured out it was Doug who set up Dollar Bill, everything would be ok. Bucky would be in the club and on the streets for one reason, to watch Doug's back while keeping an eye on the boys in the crew period. If anyone got out of line, Bucky would do them for Doug in a heartbeat.

Then there is Fred Gunner, who resides in the Shadybrook Retirement Home, in Westchester. On the first of the month of every month, Doug takes a ride up there to visit Fred. Doug, who will not admit he has always deep down inside feared and loved his father at the same time, has to pay eight hundred dollars a month and give his father three hundred for his pocket.

With all of this drama hanging over Doug's head he still had to send what he calls two crumb-snatching kids to private school, pay rent, pay off cops, pay off members of a crew who may not even like him and pay rent for an apartment that he cannot even enjoy. Someone had to suffer for Doug's woes and that person has been beautiful Sandra. Giving up hope that she would ever hear from her parents again, Sandra has come to the realization that all she has to build on is Kareem and Chaka, who are now seven years old and always puts a smile on her face every time they enter the room.

Sandra understands that she is not totally blameless when it comes to the situation she is in. Most women would have left the very first time their man put their hands on them, but this situation was a little different because Sandra had no outlets or supports. She trusted and loved Doug and he controlled her decisions and clouded her judgment. A huge mistake when you are striving for independence.

Sandra became accustomed to the lifestyle her and the kids enjoyed. Realistically, how was she ever going to pay rent in New York City? Kareem and Chaka were very intelligent and excelled in every school subject. How was Sandra going to pay for the excellent private school they attended? Deep inside she knew she could not provide for her children, as Doug was able to. So Sandra endured the smacks and sometimes the punches. The bitches, hoes and other names Doug decided to call her that day. She did it for her kids' sake, which is a little weak when you think of it, but some women stay around for dumber reasons.

One thing stayed a constant with Doug though, the way he made up with Sandra. Always asking for forgiveness for which Sandra gave. After that came the expensive gift to smooth things over for which she took. You see, she loved Doug for some reason and when you love someone, you take a lot of shit that a normal person would not. Sandra loved him but she loved her kids more and when she realized Doug did not love her kids as a father was suppose to, it made her think about how much shit was she suppose to take. Sure, he was paying for the best private school in the city and Christmas was always a gift spectacular, but he showed them very little love and something had to give.

Taking it upon herself Sandra went to all the school functions and did the things a father should do with his son and daughter. Sandra even taught them not to hate their father, but above all, to love and protect each other exclusively. Doug, who put fear in Sandra by mental and physical intimidation, had her believing he watched her every move. If she ever thought of trying to leave him, bad things would happen. Knowing Doug for this amount of time and seeing what kind of lifestyle he lived, Sandra knew that if he wanted to touch her, he could.

Doug had her and the kids on a time clock when they went out. Everything was set up for Sandra to do things at a specific time from cleaning, cooking, picking up the kids and even having sex. She had better be on time because if she were not, she would pay.

It took her two months of begging Doug who became tired of hearing her mouth to allow her to do something that gave her pleasure. He allowed her to volunteer four hours a day at a Soup kitchen that was on Jerome and Burnside Avenues. This was her outlet and a way of giving back in hope that she would receive some blessing or forgiveness for what she allowed herself to get into. From 10:00 a.m. until 2:00 p.m., Sandra was in heaven because she helped those less fortunate then herself. Sandra, from time to time though, asked herself was it not the other way around-- were they really helping her?

So now, a new phase in Doug and Sandra's life has begun. Where will it lead? Neither one of them knows, to be honest. However, they both realized that something has to give because as the old saying goes, "How many times can a master kick his dog before the dog begins to growl back?"

D.J. Murray

Chapter Thirteen
You are late

There are about two hundred people inside the community center
on a cold December day. Some in line getting served lunch and others are
at their tables eating. Sandra, who is wearing a black sweater with black
jeans to match, has her braids covered with a scarf and is wearing plastic
gloves while she serves the food. By her side is Carla Smith, a 59-year-old
black woman who started the program six years ago, by feeding people in
train stations, has now grown to where she feeds people from all over the
Bronx. The food consists of sandwiches, soup, salad, vegetables and fruit.
There are about twenty volunteer workers carrying out various tasks from
serving the food to maintaining crowd order. Serving the food brings great
joy and comfort to Sandra as she never loses her smile while serving.

"Good afternoon James and how are you?" Sandra asks the twenty-
something year old homeless man from Tremont Avenue.

Trying not to make eye contact with Sandra, he softly says, "Good
afternoon, is it possible I could have an extra piece of fruit?"

Sandra, looking at James with a smile and compassion, reaches
inside the fruit basket and gives him an extra banana.

Looking up at Sandra for about a second he manages a smile and
says, "Thank you for the fruit and for remembering my name." Sandra
nods her head as he walks to a table to eat.

As the line moves at a rapid pace, Carla returns from the pantry
room looking confused. "Sandra I know for a fact that I bought a large
container of garlic on Monday and for the life of me, I can not remember
what I did with it."

Giving a mother and daughter their lunch, Sandra replies, "Ms.
Carla, look in the pantry inside the third cabinet on the second shelf and to
your far right, it should be sitting next to the half-full jar of oregano."
Looking at Sandra with her eyebrows twisted up Carla leaves. A slim,
dark-skinned girl with twist in her hair walks up to Sandra, with tray in her
hand looking straight ahead at the clock behind Sandra. The young woman
looks no older then twenty and seems to be in pretty good physical shape.

Sandra carefully placing food on the girl's tray asks, "Good
afternoon, Rose and how are you doing on this cold, blistery day?"

"I am fine thank you."

Sandra, admiring Rose's posture, asks, "You are in great shape Rose; do you work out?"

"No, not much anymore. How do you remember my name; I do not remember telling you?"

Giving Rose a small container of apple juice, Sandra tells her, "Yes, you did three weeks ago when you first came in here; you were soaking wet from the rain."

Looking at Sandra for a second, the slim girl with the track star body walks to the back of the center and sits in a corner. Returning with the garlic in her hand is Carla, who is shaking her head as she stares at Sandra.

"Girl, you better gets you a hotline like that Ms. Cleo had." The two women share a chuckle while feeding the hungry.

* * *

With the center closed until dinner, Sandra is in the kitchen with Carla and a Spanish woman named Jasmine. They are washing and drying dishes by hand, laughing at something Ms. Carla has said. With the big, tin-like salad bowl in her hand, Sandra glances up at the clock on the wall and notices the time. Her hands starting to tremble, she drops the bowl on the floor, which in turn startles Carla and Jasmine.

"Oh, my goodness, Sandra. Baby, you alright?"

"Ms. Carla, I am really sorry, but I have to go. I have to get home, Ok?"

Jasmine, looking very concerned, rubs Sandra on her back, trying to comfort a shaking and trembling Sandra. Looking around the kitchen, Sandra quickly removes her apron, tossing it to the floor.

"Please, Sandra, tell me what is wrong; maybe we can help." Says Jasmine

"It's ok. I promise I will be back tomorrow. I just have to get home in a hurry." Watching Sandra rush out of the kitchen, the other two women just look on with concern.

* * *

Standing in the middle of the street, Sandra vigorously waves down a cab. Getting inside, she tells the cab driver her destination and asks him to hurry. Going down the Grand Concourse, the driver, caught up in a slew of red lights comes to a halt. Looking at her watch and at her surroundings, tears fall from her eyes as she now realizes that the kids are out of school and she will be late preparing dinner. Remembering that she has not been late with dinner in four months, Sandra hopes this will not be a big deal. Looking at her watch, she reads that it is now 2:20 p.m., and the lights are just turning all green down the long stretch of the Grand Concourse. Looking at the many buildings that she passes, Sandra is now counting blocks as she is now two minutes away from her building. As the driver makes a right on Bedford Park, Sandra now sees the big beige building that she calls home. As the cab stops, Sandra pulls a ten-dollar bill out of her pocket exiting the cab without taking her two dollars in change.

Pulling out her keys, Sandra enters her building, bypassing the elevator, choosing to run up the stairs instead. Taking two steps at a time, an out of breath Sandra walks quickly to her door, fumbling with her keys. Finally getting the keys in order, Sandra unlocks the three deadbolt locks and opens her door to the apartment.

"Hello, everybody I'm..." suddenly it feels as if a shotgun blast hit her chest as Sandra fights for air while grabbing her left breast. The room is spinning at about 100 miles an hour as Sandra, falling back towards the living room wall, can vaguely see Kareem and Chaka sitting on the couch, still wearing their green school uniforms. After about two seconds, everything just goes black.

*   *   *

Feeling an ice-cold gush hit her face, Sandra grasps for air as if she is drowning in Niagara Falls. Sitting up quickly, Sandra spits up water from her mouth and grabs her chest as she is in pain. Barely getting oxygen into her lungs, Sandra is able to gain some focus and can see that she is still in the living room. Now struggling to get on her hands and knees, she spots her children, who remain seated on the couch, with terrified looks on their faces. Slowly turning her head to the right, she pushes her braids out of her face and can see two large, muscle-sculpted legs in front of her. Slowly lifting her head upwards, Sandra sees Doug, who from what she can make out, is wearing nothing but a pair of black silk boxers and a pair of blue slippers. Now falling back on her backside and trying to regain her balance, Sandra jerked by Doug, forces Sandra to her feet. Smelling his gin-and-tonic breath in her nostrils, Sandra braces for the worst. Like a rag doll, he drags Sandra to the kitchen and with a show of brute force; Doug throws her in the direction of the stove, causing her to skin her hand on the floor.

"What fucking time did I tell you to come home, Sandra?"

Trying to regain her composure, Sandra avoids looking at Doug. "You said two o'clock. I am sorry, Doug." Looking down on her, the muscle-bound Doug quickly walks over to her and arches his foot to her face. Sandra raises her hand in an attempt to block the oncoming kick, but it never arrives. Instead, Doug slowly lowers his leg.

"I am going to the back and by four o'clock, my meal better be ready on that table. The next damn time I have to go pick up these kids from school, I am going to bust your ass again. Do you understand?"

"Yes, Doug, I understand." Walking away, Doug grabs Sandra's keys off the table taking them to the door. Finding a key, Doug locks the top lock on the door, locking Sandra and the kids inside.

*   *   *

Next door in her apartment is Pamela Brown, who has her ear close to the wall that is adjacent to Doug's living room. Hearing all of the commotion, Pamela says softly to herself, "I hope she kills your ass." Grabbing her keys, Pamela exits her apartment to attend her A.A. meeting.

                              *   *   *

Hearing the door to their father's room close, Kareem and Chaka rush to their mother's side to help her make it to her feet. Chaka begins to gather pots and pans while Kareem wipes Sandra's face with a towel that hangs from the refrigerator. Chaka, looking at her mother says, "Hurry, momma, hurry! We do not have much time!" Sandra, barely being able to look at her children, gives them a hug and opens the freezer, removing the food she will prepare for Doug and the rest of them.

                              *   *   *

As Sandra stands next to her children, who are both overly dressed for dinner, she examines their groomed heads and makes sure their hands are clean. Looking at the dinner that sits on the white Italian lacquer table, Sandra observes the roasted duck that is piping hot. There are vegetables, rice, baked rolls and salad sitting along side the duck. Positioning the children behind their chairs, Sandra kisses them both on the head and proceeds to go get Doug.

Sitting at a fold-up table in a bedroom, Doug is preparing his cocaine bags that he will have his men sell that night. Carefully weighing each scoop of cocaine that he sits atop the scale, Doug gently sifts the product into a small plastic Ziploc bag. Flicking the bag with his index finger, a smile comes across his face: "These young boys don't know who their dealing with."

Turning his head quickly to the door because of three light knocks, Doug coldly answers, "Who is it?"

"Doug, dinner is ready" replies Sandra.

"Go wait for me by the table; I will be there in a second"

Hearing the slow taps of Sandra's shoes, Doug wraps his last bag and gets ready to have his evening meal.

Walking into the dining room there is complete silence as Doug faintly looks at his family stand by the table waiting for him to sit. Walking over to a brown maple table, Doug stops at a beautiful, old-fashioned radio. Doug slowly turns the knobs, a light illuminates and the soft sounds of jazz music play from it. Walking over to the table, Doug takes his seat and watches Sandra walk over to him. Grabbing a white napkin, Sandra slowly unfolds it and gently lays it in Doug's lap. Stepping back to rejoin Kareem and Chaka, Sandra watches Doug prepare to eat his dinner. Cutting up his duck, Doug sticks a piece on his fork along with some vegetables and rice. Looking at his daughter, then at Sandra with suspicion, he points to the food that is on the fork at Chaka. Looking up at her mother, Chaka slowly walks over to her father, who slowly puts the food to her mouth sticking it inside. Watching Chaka chew, Doug studies the girl's throat to make sure she swallows and observes her face for any reaction. Fully satisfied Doug motions with his finger for the rest of them to sit down and eat. As the smooth voice of a woman comes through the radio, Doug savors his food. Chaka and Sandra look at each other simultaneously then at little Kareem, who is clutching a butter knife with his tiny hands. Doug, looking straight ahead, chews his food, swallows and says, "Anytime you are ready my man, anytime you are ready."

*   *   *

It is the evening, as Sandra and the kids laugh as they decorate their Christmas tree. Sandra, who is wearing a Santa clause hat, begins stringing the lights around the tree as Kareem is jumping around, tossing icicles. Chaka, who is holding candy canes in her hand, is staring straight ahead with fear in her eyes as, unknown to her mother and brother, Doug stands behind them with a candy cane in his hand. Not bothering to look behind her, Sandra stands to her feet and pulls Kareem close to her waist. Putting the candy near Sandra's, ear Doug snaps it in two, making Sandra flinch. A laughing Doug walks away and returns to his bedroom.

*   *   *

Later in the evening finds Sandra lying with the kids on their bed as they watch the last of Animal Planet on a 50-inch plasma television. Grabbing the remote control, Sandra clicks the television off.

"Ok, my precious little ones; its time for prayers and bed." As Chaka gets on her knees, a playful Kareem runs out of their room, laughing up the long hallway. Sandra, trying not to look frustrated, motions to Chaka to wait where she is. Getting ready to leave the room, Sandra sticks her head out of the bedroom door when a playful Kareem yells, "Boo, mommy!"

Sandra, grabbing her chest and acting like the little boy has frightened her, playfully grabs him and carries him to where his sister is.

Everyone becomes silent when, from another room, they hear Doug yell, "You all better take your asses to sleep back there."

Sandra, looking at her kids, motions with her finger to her mouth for them to remain silent. Watching her kids proudly say their prayers, Sandra focuses on Kareem.

"God bless Mommy and my sister, Chaka. God please let it snow on Christmas so that me, Mommy and Chaka can build a snowman, Amen."

As Sandra tucks her children away, she gives each of them a long hug and a kiss to go along with it. Chaka, who is holding her mother tight, refuses to let go. Only when Sandra uses a little more strength is she able to break herself free. Walking over to the doorway she blows them a kiss and turns the light out.

*   *   *

Now in her bed, Sandra is wearing a two-piece pajama set with thermal underwear underneath. She's burning up, but she hopes it serves as a deterrent for Doug, who is in the bathroom three feet away from her.

"Please give me the strength" she quietly whispers. She can smell the aroma of musk oil and hear the heavy footsteps coming towards the door. As the door slowly opens, Doug is wearing pajama bottoms along with a huge white gold necklace around his neck. Walking over to the bed, Doug takes a seat, causing Sandra to sink. Reaching into his pocket, he pulls out a long, thick, platinum necklace that he places on Sandra's chest.

"I know you do not believe in me anymore. But I know deep down inside, I can change to a better person. I am sorry for how I have been lately, but I have been under a lot of pressure. So please take this as an early Christmas gift."

Leaning over Sandra, Doug kisses her on the mouth and gently begins rubbing her breast. Looking at him in his eyes, she sees sadness and anger, but most of all, she sees anger.

As Doug tugs at her clothes, tears swell up in Sandra's eyes as she wonders to herself, "I am nothing but a weak woman and mother." With Doug now on top of her, Sandra turns her head towards the window where she gazes out, imagining the children and her far away from Doug.

*   *   *

As Doug sleeps like a log, a wide-awake Sandra quietly gets out of bed and puts her pajamas back on. Using the light of the moon as her guide, she walks over to her armoire that sits across the large bedroom. Getting on her hands and knees, Sandra begins to feel for something under the armoire. Looking back at her bed where Doug slowly shifts his body to another position, Sandra finds her well-kept secret. Under the armoire, she has taped a brown packaging envelope that no one is aware of. Sitting on the floor, not taking her eyes off Doug, she slowly opens the flap of the envelope with her fingernail. Gently shaking the envelope on a throw rug that sits under the armoire, Sandra reveals an abundance of expensive jewelry that consists of diamonds, gold necklaces, watches by Movado and Cartier and bracelets. Removing the platinum necklace, Sandra places it in the envelope with the rest of the jewelry Doug has given her for accepting her bruises like a good little girl. Slowly getting back into bed Sandra lays her head on her pillow and forces herself to sleep.

*   *   *

On this new day, Doug sits inside the waiting lounge of Dr. Joanne White, as he looks over some old issues of *Psychology Today.* The office is posh and upscale, which it should be for two hundred dollars a session. Doug is patting his feet to the jazz music playing low in the waiting area. Focusing his eyes on the sound of an opening door, Doug smiles at the psychiatrist he has been seeing sporadically for the past nine years. Dr. White is an Asian woman in her early fifties and Doug sees her to help him cope with his mother's suicide a while back. Walking over to Doug, Dr. White greets him with a handshake and shows him to her office.

Sitting on a beautiful leather couch, Doug studies the doctor as she opens her pad and takes out an expensive gold pen. The walls covered with cherry oak wood, while fresh flowers sit on tables inside the room. On the wall behind the doctor's desk sits laminated plaques of her numerous degrees. The floor covered with beige plush carpeting. On the wall sits a 35-inch plasma television and DVD player to match. Dr. White has spared no expense.

"First off Doug, how have you been since the last time we met?"

Smiling at the doctor, Doug answers, "I have been fine and the exercises you gave me have helped a lot."

Scribbling on her pad, Dr. White continues, "What about visiting your mother's grave site? Have you thought about that?"

"Well, that is the good news, doctor; I have gone to see her twice and both times seemed to relieve the stress that we discussed last time."

Happy with his compliance in treatment, Dr. White says, "Doug that is fantastic; you do not know how proud I am of you. That is a really big step you have taken in releasing the anger and fear that has been inside you for a very long time."

Knowing that you had someone believing in your bullshit, you could tell most quacks anything and they would believe you. As long as it fed their ego, you could lie until your nose fell off, they would not know the difference. Doug gradually knew his doctor more after each visit, feeling all along that he was nothing but a guinea pig for her psychological bullshit and if she could prove that he was making progress, it would validate her skills as a psychiatrist. While on the other side, Doug also knew that as long as he kept his visits it could payoff for him in the end. Like serial killers who get off because their psychiatrist proves them sick, so could Doug if he ever got in a jam.

"Dr. White, I do not know if this helps any, but I also went to see my father last week and we discussed some things concerning my mother. I also told him that with a little more time and healing, I could forgive him also."

Shaking her head in amazement, Dr. White says, "You are truly amazing Doug and you should be proud of yourself. I remember a while back at one of our sessions; you said you thought your father ruined your chances of ever being a good husband and father. Well, in my opinion Doug, I truly believe with the progress you have made, one day you are going to make a great husband and dad." A smiling Doug looks at the grandfather clock and sees that he has twenty more minutes to bullshit the Harvard graduate, so he does.

*   *   *

Looking at her watch, Sandra is well aware that she has some time to spare with her shopping. Pushing her cart down the aisle, Sandra walks past all the food that contains sugar and high in fat, the kind she loves by the way and makes her way into a section that shelves organic food. As she walks to her destination, Sandra jumps with fear as her cart is hit from the side by a laughing Pamela.

"Hey Sandra, you have got to keep your eyes on the road girl."
Feeling relieved Sandra looks inside Pamela's basket and is very envious. Banana crunch ice cream, Entenmanns's chocolate donuts and chicken

fingers, just to name a few. Wondering how in the hell does Pamela keep her body so tight, Sandra finally stops staring at the food.

"Hi Pamela, how are you doing?"

Noticing Sandra staring at her junk food, she says, "You know, anytime you want to come over, watch the stories and pig out with me, you are welcome, right?"

"I know I have not been very neighborly Pamela, and I am sorry for that, but your invitation sounds nice; maybe one day we can."

"Your kids eat Brussels spouts and drink soybean milk? What is that, squash? Now Sandra, I know you eat some Popeye's fried chicken?"

Trying unsuccessfully to hold her laugh in, Sandra responds, "My goodness, I have not had fried chicken in a while. That sounds good right about now."

Pamela, looking at Sandra with a smile but with a touch of sadness and Sandra feeling it also, tells her, "Well, Sandra. like I said, when your ready to free yourself, you and the kids knock on my door, I will show you what a good time is all about."

Sandra, smiling and trying to hold back the tears swelling in her eyes touches Pamela on the hand and walks to the organic section to purchase her goods. Looking behind her secretly, Pamela stares at Sandra and puts on her sunglasses to hide the tears in her own eyes.

*　　*　　*

Like most kids do at Kareem and Chaka's age, when their mother arrives home from grocery shopping, they surround her, waiting to see what comes out of the grocery bags and they are no exception to the rule. Chaka, who gladly helps her mom, puts things where they normally go while Kareem's eyes widen every time Sandra removes the bags contents, looks on in disappointed by the sight of vegetables and liver. Looking and making sure Doug is not around, Sandra pulls out a half gallon of banana crunch ice cream, which brings silent jubilation from the two children. Moving frozen vegetables and meat inside the freezer, Sandra hides the ice cream in the back and then camouflages it with the bags of frozen food. Looking at her children with a smile, she puts her finger to her mouth, letting her kids know that this is their secret. As Sandra smiles, she sees that her children are content on keeping the ice cream a secret.

Handing each child a plastic spoon, Sandra says, "Let's meet under the bed at eight o'clock tonight and don't be late, Ok?"

Getting a smile from both of her children, who are the spitting image of Sandra, they respond, "We won't be late, Mommy." As they return to the living room floor to continue their painting of their mother and them in the park on a sunny day, Sandra continues unpacking the groceries.

*　　*　　*

The atmosphere at dinner was quiet and calm. Sandra prepared lamb chops smothered in apricot sauce, served with linguine and broccoli. The kids, for once, did not complain about only being able to drink water and not soda, as they both, for a change, cleaned their plates. Sandra made sure Doug got the best lamb chops and his water glass had four ice cubes like he demanded and when it was half-empty, she would instantly refill on the spot. Doug seemed a little more at ease at the dinner table as he even asked the kids how school was going, something he never did. Sandra and the kids made sure they cleaned the dishes; therefore, Doug could not complain. Yes, all was well in the Gunner apartment and it has not been that way in a while.

*　　*　　*

As Kareem and Chaka are lying on the floor with half of their bodies under the bed, they silently hug and smile as they wait with spoons in their hands for Sandra to bring them their ice cream. Kareem, who has now gotten to his feet, is doing a little dance. An angry Chaka bangs him on his foot and whispers angrily, "Get your ass back under this bed." Not wanting to feel the wrath of his seven-year-old sibling, Kareem obeys his sister.

Sandra is on the toilet reading an issue of *Jet* magazine when her attention is broken as she hears the heavy footsteps of Doug walking past the bathroom heading to the kitchen. Still listening, Sandra gets back to admiring an R&B hunk that is featured in the magazine. Her attention is drawn away as she hears a loud slamming of what sounds like the refrigerator door. Sitting on the toilet and getting tense, Sandra lowers the magazine as she can now hear Doug returning, but this time at a much quicker pace as his footsteps pound on the wooden floor much harder. He stops at the bathroom door, as Sandra has now placed the magazine in front of her on the white tiled floor. Her heart is ready to jump out of her chest as she begins to perspire. Doug's footsteps sound as if he is returning to the bedroom and Sandra feeling a load off her shoulders, leans her head on the cold bathroom wall.

BANG! The door is busted open and standing in front of Sandra is a sweaty, muscle-bound Doug, breathing hard with his eyes red from smoking reefer. He holds a box of Banana Crunch ice cream in his hand.

"Doug, please. I am sorry, it was for the…"

Missing her head by a fraction of an inch, the box of ice cream goes by Sandra crashing into the window knocking down cologne and shampoo. Doug, who has his foot pressed against her thigh, knocks Sandra off the toilet and onto the floor.

"What the fuck did I tell you about bringing this shit in my house, bitch?"

Sandra, trying to push Doug's foot off her aching leg, cannot budge it. "Doug, you are hurting me, stop!" Reaching down, he grabs Sandra by her braids. Lifting her up, Doug throws her into the bathtub. Sandra, having the presence of mind, grabs on to the shower curtain in an attempt to break her fall. Still falling back, she hits her head on the metal sprout, opening a slight gash on the back of her head:

"I am the boss, bitch! I have the power. Do you understand me?!"

Reaching in the tub, Doug grabs Sandra by her arm and flings her into the wall, causing her to break the towel rack with her back.

"Doug, just let us go, please. Just let us go!"

Breathing hard and fast, Doug looks down on her and says, "Go ahead. You go bitch, but those are my kids and they are not going anywhere! I pay for everything in this motherfucker and everybody owes me! What you gonna do without me? You are too stupid to make it without me! Go ahead and try to leave me, see what happens!"

Sandra, lying on the floor, holding the back of her head can now see the blood from it on her hand. Looking over at the toilet, she spots the ice cream. As Doug watches her slowly begin to crawl in that direction, he is somewhat amazed and shocked to see Sandra grab the partially melted ice cream. Looking down on Sandra, Doug is wearing a face of curiosity as he watches Sandra crawl on her hands and knees in an attempt to exit the bathroom.

"Kareem and Chaka, Mommy's coming with your ice cream!" With half of her body out in the hallway, Sandra grimaces in pain as she slowly makes it to her feet. With her face directly in front of Doug's sweaty chest, she tries to move around him without touching his body.

"You ain't giving them shit. Give me that damn ice cream!" Reaching for the box, a defiant Sandra snatches the ice cream away from Doug, who, in a fit of rage, knocks it out of her hand and pushes her into the wall so hard that plaster can be heard crumbling from within. Sandra, falling to the floor, moans and lays motionless.

Looking down on her, Doug says, "Like I said, you are weak and dumb. You can do nothing to me or without me. Keep your ass on the floor where you belong." As Doug walks away, he reaches down grabbing the ice cream and throws it in the waste basket that sits in the kid's room.

Walking back to his bedroom, Doug slams and locks the door. Running from their bedroom, coming to the aid of their mother, Chaka and Kareem rub Sandra's face as Chaka begins to cry. Sandra, hearing her daughter, reaches up with her hand and begins to caress her hair. Kareem, who is standing over his mother, breaks his plastic spoon, holding just a jagged piece of plastic. Kareem begins to walk in the direction of his father's room when a hoarse and weak Sandra says, "No baby you are better than him. Our time will come soon." Listening to his mother, Kareem returns and stands near Sandra and Chaka in a protective stance.

Chapter Fourteen
The Great Escape

Getting out of Doug's truck, Sandra walks towards the community center to feed lunch to the homeless and less fortunate. Still grimacing from the ice cream incident two weeks ago, Sandra looks at her watch and calculates that Christmas is exactly three weeks away.

"Do not be late picking up those kids, Sandra. I am dead serious," says Doug. Not saying a word, Sandra enters the center.

*   *   *

While taking her coat off in the basement supply room, Sandra feels the back of her head and gently rubs the cut that she sustained from Doug. Taking a seat, Sandra looks at her watch and sees that she has forty-five minutes before people would start to arrive. Bringing her attention to the footsteps coming from the hallway, Sandra stands with a serious look on her face. Entering the room is Ms. Carla and a skinny white man in his sixties named Peter Smith.

"Hi, Sandra. This is the gentleman I was telling you about, Mr. Smith. Peter, this is Sandra, my friend."

As Sandra and Peter shake hands, Carla leaves the room so they can be alone.

"I will cut right to the chase Sandra, whatever I estimate your merchandise to be worth will be a market value. The price that I give you will be fair and honest. I collect ten percent of the fair price in cash and there is no room for negotiations; do we understand each other?"

Sandra, remembering the slime ball Jeffery she dealt with involving the check from the pageant that turned out to be phony, was fully aware she had to be extra cautious when dealing with people from this point on.

"Listen, Mr. Smith. I really appreciate you taking time from your busy schedule to come all the way uptown to see me. I really hope you understand that I can only let you estimate what I have right here and not at your store. I trust that you will be fair with me, and I have no problem with your ten percent fee. When you give me a price, I will bring the merchandise back here the next day and we can exchange my possessions for the cash," says Sandra.

Shaking his head in agreement, the man with wrinkles covering his face reaches into his pocket and removes a small eye scope. "Ok, let us see what you have," says Peter. Reaching with both her hands, Sandra removes the brown envelope from the back of her pants waistline and slowly empties the contents on a small green table that sits in the room. Taking a seat, Sandra anxiously watches the man look carefully at her things and from time to time writes on a small yellow pad. Sandra, who now is leaning forward, looks at each piece of merchandise that Doug has given her, remembering what pain she had to endure physically and emotionally to receive it.

Leaping out of her seat in sheer terror, Sandra stands in front of the old man blocking the view of a startled Jasmine, who has entered the room without knocking.

"Oh Sandra, I am so sorry I did not realize you were using the room; I just wanted to sit these plates in the closet," Jasmine says.

Looking behind her, Sandra can see that the old man is a little nervous by the way that his hands are shaking. "That is alright Jasmine; you can sit them right on the floor and when I am through, I will put them away myself."

Giving Sandra a smile, Jasmine does, while at the same time tries to sneak a glimpse at the person Sandra is trying to conceal from her. After watching Jasmine leave the room, Sandra walks to the door, locking the latch and testing the door for good measure. Looking at Peter, who is wiping sweat off his forehead, Sandra walks over to a refrigerator and retrieves the man a bottle of water.

"Here you go, Mr. Smith. Please continue," requests Sandra. Taking a sip of water, which seems to calm him down, the old man, continues to estimate Sandra's goods.

*   *   *

It has been about an hour, Mr. Smith is using his calculator and notepad, adding up figures while Sandra sits on an old loveseat and waits. After a few moments, the old man slowly rises to his feet and stretches, letting out a moan.

"Sandra, you have some very nice pieces here and based on what I have decided to be true and fair, I would be willing to offer you thirty-two thousand dollars minus thirty-two hundred, which covers my fee," says Mr. Smith.

Trying to put on the best possible poker face that she can, Sandra studies the pieces that are on the table and answers, "That seems to be fair Mr. Smith; we have a deal."

As the two of them meet in the center of the floor, they shake hands and smile. "Sandra today is Tuesday, so how about if we meet at this same time and location on Friday so we can complete the transaction."

Sandra, who grimaces at the pain coming from her back, responds, "Friday will be fine, Mr. Smith. I will see you then." Opening the door for the man, Sandra watches him leave and closes the door behind him. Locking it again, she walks back over to the table and begins to put her jewelry back inside her envelope. Putting it back down inside her pants, Sandra covers the bulk coming from the envelope with her sweater. Fixing her braids and wiping her pants Sandra, puts away the dishes Jasmine left, but before doing so, Sandra shakes her fist to the sky saying, "Thank you."

Making her way upstairs, Sandra puts a smile on her face, as she can smell the sweet aroma of Ms. Carla's cooking. The dining area is busy as usual as the men who volunteer are setting up the tables and chairs while others begin bringing out the lunch for the day. Waving to everyone, Sandra makes it over to the kitchen area where Ms. Carla is handing out pans of food to be placed on the tables.

"Everything ok, Sandra baby?" asks Ms. Carla.

Rubbing the grey-haired woman's shoulder, Sandra answers, "Everything went fine and thank you so much for your help." Passing a long pan of vegetables to a volunteer, Ms. Carla gives Sandra a quick squeeze.

Walking out of the kitchen holding a pan of tossed salad is Jasmine, who looks at Sandra and smiles. "Sandra, I am sorry about barging in earlier on you. I should have known better to knock.

"Don't worry Jasmine. It's ok; no harm was done" says Sandra. The two women exchange smiles and continue helping Ms. Carla.

*   *   *

It is 3:00 a.m. on Wednesday and Sandra is sitting in the living room on the computer while Doug, who arrived home at midnight smelling like Alize, is dead asleep. To make sure of it, Sandra even held back her vomit long enough so that she could allow Doug to have a 15-minute sex session with her. Looking at the screen, Sandra with her credit card pays for a reservation for her and the kids to Virginia Beach on December 11 at 10:35 p.m. from Kennedy airport. Knowing that Doug has planned some type of get together for his friends at the club at 11:00 p.m., Sandra is fully aware that he likes to be at least three hours ahead with his planning, so by the time her and the kids can catch a cab out to the airport, he should be at his club. Reading an e-mail that was sent to her earlier in the evening from a real estate company in Virginia Beach, it has been confirmed that they have vacancies in a nice apartment complex that had been built sometime last year. Looking at the clock on the computer, Sandra decides that she cannot stay online for too long, so she deletes the e-mail and logs off. Now going into the "C" drive, Sandra erases the history for all activity for that day and deletes the web sites she has been on. Shutting down the computer, Sandra quickly and quietly returns to bed.

As Doug drives Sandra and the kids to school, she looks at her kids sitting behind her from the rearview window with somber looks on their faces. Understanding the despair and anger they must be feeling, Sandra begins, "Hey, Kareem…knock knock"

Smiling at his mother, he answers, "Who's there?"

Turning down the radio, Doug says, "I am here and I am trying to listen to the goddamn music, so can your please shut the hell up." Kareem cuts his eyes at his father from the backseat and is silent again while Sandra looks straight ahead.

Pulling up to the school, there are about sixty kids all bundled up and dressed in their green uniforms. As Sandra gets the kids out of the car, Doug tells her, "Sandra I can not take you home, a bus will be on that corner in fourteen minutes, so make sure your ass is on it. At nine-thirty I will blow the horn to take you to feed your animals, so you make sure your ass is home waiting for me do you understand?"

"Yes, Doug. I understand" Sandra answers. Getting out of the Cadillac Escalade, Chaka overhears one of the children proclaim, "Man, that is a nice truck; they must have it made." Sandra looking at the child, then at Chaka says, "If they only knew."

Kissing them on their cheeks and watching them enter the classroom, Sandra hurries to the main office. Phones are ringing and women in their forties are helping students with different issues. Looking at her watch, Sandra knows that Doug has left her with nothing but a Meterocard and realizes she must hurry.

"Excuse me, ma'am. Who do I need to speak to in regards to getting school records sent to another state?" Sandra asks the black woman who is writing on a pad.

Not even looking up at Sandra, she responds, "You must give us two weeks notice and provide us with an official school letter where the child will be attending so that the necessary paperwork can be sent."

Looking at her watch, Sandra asks, "Well, two weeks is too late because we are planning to move in a few days and I was hoping someone could help me?"

Looking up at Sandra, the woman has a look of "You must be kidding" on her face. "Like I said, we need two weeks notice. The assistant principal, Ms. Duncan, should be here in about an hour; maybe she can do something for you."

With her watch telling her she has seven minutes until her bus arrives, Sandra says, "Ok, thank you. I will try back then." Knowing that their escape came down to timing, Sandra understood she would just have to pull the kids out and deal with the school records when they arrived in Virginia. Fixing her coat, Sandra exits the school and hurries to the bus stop.

*   *   *

Sitting in the bedroom, Sandra is carefully packing away a three-day supply of clothing for the kids and herself. Figuring that with the money she will get from Mr. Smith, buying the kids new clothes will not be a problem and with the prices being much cheaper in Virginia, she could buy them more. Removing a bag from the top of her closet, Sandra takes out brand new tooth brushes, toothpaste, a couple of coloring books, crayons and a deck of cards, putting them in the small carry-on suitcase. Closing the suitcase and putting it in the back of the closet, Sandra conceals it with her winter coats and sweaters. Closing the closet door and walking over to her dresser mirror, Sandra fixes her hair and clothes, taking a deep breath. "Everything is going to work out; just don't panic. Just be cool, tomorrow I will have my money and we will be away from here," Sandra says. Quickly turning her head to the window, she hears the horn blowing. Grabbing her coat and keys, Sandra hurries to get her ride from Doug to serve lunch to her friends.

*   *   *

It is Friday; Sandra is home from dropping the kids off at school looks at her watch that reads 9:35. Fully aware that in about an hour she should have a little over thirty thousand dollars for a new beginning with her children, but most importantly, away from the only man she loved and feared: Doug. The only problem she was dealing with at this moment was the bastard is sitting in a chair right across from her and the jewelry was under the armoire where Doug seemed to be guarding. The room is silent except for Doug, who is biting on a pretzel stick and making loud chewing noises. He always prided himself on leaving on time and sometimes a little earlier. So if he told her to get ready, how could Sandra get to the stash right in front of him? Sandra felt the beads of sweat begin to form on her forehead and she knew if Doug saw that, a thousand questions would soon follow. She had to do something even if it meant taking a small beat down because this was possibly her only chance. Slowly getting up from the bed, Sandra walks to the door.

"Where the fuck are you going, Sandra? It is almost time to go."

"I am a little thirsty; I need to get some water," Sandra answers. Staring at her for minute, Doug takes another bite of his pretzel and looks away from her. Sandra exits to the kitchen, trying not to look suspicious.

Getting water from a pitcher inside the refrigerator, Sandra looks at the cat clock with the eyes moving from side to side. She always hated that clock because the cat was a reminder of how much time she wasted with Doug. Not knowing what to do, Sandra bites her bottom lip and cannot help but to let the tears swell up in her eyes. Putting the water back inside, Sandra sees something that gives her an idea. There is a whole glass bottle of protein drink that Doug spends $150.00 a bottle on once a month. Chaos causes chaos even if it meant a beat down because what more could he do to her that he has not already done? Looking behind her to make sure, she was still alone, Sandra slowly nudges the glass pitcher inch by inch along the shelf until SMASH!

"What the hell was that!" yells Doug from the bedroom in the back.

Sandra, wondering if she did the right thing, looks at the thick purple liquid that has splashed all over the white kitchen floor. "I spilled your drink by accident," responds Sandra. Moving to the side and standing next to the refrigerator, she hears the loud and heavy footsteps of the beast arriving. Standing at the doorway of the kitchen wearing a designer sweat suit, Doug looks at the mess and then at Sandra with a pissed off stare. Walking slowly over to her, Doug stands with his hands on his hips, not saying a word while Sandra is flinching, slightly trying to anticipate what is coming.

"Sandra, get a fucking mop and clean this shit up. You have six minutes before I have to leave and drop you off. If it is not cleaned up, I promise I will use your head as a mop," says Doug. Walking away, Sandra goes to the bathroom where the mop and bucket is. Looking in the dining room mirror in front of her, Sandra notices that Doug is opening a roll of paper towels, laying them on the floor and now realizes that this is her chance.

Quickly grabbing the bucket from behind the bathroom door, Sandra sits it in the tub and begins filling it with water. While the bucket is filling up, Sandra runs to the bedroom.

Breathing hard but silently, if that is possible, she quickly kneels down and reaches under the armoire, scraping her knuckles on the wood, but still manages to pull the envelope from the armoire, which was being held by masking tape. Quickly stuffing it down the back of her pants, Sandra covers it with her sweater. Hearing an agitated Doug walking towards the bedroom, Sandra steps quickly to the bathroom, just missing his eyesight. Turning off the water and picking up the bucket, Sandra grabs the mop and begins to walk past Doug towards the kitchen, focusing on the floor and not Doug's stone-angry face.

"Hurry the hell up, Sandra," he yells, causing Sandra to flinch, almost spilling some of the water.

* * *

Inside Doug's truck trying to sit straight up in her seat, Sandra is beginning to squirm a little because of the envelope sticking her in the back. Knowing that they are a minute away, Sandra sucks it up and handles the pointy edge sticking in her back. Pulling up to the community center, Doug stops the truck so Sandra can exit while, at the same time, he admires Rose Garden, who is standing by the door wearing a heavy coat. As Sandra walks up to Rose, she gives her a hug and begins to walk inside when Doug yells from his truck, "Sandra, come here!"

Motioning to Rose to get out of the cold, Sandra walks over to the truck. "Yes Doug?"

"Who is that girl that you just spoke to?" Doug asks.

"She is just a girl that comes in to eat lunch that is all."

Looking at Sandra with anger, Doug says "What is her goddamn name and how old is she, Sandra? I did not ask you that. Obviously, she eats here; I am not stupid. I said what is her name?"

"Her name is Rose," Sandra answers.

Doug rubs his chin and a small grin comes across his face as he thinks about Rose. "Yeah, ok. You go inside now and feed the animals. You just make sure you are not late picking up those kids." Shaking her head, Sandra walks away from the truck and inside the center.

Walking to the coat room, Sandra starts to hang up her coat when Rose enters. Looking very cold and hungry, Rose manages a smile when she looks at Sandra.

"Ms. Sandra, I know how busy things can get for you here, but I saw two of the workers bringing a Christmas tree and decorations in here right before you came, I was wondering if I could help decorate the tree?"

Sandra, feeling so much pressure and anxiety on her shoulders, felt like she needed to feel human again and maybe decorating that tree with this broken young woman could help the both of them. "I tell you what Rose, after lunch I think I can sneak away for a couple of minutes. You and I can work on the tree then, Ok?"

Smiling and trying not to show it too much, a happy Rose answers, "Ok, Ms. Sandra, thanks." Turning and exiting the room, Sandra looks at her watch and sees that in about forty-five minutes, Mr. Smith would be here with the money for the exchange of the jewelry.

* * *

Like always, Sandra is standing behind the many long tables with other volunteers serving lunch to the many people entering on this Friday. Standing to her right is Jasmine, who from time to time, rubs her wrist.

Sandra, who takes notice, asks, "Jasmine, you ok? You have been rubbing at that wrist since you got here this morning."

"Oh, no, Sandra. It's fine. I just banged it on the dresser by accident last night. It is a little sore but it will be ok."

Looking at Jasmine with a little concern and suspicion, Sandra, not wanting to pry, smiles and continues to serve food. Neatly placing mashed potatoes on a little girl's tray, Sandra looks toward the exit leading to the basement where she sees Ms. Carla slowly waving to her to come over. Looking around and making sure no one else is watching Sandra sits her large spoon down.

"Jasmine, do you think you could cover for me for a few minutes?" Grabbing Sandra's spoon Jasmine smiles and nods yes.

Meeting Ms. Carla at the staircase, Sandra has a look of anxiety and of jubilation. "Sandra baby, Mr. Jones is downstairs waiting for you. Will you be ok?" asks Carla.

Grabbing Carla's hand, Sandra smiles at the grey-haired woman and kisses her on the cheek. "I am going to be fine, thank you for all of the support and kindness you have shown me since I started here. You will never know what it has meant to me," Sandra responds. As the two women share another embrace, Sandra begins her walk down the steps leading to the basement. Like always, the basement is warm and a little dim but still illuminated enough to function. Walking towards the storage door, Sandra reaches behind her and removes the envelope that she has been hiding since this morning. For some strange reason, a little pride enters Sandra because as bad as the corner of the envelope stuck her in the back, Sandra never rubbed or attempted to remove the nuisance. Maybe she wondered if this was a sign of something good happening. Wiping her face from the little sweat beads popping up on her forehead; Sandra gently turns the doorknob, entering the room.

Looking up at Sandra with a gentle smile on his face and an old pair of bifocals is Mr. Smith. Sitting at the small table, he clutches a very old but well maintained brown bag that you would see doctors carry to people's homes on visits.

"Good day, Ms. Lyte and how are you?"

Holding her envelope tightly with two hands, a now less worrisome Sandra replies, "I am doing fine and how about you?"

"I am fine, just preparing for the holidays. Please take a seat so we can get down to business?" Sandra grabs an old wooden chair and sits across from the old man as he begins to reveal crisp clean stacks of one hundred dollar bills brand new from the U.S. treasury.

"Ms. Lyte, this is your total share of twenty-eight thousand eight hundred dollars and this is my share of three thousand two hundred dollars." Sandra, staring at the stack of money sitting on the table, is almost hypnotized when she is brought back by the sound of Mr. Smith clearing his throat. Sandra, feeling a little embarrassed, reaches down and grabs the envelope that contains her freedom from the years of hell she has suffered. Slowly opening the envelope, Sandra gently pours the contents on the table. The room is spinning and Sandra's head is pounding as if someone has smacked her with a baseball bat. A shocked red-faced Mr. Smith stares at the table where copper and aluminum scrap metal lies. Sandra, holding her mouth and rocking back and fourth in her chair, begins to sob uncontrollably. The old man quickly grabs his stacks of money, putting them back into his bag and looking around the room suspiciously as if at any moment someone would bust into the room and rob him. Sandra, reaching towards the dirty scrap metal, asks, "Why, God, why!?" Gathering his possessions, Mr. Smith hurries toward the door, unlocks it, and gets ready to exit when he stops and looks at a fallen Sandra, who is now sitting on the floor in disbelief.

Staring at the metal in front of her, Sandra wonders if this is some kind of punishment or torment, she must go through. Thoughts run through her mind as she tries to figure out who has she wronged in her life to deserve what she is going through now. After Sandra fiddles with the metal, the door slowly opens and Ms. Carla walks in letting the smile she has on her face disappear as she looks at Sandra sitting on the floor slowly shaking her head.

Slowly walking over, Carla strains to bend down in front of Sandra. "Baby, what happened?"

Slowly lifting her head, Sandra with her swollen red eyes, looks at the woman and says, "I am being punished. I am being punished and maybe I deserve to be." Stretching out her arms, Carla grabs Sandra and slowly begins to stroke her head.

* * *

With the dishes washed and the garbage being disposed of, a few volunteers remain to help with small miscellaneous items. Sandra, who some how got the strength to finish her day and even kept her promise to Rose to decorate the Christmas tree puts on her coat. Sandra stares at the smile on Rose's face as she admires the seven-foot imitation pine tree. Sandra, realizing that she will have to return home and face Doug, is not concerned with the possibility of another beating because that was a forgone conclusion. What really was on her mind was how did he find out? Who or what gave her in? What was not easy for her to swallow was how he stayed on point. Sandra decides it is time to pick up the kids and face the beast. She leaves the pantry undetected.

* * *

It is 10:00 p.m. and Sandra sits in the living room looking at the walls that surround her, while waiting for Doug to come out of his lab where he has been making his product for the last eight hours. The kids were fast asleep which is very important. She did not want the kids subjected to what would happen. Sandra realizes that she has intelligent children who did not have to see the actual beatings, only the results to understand what mommy was going through. There it is the squeaking of the door and the footsteps of the beast. Sandra, sitting on the couch looking straight ahead, tries not to notice the large obstacle now sitting in front of her, but how could she not. Would this be the last of many beatings? Would she awaken as she has from the others? On the other hand, will she finally meet her maker? Sandra was about to find out.

"Baby, I want you to know that I can not let you go. You are a part of me and you know too much about me. As I told you a while ago Sandra, I know every move you make before you do. I really do not care how people perceive me or my lifestyle because I understand my intelligence and my limitations and Sandra, you don't understand yours," a relatively calm Doug says.

"You see Sandra; dealing with me is not a mystery. I am what I am…no more no less and you knew this so do not act stupid. Any strong, independent woman would have walked away years ago, but you elected to stay for the lifestyle. Sandra, you are weak and unappreciative, many hood rats would relish being where you are. You are too stupid to see and appreciate a man like me. If you did as I told you, do you think I would have touched a hair on your head for the past seven years? Sit back and think, whenever I disciplined you it was because of some dumb shit you did," Doug says. Taking a sip of some white wine, Doug continues "Like this last shit you tried to pull. Saving the jewelry and trying to pawn it, which I have to admit was pretty smart. Nevertheless, baby you have to realize even when I sleep, I am awake. I saw every time when I gave you something how you stashed it. I bet you are asking yourself how I knew about your little plan to get some cash and head to Virginia Beach to your nice new apartment. Well guess what? When a woman does not enjoy my sex anymore, I do not get upset; I just find another. That is what I did Sandra with a nice Spanish mommy named Jasmine. You probably know her; she serves the animals right along side of you."

Sandra, for the first time, flinches with emotion. Looking up at a grinning Doug, she cannot believe her ears, but her hearing is perfect. "I told you, Sandra. I may not have your little journalism bullshit degree, but I am street savvy and have a "think-ahead" attitude. Now, I believe you are going to go after her on Monday, but you will not get the chance because as of today, I had her removed. But ask yourself, did I plant someone else in her place? Maybe or maybe not" says, Doug.

Doug, reaching under his chair, pulls out a folder that contains paper and slowly begins to open it. "Baby, I had the feeling that you would start to use my computer, so look what I did," Doug says as he removes the sheet of paper. Holding it up in front of Sandra's face, a smiling Doug watches her eyes move from side to side as she reads her internet activity on the night she bought her airline tickets. "Isn't technology a motherfucker, baby? I never knew you could watch and take pictures of other people's internet activity until I watched "Jerry" on television one morning. I went out and bought myself a program for your sneaky ass. I know about the airline tickets, the e-mails to the property owner in Virginia...shit, baby, I even saw those dark, fine-ass brothers you have been looking at in those online muscle calendars. Damn, Boo, I stay in shape; you do not love me no more? Doug asks.

Sandra can only sit still in absorb the humiliation and torment as Doug shows her pictures of everything she has done on the internet. Sticking out his hand, Doug calmly revokes Sandra's wallet containing her New York State ID, bankcard, credit card and even her Virginia driver's license. Taking away her cell phone, Doug says, "At this point and time, you will be on lockdown a little harder now, baby. Your cell phone belongs to me and I will be sure to have someone always watching when you pick those kids up. Now this is the last thing I am going to say to you. Sandra, you are stupid and weak, we agree?"

Sandra answers in a low, meek voice, "Yes, I am."

"Very good baby, now we are getting somewhere. Therefore, I want you to listen to me very carefully. Christmas is only two weeks away and I love Christmas. Therefore, either two things will happen for the holidays: you will be on your best behavior and the kids will have the biggest Christmas they could ever imagine. On the other hand, baby and I want you to listen carefully because you know I do not bullshit. You can try to fuck with me again and I promise you, when those crumb snatchers wake up to rush to the Christmas tree to open their little neatly wrapped gifts, they will find Mommy instead with a bullet in her fucking head. Do you understand boo? Looking into Doug's eyes, Sandra tries to find some type of glimmer of doubt, for which she can turn into hope, but she does not; all she can see is a pair of cold brown eyes.

As Doug gets up with his glass of wine and folder, he begins to walk away when, with his right hand, he backslaps Sandra, causing her to fall off the couch and onto the floor. As Doug heads back to his bedroom, Sandra holds her now bleeding bottom lip and says quietly "He is right, I am weak and stupid."

Chapter Fifteen
Kids, Let's Go For a Ride

It is Saturday morning and Sandra watches from the fourth floor window as Doug gets the kids inside the truck to visit his dad at The Shadybrook Retirement Home in Westchester, New York. With Doug putting a block on the phone and taking away her cell phone, Sandra could only hope he would have the decency to call her when they arrived. Putting the palm of her hand on the cold, frosted windowpane, Sandra waves goodbye to her babies as the truck leaves from in front of the building. Looking around the large but empty apartment, trying to keep herself upbeat, Sandra turns on the radio. Looking over at the door, she knows that she will spend the rest of her day inside the apartment because of the fear of Doug's street surveillance.

*　*　*

There is little traffic on the north side of The Hutchinson River Parkway as Doug is making great time. Looking from his rearview mirror, Doug can see Kareem opening up a granola bar while Chaka looks at Kareem as if he is crazy with her mouth wide open.

"Boy, what the hell do you think you are doing? You know damn well I do not allow food in this truck."

Giving his father a sarcastic look, the seven year old tyke chomps down on the granola bar, creating a loud crunch and causing crumbs to scatter on the Escalades cream leather interior.

"You little bastard, I know you heard me! Put that damn bar down!"

Staring at his father with hatred that no child should have inside him, Kareem replies, "Why should I listen to you? You hit my mommy!" Chaka is now attempting to cover her brother's mouth with her hand, but it is to no avail as Kareem continues, "I know what you do to my mother and when I get big I am…"

The children's heads and bodies violently jerk forward as Doug stomps hard on his brakes bringing his vehicle to a screeching halt in the center lane of the highway. Doug, snapping his huge torso violently in the direction of Kareem, shouts, "When you get big, you gonna do what, you little bastard? What you gonna do? You are from the same flimsy cloth just like your dumb ass mother! Like I told you before, my man. Anytime your little ass is ready, come on!" Chaka, who now has tears in her eyes as she hears the blasting of horns from passing cars, holds her brother by his arm as he tries to lean towards Doug. As father and son stare at each other, Doug blinks first as he turns around and starts to drive. As the trio make their way to the residency, Doug takes a quick glance up at his rear view mirror and can still see a stone-faced Kareem burning two lasers through the back of his head with his menacing brown eyes. Meanwhile, Chaka looks at her brother rubbing his hand in an attempt to keep him calm.

*   *   *

Driving through the tall iron-gated entrance, which leads to the visitors parking area, Doug parks his vehicle. Exiting the truck Doug turns to Kareem and Chaka, "I don't want any running or playing inside this place. When we get inside, I want you both to sit down and keep quiet; do you understand?"

Chaka, who is sitting up straight looks into her father's eyes, answers softly, "Yes."

While Kareem is looking out the truck window admiring the trees and well manicured grass, he asks "Why are we here? Who do we know here?"

Doug, looking at the little boy as if he were an enemy instead of a son, shoots back, "You do not worry why we are here. I asked you a damn question, do you understand?"

Continuing to look out the window, Kareem answers in a nonchalant fashion, "Yeah." Getting out of the Escalade, Doug walks to the other side opening the door for the two youngsters. As Chaka takes her time climbing out of the truck, Kareem quickly jumps out and proceeds to run and jump over the low chain link fence running in a circle in the grass. Doug, who is now looking around the resident grounds to see if anyone is watching, looks furious.

Chaka, who is looking in her father's face, yells, "Kareem, come on lets go. I am going to tell Mommy you are misbehaving."

Stopping in his tracks Kareem, slowly walks over to where his father and sister stand, remaining in place.

"Get your dumb ass inside this place," snaps Doug.

"Do not call him dumb; he received three A's and two B's on his report card last week. You can even ask Mommy," responds Chaka. As the three of them walk towards the entrance door, Doug realizes that he has never seen his children's report cards from that expensive school he pays to send them to.

As Doug signs the children and himself in the big green book on the mahogany desk, the kids admire the many paintings that cover the tall walls and the statues that sit on mantles. Looking in the many rooms that they pass, the children see that most of the people are old. They also see that the hallways and floors are spotless, smelling like the dentist office where their mom takes them. Walking up a flight of stairs, Doug leads them to a large community room that has a pool table, ping pong table, three card tables and tables set up for games of chess. Doug is looking around the room where about twenty senior citizens are busy doing things from arts and craft to listening to the baseball game on the radio. Finally, Doug spots a man wearing a silk robe and designer pajamas watching an animal program on television.

"Go sit down until it is time to go," demands Doug. Walking over to a loveseat that sits against the wall, the children do as they are told. Removing the black Kango hat from his head, Doug slowly walks over to where the man with the big grey afro sits. Reaching out and tapping the man on his shoulder, Fred Gunner asks without turning around, "Where is my fucking pastrami sandwich, boy?"

Looking at his empty hands, Doug softly answers, "Sir, I am really sorry, but I was in such a rush to get here that it slipped my mind."

Sucking his teeth and slowly turning around in his swivel chair, Fred responds, "Nothing changes, right son? You are still the same sorry motherfucker that I spit out from my balls, huh?"

Taking a seat next to his father, Doug asks, "So, how have you been? Are they treating you ok?"

"You got my money man?" Fred asks. Reaching into his pocket, Doug removes some money and hands it to his father. "Also, my room is feeling a little small, so make some arrangements to get me moved to a larger room, you understand?"

Looking down at the black and white tiled floor, Doug answers, "Yes, sir. I will get on it right away." Looking over in the direction of the love seat, Fred sees Kareem and Chaka talking to each other. Slowly turning his head back in the direction of his son, he asks, "Stupid ass, tell me you did not? Those are yours?"

"Their names are…"

Interrupting, Fred says, "What did I tell you many years ago? The less baggage you carry the easier it is for you to move. Now look what you have done; you got some profit-eating, crumb-snatchers on your hands now."

Looking dumb and embarrassed, Doug, who still has not found the courage to look his father in his eyes, says, "I send them to private school and house them in a nice apartment. They eat the best of foods and I do not allow them any candy or sweets."

As Doug and Fred look at the two children, Chaka, forgetting what her father told them, gets out of her chair and walks over to two elderly women, who are playing bridge. Sitting down with them, the old women both smile at Chaka and pat her on the cheek. Reaching into her little purse that Sandra bought for her, she pulls out two sticks of sugarless gum, handing a stick to each woman. Looking as if the women have won the lottery, they smile and blush as they enjoy their treat from Chaka.

Meanwhile, Kareem following his sister's lead walks over to a table where a man who looks to be in his late sixties sits at the chess table waiting for a formidable opponent to take a seat across from him. Staring at Kareem with curiosity on his face, the old man nods to the board as to say to Kareem, "Your move." Kareem, reaching out his hand in the form of a handshake and receives one from the wrinkled old man. As Kareem makes his first move, the old man smiles with approval and makes his.

As Fred and Doug watch this, all unfold, the older Gunner says, "I see you got them trained to listen, huh boy? You married the momma, too?"

Clutching his hat in his hand, Doug exhales slowly, "No, I did not marry her, sir; we have lived together for the past eight years."

Counting his money, Fred looks at Doug, "What you gonna do when things get tight? I told you what would happen if you did not listen to me. I am about one hundred miles away from your ass, and I know for a fact things are getting tight."

"Sir, you do not have to worry; I have enough to survive for a while."

Shaking his head and looking at his son as if he was a complete idiot, Fred says, "Just survive? Is that what you have become, just a survivor? You better start living, my man, because that bullshit you call a life will not last forever, so you better start thinking ahead for yourself and fuck everybody else."

Reaching into his pocket, Doug pulls out a Movado watch, handing it to his father. "I almost forgot, Merry Christmas. I know it is still two weeks off, but I wanted to get it for you."

Looking at the watch and studying it, Fred looks back at his son and tosses the watch back at him, hitting his knee then falling to the ground. "I told you, I do not wear leather bands; I only wear metal bands. Get me what I like."

Picking the watch up off the floor Doug responds "No problem, sir."

*   *   *

After an hour of humiliation from his father, Doug begins to gather his things when he looks over at the table where Kareem is playing chess. There are a number of old men forming a circle to get a chance to beat the seven-year-old chess master. Looking to his left, he sees Chaka knitting with three elderly women, who marvel at how fast she has caught on. Doug looks at his father, who is counting the money he has received, softly saying, "Sir, I have to get going."

"Well, get going," answers Fred.

"By the way, when you come up here next month, you will bring two pastrami sandwiches instead of one. Maybe this will teach you about what is more important, like accountability."

Putting on his coat Doug responds, "No problem. I will see you next month. Kareem and Chaka let's go," says Doug.

Kareem, twisting his face with frustration, answers, "Can I finish this game please? It is almost over."

Doug, looking back at his father, can see Fred grinning and shaking his head slowly. Thinking back to when he was a young boy, Doug clearly knows what that gesture meant: "You have no control and on top of that, you are weak." Walking away from his father, Doug first walks over to Chaka, takes the yarning utensils away, putting her coat on. Looking sadly at the elderly women, Chaka just waves goodbye and so do the women. Walking over to the chessboard where Kareem is in deep thought, Doug quietly says, "Kareem it is time to go; put on your coat."

"Oh, come on, sonny; let us get a chance to beat the young wizard. You should be proud of him; this kid is going places when he gets older," a wrinkled face Bob says. Not paying any attention to the old wise man, Doug gives Kareem his coat, who reluctantly puts it on. Shaking hands with the elderly men, Kareem receives numerous pats on his head. As Doug and the children begin to exit the recreational room, Chaka quickly runs over to Fred and touches him gently on his shoulder saying, "Goodbye, granddaddy."

Looking at the beautiful Chaka from the corner of his eye, Fred responds, "Goodbye and that is Mr. Gunner." Looking at him for a second or two, Chaka kisses him on the cheek, returning to Doug and Kareem.

As they exit, Kareem looks at his sister strangely and asks, "That was nasty; why did you kiss him?" Chaka, rolling her eyes at her brother, answers, "Because he is sad."

* * *

As the sun sends its rays through the windows of the Escalade, Doug looks at his rearview mirror and notices that his children are sound asleep. Dialing a number on his cell phone he gets through to Fish, who is at Doug's club.

"Hey, what's up? How much did we move last night?"

Doug's mouth drops open as he listens to Fish on the other end. "What the fuck do you mean Buster got jacked last night? By who? They got all of it? Damn. Listen, get everybody together tonight; we need a sit-down," Doug says. Hanging up his phone and throwing it in the seat next to him, Doug listens to the request of a now awakened Kareem "Can we stop at McDonalds; I'm getting hungry?"

"Hell no! I told your little ass to eat something before we left this morning! Now just wait until you get your ass home to eat!" an angry Doug answers. Not saying a word, Kareem sits back in his seat and looks out of his window.

* * *

Walking into his apartment, Doug watches his kids run and jump into the open arms of their loving mother, who is preparing lunch.

"How are my babies doing?" she excitingly asks.

Chaka, who is kissing her mother all over her face, answers proudly, "I learned how to knit a sweater today!"

"You did!? That is wonderful; I knew you were a smart girl."

Kareem, who is doing some sort of crazy dance for his mother, which makes his sister crack up laughing, tells Sandra, "I beat five men today in chess. One of them even called me a wizard."

Sandra, who smiles and looks at her son proudly, tells him, "Well, you practice enough on me. I can see why you are so good."

Meanwhile Doug, who is standing from a distance in the living room, looks on with anger in his face. Sandra, who can sense that he is standing behind her does not dare look.

"Sandra, come to the bathroom for a second," demands Doug.

"Ok, Doug, can you give me one second; I want to get their coats off and give them some hot chocolate," Sandra replies.

"Excuse me?" says Doug. Kissing the children on their cheeks Sandra walks toward Doug, who in turn leads the way to the bathroom.

Closing the door behind him, Doug turns and looks at Sandra up and down. Seeing that Sandra is wearing a corduroy skirt with no stockings, Doug slowly pins her to the front of the vanity. With a face that is dark and menacing, Doug gets close enough to Sandra so that she can smell his breath and she is clearly nervous.

Rubbing his large sweaty hands on her smooth, large, toned thighs, he asks "Do you miss your man, baby? You miss me, right?"

Doug pushing himself harder against her making Sandra grimace with pain because of her aching back. Trying to answer correctly, Sandra says, "Yes Doug, I miss you." Quickly and forcefully, he spins her around so that she now faces the mirror over the sink. With very little regards for passion and gentleness, Doug quickly jerks up Sandra's skirt, revealing blue silk panties. Looking into the mirror, Sandra grimaces at the look of the beast as he pulls her panties to one side, ripping them in the process. Biting her lip and gripping both sides of the porcelain sink, Sandra observes his facial expressions every time he thrust his penis inside her.

Trying to be strong, she thinks to herself how Doug has never made true love to her and how she finds him repulsive. She only hopes this rape will be over soon. As he pushes himself harder and farther inside her, Sandra looks at the toothbrush holder and spots a disposable razor he uses to keep his large skull clean and for a split second Sandra wonders to herself, "It is right there Sandra. Grab it and at the precise moment, when he releases his nasty, slimy sewage inside you, decapitate the nasty serpent attached to his balls. Then you can grab the kids and just go. Wake up stupid! You know you will only have one chance and if you blow this chance, he will definitely break your neck while your skirt is still up. Do you want this for your kids? Just deal with this. It is almost over, just look at the ugly ass faces he is making. Just use your head and think of a better plan."

Moaning louder Doug pulls out of Sandra and releases himself on her skirt. Pulling up his pants, Doug smacks Sandra on the backside, which makes a loud noise. Before exiting, Doug says, "Hurry up and get my lunch ready; I am hungry." Looking at herself in the mirror, Sandra softly says to herself, "Yep Sandra, you are pathetic. Now go do what Massa told you to do."

Chapter Sixteen
Can't Beat 'Um, Join 'Um

The Harlem streets are paved with fresh white snow thanks to the nor'easter that has swooped down on the city this evening. Driving slowly and carefully, Doug turns up his wipers to help his vision, wondering what happened Friday night to his friends as they peddled his product on his corners. Not wanting to speculate or assume Doug was sure about one thing: He had to get his men back out there because his lifestyle costs money. Pulling up to his nightclub, Doug gets out of his vehicle and finds the key to his club. Covering his face from the wind-blown snow, Doug quickly sticks his key in the door and walks inside his quiet and dark club, which, to the disappointment of many, is closed tonight.

Brushing his coat off and stomping the snow off his feet, Doug proceeds to walk to the back of the club to his office. Admiring and appreciating how well the staff keeps the place clean and managed, Doug removes his coat and sits it across a bar stool. Getting closer to the room, Doug calls out for his men, "Yo Fish, Troy, yo Buster," but gets no response. Feeling a little suspicious, Doug feels for his gun, which is in the back of his pants waist line. Walking into his office, Doug is startled and confused but still has the state of mind to reach for his weapon.

"Doug, my brother please don't," the man dressed in all black sitting at Doug's desk says. From Doug's left and right, two men standing six feet, six inches tall wearing white full length cashmere coats point silver pump shotguns to his head. Letting his senses take over, Doug lowers his hands to his sides.

"That's right, brother. Just relax and all will be fine. It is almost Christmas and we want you to spend many more with the one's near and dear to your heart." Looking around rapidly with his eyes, Doug takes a deep breath. "Who are you and what do you want? Better yet, how did you get the fuck in here and where are my men?"

Removing his sunglasses, the man in black with light hazel eyes and no eyebrows responds, "Ok, Doug, here we go. My name is X. and I represent the Lords of the Underground. We control ninety-one percent of all the drugs on the street. From cocaine, smack, marijuana, ecstasy and crack. If someone is getting high in this city, chances are it came through us. As far as what we want, Doug; we want you. We have watched you since you visited one of our distributors Mario Chavez. You remember him, right?" Doug looks at the man with curiosity and fear but mostly fear because after sitting under the hot lights in the room, Mr. X has not one drop of perspiration on his forehead.

"Your organization killed him? I lost sixty percent of my profit because of that shit!" Mr. X motions with his fingers for his men to lower their weapons. "Business is business Doug and Mario went beyond the organization's rules when it came to promoting on the side. He never asked for permission and he was very dishonest in sharing his new mule...you."

Taking a seat in front of his desk, Doug looks around the room: "Come on Doug. I admire intelligence and right now for a kid who started with nothing, who now enjoys the many things that you have, you are not getting the big picture. We just cut out your middle man, the guy who was getting seventy percent of your profits. If you make some long, hard decisions, there is a slight chance you could be making a lot more without him."

Trying to picture what he could do with better profits, Doug says, "Tonight I was suppose to have a meeting with my men about how and who robbed them. Well, I already know now who did that, but my other concern is for my men."

Standing up out of his chair and removing his coat, Mr. X. takes his seat again. "Doug, I have some good news and some bad news; I will give you the bad news first because I believe in silver linings. When we entered the club, your men had not arrived yet, so we waited. When they did your friend, Troy began to act very immature and disrespectful by pulling his gun and spitting on my shoes. A very nasty act that we dealt with swiftly." Reaching under the desk, Mr. X reveals a mid-size cardboard box that he begins to open. Slowly opening the flaps on the box, he slides it forward to Doug, who is now looking very apprehensive about looking inside. Looking at the men that are in the room with him, Doug slowly pulls the box close to him, swallows and looks inside. Jumping out of his seat while pushing the box to the floor, Doug stares at the contents of the box with disgust.

"Calm down Doug and let me explain the scene to you. Troy pulled his gun out with that hand. While that pinkish slime of mass is, his lips and tongue. That is what he used to create the saliva he so rudely spit on my fifteen hundred dollar shoes."

A sobbing Doug cannot hold back his emotions: "You did not have to do this. He had a wife. He was a good man"

Looking at Doug as if he was a child, Mr. X. shakes his head, "Hey Doug pull yourself together. He had a choice; Troy could have been a gentleman and lived or he could have been rude and died. He chose the latter. Besides, his wife was not that stupid; we ran a background check on Troy and that wife of his who had a substantial insurance policy on him, so she understood his lifestyle. So please wipe your eyes; you look weak. Now, as far as your friends Buster and Fish go, listen up. Some time ago, he killed a man on Fish's command by the name of Willie Parker, who owned a meat market in the Bronx. All because Fish thought, he was out of line at some meeting he held. Now you look a little shocked because I know so much, so I will tell you why I am so informed. Fish has worked for us long before you met Chavez; that is the reason why he had those contacts for you. His mistake was made when he gave the hit on Willie. Fish had no authority to give such orders; why he would be that stupid is unknown to me. Therefore, Because of the rudeness of your men, they had to pay for past sins. So your man Buster is now being grinded up in Willie's meat market as we speak for pulling the trigger."

Feeling as if the room is spinning, Doug, looking at the ground, asks, "So that leaves Fish; where is he?"

Motioning to one of his cronies, who leaves the room, Mr. X. looks amusingly at an obvious shaken Doug.

"Ah, here is our friend now," says Mr. X. as Doug can hear the sound of rolling wheels. What enters the room is a leather chair with a badly beaten Fish wearing nothing but his underwear. Fish's face beaten unrecognizable and his right leg broke in at least three areas moans like an infant. His hands look like pulverized stumps because they have been smashed with a sledgehammer. His eyes are swollen shut and his lips mangled causing him to spit up blood.

"Doug, let me be the first to tell you that this is cruel, without a doubt, but this is a business and like any business, rules and regulations have to be abided by. Fish, was treated well by this organization and so was his family because we believe in loyalty not only for our workers but also for their loved ones. So when a person who is treated as well as Fish has been over the years, there is no excuse for his stupidity and that stupidity is on display for you tonight Doug," says Mr. X.

With his mouth gone dry and his eyes fixed on his childhood friend, who unknown to Doug, lived a hell of a secret life, Doug cannot think straight. "Please, get him to a hospital and I will listen to your proposal. I just ask you kindly that you please get him some help; he does not deserve to die like this please," pleads Doug.

As Mr. X. nods his head, the same man that wheeled Fish in the room pulls him out backwards. As fish is pulled away, Doug looks at the man that fought and worked with him side-by-side for so many years. As Fish is no longer in Doug's sight, he can only hear the sounds of the chair's wheels squeak on the floor until after a moment he can no longer.

* * *

It has been about twenty minutes now and silence is golden inside Doug's office. The only thing that has changed is Doug has been given a drink and a grilled chicken salad that he has not touched. Looking at Doug and his untouched salad, Mr. X. breaks the silence: "Doug, tonight we have witnessed much and learned a lot. So now before I let you go home, let me lay it on the table for you. We all agree that my employers are in charge of this city and very soon, most of the entire east coast. The canals that feed and furnish you are closing up real fast. What you have on your side are your brains and your will to eat, which we admire. The proposal I am offering to you is an interesting one at that. We offer you a position in our organization on the entry level as a worker that we will pay handsomely for hard work. You will also have a great opportunity for advancement."

Doug, doing his best to regain his composure, asks, "Like anything in life, I am well aware that nothing is free. If I was interested in becoming a part of your organization, what would I have to do?"

"Doug, we realize you are not stupid, we know that you have some very high ranking police on your payroll. They have no idea how quickly we have risen in the ranks, but sooner or later, they will. We want this to be a nice transition for all and the last thing we want is a firefight with the cops. Therefore, if you would become a part of our organization, we would continue to help you fund them, as you have done. For exchange for our funds, you would give us information on the higher ranking officers, such as their family history, who they shake down and the judges they get their search warrants from."

Doug, looking and feeling a little bit more confident that not only could he leave his club tonight with his life but very possibly a new start, asks, "I am pretty sure there is another stipulation involved, right?"

Smiling at Doug with a "you bet your ass there is" look Mr. X. answers, "Yes Doug and it comes with a deadline attached to it also. The start up money for joining the organization is one million dollars and you have until New Year's Day to have the money. If you do not make the deadline, the deal is off and you will be lucky to sell a nickel bag on an abandoned corner in Staten Island. Which in turn means you will lose everything you have and that father of yours that you pay so dearly for to stay in that upscale retirement home; well; I wonder how it would make you feel to see him living in a cardboard box. Therefore, Doug, you have what looks like a mixture of a dilemma and opportunity on your hands. Either way, the clock is ticking."

Getting up from his chair, Mr. X. puts his coat on while one of the guards in the cashmere coat slowly opens the door. Before exiting, Mr. X reaches into his coat pocket and slides a white card in front of Doug. Slowly picking the card up, Doug reads a telephone number on the card.

"Doug, listen very carefully; the phone number on that card is a private and exclusive number. You will only have one chance to dial that number and that will be to inform us of your answer. If you do not call, the organization will assume that you will not be joining us." Before Mr. X. leaves the room, he pats Doug on the shoulder and takes away the grilled chicken salad that he never touched.

"Waste not, want not," Mr. X says as he exits. Sitting in his office wondering what just happened to his friends and most importantly to him,

Doug looks at the card with the phone number on it and remembers what his father asked him at the retirement home: "Do you want to live or just survive?" Looking at the card again, Doug says to himself in a low tone, "Let's see what you are made of Doug." Getting up from his chair, Doug turns off his office light and exits his empty club.

*　　*　　*

The weather was bad, but Doug is home in his apartment, which is dark and quiet. Walking slowly from his living room, he makes it without much noise to his children's bedroom. Slowly opening the door, Doug can see that the nightlight is on, giving a dim illumination in the room. Looking over at the kid's bed, he sees Chaka lying on Sandra's chest while Kareem lays on the both of them, as if he were shielding them from some kind of danger. Looking at the situation for another minute, Doug slowly closes the door and walks away.

Sitting on his bed, Doug is in deep thought, wondering what has to be done on both fronts. How does he get the money together and what must he do if he could not get the money. Putting his head on his pillow, Doug can think no more as he quickly falls asleep.

Chapter Seventeen
Bad Decisions, Horrible Circumstances

With only a week until Christmas Doug has used every source available to the raise cash for the proposition. Doug with total liquidation of all he has, including the jewelry and coats he purchased for Sandra put together roughly $250,000.00. Not nearly, enough to join what possibly could be the most powerful moneymaking machine in New York history, from a street perspective. Doug knew he was smart and he did not need a flunky like Mr. X. to tell him this. With the question still ringing in his mind from his father, "Do you want to live or just survive?" Doug thought about a wolf he saw on an animal program that waited five days in one spot before it went in for a kill. The wolf knew this would be his last opportunity to eat well, so he literally starved himself to death just to make the perfect kill. Sitting in his office on this cold, blistery morning, Doug decided he would be that wolf, but wolves need weak prey and Doug already decided what to hunt. Picking up his phone Doug dialed an old wolf to form a pack: his old friend Bucky.

*   *   *

In a snow-covered parking lot sitting inside a black van at the Bay Plaza Shopping Mall in the Bronx are Doug, Bucky, Al and Clyde. Doug, being the youngest of the four, considered them old school but in a good way. They were smart, hungry and fearless. The last credential was very important because when a transaction like this seemed so simple and clean-cut, it was not. Looking at his watch, Doug reads 1:59 a.m. Pulling out his weapon and checking it, Doug is satisfied. With a briefcase on his lap that contains $250,000.00, Doug has calculated that with the amount of keys he would steal tonight, he would have little problem selling it back on the street while combining it with the money on his lap, he would easily reach his goal. Looking at the entrance next to "Checker's", Doug spots the white Lexus as it pulls in and stops 100 feet away. Not to dare and insult his crew, Doug does not ask if they are ready; he just nods his head and flashes his lights three times. The Lexus, in turn, does the same slowly driving up to where Doug and his crew are parked.

Simultaneously the doors of both vehicles open and both crews

exit with each leader holding a suitcase. Looking around, Doug looks at
Michael Marino, an Italian cat from Bensonhurst Brooklyn, who cannot be
anymore than twenty-three years old. Standing alongside of him are three
more Italian guys about the same age. Scouting his prey, Doug can see
that they're wearing nice coats with suits and shoes. In the dead of winter
with so many ice spots in the parking lot, Doug knew these people were
not dressed for warfare. With his men wearing sweat suits and gortex
hiking boots, Doug's crew was prepared. After each posse checks each
other out the two leaders, come face to face.

"Thank you Doug, for being on time; I was a little worried with
how your people are always late for everything and all," Michael says.

Drawing a few chuckles from his crew, the young Italian looks
behind him and smiles. "I know what you mean partner; we are always
late for everything," responds Doug.

Michael, who obviously is feeling his oats, says, "Let's get
something straight; we ain't partners or friends. The only thing happening
is a nice simple transaction that I would like to get done right now so I can
get the hell out of the Bronx."

"Fair enough; let's get it done. We will open up at the same time,
Ok?" asks Doug.

Not taking his eyes off Doug, the now serious looking Michael
snaps open his briefcase and slowly opens it, revealing neatly packaged
bundles of pure cocaine. Doug, looking cool as ever, slowly opens his and
shows Michael the cash, which is neatly stacked in one hundred dollar
bundles. Slowly exchanging briefcases, each man inspects his product, one
by tasting and the other by speed counting. Looking up at each other, they
reluctantly nod their heads in agreement then close their briefcases.
Looking at his car, which is about 40 feet away, Michael spots a young
teenager circling around his vehicle.

"Hey, what the fuck are you looking at!?" yells Michael. The
young kid holds up his arms and begins to shake his head side-to-side
when he yells back, "Sorry, mister. I was just admiring it. I did not know it
was yours, sorry!" Michael nods to one of his men, who pulls out his
weapon and begins to walk toward the teenager, when the young man
turns and runs out of the parking lot.

"What the fuck is this, Doug?" asks Michael.

"Take it easy, man. He was just some kid looking at your ride, that
is all, relax." Looking suspicious and angry, Michael quickly grabs his
money and motions to his men to back up. As they do, Doug picks up his
suitcase watching his men pull their weapons leading him back to the van.
As each team of men enters their vehicle, they sit and watch each other.

Michael, looking at the money in the briefcase, smiles and begins
to chuckle with his men, "Stupid ass eggplant; he never saw it coming.
Let's pull out first, boys; I have a feeling they are going to be very angry."
As Michael starts his car and begins to back up there is a loud bang.

"Holy shit what the fuck!" As the men all look up, they are blinded by the oncoming van being driven by Doug. Letting out a blood-curdling scream, Michael and his partner sitting in front with him hold up their hands as the van crashes head-on with the Lexus, causing the air bags to deploy, hitting them hard in the face.

"Let's do it!" yells Doug, who with his band of men, jump out of the van and rush the totaled Lexus. Without hesitation, Bucky and his friends fire upon the passengers in the back seat before they can even pull their weapons. Doug fires and kills Michael's friend that sits next to him, leaving a dazed and bloodied Michael, still clutching the suitcase with his hand. Motioning to his men to get back in the van, Doug hurries to the driver's side of the Lexus to meet Michael. Punching the injured man in the face, Doug grabs the suitcase that contains his money and looks down at the blown out tires of the Lexus, which have spikes under them that the teenager put there for a small fee.

"I guess I am on time, huh Mike?" asks Doug. Gasping for air, Michael responds, "Fuck you." Doug smiles and stares at Michael one last time before pumping bullets into his body. Hurrying back to the van, Doug enters and drives towards the exit leading to I-95 South.

Michael, with blood coming from his mouth, is on his last seconds of life when he reaches into his coat pocket and removes a small red detonator. Looking at the black van speeding away, a dying and bloodied Michael gives one last smile, presses the button and quietly dies.

As an excited Doug, heads up the ramp that leads to the nearly empty highway, there is an explosion that comes from the briefcase filled with cocaine. As the van comes to a complete stop, the four men are coughing and gasping for air as the van fills with a white powdery dust. Doug, rolling down his window, allowing fresh air to enter, helps him gain some vision. Looking at his hands and clothes, Doug cannot believe his eyes. The van and the men are covered with cocaine, and the suitcase is practically destroyed. Bucky wiping his mouth and eyes yells, "Doug, get the hell out of here before someone catches us!" Grabbing the steering wheel, Doug looks at his white hands and drives on the highway back to his club. As the cold winter air hits the face of a dejected Doug, he knows of only two things at this moment, lose the van and arrange for his only and last resort to raise his money.

*   *   *

Standing in his shower, Doug lets the warm water hit his baldhead and run down his back. "Do you want to live or just survive?" he quietly asks himself as he turns the water off and exits the shower. Looking in the mirror, a wet Doug answers himself, "It is time for a new beginning and I want to live." Picking up his phone that is on the sink, Doug dials the number of his long-time associate, Detective Tommy Davis.

"Good morning, it's me, Doug. Listen, I have a proposal for you that involves a nice piece of change and I was wondering if we could meet

at our usual spot this afternoon? Ok, very well. I will see you then, later."
Hanging up his phone, Doug listens through his bathroom door as he hears
Chaka and Kareem laughing in the kitchen with Sandra.

* * *

In a beautiful five thousand square foot house in Bensonhurst,
Brooklyn Tony Marino head of the Russo crime family lays in bed asleep
with his wife Connie, when his phone begins to ring. Moving around
under his goose-down comforter, Tony reaches over his wife and grabs his
phone on the third ring. Clearing his throat, he answers, "Hello? Yes this
is he. Oh no, Oh please no!"

A frightened Connie quickly sits up in bed, holding her mouth with
one hand and grabbing her husband with the other. As Tony begins to sob
uncontrollably, his wife tenderly asks, "Honey, what is it? Please answer
me, what is it?"

Putting the phone back on its base, a red-eyed Tony slowly turns to
his wife, who is now shaking and answers, " Honey that was the city
morgue; they want us to come down right away. Baby; they say Michael is
there." As Connie screams, Tony grabs his wife, trying to comfort her. As
the two of them cry together, 16-year-old daughter Kathy bursts into the
room with a look of fear on her face, yelling, "What happened? Mom and
Dad what happened? Kathy, sitting on the bed with her parents, forms a
tiny huddle of support.

* * *

Inside the Boston Road diner Doug and Tommy sip on cappuccino
and are eating English muffins. Doug reaching under the table gives the
detective an envelope that is four inches thick. "Do we have all bases
covered, Tommy?

Looking discreetly in the envelope, Tommy lets a grin come across
his face, "All bases are covered, just understand that after this, we will
severe our alliances for a while. Doug, I have to ask, are you sure about
this?"

Sipping from his cup, Doug nods his head yes. "I have never been
more sure about anything. I appreciate your services." The two men shake
hands finishing off their food and drinks. Doug, removing himself from
the table, throws a twenty-dollar bill down to cover the food and exits.

Dialing on his phone, Tommy speaks to one of his associates,
"Yeah, it's me. Everything is a go; we have the green light. Just let the
other two men know, we will meet up at my place to discuss the situation.
Oh, by the way, did you hear about Michael Marino? Yeah, I know. It
could not happen to a better grease ball." Hanging up his phone, Tommy
slithers out of the booth, exiting the restaurant.

Chapter Eighteen
Merry Christmas

It is Christmas morning and Doug is in the bedroom closet kneeling over a safe that he had installed into the floor. Slowly turning the dial from right to left, he opens the safe door and studies a leather binder that contains DVD's that are marked with dates and events. Carefully zipping the binder shut, Doug puts them inside the safe, closes the door and spins the combination dial to ensure their security. Brushing off his knees after standing up, Doug turns off the light inside the closet then turns around and is startled, as Sandra is standing right behind him.

"Oh shit!" says Doug.

"Merry Christmas Doug; I am sorry, did I scare you?"

Looking at Sandra with an expression on his face as if he has been doing something wrong, Doug closes the door, "How long have you been standing behind me, Sandra?"

"Not long at all. I just heard some rambling and I thought it was the kids, so I got up to see. Merry Christmas once again."

Looking at Sandra, Doug begins to gain his composure and says, "Won't you go wake them up so they can open their gifts." Walking off to the living room, Doug gives Sandra a smile and in turn, she does the same. Sandra, walking to the kids' bedroom, feels like a kid herself.

As Kareem and Chaka are lead to the living room by Sandra, who is smiling from ear-to-ear at her bundles of joy, who still have cold in their eyes, Doug stands by the couch, looking at the children's expressions as they spot the many gifts that await them under the tree.

"Merry Christmas Boo Boo's; look what Santa bought you," Sandra says. Finally focusing in on the colorful packages, the two children look at each other and now realize what day it is. Grabbing and hugging each other, they both run into the arms of their mother. Doug, taking in the whole scene, sits on the couch and says, "Merry Christmas, kids."

Sandra, turning the children to face Doug, asks them, "What do you say to your father?"

Looking up at Doug, they respond together, "Merry Christmas." Kissing them both on their cheeks, Sandra releases them and watches as they begin to happily rip open their many presents.

"Doug, would it bother you if I put on some Christmas music?" Looking at the kids laugh and hug each other with the surprise of each newly discovered toy, Doug says "Sure, Sandra, no problem; turn on your Christmas music." Sandra finds a red Christmas hat and puts it on her head, which brings laughter from Chaka. Putting in a CD of R&B singers performing different Christmas carols, Sandra walks over to the tree and once again kisses her children, taking a seat next to them to share in their happiness. Looking at his watch, a subdued Doug gets up from the couch, grabbing his coat and putting it on.

"Sandra listen they have toys that need batteries and I forgot to get them. I will run out to get them and be right back." Looking at Doug while at the same time trying not to say or relay with facial expressions anything that could spoil the moment, Sandra says, "Ok, we will be right here." Removing his keys from his pocket, Doug begins to exit the apartment, but before he does, he takes one more look at Sandra and the kids sitting by the Christmas tree.

*   *   *

It has been about an hour now and Doug still has not returned with the batteries. Sipping on a cup of eggnog, Sandra starts to gather up shreds of wrapping paper, putting it inside a black garbage bag.

"Come on, kids. You still have a whole lot more to unwrap, so let's go." Giving the children a cup of orange juice and a breakfast bar, Sandra can hear the locks on the door begin to turn as Doug is returning with the batteries. Hearing the door close, Sandra bends her head towards the hallway, "Doug, are you back? We are still in the living room opening gifts. Do you have the batteries? Doug?" Sandra slowly walks past the kids, who are oblivious to her concerns, and cautiously begins to walk towards the door when in a mad rush; four large masked men dressed in black, wearing ski masks knock Sandra backwards to the floor.

"Kareem and Chaka run to your room, run!" a terrified Sandra screams. The children, however, do not run because they never had a chance as two of the men grab one child each covering their mouths. As Sandra makes it to her feet, she attempts to run in the direction of the kids when one of the assailants trips her, causing her to fall into the Christmas tree. One of the men turns up the volume to drown out the noise in the apartment. Sandra looking to her left can see that her children are terrified as they kick and squirm while being held by the two men. Looking to the right, Sandra looks under the tree and grabs a radio that belongs to Kareem. Now grabbed by her hair by one of the men, Sandra swings with all her mite, striking him across his face. Cutting through his mask Sandra leaves a long jagged gash. Falling backwards, holding his face the attacker screams in agony. Seeing that her children are very close to her possible rescue attempt, Sandra, who has no expression of fear anymore but one of determination, begins to rush at the man holding Chaka. With a sudden jolt of force, Sandra crumbles to the floor from a sharp kick to her ribs. Never knowing what broken ribs felt like, Sandra is positive that hers' are because at this moment, she can hardly breathe. The man that is cut rushes towards Sandra, kicking her in the face with the bottom of his black cowboy boot, causing her to violently sprawl out in the middle of the floor. Kareem, who is going berserk in his assailant's arms, manages to bite down on his arm, making the giant figure jerk his arm back and smack Kareem hard across the face.

"Listen, enough of this shit; someone is going to hear us. Let's get this over with," says the assailant who kicked Sandra in the ribs. As one of the assailants grabs Sandra by her arm, he drags her over to the couch where she can see her children being held by the window. Making a very feeble but brave attempt to get up again, Sandra can feel the hard and painful pressure of a boot pushing her back down to the floor. An assailant grabbing Sandra by her braids yanks her head up violently, putting a large amount of strain on her neck.

"Look at this, baby!" he demands. Watching in disbelief and horror, Sandra watches as the living room window is opened, sending a cold and blustery wind chill through the room and across her face. Looking at her beautiful daughter, Chaka being carried towards the window, Sandra moans and manages to stretch one of her arms out towards her daughter: "No, please. Not my baby!" with tears streaming down both their faces, Sandra and Chaka's eyes meet and lock while the only thing that can come across Sandra's mind is holding her daughter in the operating room on the day she was born. Watching as the animal holding, her daughter twists around as if he was throwing a discus in the Olympics, tosses Chaka out of the fourth floor window. Feeling the warm sensation of her urine coming from her body, Sandra lowers her head as she can feel herself losing awareness, but just as she tries to close her eyes from what is coming next, Sandra is slapped across the face and made to watch. Kareem, who always tried to protect her, is fighting to get loose and make it to her. Her little man, who is kicking and punching, miraculously almost squirms loose, but cannot because of the power of his assailant. With very little strength left in her body, Sandra lowers her head to the floor and watches as her little warrior is sent to meet his sister.

"We have got to get out of here," one assailant yells over the song "Jingle Bell Rock," coming from the speakers. As three of the men hurry to the hallway that leads to the door, the man who has been holding Sandra down yanks her head up by her braids and reaches down with a military solid steel knife, pressing it against Sandra's throat. Catatonic and in total shock, Sandra manages to see two things: a white wrist and a green dragon. As the dragon moves slowly across her face, she feels the suffering and torment start to leave her body as her throat is slit open. With her eyes slowly closing for what she believes to be the last time,

Sandra's head falls with a thud on the oak wood floor.

* * *

Pamela Brown is returning from the neighborhood bodega with a few things for her little private Christmas dinner. While climbing the stairs between the second and third floor, she looks up in sheer fright as four masked men are rumbling down the stairs in her direction. Not being quick enough to get out of the way, Pamela is shoved into the staircase wall, causing her to hit her back and drop her bags. Sitting on a step looking down and listening to the men as they make it to the first floor where they exit the building, Pamela bends her head upward in the direction of her floor.

Holding her bags, Pamela stands in the middle of the fourth floor hallway where she stares at two apartment doors. Looking at her door, which is locked, she slowly and silently removes her keys. Trying to take that first step forward to her door, something will not allow her to do it as she stares at the slightly opened door of apartment 4B. As "Silent Night" plays from the inside of the apartment, Pamela gathers the courage from somewhere deep inside her to take that first step towards Sandra's door. With much apprehension, Pamela knocks on the door three times, which causes the door to open a little more.

"Sandra, are you there?" asks Pamela. Feeling the hair on the back of her neck stand, she sticks her head halfway in the door: "Sandra, Merry Christmas, are you there?" Now shaking a little, Pamela slides her body between the door and finds herself inside the long, dark hallway. As the stereo completes the play list of songs, there is a deafening silence. Setting her bags slowly and quietly as possible on the floor, Pamela makes her way down the hallway. Seeing the light coming from the living room a few steps ahead, she walks through the entrance and immediately her attention is drawn to the brown curtains that push back in forth because of the cold wind coming from outside. Looking to her right, Pamela can see the many toys that sit under the Christmas tree and the many more that remain unopened. Slowly turning to her left, Pamela screams so loud that people throughout the building open their windows to see what is causing the commotion. Holding her mouth while falling to her knees, Pamela looks in horror as she comes across Sandra, who is lying in a pool of blood.

"Sandra, please no, Sandra. Somebody help us! Somebody help us!" Pamela yells as she crawls over to her friend and neighbor. Kneeling in the blood, Pamela rubs Sandra's head as she tries to find a pulse. Feeling a light pulsating throb coming from Sandra's neck, Pamela quickly removes her coat and sweater, resting Sandra's head on the coat while wrapping the sweater with pressure on Sandra's ugly opened wound.

"Please, somebody, help us, please! She yells while holding the unconscious Sandra in her arms. Pamela's heart rate jumps higher as she hears footsteps running into the apartment. Looking up with fear in her eyes she sees that it's Luis, the building's superintendent.

"Oh God, Luis. Call an ambulance, please; she is dying!" Pamela demands. "Oh shit, where are the kids? Where are the kids?" Luis, walking over to Pamela, tries to comfort her: "Pamela, I called the police and the ambulance, but I will call again!" As he dials 911 on his phone, Pamela is softly kissing Sandra on her head and from a distance; they can hear the sirens getting closer. Luis walks over to the window to close it when he hears screams coming from the back alley of the building. Looking out of the window, the short Spanish man quickly pulls his head back in and cannot help but to let the breakfast he had earlier come up from his stomach exiting his mouth onto the floor.

"Luis, what did you see?" asks Pamela. Letting his body slump to the floor, the now sobbing man responds, "It's her kids" Pamela is now crying harder as she rocks Sandra back and fourth. Busting into the apartment are EMS workers, who are holding all kinds of medical equipment. A worker quickly grabs on to Pamela: "Ok miss, you have got to let us take over from here, please!" Luis, who is still crying, gently grabs Pamela and pulls her to the side so that they may attend to Sandra. "Let's move; her pressure is going! Close her up, and let's move! Heart rate is dropping!" yells the EMS worker. As Pamela and Luis watch as the medical unit hooks tubes and machines to Sandra, they put her on a stretcher and quickly rush out of the apartment.

An EMS worker quickly turns to Pamela and Luis, "We are going to need you two to come down to the hospital because your friend has lost a lot of blood. We need to see if anyone of you can donate." A quivering Pamela shakes her head up and down quickly in agreement.

* * *

Outside in front of the building, there is pandemonium and outrage as police cars line up throughout the street. Uniform officers are asking numerous tenants questions and from a distance cries of anguish can be heard as Sandra is wheeled out of her building by the paramedics with Pamela by her side. A black sedan with a flashing light in its window quickly pulls up to the building. Exiting the car are Detectives Tommy Davis and Joseph McCarthy. Observing the scene carefully, they walk over and look at Sandra, who is about to be lifted into the ambulance.

"Is she gonna make it?" Detective Davis asks the EMS worker, who is frantically trying to get in the vehicle.

"I really do not think so; she has lost a lot of blood, all we can do is get to the hospital quickly, her life depends on it." As Pamela gets ready to enter the ambulance from the back, Doug's truck is now pulling up in front of his building. As the crowd looks and points at him, Doug examines the scene with his eyes when he hears an old woman still dressed in her pajamas and wearing an old red coat yell, "Oh, God, no! Not the babies!" Everyone is now focused on another set of emergency workers carrying out the small bodies of Kareem and Chaka, who are inside what looks like black plastic duffel bags.

Doug, looking over at the alleyway, drops his bags of batteries and begins to run towards his children: "No! Please no please! My children!" Getting closer to their bodies, Doug is grabbed by three uniformed officers and gently subdued.

"I am so sorry, sir, but we cannot let you see them like this right now. We are so sorry," says one of the officers. Doug, who has fallen to his knees, begins to sob out loudly as onlookers also cry expressing their sympathy.

"Where is my lady, Sandra?" he cries. People are pointing at the EMS truck that is now turning the corner.

"Sir, your wife is being taken to Bronx North Central Hospital," says another officer. As Doug begins to turn and walk towards his truck, he is confronted by Detectives Davis and McCarthy, who have somber looks on their faces.

"Doug, hello I am Detective Tommy Davis and this is Detective Joseph McCarthy, we want to express our deepest sympathy to you and your family. We want to give you our cards so that we can speak to you as soon as possible while this is fresh. We suggest that you go to the hospital to be with your woman friend and as soon as anything comes up you will be the first to know. Also, we would like to let you know that we will be the lead detectives on this case, so please believe and trust us that whoever did this horrible crime will be caught and prosecuted to the highest extent of the law." As the officers shake Doug's, hand they lead him to his vehicle so that he can hurry to the hospital. As the detectives watch Doug speed off, Detective McCarthy rubs the fresh bandage on the left side of his cheek that has been cut.

"Damn this hurts." Looking at his partner, Detective Davis responds, "Look at it this way partner, consider it a very expensive battle scar."

                              *   *   *

The waiting room is jam packed with people who are there to support Sandra. Ms. Carla and people who volunteer at the food pantry are standing together in prayer. Pamela and Luis are sitting with a nurse with their sleeves rolled up ready to give blood. The nurses are checking to see if anyone else has the right type of blood to donate to Sandra. Rose has quietly entered the waiting area and has taken a seat in a corner where no one can notice her. In all there has to be about twenty-five people in the room talking, crying and praying when the room comes to a hush with the sight of Doug, who is very surprised himself by the number of people there to support Sandra. One by one, neighbors approach Doug with a hug as a show of support.

"Hi my name is Carla, and Sandra helped me so much at the pantry, we all want to give our deepest sympathy for your loss."

With a somber look on his face, Doug responds, "Thank you all for your support, but I have to see Sandra right now." As Doug receives the last of the handshakes and hugs, his eyes lock up with the only person that has not expressed sympathy towards him and that is Pamela, who stands on the wall holding a cotton ball on her arm where blood was drawn. As their eyes remain locked, they look away in the direction of Dr. Mackey, who has entered holding a clipboard.

"Who is the next of kin to Sandra?" Doug, stepping up to the forefront, says "That would be me. Is she going to be alright?"

Looking over his charts the doctor looks somberly at Doug: "Right now sir, Ms. Lyte has lost a lot of blood and her heart rate is unstable. The nurses have informed me that this woman, Pamela Brown, has O type blood, which is somewhat rare because of its ability to donate universally. Sandra is also O type, which means she can only receive from a person with type O. So, Doug, as you can see, we do not have time to waste; we need to really get Ms. Brown inside for a transfusion and even after that, you have to understand the next twelve hours will be critical." Doug, who has turned to Pamela, says, "Please, Pamela help her" Not even looking at Doug or responding to him, she walks right to the doctor.

"I am ready, Dr. Mackey."

Pamela is letting the tears come down her face as she is lying next to an unconscious Sandra, who has about a hundred tubes coming out of her mouth, arms and nose. As the nurses lay Pamela on the bed next to her friend, they begin getting ready for the transfusion. As the nurse wipes her arm and inserts the tubing, Pamela watches her blood enter a filtering device that she hopes can enter Sandra's body. Listening to the beeping of the heart monitor, all Pamela can do is hope and pray that Sandra will live to see another day.

Chapter Nineteen
Now On To More Important Matters

New Year's Day finds Doug standing in front of his mirror in his empty and quiet apartment. Not staying there much since the horrible incident one week ago, Doug had a cleaning service come in and thoroughly clean the apartment.

Without remorse or regards, he even had Chaka and Kareem's toys and clothes thrown away, trying to erase all sentimental value. With one million dollars in life insurance in his possession, Doug spared no expense when it came down to his children's funeral. With no sense of shame or embarrassment, many people came to witness the children buried on top of each other in the same plot of land with their tiny bodies squeezed inside two unfinished pine boxes that a dog owner would not use for his pet.

The flowers that adorned their caskets came from the local bodega. Doug spent the minimum amount of money on their tombstones. Just their names, dates of birth and the date of death engraved them.

Doug was now preparing for his new life with the Lords of the Underground. Dressed in a very conservative suit with shoes to match, Doug looks inside the suitcase at the clean and neatly stacked blood money that he would turn over for his entry into the organization.

Picking up the card that Mr. X. gave him a few weeks ago, Doug dials the number from his cell phone, "This is Doug. I am calling for the sit down. Yes, I have it, I have it all. Yes, I know where it is. Very good. I will be there at three o'clock. Ok, goodbye." Letting a smile come across his face, Doug looks at himself up and down from head to toe, making sure he looks perfectly debonair for the meeting.

* * *

As the Plaza Hotel worker takes the keys to his vehicle, a stunning black sister named Gloria greets Doug.

"Good afternoon Mr. Gunner. My name is Gloria Henderson and I would like to welcome you to the Plaza Hotel. If you follow me, I will take you to meet with my associates." Doug cannot help not to look at the elegance of the woman as he follows her to the elevator. Riding the elevator to the fifteenth floor, Doug can only think about the possibility of his new life. As the elevator doors open, Doug is taken to a luxury suite.

As Gloria and Doug stand in the living room, a man dressed in a white suit enters with a huge smile on his face.

"Good day Doug. How are you today?" Walking over to Doug, the man greets him with a handshake and nods his head at Gloria, who smiles and exits the suite.

"Doug, please sit down; my associates will see you in a few minutes. Meanwhile, please enjoy this entrée that we have prepared especially for you. As a waiter removes the cover from the trays that sit on a table in the dining area, offering Doug lobster, Alaskan crab legs, roast beef and pouched salmon. As the waiter prepares his choice of meal, which is lobster, Doug begins to eat his meal, while sipping on Johnny Walker blue.

*   *   *

After his meal, Doug walked to another suite on the same floor where he sat on a couch. Entering the room are two black men looking to be in their early forties. Both men are well dressed and groomed, looking as if they stepped off a GQ magazine cover. Taking a seat on a couch opposite Doug, one of the men pulls out a long Cuban cigar and runs his tongue across it while the other man pulls out a lighter and proceeds to light the cigar.

"Doug, can we have our money please?" asks one of the men who is wearing a tan colored suit. Grabbing the suitcase, Doug slowly hands it to the man. Opening the suitcase, the two men examine the money inside and close it back up, setting it between the both of them.

"Doug, my name is Mr. Brown and this is Mr. Green, we would like you to think of us as your sponsors. This basically means that we are putting our trust in you and our reputations on the line with the organization that you will prove to be a worthwhile acquisition."

Doug, paying close attention, responds, "I want to thank you for the chance of becoming a member and I promise you I will not let you down."

Mr. Brown, nodding his head at Doug, says, "First of all, Doug, never make promises because when you do, you automatically put yourself in debt to someone and that is not intelligent. Secondly, if you are not beneficial to us, please understand that you will not be letting us down; you will be letting yourself down. Always remember Doug your actions and decisions might reflect on our judgment of character, but it will definitely impact your life even more."

Feeling isolated and alone, Doug realizes for the first time since he has been involved in the game, he is not calling any shots. Doug recognizes that these cats are serious and in a polite kind of way, they were letting him know that the organization does not believe in erasers to correct mistakes. You had better be on your toes when it came down to business because if you were not, chances are you would be out of business for good.

"Doug, I want to make something very clear to you, Lords of the Underground, do not tolerate loose ends and I will make myself clear by what I mean by 'loose ends.' If by any chance you have bodies, cases, unpaid debt, broken promises, vendettas or even an unhappy woman, do not bring it to us because we do not want any part of it. It is your problem from your past life and it is your duty to handle these affairs before you enter the matrimony of our organization. As of this moment, your life has begun, but it is up to you on how you want this transition to go; either smooth or bumpy," says Mr. Brown.

Nodding in agreement, Doug responds. "Without a doubt, I fully understand and accept the terms of the agreement. As a new employee, I am ready and eager to do all I can to make myself a profitable asset."

Reaching and grabbing a duffel bag off the Italian marble table, Mr. Green gives Doug the bag: "Doug, inside that bag you will find an untraceable disposable phone, twenty-five thousand dollars in cash and keys to a brand new vehicle that awaits you in the parking garage of this hotel. At this moment Doug, I want you to think of yourself as one of a thousand ants that spends the day working to please the Queen. As a worker Doug your task is to carry out our instructions to the finest detail and always bring us back a profit. You will never use your phone to make calls, only to receive them from us. Your car is strictly for transportation, not for women or any other childish use. Your money is your livelihood, so spend it wisely. In the next three days, we will contact you at noon for your first assignment, so please stay on point because we will only call once. If you miss the call, you lose the assignment and the wages that go with it. You will not get another call for three weeks and by that time, you will be hungry again. Continue to show sloppiness and you are done. Do I make myself clear?"

Feeling rejuvenated by this opportunity, Doug says, "I understand clearly what you have said and I will be ready when the call comes in."

A smiling Mr. Brown says, "It has been a long productive meeting Doug and I really hope this relationship will be productive for everyone involved. Therefore, it is time Mr. Green and I head back to let the organization know that we have a new employee. Doug I want you to get a taste of how we treat our employees. I want you to enjoy this suite here in The Plaza for the rest of the day. Whatever you need, just charge it to the room and the organization will cover it. Also, here are two tickets to the Broadway show *Phantom of the Opera*. I have seen it twice and enjoyed it more each time. One more thing, Doug…"

Mr. Brown Dials a number from his phone and Gloria enters the suite with two black sisters that look like runway models, except they have bodies like amazons. The two women both dressed in designer pinstriped suits have smiles on their faces as they look at Doug.

"Doug this is Jayne and Samantha; they will be your guests tonight and will love to spend some time getting to know you a little better. I hope you do not mind the company?" asks Mr. Brown.

Doug, who cannot help but to smile responds, "Not at all; it would be my pleasure to have them join me tonight."

As everyone stands and exchanges handshakes, Mr. Green, Mr. Brown and Gloria exit the room, leaving Doug with his guests for the night. Without saying a word, the two women walk up to Doug, kiss him on the mouth at the same time, and slowly begin to remove their clothes. Gently and slowly forcing Doug to sit on the coach, the women put on a sex show for Doug that even he has to admire. While sitting there on the couch with a huge erection, something continues to pop up in his head. Doug thought about the "loose ends" he had to take care of. Doug knew if he really wanted a new beginning, the "loose ends" had to be disposed of at all cost. This was Doug's last and final chance of scratching his way back to the top. As dismal as that sounded though, Doug did not let it get him down because the one thing he had that no one could take from him was his will to achieve at all cost. True, these men in the organization were elaborate, but they got that way by being hungry and ambitious. In Doug's mind, who was more hungry and ambitious than he? With his mind focused back on his dates for the night, Doug smiles as the women climb on top of him, removing his clothing.

Chapter Twenty
Loose Ends Starting To Form a Noose

A table lamp that sits next to Sandra's bed lights the hospital room. It has been nine days since that horrible Christmas morning, when Sandra experienced what no human being should ever have to go through. The news coverage lasted about three days, but as usual, when dealing with certain neighborhoods and individuals, when a crime is unsolved it becomes just another cold case file. Balloons and flowers fill Sandra's room that came from caring individuals from her building and the pantry where she volunteered. There is only one tube in Sandra's arm as the doctors said her recovery has been nothing short of a miracle. During this time, her main support system as she has continued to fall in and out of consciousness has been Pamela. Reading to Sandra and fixing her hair has become a regular routine. A couple of the nurses have explained to Pamela that Sandra's scar would always remain and she will soon remember what happened to her children and would need psychological therapy that would last months, maybe years. Doug has not visited Sandra once since he left her in the hospital, which made Pamela try to come up with about a thousand reasons why. Pamela has noticed the quiet young woman named Rose who comes by to look at Sandra through the door at different times of the night. Pamela always wondered how she got by security but did not think too much about it; she just thought it was nice to see that Rose cared. As Pamela looks at her watch and sees that it is four in the morning, she takes out her picture of her son, Derrick, kissing it softly and laying her head on Sandra's stomach while closing her eyes, drifting off into a light sleep.

* * *

At the "Checkers" hamburger spot in the Bay Plaza Shopping Mall, with the drive-through window closed people are waiting and wondering why they cannot order food at two o'clock in the afternoon. Getting inpatient, the majority of them begin to drive over to a nearby Burger King, which is about three hundred yards away.

Inside the restaurant in the back of the supply room, there are twelve workers, which includes two managers and ten regular shift workers. They range between the ages of seventeen and thirty-five. All sitting against a wall, they are face-to-face with Tony Marino, the reputed crime boss. They all know whom Tony is, obviously by the tears streaming from everyone's eyes. The room is silent but filled with tension and fear because standing with Tony is a few of his soldiers, who look as if they have not beaten anyone in a while.

Tony, stepping forward, says, "You all know who I am. However, what you may not know is that I am a loving husband and father who cares about my family very deeply. Now I am here today with you because I know you all have families that you care about, so I think you can relate to what I am going to say. I know this restaurant operates twenty-four hours a day. On a few days before Christmas, in this same parking lot, there was a tragic shooting that took the life of my son."

All the workers are trying to look away from Tony, but some cannot help themselves because of the yellow rain gear that sits on the floor along with the two chainsaws.

"Now, what I want you to know is that I am not a monster; just a businessman. So as bad as this scene may look right now, I want you to understand that I want you all to go home and continue to live your lives as usual. But before I can let you do that, I need some answers that could possibly help me and my family," says Tony.

A shaking and now sobbing Spanish girl named Michelle raises her hand. Tony, taking notice nods his head to her with a slight smile.

"Sir, I am really sorry about your son, but I did not see anything because I was not here. Sir, I am just sixteen years old; can I please go home? Please?"

Looking at the girl with some compassion, Tony answers, "Please do not cry, sweetheart. I have a daughter your age at home, so please understand that having you in this situation really pains me and I promise you that once I get my answers, everyone will be free to go."

*   *   *

Thirty minutes have gone by; Tony has shown patience and understanding as he has questioned everyone about what happened on the night of his son's murder. Feeling as if he will not get anywhere, Tony nods to one of his soldiers who begin to put on the rain gear. Chaos now ensues, as the workers, who are all sitting with their feet bound together, are now sobbing louder and begging for their lives. Tony, who no longer is smiling, looks at them all from one end of the room to the other:

"All I wanted was your help today. Everyone in this room knows the police will not help me because of who I am. They are probably gloating because of my loss. So, please I beg of you--somebody please do not allow me to change your lives the way mine has been changed."

Looking around the room and now just seeing frightened faces, Tony nods to his soldier in the rain gear, who in turn walks over and grabs one of the managers named Alfred, a skinny man about thirty years old. The workers are crying as a terrified Alfred is trembling while being held to the floor face down by the other soldier's foot. With the sounds of a cranking chainsaw now starting, Alfred is urinating on himself as he can hear the motor running and smell the fumes it gives off. As the blade heads towards Alfred's neck, he closes his eyes and begins to pray to himself.

"Wait oh God please wait!" yells eighteen-year-old Tasha.

Tony looking at the distraught black girls' face, motions with his finger to his man. Turning off the chainsaw, the two men pick Alfred off the floor and help him to sit up. Walking over to Tasha and pulling out a handkerchief, Tony gently wipes her face clean of tears and sweat. Looking deeply into Tasha's eyes, he asks, "Sweetheart, do you have something you would like to say? Take your time."

Bravely gathering herself together and taking a swallow, the young girl begins, "I was emptying the trash that night when I heard some yelling coming from the parking lot. I was a little nervous while at the same time, very cold, so I stayed close to the door entrance where it was warm. When I sat the garbage in the bin that is when I heard a loud crash, which sounded like two cars hitting each other. After that a few seconds went by, and that is when I heard the gunfire."

Tony, looking at the young girl and never taking his eyes off of her simply because he believed he was an expert at knowing if a person was lying or telling the truth, gives her a bottle of water.

"Please Tasha, tell me what happened after that."

Taking a small sip of water and looking at her fellow workers as they stare back at her, knowing that their lives may depend on her, says, "After the gunfire, I wanted to go downstairs and get Alfred, but I knew he was counting inventory. With us being the only two there, I did not want to leave the counter unattended. I was so scared, but something kept pushing me to go look. I slowly stuck my head from around the wall of the restaurant. I saw a tall and big, bald black man standing by the driver's side of the car with a gun pointed to the driver. He fired about two or three times into the car. After that, he reached inside the car and removed a black briefcase.

"Tasha, did you get a clear look at his face or did you hear anything said?" asks Tony.

"No, I am really sorry. I could not get a clear look; it was dark and the lighting in the parking lot is not great. As far as any words, being said no sir. I did not," Tasha says.

Looking a little frustrated because the description Tasha has given him fits almost anyone in the five boroughs, Tony takes a long deep breath and exhales.

"No wait!" says Tasha. Everyone in the room is laser-focused back on Tasha as if she has found the cure for the common cold. "I did hear something. When the big man with the suitcase was staring at the person he just shot, I heard one of the guys yell from the van they were in,"Come on Doug, Let's go!" That is when the man named Doug got in the van and sped off."

"Tasha, I am pretty sure the police asked you the same questions that I did, so tell me, sweetheart, why did you keep this away from the police?" asks Tony.

Taking another sip of her water, Tasha continues, "I had a brother that, if alive today, would be in college; he was very smart. Four years ago, my brother was shot for holding a bottle of orange juice in a black plastic bag. Two cops investigating a robbery in my building thought he had a gun they never found. My brother died in my mother's arms. The trial found them not guilty because the jury said it was an accident committed by two decorated cops. I will never help or rely on the police department for as long as I live. Once again, I am sorry about what happened to your son, but I was scared and not willing to help the cops."

Looking at the workers in the room, Tony motions to his men and they begin to untie the staff's feet, helping them to stand. "Tasha, you are a brave, young girl and I am sorry about your brother. I hope you and the rest of your coworkers understand that this was personal to my family and me. I had no other choice but to go to this extreme. When we leave, you can go on with your lives as usual," says Tony.

As the men pick up their tools of destruction, they exit the restaurant with their boss. Feeling like a ton of bricks have been moved from their chest, the workers at the hamburger restaurant hug and sob together as a few walk over to a still shaken Alfred to offer comfort.

Tasha, looking at everyone, says, "We need to all go home and never tell anyone about what almost happened here today." All the workers gather their belongings and go home for the rest of the day.

*   *   *

Back inside the hospital room, Pamela is now awake but still resting on Sandra's stomach asks, "Why couldn't you just leave, girl? You could have brought those little angels of yours to my place and we could have figured something out. I had everything all worked out for us to enjoy our time together. I had banana crunch ice cream in the freezer along with tacos and chili for the kids. We could have watched the stories together and figured out who was dishing out the dirt. I could have told you about my little baby, Derrick and showed you all of his pictures. I could have been your ear to listen and try to understand all that you went through living in that hellhole. I am no angel either Sandra, because I heard your suffering and I did nothing about it. I was scared and somewhat of a coward not to speak up and now, it is too late. I just hope one day, when you are able and well, you can find it in your heart to forgive me."

As tears leave her eyes, Pamela feels her face moving up and down a little bit faster. As she begins to lift her head, she shivers as Sandra's smooth hand rubs her face and head, stroking it gently. Lifting her head and turning it slowly in Sandra's direction, Pamela can see the determination of a woman who has lost it all except her will to live. Looking at Sandra with complete awe, Pamela can barely hear her trying to speak. Not saying a word, Pamela gathers herself on the bed and brings her ear close to Sandra's mouth to make out what she is trying to say.

Sandra, slowly pulling oxygen in her body, gathers the strength to speak: "Get me away from here...the dragon is coming for me. The dragon will find me here...get me away from here."

As Sandra, who is exhausted, lies back on her pillow, Pamela stands to her feet looking at Sandra, responds, "Don't worry my sister I will get you out of here."

Chapter Twenty-One
Checking Out

Inside a roach-infested Queens flat is Detective Tony Harris, who sits on his couch checking his unregistered silver-plated, semi-automatic weapon that he feeds a clip of fourteen bullets. Taking a sip of hot beer that has been on his dusty coffee table from earlier, the twelve-year veteran can only hear the command and reassurance of his fellow detective, Tommy Davis:

"It doesn't matter if she survives because she could never identify us and secondly, her mental state would be so screwed up she could never face the challenge of revisiting that day again, so just relax."

Tony knew that was easier said then done and besides, he did not get to become a detective by playing it safe; he got there because he believed in his instincts and those instincts told him Sandra, as a dead corpse, was better than a live one with the will to seek justice. Besides, Tony figured it was easy for Tommy Davis to tell him to relax; he was the only one in the apartment that day with no blood on his hands. All he did was give orders and turn the volume up on the radio. No, Tony was going by his instincts tonight and those instincts said he needed to let Sandra smell the downy on the pillowcase she laid her head on. Looking at his watch, he felt this was the perfect time to pay her a visit. Because of the graveyard shift, no one would even notice he was there or, for that matter, notice she was gone. Tossing the pornographic magazine off his lap, Detective Harris inserts his weapon in his holster, kisses his magic dragon on his wrist and exits his apartment to pay Sandra a visit.

*   *   *

The hospital is cryptic with its quiet and comatose aura. There are not many doctors and nurses on duty tonight maybe because of the snow or just only the unlucky get to work this shift. Inside the emergency waiting room, only a handful of people sit with fever, cuts and bruises. At the nurses' station, there is only one nurse and she is too busy flirting with the porter to see anything right away. The majority of the patients are asleep in their beds, waiting for daybreak and hoping loved ones will visit while others hope to go home.

In room 613, Pamela is gathering up Sandra's personal belongings while Sandra sits on her bed holding her neck and letting the tears fall from her eyes, thinking about her babies who are no more. Still wearing her hospital gown, Sandra, watching Pamela stuff her duffel bag to its full capacity, makes a feeble attempt trying to put her jeans on. Moving as if she was seventy-five years old, Sandra can barely bend down to put her legs into her pants. Taking deep breaths, she tries again but to no avail. Looking behind her, Pamela can only feel hurt and despair, watching this once vibrant woman with so much of her life ahead of her reduced to this.

"Sandra, try not to do so much, ok? I will be right there in a minute; I just want to make sure I have everything," Pamela whispers. Accepting that she is helpless, Sandra listens and gives up. Sitting on her bed while Pamela slowly slips her gown off, Sandra lowers her head as Pamela puts on her sweater and then her jeans. Looking around, Pamela finds a clean pair of white socks that she gently puts on her friend's feet.

"Sandra baby, In a few minutes, we will be getting out of here," says Pamela.

*   *   *

Parking his car in the hospital parking lot is a stone-faced Tony Harris, who looks up at the Bronx North Central Hospital that stands before him. Looking at his watch it is about three hours before daybreak, Tony adjust his coat collar and puts on the same pair of black leather gloves that he used to open Sandra's throat and enters the hospital to finish the job.

*   *   *

With Sandra, all bundled up and ready to go, Pamela quietly uses her cell phone to call a cab.

"Sandra sweetheart I will be right back; I just want to make sure the coast is clear," Pamela whispers. Watching as Pamela exits the room, Sandra sits in a wheelchair wondering to herself why Doug had not been by to visit her. She knew he never loved her or the kids, but just out of sympathy, Sandra figured that would justify one visit. Putting the thought out of her mind, Sandra refocuses on getting out of the hospital because she did not care what anyone thought or believed; she could feel the dragon looking for her to finish what he did not previously. You do not slaughter a family and leave loose ends.

Turning her head and snapping back to reality, Sandra looks at Pamela, who has a look of purpose on her face, "Ok Sandra, you have everything? We have to move right now because the cab will be here in ten minutes." Sandra, sitting in her chair, takes a deep breath and lets Pamela lead her out the hospital room.

Making a sharp left and walking away from the nurses' station, Pamela pushes Sandra towards the intensive care ward that has another set of elevators on the north side. Looking cautiously from side to side, Pamela gently opens the swinging doors with the wheels of the wheelchair. Now in the other ward, Pamela makes a sharp right as she can see two security guards having a coffee break. Making her way to the elevators, Pamela breathes a sigh of relief as she pushes the button, waiting along with Sandra.

* * *

Riding on the elevator, Detective Harris adjusts his gloves on his hands and waits for the elevator doors to open on the sixth floor. Knowing that the hospital would be on a skeleton crew, Harris believes that his mission should be quick and without difficulty. As the doors open, he steps out and walks towards the nurses' station. Walking along the ward, Harris quickly glances into rooms where the doors are open; hoping that maybe he would locate Sandra without having to ask a nurse because he figured the less he got noticed the better.

* * *

\ Pamela is getting frustrated at this point, because twice an elevator has stopped at their floor and both times custodians had them filled to capacity with mops, buckets and other cleaning supplies. Looking around the floor, Pamela decides to walk back to the west wing where Sandra's room is and sneak on those elevators. It is a huge risk because what if a nurse notifies security if Pamela's reasoning is not good enough for removing Sandra. Knowing she only had a few minutes until the cab arrived, she has no choice because Sandra is in no condition to walk down six flights of steps. "Hang in there girl, I will get us out of here" Pamela promises.

* * *

Detective Harris, walking down the quiet corridor, now finds himself upon the nurses' station where Nurse Collins, a young, attractive white woman in her early twenties, sits reading a magazine. Putting a smile on his face, Harris slowly and calmly approaches the unsuspecting nurse with his badge in his hand greeting her, "Good morning nurse, I am Detective Harris of the homicide squad and I am looking for a Sandra Lyte, who I believe is on this floor. I know it is very early in the morning, but I will only be a few moments and my questions are crucial to our investigation."

As the nurse types in Sandra's name, she looks at Harris with a pupil's crush answering, "Detective, Sandra Lyte is located in room six thirteen, but I really do not want to get in any trouble; I am kind of like new on the job. So please, if you could make this as short as possible, I would appreciate it."

Putting on the charm, Harris smiles at the nurse, briefly rubbing her hand, "I promise I will make it quick and it will be our secret." Pointing him in the direction of the room, the smile on Harris's face leaves as he prepares to kill Sandra and now he is convinced he will have to do the same to the nurse.

Slowly opening the door, Harris sticks his head in seeing the curtain pulled around the bed. Stepping inside the room, he gently closes the door and walks towards Sandra's bed. As Harris gets closer to the bed, he reaches up with his hand and slowly pulls the curtain back with a smile on his face: "I never miss twice, bitch" he whispers to himself. The smile on his face slowly disappears and sweat beads start to form on Harris's forehead. Seeing that Sandra is gone, the detective looks around the room in an almost state of panic. Staring at the empty bed for a few more seconds, Harris quickly exits the room.

Walking back to the nurses' station, Harris stands by the desk in a daze-like state and stares around the ward, hoping to see something or someone.

"Detective, that was quick; did you get the information you were looking for?" asks Nurse Collins.

Realizing that he cannot give himself away by wearing his frustration on his face, Harris responds, "Nurse, Sandra Lyte is not in her room. Did you see anyone leave with her? Did anyone come visit her today? Can you check your visitor's log, please?" As Nurse Collins looks over her log, Harris, with his badge now in his hand, looks over to the elevator banks that are about sixty feet away. Looking closer, he sees a woman in a wheelchair and another woman standing with her. Walking away from the nurses' station, Harris tunes out the nurse, who is trying to tell him who was the last person to visit Sandra.

"Excuse me, ladies!" Harris yells towards the elevator.

Pamela, looking up, can see Harris walking towards them with his hand rose revealing a badge. Sandra, who is trying to keep herself up and awake, is somewhat drowsy because of all the medication that she has taken since her stay in the hospital. Looking up, Sandra sees the dragon on Harris's wrist and begins to tremble. Using all of the strength she can muster from her throat, Sandra, in a raspy, dry voice, proclaims, "The dragon is here! The dragon is here!"

As the eyes of Pamela and Harris's lock, the red light over the elevator door illuminates and rings signifying down. "Stay right there; I need to talk to you!" demands Harris. As the doors open, Pamela quickly spins Sandra around in the chair and begins to enter the elevator. "I am an officer. Do not move!" yells Harris as he sprints towards the elevator.

Pamela is frantically pushing the lobby button and the closed button at once when the elevator doors begin to close. Hearing the footsteps of Harris getting closer, Sandra shakes even more. As the doors close, Pamela gets a quick and brief glance of the well-built man, who is now pursuing them.

Standing in front of the closed doors, Harris looks up and sees that the elevator is going down. Looking around the ward, he locates a door that leads to some steps. Running quickly, Harris pushes the door violently and begins to run downstairs, hoping to catch his prey.

Still pushing hard on the lobby level button, hoping the elevator would not stop, Pamela with her other hand, holds on to Sandra's face, trying to keep her calm. Looking up at the digital screen and watching the numbers slowly descend, Pamela reaches into her purse and removes her house keys, holding them inside her hand in such a way that two of the keys protrude between her fingers, creating a jabbing weapon. The elevator screen reads lobby and as the doors open slowly, Pamela braces herself while putting more of her body weight on the back of the wheelchair, making sure to get a good push out the door.

*   *   *

Picking himself up off the first-floor steps, Harris looks at the orange soda that someone spilled. Rubbing his sore ankle, he hurries down the last flight of stairs leading to the lobby level. Not paying any attention to the sign on the door that reads "EMERGENCY EXIT ONLY- ALARM WILL SOUND," Harris pushes the red arm on the door and in an instant, bells are ringing. Ignoring the alarm, Harris limps out of hallway and into the back of the lobby where he sees Pamela and Sandra exiting the elevator: "Stop! I said stop, bitches!" Harris yells at the top of his lungs.

Frantically pushing Sandra towards the three revolving doors leading to the street, Pamela turns and looks for the yelling voice that she somehow hears over the ringing alarm. Looking behind her, she sees Detective Harris, who is limping towards them with his gun showing at his side. With all her strength, Pamela pushes forward and now can spot the Lincoln Towncar cab parked outside near the curb. Not bothering to look behind her, Pamela is pushing Sandra as fast as she can as she is now at the security desk where three guards are trying to decide why the alarm has went off. Hearing Detective Harris's screams get louder, which meant he was closer, Pamela can only think of one thing: "Please help us! That man's got a weapon; he's trying to kill us!" she yells at the three security guards. With that, the three guards look at Pamela and then at the limping man coming towards them, who looks like a sweating maniac.

"Get out of here now!" a husky guard named Bernard yells at Pamela and Sandra. Pulling out his mace and nightstick, Bernard lets his two fellow guards know, "Oh yeah, fellas; we got some action, let's take his ass down." As the three guards run towards the detective, Pamela pushes Sandra outside the door into the cold winter morning where the wind is howling.

Looking for the cab, Pamela spots him beginning to drive away from the hospital entrance. "Taxi, Right here!" Pamela yells, causing the red brake lights to illuminate. "Come on Sandra; let's go!" pushing Sandra as fast as she can, Pamela makes it to the back door where she quickly opens it and uses all her strength to push Sandra inside the cab. Sandra, who is feeling helpless, uses all of the muscles in her body to crawl inside the back seat of the cab. Seeing that Sandra is safely inside the cab, Pamela opens the front door on the passenger side. Before getting inside though, she takes a quick peak at the revolving doors of the hospital and can see the guards wrestling with Harris on the floor. Getting inside the cab, Pamela looks at the Spanish driver and pleads, "Jerome Ave. on the corner of Burnside Ave. Please hurry!"

As the guards finally subdue a ranting Harris, a shocked Bernard notices Harris's badge and weapon for which he demands his partners, "Oh shit! Everybody calm down! This guys a cop!" As the other two guards look at Bernard and then at a furious, red-faced Detective Harris, they all slowly release him, moving away leaving him on the cold tiled lobby floor.

"You are fucking idiots! I was yelling at you three assholes that I was a cop! I am telling you not only will you lose your jobs; you will be arrested for obstructing an officer. As the three guards stand in silence, Harris makes it to his feet, looking towards the revolving doors where he was inches away from capturing not only Sandra but Pamela also.

"This ain't over. This ain't over by a long shot," the sweaty detective says.

*   *   *

As the cab pulls up to the pantry where Sandra volunteered, Pamela quickly exits the cab and runs to open the other door where Sandra sits. Carefully grabbing onto her, Pamela slowly assists her out of the cab.

"Sandra, are you ok baby?" Pamela asks. Still trying to catch her breath, Sandra slowly nods her head up and down.

Walking over to the driver's side of the cab, Pamela removes a twenty-dollar bill from her pocket and gives it to the driver: "You did a great job in this bad weather. Keep the change and thank you," says Pamela.

Taking the twenty, the smiling cabby responds, "No problem, Mommy, thank you."

As the car pulls away, Pamela grabs Sandra's bag and walks towards the delivery entrance door of the pantry. As Pamela knocks three times on the door, she hugs Sandra in an attempt to keep her warm. Hearing the turning and clicking of locks, there is a heavy pull of the door, forcing it to open. Standing on the other side with welcoming smiles is Ms. Carla and Rose Garden. All four women hug and embrace each other as they assist Sandra into the pantry.

Helping Sandra get her coat off, the women sit at a table covered with breakfast food. Shaking from their ordeal, Sandra looks up at Pamela, hoarsely saying, "I will never be able to repay you Pamela. You saved my life."

Pamela, reaching across the table, rubs Sandra on her sweaty forehead and says, "You don't owe me anything; you are my sister." Ms. Carla making everyone grasp hands around the table, leads in grace before eating.

Chapter Twenty-Two
A Discovery at the House of Horrors

A week has passed and Sandra is sitting on an old cot that Carla had stored away in the basement. Next to her is Pamela who says, "I do not want to bombard you with too many questions, Sandra, because I do not want you straining your throat. Do you plan to see a counselor to begin helping you through this ordeal? Sandra, you have not had the chance to sort through the horrific death of your babies."

Looking straight ahead at the cinder block wall, Sandra gently clears her throat, "My life, Pamela, is over. My dreams of raising my children are over. My dreams of starting a career, being a devoted partner and wife to someone is over. My trust in the people of this world is over. I fully accept that my parents hate me and want nothing to do with me. Pamela I even accept that I have never done anything malicious to anyone in my life, but someone wants to kill me and chances are they will probably succeed. You know what I will never accept, though? To die knowing I never tried to bring my children's killers to justice. That would be a shameful and cowardly way to leave this earth."

Pamela, listening intently to every word that comes out of Sandra's mouth, while getting the nerves to share her secret, says, "Listen to me, please? I lost Derrick many years ago because of my stupidity and selfishness. For many years, I needed someone to talk to and a shoulder for support. Sometimes it helped and other times it did not, but at least I had the assurance of knowing I could go somewhere. Sandra, you have suffered and gone through more than what the average person would ever face in a lifetime. Trust me; you have to seek counseling now and I will help you"

Looking at Pamela, trying not to seem as if all that she just said has went through one ear and out the other; Sandra grabs the faithful woman's hand: "Pamela, I want to let you know and please never forget this, ok? I love you for being a friend to me from the day we met, until this very moment. Please understand that I mean no harm, but at this moment fuck a counselor. The reality Pamela is that more than likely, I could die before even finding out the truth about Kareem and Chaka, but you see Pamela, I do not care anymore. What can they take from me now? I was always told by my father and Doug, who I thought I loved, that I was useless and was not worth a pile of shit. You know what Pamela? Looking back at my life, maybe I am not. I could not even get the courage to get my children out of a violent environment. What kind of mother was I? Therefore, all I have left Pamela is vengeance .Chances are I will probably screw this up, but be forewarned; I will die trying. I will not visit my children's resting place without trying to make amends first. I miss my babies; what did they do to deserve this"

As Sandra begins to cry uncontrollably, Pamela hugs the sobbing Sandra and rocks her slowly. "Whatever you need me to do let me know. Whatever you need me to do, I am here," Pamela whispers into her friend's ear. Now standing at the door and looking on in silence are Carla and Rose, who by the look in their eyes, want to help Sandra as well, but at this moment have no idea what to do. Calming herself down, Sandra gently pulls away from Pamela and wipes her face with a napkin.

"Has anyone heard or seen from Doug?" Sandra asks. Looking, as all three women shake their heads no, Sandra continues, "Who arranged for Kareem and Chaka's burials?" Stepping forward Carla answers, "Doug did that, Sandra. To be honest with you, I wish he would not have, though. Your children deserved a better service than what he gave them. At least they knew you loved them."

Rose, stepping forward with her head tilted to the ground, begins to cry, "I hate him. He is a wasted sperm. Doug cares about no one but himself."

As Carla now tries to comfort Rose, a now subdued Sandra stands on her own. "Pamela while you were at home, have you heard him come or go since the funeral?" asks Sandra.

As Pamela sits and takes a few moments to ponder the question, she answers, "Come to think of it, Sandra, no I have not heard him come or leave since the funeral."

"Pamela, did you really mean what you said about helping me?"

"Of course I did. Anything you need I am here for you."

Sandra, looking straight into Pamela's eyes, says, "Help me get back into his apartment; I need to gather a few things." All three women are looking at Sandra as if she has just completely lost her mind.

"Sandra, you can not be serious, girl. Please take my advice and seek out counseling before you dare enter that place again. I do not have much, but I will pick you up some things and I am pretty sure Ms. Carla would not mind you staying here, but Sandra you can not go back there," pleads Pamela.

Looking at her friend with rage in her eyes, Sandra responds, "You just said not even a minute ago that you would help me in any way that you could. So, I ask you one more fucking time; Pamela, will you help me get into Doug's apartment?" Looking at Carla and Rose for help but seeing none was available,

Pamela fearing she would lose the trust of Sandra if she answered wrong, says, "Yes Sandra, I will help you. Do you have a plan to get inside without being found out?"

"Yes, Pamela. I have a plan, but for this plan to work, I need you to do exactly what I say, Ok?"

Pamela, feeling queasy inside her stomach, answers, "Yes, I understand and I will do exactly as you tell me."

Looking at her friends in the small and chilly room, Sandra says, "If you all do not mind, I need a few moments to myself just to think. So, if you could excuse me I would appreciate it." As everyone exits the room, Sandra sits on the cot and stares at the ceiling: "This is for you babies." Rubbing her neck, Sandra thinks hard about how she will go about finding some answers.

*   *   *

Entering the second week since Sandra left the hospital, as she had promised her children she has been digging for information. Spending hours down at the precinct, she has been trying to get information about the ongoing investigation but has turned up nothing new.

Speaking with Detective Sam Daniels, who Sandra found to be quite polite, she found it strange how he spilled his coffee when she walked into the large office. His reaction evaporated quickly from her mind because her main concern was getting any information on her case as quickly as possible. Giving the detective all of the details of that Christmas day was crucial to Sandra, who even explained to the detective about the man with the dragon tattoo who cut her throat and made a visit at the hospital two weeks ago. Showing compassion and understanding, Detective Daniels reassured Sandra that they are doing everything possible to bring her children's killers to justice. Somewhat satisfied with the detective's position, Sandra would take his card and leave the precinct, feeling as if the ball was rolling in the right direction.

Unknown to Sandra though, was that when she left the stationhouse, Detective Daniels wasted no time and called Detective Davis explaining the two major problems that had arisen: Sandra's memory to detail and Tony Harris's dumb ass decision to visit Sandra in the hospital.

*   *   *

Sandra's watch reads 1:00 a.m. on Tuesday morning and by the sounds coming from the walls of the basement, the wind was howling. Told by Pamela that Doug has not been home since she has been back at her apartment; Sandra has decided that this was the right moment for her to return to the scene of her bloody Christmas. The plan was for Pamela to sit by her phone in the kitchen and look out of her window, which was directly over the one-way street leading to the building. What was great about Pamela's view was that it gave her a clear projection for about three blocks and everyone knew Doug was in love with his black Escalade. No one in this neighborhood had a black Escalade, so chances were if Pamela spotted one, it would belong to Doug. There was always the possibility of

human error. What if somehow Pamela missed the car? This almost
seemed impossible, but they had a back up set of eyes that belonged to
Rose, who begged Sandra to let her help. Rose would stand inside a
building hallway by the door where Doug would have to make a right turn
to enter the street leading to his building. With Pamela's cell phone, Rose
would dial Pamela's home telephone number if she saw anything that
resembled Doug's vehicle. Once Pamela received that phone call, she
would make sure it was Doug. Once Pamela made a positive
identification, she would call Ms. Carla's cell phone that Sandra borrowed
and Sandra would have adequate time to exit the apartment, locking the
door behind her and enter Pamela's apartment, which was right next door.
If all of this went to plan, then they would call Rose and tell her to go back
to the pantry where Carla had a bed set up for her to sleep.

Knowing that Doug was not a stay-at-home type of man, Pamela
and Sandra would drink coffee all night sitting by the door listening for
Doug to leave. When that happened, Sandra would return to the pantry
with her possessions, which included her wallet and cell phone that Doug
had taken from her. Hoping it was in the same place where he hid it from
her, Sandra could withdraw the three thousand dollars she had
accumulated from the many ass beatings she absorbed. She figured maybe
she could get a fresh start in a little kitchenette apartment somewhere
away from the house of horrors. That goal was so far away right now
because what she was attempting to do was almost suicidal. What if the
dragon and his friends were waiting for her like a pack of wolves waiting
for a deer to return to her drinking pond? Deep down Sandra knew Pamela
was right about seeking counseling and letting the detectives do their jobs.
Sandra figured to herself who was she? She could not even muster the
wisdom to recognize the warning sign to protect and shield her children
from the violence and abuse of Doug Gunner.

Looking at the cell phone, which is fully charged, Sandra did her
best to push the negativity from her mind and focus back on the task:
Getting in and out of the apartment as quickly as possible with her
important possessions. Just maybe, she thought to herself, after all she has
been through, a blessing could be sent down to her and maybe she would
find a clue or sign that the detectives missed that would lead to the capture
of Kareem and Chaka's killers.

Quickly jumping to her feet as if someone has stuck a pin in her
butt, Sandra looks at the cell phone, which is now ringing. Looking at the
blue illuminated glass, Sandra reads the caller id, which indicates it is
Pamela calling. Taking a deep breath, Sandra slowly flips the receiver:
"Hello...Thank you Pamela. I am on my way...Do not worry; I will be
careful." Hanging up her phone, Sandra begins to put on her coat, hat and
scarf. Making sure that she has her keys in her jean pocket, she walks out
the door of her little room, looking back at the cot that Carla was nice
enough to give her. At that very intense moment, Sandra realizes that she
may not return to this room. Pushing that thought out of her mind, Sandra

turns the light off and closes the door.

Walking towards the side door of the pantry, Sandra can see Carla waiting for her with a smile of concern, but nevertheless, it is still a smile. Looking outside the open door, Sandra can see the cab waiting for her, ready to take her to the apartment. Without saying a word to each other, Sandra and Carla hug each other for a moment, both fighting back tears.

"I love you, Ms. Carla and I always will."

"I love you too baby and you call me Mom, Ok? You are the daughter I always wanted." Slowly releasing each other, they give one more look before Sandra heads out into the dead of night, stepping inside the car and driving off. Ms. Carla stands at her door watching the backlights of the car until she can see them no more.

*   *   *

Now five blocks away from her destination, Sandra now thinks to herself, "What if he changed the locks? Or what if someone in the building sees me and tells him?" Pushing those thoughts not totally out of her mind but way in the back of it, Sandra focuses on her objective and doing it as fast as possible. As the cab gets closer to the building, Sandra makes the driver stop at the alleyway that leads to a back entrance of the building. Paying the cabby, Sandra exits the cab and stares up at the brown building.

As Sandra enters the alleyway, a cold chill sends shivers throughout her body as she realizes that somewhere in this area; her children's bodies landed ending their hopes and dreams forever. Doing everything within her power to control her emotions, Sandra walks straight towards the steel steps that will take her to the back entrance of the building. With one-step at a time, the coldness from the steps runs through the soles of her shoes to the top of her now throbbing head. After each step, something in the back of her mind is trying to convince her that she is over her head. With determination, Sandra continues to climb until she stands at the top of the steps in front of the large, steel, grey door. Reaching into her pocket, she removes her keys that would lead possibly to her getting justice.

"Turn the key and get this over with, Sandra," she said quietly to herself. Taking a deep breath, she slowly pushes the door open and sees the mailbox where Kareem always opened and removed the mail for her. Looking straight ahead, Sandra walks up three small steps looking at the elevator and then at the staircase, which is at the right of the elevator. Realizing getting on the elevator would put her in a confined space with the possibility of being stuck or noticed, Sandra decides to walk up. Grabbing onto the banister, Sandra quietly begins her journey up to where it all ended. With the first step came a slap in the face. With another step came the name-calling of "bitch and stupid" and with another step came the hair pulling and crashing into walls. With another step, came the looks of confusion in her children's faces as they wondered why did Mommy have to go through this? With the next step came the nasty drunken sex that she endured for years. With the next step came the belief that she was useless and weak, adding nothing positive to the life of her kids or herself. Then the last step that had Sandra six feet away from the apartment door was the image of Chaka reaching out to her for help and Kareem fighting with all of his strength to free himself to help his mother. Then it hit Sandra like a ton of bricks all at once; as much as she blamed herself and she really did, she now realized that she hated Doug. She not only hated him, she wished things on him now that her minister father told her many lives ago that God would not approve of. She could not help it, though; the hatred filled her body the closer she got to the door. Now a sick thought entered her head; in a way, she hoped she would find Doug asleep right now so she could stab or burn him to death so that he could feel a small portion of what she was dealing with. Looking at the peephole of Pamela's door, Sandra cannot swear by it but she can almost see the eye of her friend, as usual, looking out for her. Sliding the key into the top lock, Sandra turns until she hears the clicking sound. Now for the middle lock, this had to be jiggled a little until it made a clicking sound. Finally, there was the lock on the doorknob that she only has to turn halfway to the left and with that, Sandra gives the door a slight push gaining access to her personal hellhole.

Looking down the long, dark hallway that only gets light from the opening of the door, Sandra ignores the heavy footsteps of the dragon and his accomplices running inside, rushing the kids and herself on Christmas. Closing the door as quietly as possible, Sandra locks the door and reaches for the light switch in the hallway. Being able to see what is in front of her now, Sandra slowly and cautiously walks up the hallway that leads to the living room. Remembering as if it was yesterday, she walks over to the big lamp that sits on the end table and turns it on. Looking around, Sandra can see that the Christmas tree and all the gifts that were under it are gone. The blood that poured out of her throat onto the wooden floor is gone. In fact, the apartment cleaned spotless, gives off an eerie lemon smell.

"Get in and out; you are wasting time," Sandra reminds herself. Turning her back to the living room, Sandra is frozen by the voices coming from the window: "Help us, Mommy! Help us! Come with us, Mommy. Don't leave!" frozen in her steps, Sandra's legs feel as if they weigh two tons each, as she cannot move them. Sandra feels the sweat and anxiety build up inside her.

"Get away from the window and out of this room. It is not them; they know your purpose and they understand. They know you love them. Now get out of this room because time is wasting," Sandra tells herself. Feeling like she is pulling a small car, Sandra manages to get away from the room and the voices pleading to her.

Now inside the bedroom, Sandra is determined to accomplish her task quickly and effectively. Looking through the dresser drawers for her wallet and not finding it in the nightstands, she now swiftly looks inside the armoire drawers, finding instead Doug's underwear and shirts. Putting the thought out of her mind of him throwing her things out, Sandra walks to the closet and gently pushes the many expensive suits and coats to the side in order to look on top of the shelves. Moving the shoeboxes from one side to the other, all Sandra finds are automatic weapons and some pornographic DVD's. Feeling as if her time is running out, Sandra becomes somewhat dejected and lowers herself on her knees in the closet, hoping Doug had mistakenly thrown something on the floor. Moving more shoeboxes to the side, Sandra is now leaning in the closet when she feels a bump on the closet floor. Feeling with both of her hands, Sandra pulls on a ring that lifts a wooden plank, revealing the safe Sandra saw Doug open on Christmas morning. Looking at the safe with deep thought, Sandra pushes everything out of her mind and focuses on the three numbers that Doug dialed that morning.

"You can do this, but you must hurry," Sandra's inner voice tells her. With the only light coming from the brightness of the full moon, Sandra turns on the closet light and kneels down. Putting her face inches away from the safe knob, she can see Doug dialing those three sets of numbers from right to left and right again. With her right hand, Sandra turns the knob slowly stopping at 33. Turning back one full rotation, she now stops at 14. Finally, turning the knob slowly to the right again, she stops at 26 and exhales. Looking at the silver handle, Sandra grabs onto it and closes her eyes. With her eyes still closed consciously hoping and praying, Sandra gently pulls the handle in the down position when she hears a "clicking sound." Slowly pulling the safe door open, Sandra gazes inside and looks at the contents of the safe. Inside is a small black case that Sandra removes and unzips, finding what looks like ten gold DVD's. She quickly zips the case back up and sets it between her thighs. Moving bundles of money that are in the safe out of the way, she finds her wallet and her cell phone. Quickly grabbing them, Sandra frantically looks through the wallets contents and finds everything is still there. Most importantly, Sandra's bankcard is still there, which is the key for her getting a new place. Paying no attention to the money, two guns and the bag of reefer, Sandra closes the safe, spins the knob and makes sure it is locked. Remembering exactly how the shoes were placed, Sandra closes the wooden plank that hides the safe and puts the shoes back.

* * *

As Rose stands in the hallway of the cold building looking out of the front door, she is unaware of the red Lincoln Navigator that has just sped past her. Holding Pamela's phone in her hand, Rose continues to wait.

Sitting at her window wide awake and alert, Pamela looks at her watch and can see that it has been twenty minutes since Sandra entered the apartment. Now standing and looking out of her window, Pamela looks at her telephone, wondering if it works and then realizes that is a stupid thought knowing that as long as she can remember she has never been late with a bill payment. Walking closer to her window, Pamela takes notice to a red truck coming to a rolling stop and then beginning to park in front of the building. With a concerned look on her face, Pamela watches two women exit the truck first. They seem to be laughing and giggling with one another. Pamela's face of concern turns to horror as Doug gets out of the driver's side of the truck holding a suitcase. Quickly running over to her phone, Pamela calls Sandra, which she instructed Sandra to make sure Ms. Carla's phone was on vibrate.

Speaking as low as possible, while at the same time watching all three of them walk up the courtyard steps leading to the front door, Pamela says, "Sandra, get the hell out now; Doug's on his way upstairs. Please hurry up. I am going to open my door right now. Hurry" Running to her door, Pamela quickly turns her locks and opens the door. From a distance, Pamela can hear the three of them talking on what seems like the first floor.

Exiting the apartment is Sandra with the black DVD case under her arm and the keys to the apartment. Swiftly and quietly, Sandra locks all three locks, having to jiggle the middle lock just a touch. Hearing the footsteps and talking getting closer and clearer, Sandra begins to tremble and almost freezes in her steps when Pamela grabs her by the arm snatching her into the apartment with neither woman noticing the piece of paper that lays on the ground, falling from the top of Doug's apartment door.

Pushing Sandra towards the kitchen, Pamela locks her door and holds her breath as she can clearly hear Doug and his two playmates making their way to his apartment. As Sandra sits on the kitchen floor with her head buried inside her hands, Pamela stands by her door, listening to Doug take out his keys.

Looking at his keys, Doug takes notice to the white-tiled hallway floor. Bending down, he picks up a small yellow piece of folded paper and turns to the two women. With his hand, he gestures to the both of them to go stand one floor below. Pulling out his gun, Doug opens his apartment door and cautiously enters his apartment.

As a couple of minutes pass by, Doug opens up his apartment door: "Ladies, everything is cool. Come on up."

With looks of concern on their faces, one of the girls, whose name is Bernice, asks, "Doug, baby, you sure everything is Ok?"

Looking at the woman with a bit of anger, Doug says, "What did I just say? Just bring your asses in here now."

Hearing Doug's apartment door close, Pamela lets out a long sigh and turns to Sandra, who is still sitting on the kitchen floor. Walking over to Sandra, Pamela gets on the floor giving her a long hug. Looking at Pamela, Sandra says, "Please call Rose and tell her we are Ok and she did really well." Without hesitation, Pamela does just that.

Chapter Twenty-Three
Dirty Deeds

Covering his eyes from the bright sunlight coming from his bedroom window, Doug gathers his thoughts as he lies in bed. Looking at both sides of his bed, Doug realizes that he put Bernice and Sharon out when it was still dark but cannot seem to recall doing so. Slowly getting out of his bed, Doug begins to walk to his bathroom when he suddenly stops in takes notice to his nightstand. On the nightstand is the yellow piece of paper that he picked up off the hallway floor. Looking at the paper for another few seconds, Doug goes to the bathroom.

Standing at the doorway of his bedroom, Doug, with a slight look of amusement on his face, scopes the entire room from left to right. Trying to decide if he should make some breakfast, an overwhelming feeling of paranoia comes over him, Doug turns and starts to walk to his kitchen and then stops. Walking over to his nightstand, he checks inside and sees that everything is in place. Now checking the other nightstand and the armoire, Doug is satisfied and walks to his kitchen to make himself some breakfast.

*   *   *

Looking at the garbage that he has prepared, Doug pans around the dining room looking at the three empty chairs where Sandra, Kareem and Chaka sat just a month ago. Then, in an instant, visions come to his head of the doctor asking him if he was sure, he wanted to wait outside the operating room, losing the chance to see his kids brought into the world. He only visited Sandra and the kids once, that was to bring them home. As the kids grew in those dining room chairs, Doug had no memories of taking Kareem to play basketball or baseball, not even teaching him how to ride a bike. Sandra was the one who did all of those things. Doug looks at the other chair where every morning Chaka would fight and struggle to get herself seated to eat and she would gaze at him, hoping he would help her, but the help only came from Sandra as usual. Focusing back on the garbage on his plate, Doug remembers how well Sandra could cook and deep down inside he loved her meals. Pushing the slop that he has prepared away from him Doug says, "What did anyone ever do for me? I gave and everybody took! Nobody ever gave me anything!" Getting up from the table, he still sees the three people that never did him any harm. Not wanting to give into regrets, sorrows and disappointment Doug exits to take a shower and never looks back.

Standing in front of his closet, wearing nothing but his bathrobe, Doug looks over his wardrobe, trying to decide what he will wear. Pulling out his beige two-piece suit, Doug finds the shoes and shirt to match. Closing his closet door, Doug turns on some soft music and begins to get dressed.

*   *   *

It is a little before ten in the morning and Doug is prepared to head out to make his afternoon meeting when once again; he stops and looks at the piece of paper that sits atop of his nightstand. Deep inside Doug feels he has not looked at every hiding space and stares at the closet door. Removing his jacket and feeling anxiety pumping through his body, Doug walks over to his closet, opens the door and enters. Turning on the light inside, Doug slowly removes the many boxes of shoes that sit on the floor. Now just looking at the plank of wood with the metal ring on it, Doug gently grabs it and slowly pulls it up, revealing his safe. Arching his body so that he can get closer, Doug begins slowly turning the dial from right to left and back to right, unknown to Doug just as Sandra did eight hours ago. Doug slowly turns the handle and lifts the safe door. Falling back and hitting his back on the closet door looking as if he has just seen not one ghost but three, Doug can feel the saliva fall from his mouth. Tears, for the first time in many years, fill the eyes of the man built like a piece of steel. Trying to gather himself is difficult, because the closet feels as if it is spinning three hundred miles an hour. Holding his throbbing baldhead in his hands, Doug finally is able to sit up on his knees. Kneeling back over the safe, Doug removes the weapons, reefer and the four thick stacks of one hundred dollar bills. Looking at an empty safe, Doug feels as if he is having a nervous breakdown. Not really taking notice that Sandra's wallet is gone, Doug sobs like a six-year-old boy who has lost his toy marbles: "What the fuck! Not my DVD's, who in the fuck took my DVD's?"

Now struggling to make it to his feet, Doug exits his closet and plops himself on the bed with a thud. Looking around his room, the only word that comes to his head is "leverage." It took him years to build it up and just like that, his advantage was gone. Without it, Doug knew if things hit the fan, it would be over for him. Looking at his watch, Doug realizes that he should have been out the door already heading to his meeting. As he slowly begins to put on his jacket and grab his car keys, it is now obvious to Doug that someone has been in his apartment and the yellow paper was not lying to him. Putting everything back in the safe, Doug does the best that he can to pull himself together. Looking back at his bedroom, Doug begins to exit while, at the same time, his brain is working five times harder than usual.

Sitting in his car and driving down Webster Ave., getting ready to get on the Cross Bronx expressway, Doug grabs his phone and scans for the telephone number for North Bronx Central Hospital.

"Yes, this is Doug Gunner. I am calling to find out about the condition of a patient by the name of Sandra Lyte. She was admitted in your hospital on Christmas day. No problem, I can hold. She left unauthorized two weeks ago. Listen, how can someone just leave the hospital without anyone seeing her? So, did anyone in the hospital notice anything strange around her room? Yeah, ok. Thanks for nothing." Hanging up his phone, Doug now enters the Cross Bronx expressway saying, "No fucking way. There has to be another answer; there has to be."

* * *

Sitting by herself in the basement, Sandra looks at the two items that she has taken from Doug's safe. Picking up the wallet, Sandra slowly examines the contents, seeing her Virginia driver's license, social security card and most importantly, her bank ATM card. Sandra looks up to the white, chipped ceiling with relief. Looking wary of the DVD case, she looks it over, wondering what could be on them. Setting it down on top of the table, Sandra slowly unzips the case and opens it, to find ten gold discs secured in plastic sleeves. Flipping the plastic pages, Sandra reads what is on each disc: "April 23, sexcapade; May 16, orgy time; January 1, pretty young bondage girls; and other dates and names of sexual parties are written on the discs.

Sandra, turning the last sleeve, begins to close the book when she cannot help but to notice a small bulk inside the last sleeve. Feeling with her fingers, she finds the opening where the disc can be removed and feels what seems to be paper. Carefully removing the pink colored paper, Sandra slowly unfolds the two sheets and begins to read the top of the document. The letterhead of the document reads, "National Insurance Agency Inc. Syracuse, New York 13215." Looking further down the page, Sandra now clearly sees what she is reading is a receipt for a payment of an insurance policy for $500,000.00 in the name of Chaka Lyte. With her hands starting to tremble, she quickly flips to the other pink document and sees that it reads the same thing, except on this page the insured is Kareem Lyte. Both documents name Doug as the only beneficiary and both documents have Doug's signature.

Looking at both pieces of paper, Sandra bends her head towards the floor beneath her feet: With her body beginning to tremble, Sandra once again stares at the insurance policy receipts. Looking up at the cinder block wall, Sandra quickly runs at the cot and wooden table turning them over causing a crashing noise. Grabbing hold of the wooden chair Sandra hurls it at the wall smashing it to pieces. Now grabbing at her shirt Sandra begins to dig into the fabric pulling at her skin. Staring at the receipts that now lie on the floor Sandra yells, "You no good son of a bitch, you motherfucker! Running over to a cabinet, Sandra proceeds to break dishes onto the floor. Quickly running into the room is Ms. Carla and Pamela who both wears shocked looks on their faces as they see the damage Sandra has done inside the room. Gently grabbing her from behind Pamela is able to get Sandra on the floor saying, "Ok baby, I am here, I am here" rubbing Sandra on her head in an effort to calm her down, Pamela looks up at a mystified Ms. Carla.

*　　*　　*

It has been an hour since Sandra's outburst, while Pamela and Ms. Carla have cleaned the basement; they have managed to keep Sandra cool. Never explaining what triggered her outburst Sandra has managed to hide the receipts from them both. Feeling remorseful for breaking Ms. Carla things Sandra offered to repay her, but Ms. Carla would have none of it. Holding her possessions Sandra looks at Pamela who says, "Please talk to me anytime you feel like it, I am here for you girl." Feeling grateful Sandra gives Pamela a hug as Pamela continues, "Well, I am just here to let you know that my cousin Kenny is ready to drive us to the apartment I mentioned to you a few days ago. It is pretty far from Doug, almost on the border of Yonkers, most importantly; it is very secluded with a rent you should be able to afford until you are ready to really get out of here."

Walking over to her friend, Sandra gives her a hug and a rub on the shoulders: "Ok, I am ready. I just want to say goodbye to Ms. Carla before I leave. Grabbing her two duffel bags, Sandra opens one and puts the case holding the DVD's inside.

As Pamela stands with her cousin next to his blue sedan, they watch Sandra and Carla embrace each other almost looking as if neither one of them will let go. As they end their final goodbye, Sandra reaches down and picks up her bags, when from across the street running towards Sandra is Rose. As Pamela observes the scene, she can see Sandra mouthing the words "goodbye baby" to Rose, who begins crying and pulling Sandra's arms in a gesture for her to stay. Grabbing Rose and holding her close, Sandra strokes the young woman's hair softly. Still crying uncontrollably, Rose has to be subdued by Carla, who gently but forcibly takes her into the pantry. Not wanting to look back and knowing that she would not be able to stand to see the pain on Rose's face, Sandra walks to the car where Kenny shakes her hand and puts her bags into the trunk of his car. As they drive off down Jerome Ave., a white Cadillac STS waits a few seconds, pulls off, and begins to tail them.

*　　*　　*

As Sandra, Pamela and Kenny stand on the porch of a three-family, brick house in the Riverdale section of the Bronx, a small Russian woman, looking to be in her mid sixties, opens her door and says, "Yes, how can I help you?"

Kenny, putting a smile on his face, calmly steps forward, "Hello, ma'am. My name is Kenny Brown. A few days ago I called you about the studio vacancy you advertised in the newspaper?" Looking at all three of them, the old women closes her door and yells for someone in her Russian tongue.

- 146 -

After a few seconds, a tall, slender man in his thirties comes to the door: "Yes, who come for studio?"

Sandra, slowly raising her hand, answers, "Good afternoon sir. That would be me. My name is Sandra Lyte." Looking at all three of them with some sign of suspicion, the man slowly opens the door and waves them in.

It has been just a few moments, and Sandra feels that all the place needs is a paint job and some nicer curtains. With the place being already furnished, even though the furniture was a little outdated, Sandra seems satisfied and walks over to the man whose name is Boris: "Sir, I like the place very much and would like to move in right now, if possible?"

Staring out of the small kitchen window, he turns and looks at Sandra, "One month rent, one month security and no pets, ok? You pay rent always on first of month, yes?"

Sticking out her hand to Boris, Sandra shakes the man's hand, as he does not crack a smile.

"You have a deal and I promise never to be late with the rent."

*   *   *

It is the evening and Sandra is exhausted from all of the tidying up she has done around her new place. Before Pamela and Kenny left her to be alone, Sandra got Kenny to do her one more favor and that was to drive her to a local pawnshop to purchase a television and a DVD player. What Sandra got was a little more upscale for half the price and that was a 19-inch television/DVD combo set. The set was not brand new, but it was in excellent condition, but most importantly, it spared Sandra the time of trying to figure out how to hook the two separate units up if bought separately. Sitting on her old but comfortable wooden bed that creaked a little when she moved, Sandra looks around at her surroundings and cannot help not think about how bad her life has turned out. How the many choices she made turned out to be horrible ones not only for herself but also to the ones that meant the most to any mother: her children. What was she doing here? Why not just make another run for the border and start again? She asked herself. She had not heard from the police since she made her visit a few weeks ago, so as far as Sandra was concerned, her kids' case was turning cold very fast.

Sitting on her bed a voice inside Sandra's head begins to speak, "You have been spared Sandra, not because you are special or because the world needs you. It is simply because of the dirty hand you have been dealt. You deserve a shot at redemption and with that chance; you owe it to your children to fight back. Your children never got the chance to live and grow like they deserved to." Sandra, hearing the voice, tries to drown it out by looking at the pictures on the kitchen wall. The voice just gets louder: "You see Sandra, in spite of what you have always been told for the past seven years about how dumb and weak you are, I will no longer let you use that as an excuse to keep running and hiding from finding the truth. No, that shit stops today! Today the mission begins and the tears end. You will find those responsible for killing your children no matter what it takes. However, Sandra, I do promise you this: if you try to run away, give up or give in to excuses, make no mistake; I will haunt and torment your mind until you die. I will never go away and will always remind you of how you crumbled in the face of adversity. When you had one last chance to do what was right for your children, you weltered. I will also make you realize that you did not love your children because even in their deaths, you would not stand up to protect them. Then those beautiful seven years of love, your children abundantly poured out to you will turn to infinite hatred because they will soon begin to talk to you also, not of how they miss and love you but how they despise you because of your weakness. Sandra, now I will go away to give you time to think about your next move, speak to you later."

As Sandra sits on her bed, the room once lit by the setting winter sun is now dark, and the only thing that Sandra can clearly make out is the black DVD case that sits atop her bedside dresser. Getting up from the bed Sandra walks over to the dresser, grabs the black case, and walks to her television set where she sits down and turns on the television set. From reading the manual that the pawnshop owner gave her, Sandra pressed the AV button on the television, which bought her to a black screen that flashed, "No Disc." Looking at the buttons on the DVD part of the set, Sandra locates and pushes the open button, causing the door to slide forward. Slowly unzipping the case, Sandra looks through the various discs, finally choosing one that says, "Sexcapade." Loading it into the player and pressing play, Sandra adjusts the sound and watches.

As clear as day, there is Doug in some apartment that Sandra cannot make out. There is food and champagne in the living room. Not taking her eyes off the screen, Sandra watches as black and white men enter the apartment. It is hard for Sandra to make out who the men are because of the angle and blurriness of the overhead camera shot. Looking at the fast forward button, Sandra speeds the disc ahead hoping to see something better, but she only finds various scenes of the men having sex with different women. Growing a little frustrated, Sandra begins to remove the disc and try another when she observes a black man putting his clothes on in one of the rooms. It is not the clothes that caught her attention, but the badge he puts around his neck. Looking more closely and intently at the screen, Sandra is positive that it is a police badge. The black man, who Sandra still cannot make out, is balding on the top of his head. Watching the man walk over to the Chinese girl who he had sex with, he gives her one last kiss. Putting on his gun holster, he walks out of the room. Temporarily stopping the player Sandra grabs a notepad and a pen to write down what she has observed. Pressing the pause button again, Sandra continues to watch.

* * *

After spending almost three hours of stopping and rewinding the DVD player, Sandra has done her best to observe and memorize everything she feels is important. Looking over her notes, Sandra has written that she is positive that the men on the discs are part of law enforcement, but at what level, Sandra is not clear. What she hopes, though, is that the next set of discs that she will watch are a lot clearer and concrete. Feeling hungry, but not at all tired anymore Sandra walks to her kitchen and prepares a sandwich.

*   *   *

Six hours have vanished with a blink of an eye and looking at the window, Sandra can hear the sound of garbage trucks rolling down the street. The sun has not begun to rise yet, but with the chirping of the sparrows, it will rise soon. Taking a sip of warm soda, Sandra wipes her dry and drooping eyes with a wet rag. On the floor, lies about nine candy bar wrappers and empty cans of soda. On Sandra's lap sits her pad that, to her total disappointment, contains only one page of notes with a few thoughts that could help solve the crime of "her" century. She has scanned through seven discs and only gained insight about a few things; Doug was pretty clever in many ways, making sure he had law enforcement on his side for protection while at the same time obtaining dirt on them just in case they came after him. As for the law enforcement officers, they were near-sighted in doing all of this illegal activity, knowing it was wrong and could jeopardize their careers. Finally, Sandra is now fully aware that if she was going all the way with this, she had somewhat of legitimate proof and identification of the men on these discs. A southern girl from Virginia was about to bring a lot of important people down and, at the same time, maybe finding the truth involving Kareem and Chaka's murders. However, unfortunately all nine discs had terrible camera shots and grainy pictures. The only reason Sandra was able to make out Doug was that his dumb ass at times looked directly into the camera. Now looking down at the final disc that reads, "Pretty young bondage girls," Sandra loads it in the player.

As forty-five minutes of viewing by Sandra has passed, the sun begins to rise and Sandra's pencil is moving quickly across the paper because to her surprise, this last disc for some reason is clear as the blue sky. The views are no longer overhead but at face and shoulder level where she can make out without a doubt everyone's identity and burn that image in her mind. So far, Sandra has not seen anything special happen yet, except for the men and Doug sitting around eating, drinking and snorting blow. Getting up but not turning the player off, Sandra quickly runs to the bathroom with a glass in her hand.

Opening the door to the sound of a flushing toilet, Sandra walks back to her chair with a fresh glass of water. Focusing her eyes back on the television, her eyes widen as she mistakenly drops her glass of water. Getting closer to the television screen, Sandra falls to her knees as she witnesses a smiling Doug parading a shaking and crying Rose around on a leash in front of law enforcement officers.

"Oh my goodness no, Rose, how did he get to you?" Sandra asks herself aloud. Not being able to move or turn away from the image on the screen, Sandra looks on as Doug forces the terrified Rose to remove her clothes as the men who have formed a small circle around her wave their arms in the air as they poke and spank her small petite body. Forcing Rose by the collar around her neck to the floor, the naked young woman is sobbing obviously pleading to be let go. Doug, with his free hand, smacks Rose across the head, knocking her to the floor causing Sandra to shiver. "You son of a bitch!" Sandra blurts out, as her face turns red. Sitting in an upright position, Sandra rocks back and forth, continuing to watch as a much older woman, maybe in her late thirties, enters the room wearing a black dominatrix suit. The woman is dark-skinned and has blonde hair. As Doug smacks the woman on her backside, he gives her the leash that holds Rose.

*   *   *

After sixty minutes of watching Rose being sexually assaulted and conquered by the "Dominatrix bitch" Sandra at this point, does not know where her pain comes from most. Knowing now why Rose hated Doug so much or because she sat through the ordeal, never turning her head away from the television. This made Sandra ask herself a question: "Am I becoming numb to all of this pain and suffering that I have witnessed?"

Then just as quickly, as she asked herself that question, the voice that had told her how things were going to be from now on answered, "No Sandra, not numb but stronger and wiser. The pain and sorrow you feel for Rose is right. Turn that pain and sorrow into ambition and determination" Just like that, the voice was gone.

Looking at the DVD counter on the television, Sandra has noticed from the past disc that they only ran for about one-and-a-half hours long, and by her calculations, there would be about maybe three or four minutes left to view. The dominant woman who Sandra began to despise is dragging a sweaty and naked almost zombie-like Rose out of the room. As hard as it was, Sandra continued to write and take notes when she noticed something in the living room that caused Sandra to shiver. One of the men, a white man, out of drunkenness jumps up from the coach removing his hat begins to jump up and down, causing the others around him, including Doug, to laugh. The man removes his sweater and undershirt, revealing a well-chiseled body. What put Sandra in a shock-like state is what Sandra saw plastered on the man's right wrist: a tattoo of a large, fire-breathing dragon. The dragon that held her down and made her watch the murder of her children, the dragon who opened her throat leaving her to die, the dragon that chased Pamela and her in the hospital, is the same fucking dragon that is eating with that bastard Doug.

The DVD ends with the man with the pet dragon dancing on Doug's couch. Sandra sits on the floor snapping a number two pencil in her hands, staring at the frozen image on the screen.

Chapter Twenty-Four
Doug Mixes Past With The Present

Sitting in front of his new superior, Doug listens intently to orders and objectives instructed. Looking around and admiring the large apartment that sits on 72nd and Park Ave., Doug tries to keep focused on his job at hand.

Mr. X., sitting at a large ivory desk in the living room painted all white, informs Doug, "In a four hour span, you will meet with three men at three different locations throughout the five boroughs. Each man will give you one-third of two million dollars in exchange for a special key. After the last pick-up, you will bring the two million dollars to me at another location that I will disclose to you later."

Listening and looking at Mr. X, Doug does not respond right away; instead, he lets his thoughts wander: "Four hours, three meetings, I have to fit my selling time into finding my discs. I have to locate that bitch Sandra. I cannot prove it yet, but I know my hunches are leading me in the right direction. Just have to flush her ass out, that's all."

Mr. X snaps his fingers to get Doug's attention: "Excuse me, Doug. Are you ok? Are you with me? You have a very important task, so I suggest you listen carefully. When these men give you the money, you are to turn over a key to them. The first man from the Bronx will get a red key while the man in Brooklyn will get a blue key and finally the man in Queens will get a black key. After each drop, you will do as I instructed, you understand?"

"Yes, I understand clearly," Doug, says.

Looking at Doug as he takes a sip of cappuccino, Mr. X responds, "Doug, when we first met, I told you in order to be successful in this organization, your mind had to be clear and all past debts in your past life had to be taken care of before you worked for us; do you remember?"

Shaking his head yes, Doug says, "I assure you, my mind is clear, and I am ready for this assignment."

"Doug, do not try to reassure me or the organization of anything. You just keep telling yourself that. I would like to discuss your performance so far. To this date, we have been satisfied in the way you have followed our instructions. We also understand that we have been keeping you regulated to your club for the past month, selling our product and entertaining our clients. We just want you to know that we thank you for your cooperation in handling the situation. We just want to let you know that as long as you continue to perform at your very best, we will continue to reward you as we have with your new vehicle."

Doug, looking intently into his boss' eyes, as he speaks, knows that this meeting is ending. Reaching down by the chair he is sitting in, he grabs a grey briefcase and gently sets it atop the desk in front of Mr. X, who motions over to his lieutenant who goes by the name Blue. Spinning the briefcase towards him, Blue slowly opens it and turns it back to his boss for inspection.

"One hundred and fifty thousand right Doug?"

"Yes that is correct one hundred and fifty thousand."

Reaching inside the briefcase, Mr. X removes twenty-two thousand five hundred dollars and slides it across the table to Doug. "Here is your fifteen percent and this meeting is over. Remember what we discussed, and I will see you at our next meeting." Standing up from his chair, Doug shakes his boss' hand and leaves the plush apartment, making his way down to the garage where his Navigator awaits.

*   *   *

Driving down the cold but sunny streets of Manhattan, Doug heads for home, needing to get some rest before he begins his night of work at his club. Driving up Broadway and making his way to the 145th Street Bridge, the only word on Doug's mind was "leverage" because he knew the man with the most advantages stayed out of jail. At this very moment, he knew that he had lost a huge part of his and what pounded at his head even more was the fact that he possibly lost that advantage to some dumb bitch with a nice body he should have dumped seven years ago.

Going across the bridge leading him back to the Bronx, all he could hear was his father's voice: "They are only to hump and pump--no more, no less."

Shaking his head back and forth, Doug pounds his steering wheel and presses a button, which dials a number. As a phone rings, a voice answers on the second ring: "Yeah, what's up?"

"Bucky, what's up? This is Doug. Listen, I need to ask you something, have you seen or run into anyone who has seen Sandra?" Doug asks.

"No dog, I thought she was still in the hospital?"

Stopping at a red light on the Grand Concourse, Doug says, "No, Bucky. It has come to my understanding that she has checked herself out, and I am very worried about my Boo, man. I need to find her and make sure she is ok. Listen Bucky, please do me a favor man; put the word out on the street and when you are out there, please call me right away if you here or see anything, brother. This shit is killing me now; where the hell could she be?"

"Yo, dog. You just stay calm, Ok. I will put the word out and trust me; we will find her. You just stay calm."

Doug, with a convincing smile, says, "Thanks, brother. I will talk to you later, one."

"One, Doug."

Pressing the receiver button on the steering wheel, Doug is about three minutes away from his apartment when he says to himself, "Sandra baby, we will soon see if my hunch is right or wrong. For your sake, you better hope I am wrong because if I am not, baby, your ass is through this time and I will personally make sure the job gets done correctly." Pulling up to his building, Doug rolls his eyes and sucks his teeth because sitting on his stoop reading a newspaper with a cup of coffee is Detective Tommy Davis.

"Shit, I am dead fucking tired. What the hell does he want?"

Exiting his vehicle, Doug puts on a fake smile and charm, walking towards Tommy.

"Detective, what do I owe this honor?"

Tommy, looking up, smiles right back at Doug and gives him a look of phoniness. "It has been a little while since I have spoken to my brother from another mother and last I noticed, that check them folks pay me at the department ain't supporting my lifestyle," responds Tommy.

Leaning on a concrete pillar, Doug, who is about to fall on his face from exhaustion, says, "Listen Tommy, I know shit has not been rolling in like the old days, but things have been a little tight for a brother."

Taking a sip of his coffee and gazing at Doug's brand-spanking-new red Navigator, Tommy says, "Man, who you telling about tough? The old woman asked me for her three hundred dollar day spa money and I had to tell her for the time being she would have to go around the corner to the Korean woman and she almost took my damn head off. Doug, brother please, the last thing I want to hear about is how tough things are for you. Not once have I harassed you with phone calls or visits, but now I am getting a little hungry and I want to eat baby."

Knowing this day would come; Doug stares at the detective seeing him as a crack addict that begins to know your every move. When you make a move, there his ass is standing at the train station or the bus stop waiting for you with his hand sticking out. Gazing at his truck, that word entered his mind again: "leverage."

Doug was starting to come to grips with his reality that he was losing it. "Listen Tommy, I got a little something, but you are going to have to give me a little space partner until things heat up again." Reaching into his pocket, Doug pulls out a roll of hundred dollar bills, giving Tommy some. "Tommy, this is twenty-five hundred and like I said, when things heat up, you know I will look out for you."

Tommy, looking at the money as if he did not receive the Christmas gift under the tree that he expected, smiles and begins to put his newspaper under his arm. Getting up from the steps and holding his arms up to the sky while stretching, Tommy says, "Ok, partner, being that we cool and shit, I am going to give you some room. You won't have to worry about my soldiers coming around messing with you; just continue to have a little something for me every week, cool?"

Looking at his watch, Doug can feel his eyes getting heavier as each second goes by. "Ok Tommy, no problem, but we cannot meet in front of my place like this. When I have your stash, I will call you to set up an exchange." Tommy smacks Doug on the back and enters his car. Starting the engine, Doug gets a wave and smile from the detective before he drives off down the street. Before going upstairs, Doug can only think of two things right now. One of them was how long was Tommy waiting for him on these steps? It was only like thirty-three degrees outside; he had to be freezing. Then Doug realized that Tommy was like a crack addict, except his crack was money and just like any addict, they will do whatever it takes to get their fix. That bothered Doug because what would Tommy do next wait by his door the following week? The second thing that concerned Doug was what Tommy said about his soldiers staying away and not making any visits. If the money got slow were they to start shaking him down? Of course, they would. Removing his keys from his pocket, Doug begins to walk up his steps, making his way into his building.

* * *

Looking at the mail he just took out from his mailbox, Doug can no longer fight it. Throwing the mail on his living room coffee table, he plops himself on the sofa, removing his shoes and begins to shut his eyes when something flashes inside his head: the mail. Sitting up on the couch, Doug reaches for the pile of envelopes with a newfound energy, scanning through it quickly his eyes focus on a blue envelope. Looking at the piece of mail like it was a winning lottery ticket, Doug begins to open Sandra's cell phone bill. Seeing that she owes fifty-two dollars, Doug flips through the pages until he comes upon the list of numbers that she has dialed during this billing period. Looking at the list of numbers, Doug can clearly see she has made many calls during the late night and the dates indicate this was right before he took her phone away. Two numbers stick out, though, and they are both 718 numbers. Finding a boost of energy, Doug gets up to retrieve his cordless phone that sits on his television set. Looking at one of the frequently dialed numbers, Doug dials it and places his hands over the receiver. Listening for an answer, on the third ring, he gets one.

"Good afternoon, Burnside Pantry, this is Carla. Hello? Hello? Hey, it is your dime." Doug, hearing a click from the other end of the line, holds on to the phone and now wears a big thinking cap, trying to understand why Sandra, even though she volunteered at that pantry; why did she make all these calls at strange times of the night? Now looking at the other number, Doug dials that one also and waits as he listens to the phone ring four, five, and finally six times with no answer, not even an answering machine. Hanging up his phone, Doug takes a walk to his living room wall to admire one of his paintings he purchased a few years ago. Pushing the redial button, Doug stares at the picture while listening to the rings again when something dawns on him. Listening more intently, Doug swears he can hear a ringing phone from the other side of his wall. With the phone still in his hand, Doug slowly leans toward his living room wall, pressing his ear against it and sure enough, though it may be low, he can hear a ringing phone. Pressing the off button on his phone, Doug wears a look of curiosity, as he can no longer hear the ringing through the wall. Pressing redial again, Doug now can hear the ringing as if it has gotten louder and clearer. Doug hangs up and redials three more times to reassure himself that he is not crazy: sure enough, his discovery is true. Doug tosses the phone on the couch, staring at the wall with anger and admiration mixed in saying, "Ok, bitch. I think you just fucked up. I'm not totally sure, but soon enough I will find out and if you did fuck up with me, all of you fucked up with me."

Chapter Twenty-Five
Sandra Moves Forward

It is Saturday afternoon, 3:00 p.m. to be exact and Sandra, who has just awakened from a nine-hour nap, still has all of her notes etched in her mind and on paper from what she witnessed on Doug's DVD collection. She has also figured something else out while getting a fresh shower and clothes prepared. Doug is not stupid because sooner or later, he is going to narrow down all those around him who he suspects could have entered the apartment and taken his DVDs. Figuring out how that person got into his safe was not important to him though, because all he wanted to do is catch the individual and make that person suffer. The other thing that Sandra figured to be true was that those discs were very important to Doug simply because as long as she has known him, Sandra knew that Doug enjoyed the upper hand. As long as he held those discs with the cops engaged in illegal activity, Doug held an advantage just in case he got in trouble. Without the discs, his word carried little weight in a court of law if he was busted. Looking at her watch, Sandra hurried to get herself together because soon after waking up, she called Pamela on her cell and asked her to come over for lunch and a meeting. Pamela, a person being a stickler for time, would be there in about thirty minutes. Grabbing her personals, Sandra enters the bathroom.

*   *   *

As Sandra and Pamela sit at the small dinette table, they eat hero sandwiches in silence while drinking diet soda. Feeling as if the Saturday has come and gone based on the sun beginning to set over the quiet Bronx Street, Pamela, looking at her friend, can tell she has a lot on her mind and makes an attempt to get her to open up.

"So, girl, how do you like your new surroundings?"

Taking a swig of her soda, Sandra responds, "I think I finally know why things happened on Christmas Day Pamela."

Finishing her sandwich, Pamela adjusts her chair so that she is facing Sandra and looking deep into her eyes. "Ok, baby. You tell me why and take your time."

"Pamela, I have spent about ten hours straight, maybe more--I cannot be sure, studying what I took from Doug's apartment that night. You see this leather case? It contains discs of Doug and people who work for the police department doing some terrible shit that could get a lot of important people locked up."

Sandra, slowly sliding the disc towards her, watches Pamela open it slowly, reading the titles and dates of each disc. "Sandra, please tell me what you saw and what does it all have to do with Christmas Day? Because if it can help you bring those bastards responsible for Kareem and Chaka you have to do something right away."

Standing up from her chair, Sandra slowly paces back and forth in the small cooking area as she explains, "First of all, Pamela, what I am about to discuss with you can go no further than this room because you are the only person I can trust, ok?"

Pamela, nodding her head, is hanging on every word coming from Sandra's mouth.

"Also in this disc holder I found a set of insurance policy receipts totaling one million dollars made out in Kareem and Chaka's name with Doug as the sole beneficiary. He never discussed these policies with me and I never remembered any insurance agent coming to the apartment when I was there."

"Wait a minute" Pamela says who is in disbelief. "Sandra are you telling me that Doug is responsible for the deaths of his own children?"

"Yes Pamela that motherfucker had my babies slaughtered for the fucking money! You hear me Pamela? As Sandra's, voice rises with anger. "He killed my babies for fucking money!"

Pamela leaps out of her chair with anger burning from her eyes saying, "What the fuck are we waiting for? Let us deal with that cold-hearted bastard right now! I know where I can get a burner. Let us blow his motherfucking brains out!

Sandra almost giving in to the temptation calms Pamela down. "Pamela, that would be too merciful for that son of a bitch. I got other plans for his monkey-ass that will include pain and suffering, as he has never felt. When it all goes down I will be there and that son of a bitch will have no choice but to look into my eyes before he goes to hell, that I promise. I know you think I should react now but this will take time and patience. Are you with me Pamela?"

Pamela looking Sandra straight in her eyes says, "All the way sister."

Pamela, calming herself down, continues to listen to Sandra, who now has determination written on her face continues, " Pamela on one of the last discs I watched, Doug had Rose on a dog leash, on her hands and knees performing sex acts. While those motherfucker's stood their watching as she cried and begged them to stop. That is why she said she hated Doug and that he was a bad man. How could she be so brave and help us Pamela when she holds so much pain inside her?"

Pamela grabs a napkin from the table and wipes her eyes. "Sandra, maybe that's just it baby…maybe Rose's way of dealing with all that she has been through is her helping you and bonding with you. Obviously she knew more about Doug then we were aware of."

Leaning up against the refrigerator Sandra continues, "On the last disc I watched, there was a man that I recognized from Christmas Day."

Quickly jumping out of her chair, Pamela grabs Sandra by the shoulders, "Oh shit, Who Sandra?"

Looking at Pamela and seeing that she is mad as hell, Sandra explains, "When those men ambushed us on Christmas, they all had on black clothes and black masks to match, so I could never match a face to them. What I vividly remember is the hand that went across my face as he slit my throat. Pamela, on his wrist was a tattoo of a green dragon. Just like the one on the man's wrist in the hospital chasing us do you remember him?"

Twisting her face in thought, Pamela answers, "Yes, Sandra, I remember him."

Walking slowly over to Sandra, Pamela slowly and gently rubs her fingers across Sandra's freshly scarred throat. "Sandra, let us sit down and take a break from all this shit. We are gonna make ourselves sick."

Shaking her head, Sandra answers, "No, I want to continue. On the last disc that I watched when they humiliated Rose, a man stood up and applauded, taking off his shirt. While the majority of the discs are a bit fuzzy and shot at poor angles, this disc was perfect in every way. On this man's wrist was the tattoo, while clipped to his waistband was a gun and a police shield. Pamela, I cannot totally prove it yet, but I am pretty positive Doug and these men are responsible for what happened to my children."

Pamela, continues to study Sandra's face defiantly says, "No, Sandra don't you dare doubt yourself or your feelings; they did this shit, and I am going to help you figure out how to get their fucking asses back."

*　　*　　*

It is 10:00 p.m. and Sandra has been sitting by her window looking at pictures of Kareem and Chaka while Pamela has been looking angrily at DVD's of Doug and the detectives. Turning off the television after witnessing what was done to Rose, Pamela, who feels numb throughout her body, walks back over to the dinette table and stares at the stove:

"Sandra, you are right in waiting. We cannot go to the police because they have that secret blue wall bullshit. We have to figure out how to get this information into the right set of hands. We also have to watch our backs because I am pretty sure sooner or later, Doug will put all of this together and will begin searching for his discs."

Setting the pictures back inside a shoebox, Sandra, trying her best to push the fear that she still has of Doug from her mind, says, "I have a few ideas on what we can do Pamela, but the first thing I must do is get these discs into the right hands, and I think I know someone. Her name is Maria Copper, the special investigative reporter on channel four. She is always getting shady companies and people in trouble by exposing their wrongdoings. I remember last year when she got those meat markets in Hunt's Point closed down because of the bad meat they were selling to the supermarkets in the poorer neighborhoods. My plan is to give her a call as soon as possible next week."

Walking over to Sandra a serious looking Pamela says, "I want you to know and realize something, ok? This is some deep shit we are about to get involved in. Once we set one foot into motion, there is no turning back. Now I want to tell you this also Sandra: I love you and as I said before, no one in this world is going to convince me that you deserved what happened to you. Understand that once this ball starts to roll, it is going to pick up some nasty shit along the way and you cannot let it scare or intimidate you. You have to promise me that you will not give up, ok? As long as you stay strong, I am with you all the way."

"I love you too Pamela, thank you for all of the help and support you have given me and no, I will not give up because this is not about me anymore; it is about my two babies."

As both women embrace each other at the dinette table, the unpredictability of the unknown enters their minds and bodies, but at the same time, a power of love and determination bonds them together pushing all fear away. Slowly letting go of each other, Sandra looks into Pamela's eyes:

"Pamela, I promised myself that I would not do this until I brought my children's killers to justice, but I miss them so much and my heart aches so much. I need to visit them; I need to speak to them, Pamela."

"Sandra, are you sure you are ready for this? You do not have any idea what visiting those gravesites could do to your mind; it could crush you and cause you to abandon the whole plan. Can you handle that?"

Grabbing Pamela by the hand, Sandra says, "I thought that at one time also that is why I said to myself that I would not visit them until this was done. Now I realize that decision was the wrong one because of the danger and seriousness of this matter. Pamela, I want to see them for strength and comfort, so please, I do not even know where they rest, so can you tell me, please?"

Walking over to the dinette table, Pamela grabbed the pad and pen and wrote the address down. "Sandra, this is the name of the cemetery, address and location of where their plots are; do you need me to go there with you?"

"No, Pamela. This is something I have to do by myself, I will tell you when I am leaving and where I have hidden these discs. In addition, I am going to make a copy of the apartment key so that you will have one. When I get back from visiting Kareem and Chaka, I will call you and that is when you can come over so we can contact Maria Copper, ok?"

Shaking her head up and down Pamela looks at Sandra as if she is a baby chicken about to walk into a slaughterhouse, but manages to put a smile on her face. "Baby, let's call you a cab because it is getting late and it's freezing outside," says Sandra. Calling a cab, Sandra helps Pamela put on her coat and gives her one last hug as she walks her to the street from her apartment. The dispatcher told them a driver would be there in three minutes.

*　*　*

It's Sunday morning, and the air is brisk but amazingly fresh and clean. Sandra, sitting in the back of a red Towncar, is about three minutes away from the Pelham Cemetery on Earley Avenue in the Bronx. Holding two brown teddy bears in her hand and a small bouquet of flowers in the other, Sandra is doing her best to hold it together as she can now see the entrance gates of the cemetery. As the driver pulls inside the cemetery, Sandra hands the man a piece of paper, with the plot number and directions of where her children rest. As the car slowly moves on the asphalt driveway, Sandra gazes at the fancy and large monuments and headstones that families have adorned on the gravesites of their loved ones. As the car comes to a slow halt, the driver turns to face Sandra:

"Miss, I think this is the location. Would you like me to wait here for you?"

"No, sir that will not be necessary; I have your company card, so I will call. Thank you very much; you are a good driver." Getting out of the car and watching it drive away, Sandra looks at the instructions that Pamela wrote down for her while walking towards Kareem and Chaka's resting place. Buttoning her coat collar to protect her neck from the sudden burst of wind, Sandra removes her sunglasses and looks at the two concrete tombstones that have her children's names with dates of births and deaths on them. Letting a smile come on her face, Sandra slowly walks to and kneels at the tombstones, wiping some old snow from the top of them. Laying the teddy bears on the ground, Sandra divides the flowers between the two children. The sky is becoming very cloudy, as the wind has begun to pick up, making thirty-two degrees, feel like fifteen. Looking at the dates of her children's short existence on the tombstones, Sandra feels it is not fair that she stands above ground while her precious little ones are below it. Deep inside, Sandra wishes she were with them.

"The first thing Mommy wants you to know is that I miss the both of you very much. Kareem, I hope you are taking good care of your sister and Chaka, you make sure your brother stays out of trouble because we know how mischievous he is."

Trying to hold back the tears, Sandra cannot as she looks to her far right at an elderly man standing alone at a gravesite with flowers in his hand.

"Mommy said she would hold it together, but I cannot because I miss and love you both so much. I know I should have tried harder to get us out of that place, but I had no other place to go and there was no way I could afford to give you the education that you were receiving, so I took the beatings, hoping they would stop. Instead, the beatings turned your mother into this lonely woman before you both."

Feeling as if two thousand pounds are weighing on her heart, Sandra tries to swallow but cannot because of the peach-size lump in her throat.

"I do not know if you two will ever forgive and respect me for what I allowed to happen, but I hope and pray that you will give me the chance to make up for what I allowed to happen. I want to make a promise to the both of you that I will never sleep or rest until I have used up all the energy in my mind and body to find who did this to us. I swear before the both of you that I will find them and they will pay."

Now on her knees, Sandra holds onto both of the tombstones with each hand as she cries uncontrollably. As she watches her warm tears fall into the snow and dirt, Sandra does not even feel the hand from behind her touch her shoulder.

"It's Ok, sweetheart. God has them in his Bosom and they are in a better place now." Sniffing and trying to gain some control, Sandra shivers a little at the sound of the low but positive voice. Slowly turning her head and brushing her braids away from her red, swollen eyes, Sandra looks at a frail Jewish man standing behind her.

"Please let me help you up from the snow, young lady," says the old man, who grunts but is successful in getting Sandra to her feet. "I miss my Edna also like you miss your love ones. I see they were very young and vibrant. They are probably doing much work for God right now and they know that you love and miss them, but they want you to live, like my Edna had told me last year." The old man wearing a black old coat and hat to match removes a handkerchief from his pocket gently wiping Sandra's face.

"Where did you come from?" asks a still upset Sandra.

Allowing a smile to come to his face, the old man replies, "The same as you young lady from a far off place hoping for a better life sixty-eight years ago. That is when I met my Edna and my life had never been happier until it was time for her to go. Did you have a good time with your loved ones?"

Looking down at the ground, Sandra looks back at the old man, "I enjoyed every minute with them and I made sure they knew that I loved them all the time."

With a smile on his wrinkled face, the old man says, "Well, you have done a great thing that millions of mothers in this world cannot say they have and that is a shame. They love you and will always love you, like my Edna, but you must never stop talking to them because they like that. But a time must come when you must continue on, holding them near your heart but still moving on."

Sandra, feeling a little comfort from this total stranger, reaches out and rubs his slouching shoulders: "Thank you very much for the encouragement; you are a very nice man. My name is Sandra and these are my babies, Kareem and Chaka."

"My name is Albert, it is nice to meet you Sandra and you must stay strong for them because whether you know it or not, they will always depend on you to continue to carry their legacy."

Turning and looking at the two teddy bears that sit on the gravesites, Sandra turns back to Henry and says, "I will Henry, I made them a promise that I would."

Moving closer to Sandra, the old man gently gives her a hug and whispers, "He knows your pain and will help you to make things right." Adjusting his hat and coat, the old man gives Sandra one more smile, as he begins to walk down the asphalt driveway where a tall man stands by a long limousine with the back door open. Sandra, watching him until she sees him get into his car, looks on as the driver gets in and drives out of sight. Feeling the light snow flakes that begin to fall and hit her nose, Sandra turns to her children's resting places and says, "Mommy has to go now, but I promise I will be back when this is all over, telling you how brave and strong I was in finding the bad people who did this to us. Always know mommy loves you both terribly. You both were the only people who really loved me and I will not let you both down. Mommy will see and talk to real soon, I promise." Sitting the teddy bears up straight on the tombstones, Sandra turns to walk down the driveway when her phone starts to ring.

Halfway to the entrance, she answers on the fourth ring, "Hello? You motherfucker! I know what happened you no good son of a bitch! Fuck you, you bastard! I do not want to hear shit from your ass! You just know this, you no good motherfucker, I know you killed my babies! You and those fucking dirty cops. You will all go to jail and rot like fucking animals, you son of a bitch!" Sandra's face is tomato red as spit shoots from her mouth. Some people who are paying respect to their loved ones cannot help but to stop and look at her go berserk.

*   *   *

Doug is in his truck in a parking lot listening to a woman that he has never heard use profanity before. Realizing this is not the woman he abused, Doug tries to intimidate. "Fuck you and your dead kids bitch! Who in the fuck do you think you are talking to bitch? I am going to say this shit once, so listen closely! I want my discs back right fucking now and if I do not get them back, Sandra, I promise you I will hunt your fucking ass down, open up your fucking throat and watch your ass bleed to death myself, bitch!

*   *   *

Sandra standing at the gated entrance has no tears coming down her face as she interrupts Doug, "Come get them, motherfucker! You are not anything but a fucking coward and a lowlife piece of shit! I am not afraid of your ass Doug and you know what, your stupid ass had better watch your back because unlike your dumb fucking ass, I have nothing to lose anymore. So you better hope you find me before these discs and myself find someone else, you steroid-taking motherfucker!" Hanging up her phone, Sandra waves a cab down and enters to return home.

Doug, hanging up his phone is in complete shock as his hands begin to tremble. Gaining some composure, he is able to dial a number on his cell phone putting it to his ear: "Bucky, listen to me man. You got to turn up the heat on finding Sandra; use what resources you have man, but you have to find her." Hanging up his phone, Doug starts his car and begins to drive out of the parking lot when he slams on his brakes because he almost hits a woman pushing her baby in a stroller. For the first time in Doug's life, a cold chill flooded his body after Sandra hung up the phone. Doug tried shaking that feeling but it was impossible.

Chapter Twenty-Six
Tony Marino Meet Sandra Lyte

While coming home from the cemetery, Sandra had this strange urge for banana crunch ice cream, so instead of having the cab driver let her off at her basement apartment, she stopped at the supermarket instead. With the snow beginning to fall more rapidly along with a gusty wind, Sandra was fortunate to find a cashier who was able to check her out quickly. With her venomous conversation with Doug still on her mind, Sandra tries to focus on what her new friend Albert said to her about her children. It was hard though, because she knew Doug was a persistent son of a bitch who had many associates in the city, so Sandra began to wonder was it safe for her to spend unnecessary time on the street. Looking at the items she had just purchased, Sandra thought it best that until she was ready to make her moves with the discs she would do her best to stay out of sight. Covering her face from the wind and snow, Sandra hurried home.

*   *   *

Brushing herself off and stomping her feet, Sandra walks down the well-lit hallway that leads to the door of her apartment. Walking past the slop sink closet and the electric meters, Sandra takes out her keys to unlock her door when she looks up and drops her bag. With a terrified look on her face, she does not scream or say a word; instead, she just looks at the six large Italian men who are all wearing expensive cashmere coats with suits to match. One of the men, smiling at Sandra, walks closer in her direction slowly bending down picking up her bag:

"Sandra I did not mean to frighten you. Please let me introduce myself. My name is Tony Marino and I was wondering if I could take up a few minutes of your time because I truly believe we have a lot in common and if we put our heads together, we can help one another."

Holding her bag in her hand, Sandra cannot take her eyes off Tony's men, who are very large and intimidating to the eye. "I do not know you and how did you find me? Sandra asks.

Still able to maintain his smile that reveals his perfectly white teeth, Tony says, "Sandra, I promise I will explain and answer all of your questions if you could give me just a minute of your time. I give you my word; you have nothing to fear and besides, we would not want your ice cream to melt, now would we?"

Sandra almost feels as if she has no choice in the matter and Tony is just trying to make her feel as if she does, so Sandra takes a long deep breathe then exhales, "Ok Mr. Marino, but just for a few moments and only you."

Shaking his head in agreement, Tony says, "I fully understand Sandra. Just me and please call me Tony. Men, please give Sandra and me a little privacy."

With that command the five men, who are obviously bodyguards, did as told and walked outside to their cars. Holding Sandra's bag, Tony watches her nervously open her door.

Turning on her light, Sandra quickly puts her groceries away as Tony stands and admires how Sandra as decorated such a small place so nicely. "Tony, I just have water and orange juice; may I offer you some?"

Removing his leather gloves, Tony responds, "Oh Sandra, no thank you I am fine. I really admire your creativity with your place; my wife would have a ball with your ideas."

Feeling a little at ease and feeling sure, that Tony was no associate of Doug's, a brief smile flashes across Sandra's face.

"Please have a seat at the table and you can take your coat off."

Tony, doing so, watches Sandra as she takes a seat directly across from him. "Sandra, I am not one to mince words, so I will get right to the point. My heart goes out to you in your time of loss. Not meaning any disrespect to you or purposely opening up any wounds, I am fully aware of what was done to your children and yourself. Tonight I am here to let you know that I not only feel your pain, but I also understand it."

Reaching into his Armani suit jacket pocket, Tony removes a 5x7 photo of a closed white casket. "Sandra, this is the casket of my son, Anthony Michael Marino, Jr. my only son who was murdered a few days before your children faced their sad and untimely demise. I am here Sandra because I believe the man who I have discovered through hard work, responsible for my pain is also the same man responsible for yours. Sandra that man is Doug Gunner."

Holding the photo in her hand, Sandra stares at it in silence while Tony looks on. "Sandra, I am not a stupid father, just a loving one and I know my son Michael was no angel of God, but he was still my son and the way he died at the hands of Doug I cannot forgive or forget. I am so sorry to bring my personal agendas to you during your trying times, but I really feel at this time we could help each other greatly."

Taking her eyes off the photo to look at Tony, Sandra cannot help but to feel some compassion for this man. "Tony, I have not seen or heard from Doug since the day they admitted me into the hospital. No phone calls, visits or letters. My girlfriend helped me home from the hospital, not Doug. I am sorry about the lost of your son and you too have my deepest condolences, but I have no information to give you. However, I hope for you and your family's sake, if Doug is responsible for our children's deaths, make him suffer ten times as much as we have."

Tony, reaching into his pocket, removes a business card and hands it to Sandra. "Listen, sweetheart I have many associates and friends who, through the kindness of their hearts, have elected to offer me their help in locating Doug. I have searched and located many men for lesser deeds than Doug, so I know it is just a matter of time before I locate him, but as I said to you before, any information that you gather and can pass on to me would be greatly appreciated Sandra."

Reading his card and now looking at the large but polite man, Sandra replies, "I promise you that if I call, it won't be a social one but an informative one."

Tony reaching out with his hand, gently grabs and shakes Sandra's hand as he puts on his scarf and coat. Escorting him to the entrance, Sandra unlocks and opens the door, "Take care, Sandra; you are a brave woman and may God continue to give you strength."

Nodding her head in acknowledgment, Sandra closes and locks her door. Walking back over to her dinette table, Sandra picks up, studies the business card marked Tony Marino and thinks to herself, what could have possessed Doug to shoot and kill a Mafioso's only son? Did he actually think this would just go away? Well, that was for Doug to figure out because what was on Sandra's mind at this moment was how she could use Tony as an asset in some kind of way to keep Doug away from her while she figured out what would be the safest way to get those discs to Maria Copper.

Sandra decides to simply sit down in front of her television in the dark and eat her bowl of banana crunch ice cream. It has been a long time since she has been able to enjoy just one indulgence and it could be her last, so without any more hesitation, Sandra does so.

*   *   *

It's been about an hour since Sandra sat down with her ice cream watching reruns of "The Jefferson's," but the voice that said it would torment her resurfaced in her head again and would not let her enjoy that small moment of relaxation, not even for a second. That voice wanted Sandra to know that she had work to do. "Now is not the time for enjoyment, Sandra," the voice said. "You have things to do and the planning must start right now. At this moment, you control the board and you must make your move. Bring Doug to Tony Marino and let him meet his demise. You have the bait; now just put it on the hook. Doug is desperate and he thinks you do not realize it because he has always regarded you as being stupid. Now is the time Sandra, to show him how much he has underestimated you. Get on the phone and locate your incoming calls. You will find his number and convince him that you are over your head and all you want is for him to leave you alone. Do not sound angry or upset just confused. When Doug agrees to set up this meeting, you call Tony and tell him Doug has contacted you to arrange a meeting. At that point, you will give Tony the exact time and place then you will just sit back and enjoy the show. Sandra, you must get off your ass at this very moment and act right now. Remember what I said: you have the bait, now all you have to do is act weak and defenseless reeling him in."

Sandra, sitting in front of an empty, large plastic bowl that still has the smell of banana crunch ice cream, listens as the voice slowly goes back where it came from. Looking over at her purse, Sandra walks over to it and removes her cell phone. "Shit, I have to call the post office and get my mail sent to this address instead of Doug's," says Sandra. Wondering why she just said that, Sandra shakes her head. Then just like that, the answer comes to her. "I am becoming more of a calculating thinker." Looking at her cell phone, Sandra locates Doug's number. Walking over to the sink, Sandra splashes her face with cold water and wipes it dry with a paper towel. Sitting at the dinette table, Sandra looks at her phone for a moment and presses the green button on her phone.

Doug, sitting in his living room with Jasmine naked and on his lap getting her groove on, hears his phone ring. With his eyes half closed, Doug admires the way Jasmine moves her hips from side to side. Slowly reaching for his phone on the third ring, Doug answers, "Yeah, what's up?" quickly sitting up, Doug tosses Jasmine to the side where she tumbles to the left side of Doug, almost falling off the couch. "Damn, Doug!" Jasmine yells. Raising the backside of his hand in a threatening motion, the woman quickly shuts up.

Right away, Sandra recognizes the voice of the woman that blew her only chance of escaping a while ago, posing to be a friend at the pantry. Sandra could feel her anger begin to boil but knew she had to be cool for just about five minutes.

"Doug, please pay attention to me very carefully. I want to set up a meeting so I can give you back your discs. I realize what I did was wrong and I am way over my head. Doug, I do not want anything from you; all that I ask is that you give me my freedom and allow me to move on with my life." Sandra says.

Doug, sitting and listening very carefully to Sandra's voice, can't pick up any bad vibes or reasons to believe she lying, but he still has some doubts because after all, he never expected her to have the heart and guts to steal the discs in the first place. "How the fuck do I know you are not trying to set me up, bitch? I mean you sounded very pissed off today with all of your fucking threats in all."

Sandra, clinching her teeth is doing her best to hold it together. "You know what Doug? You are going to have to trust me. All I want is my life back…nothing more and nothing less. I want to meet somewhere that is well exposed and lit where I can feel safe knowing that you will not hurt me. You know where the Valentine Avenue Park is across the street from public school nine, the same park I use to take your children. I want to meet there next Sunday at noon on the corner. I will drop the discs inside a trash bin and walk away. Doug, I am telling you that if anything happens to me, you will regret it."

Doug, feeling like he could snap Sandra's neck for giving him directives, decides to remain cool and go along with her demand. Besides, he thought to himself Sandra was nobody and knew nobody, so she was no threat. He would get what he wanted and at the same time, retain his advantage over that slimy detective Tommy Davis. He got no bad vibe from this deal, so he decided to bite. "Ok Sandra, you have got yourself a deal and I promise I will let you walk away, scouts honor."

Sandra, standing at her dinette table, responds, "Doug, you can play all you want and think I am not serious, but I am telling you that if anything happens to me, you are in a lot of trouble" feeling her heart pound faster and faster Sandra says, "Ok, Doug. You will see me on the corner dropping the disc off at noon. I will not call you anymore and please do not call me." Hanging up her phone, Sandra locates Tony Marino's card and begins to dial his number.

Doug, looking over at Jasmine, who is now sitting on the love seat smoking a joint, says quietly to himself, "I don't even need any back-up for this shit; this will be like eating cake. All I want is my discs." Getting ready to walk over to Jasmine, he hears the phone that his new organization gave him begin to ring, "Hello, this is Doug," he quietly responds.

*   *   *

Sitting at a large oak desk at his home in Greenwich Connecticut, Mr. X says "Hello Doug, Just calling to let you know that you will be picking up those three packages next Sunday starting at eight in the morning. I want the suitcase bought to me at the plaza at three in the afternoon, do you understand?"

*   *   *

With what feels like a million bullets of sweat forming on his forehead, Doug barely holds it together when answering, "Yes, I fully understand; I will deliver the keys for the currency. You can count on me...yes sir. I will see you at three." Hanging up the phone, Doug slowly exhales and takes a sip of cognac that sits on the coffee table. Looking at Jasmine, he orders, "Listen, I am busy all of a sudden; get your shit on and get out." Without uttering a word, the woman does just that.

Chapter Twenty-Seven
The Drop Off

It is a week later, Sunday morning 7:30 a.m. to be exact and Sandra, who probably slept three sound hours the night before, sits anxiously at her dinette table with her keys, cell phone and the DVD case in front of her. Immediately after agreeing with Doug concerning his discs, Sandra got on the phone with Tony, explaining almost everything to him about when and why Doug contacted her. Tony agreed and promised Sandra that he would make sure no harm would come to her. After everything went down, a car would get her away and back to her place. Sandra never explained in total detail what she was delivering to Doug because she figured it did not matter. The main objective was that she was leading Doug right to Tony and he would deal with Doug for the death of his son. Sitting at the table, Sandra did not have a sense of fear in her body or her mind, but only transformation. She started to wonder to herself was she stooping to Doug's diabolical level in going through with this plan. After all, it was a good chance this would be the last day of Doug's life and she would be somewhat responsible. All throughout her life, Sandra said to herself she had been a good person who never hurt anyone and helped everybody when asked. By going through with this plan, was she becoming as evil as Doug was? Sitting at the dinette table and thinking about the question, her inner friend showed up again.

"Sandra, I will make this short and sweet, ok? You are a good person who has suffered and endured much in the past seven years at the hands of a person who epitomizes evil. No one will miss him and in some societies Sandra, you would be a hero. Snap out of it and stop letting yourself feel sorry for this motherfucker. Remember Sandra, revenge is a dish best served cold and I will be damned if I do not make sure you feed it to Doug straight out of the motherfucking freezer. So I know and understand what you are feeling right now, but trust me; after you hear of his demise, you and your kids will rest easier."

As the voice exits her mind, Sandra looks at the photo of her children that sits atop the television and says, "Mommy will not turn back now."

As Doug drives to his first stop in the Bronx, which is the Executive Towers to be exact, he looks on the passenger seat of his vehicle and takes notice to the large silver metal suitcase that will be loaded with a little over two million dollars. Doug was trusted to deliver to his employer by 3pm this afternoon. For the first time in a while, Doug was feeling needed and he enjoyed the feeling. Never mind the fact that he did not even know the three individuals he was delivering these special keys to, it was the fact that he was apart of a special organization that trusted him with significant amounts of money. To top it off he was getting his discs back, while at the same time regaining his leverage. Doug never liked Sunday's because of what it represented, but on this particular Sunday, it all just felt right.

*   *   *

Standing in the apartment of Tito Hernandez, two large bodyguards patted Doug down. With Doug's two nickel-plated cannons located in the waist of his paints, Doug begins to remove them when Tito waives him off.

"Let him keep his weapons. I can tell it makes him feel safe," says Tito. Doug, looking around the living room, can tell Tito is gay by the huge collection of gay porn he has neatly organized in a DVD case right next to his twenty thousand dollar home theater system.

"I have your key; can we make this transaction now?" asks Doug.

"Sure Dougie, but what is the rush? Sit with me and have a cup of java."

Doug, trying to remember that this day will turn out great in a few hours, holds his temper: "My name is Doug and no thanks; let's just get this over with, please. Tito, who is wearing a skin-tight leather leopard suit, sucks his teeth and rolls his eyes at Doug while motioning to one of his large guards. As the guard leaves the room, Tito continues to stare and smile at Doug, which makes him extremely uncomfortable. The guard now reenters the living room, rolling on a food server, stacks upon stacks of clean, crisp one hundred dollar bills.

Tito, looking at Doug says, "Give me my key, you son of a bitch. I thought you wanted to be my friend."

With his eyes now shooting 357 magnum bullets at Tito, Doug is about another stupid comment away from pulling his steel and blasting gay Tito and his guards through the living room wall. Setting his suitcase on the serving tray, Doug opens it and watches the guard put the money inside. Reaching into his pocket, Doug hands over the red car key to Tito, making sure he never touches the man's hand.

"Now get the fuck out of here Doug, because you make me very sick," demands Tito. Somehow, Doug, who in the past would have smoked his ass in a second, completes the transaction and exits the apartment. Walking to the elevator, Doug removes one of his guns and cocks it just in case Tito got stupid.

Sitting in his Navigator, Doug puts the suitcase on the floor and looks at his watch. Seeing that it's 8:30 a.m., Doug feels good again knowing that the first pick-up is over and in another couple of hours, he would have his discs and completed what Mr. X had called a very important assignment. Starting up his car, Doug begins to make his way to Brooklyn for his second delivery and pick- up.

*   *   *

Ten o'clock in the morning finds Tony Marino sitting in his private social club along side four of his soldiers, who go by Frankie, Sal, Johnny and Vito, all loyal and respected workers. Sipping on cappuccino and eating bagels, the men are inspecting their weapons and listening closely to their capo.

"Sal, when she makes the drop, you start the car and get her out of there, you understand?" asks Tony.

"Yes, boss I understand. Get her out and home as soon as she makes her drop. I have the red Towncar ready; it looks just like the cabs they drive up there."

Tony, nodding his head with satisfaction, looks at his other three men: "Remember my words, ok? He is no good to me dead or shot. When he returns to his car, you move in on him quickly and get it done without drawing too much attention. If he tries to put up a fight, stun him and carry him to the car. Under no circumstances, do I want him dead, ok Johnny?"

Johnny, loading the last bullet into his clip, says, "I know you want him alive boss. I will do my best not to hurt him, yes." Feeling satisfied with his men, Tony holds his glass of cappuccino in the air to toast his men: "For Michael." His men, looking at him with some sadness on their faces, hold their glasses up and respond as one: "For Michael."

*   *   *

Eleven o'clock in the morning finds Sandra taking small sips of water from a red glass. Hoping that the water would wet her dry mouth, Sandra is disappointed because it does not. Sandra remembers what Tony told her about the red Towncar's flashing rear lights being the signal for Sandra to get in. Tony did not want Sandra to look back at Doug because he might see something in her eyes. Looking at her watch, Sandra begins to gather her coat and house keys. Glancing at the black DVD case, Sandra unzips it for the fifth time and examines its contents. Feeling satisfied, she zips it back up and looks at the clock on her wall, waiting until it reads 11:30. The door in her head opened up and Sandra could hear it coming: "Be cool, Sandra. You can do this. In another ninety minutes, you will be back home starting a new chapter in your life; all you have to do is make it through these next ninety minutes. I know you are in a zone, so I will not stay long. I just wanted to let you know how proud I am of you. Talk to you later, Sandra." As her inner companion returns to the back of her mind, Sandra calls a cab.

11:30 a.m. and Doug is inspecting the large, steel-like suitcase that sits on the passenger side seat of his SUV. Looking around Astoria Boulevard, Doug notices the many people going to church. Focusing back on the money and wondering to himself how two million dollars could fit so perfectly inside the case, it just reconfirms how organized and precise his new employers were. Looking up at the sun and feeling how warm it was becoming for a Sunday in the middle of winter, Doug cannot help but to let a good feeling inside him expose itself. The last two deliveries went beautifully, and he was right on schedule on getting his discs back. Doug had never felt guilt for anything he has done in his life, not even setting up his family. As far as he was concerned, all parties knew what they were getting into when they came together. No, it was not guilt he was feeling towards Sandra but strangely compassion. That is why after picking up the last of the money walking back to his truck; Doug decided that he would let Sandra walk. The way he saw it, what could she do to him? She was afraid and confused, probably planning to go back to Virginia. She was always weak and scared; besides, Sandra knew that at any time, Doug could reach out from the streets and touch her. He knew she did not want to live like that, so as far as he was concerned, in about twenty-five minutes, he would never see the woman he thought he loved again, so he decided it was ok to let her live.

*　*　*

It is 11:57 a.m., and Sandra is sitting in her cab on the corner of 183rd Street and Valentine Avenue. She is diagonally across from the park when her heart starts to race because she now spots Doug's red Navigator approaching. The man responsible for the deaths of the two people that loved her unconditionally. The truck has slowly come to a stop on the corner of Valentine Avenue right in front of public school nine.

Looking in the opposite direction, Sandra locates the red Towncar that Tony had promised would be there to take her home. Looking at her trembling hands, Sandra squeezes them tight in an effort to get them under control. The only words that come to her mind are "be cool" as she firmly grabs the leather case and pays the cab driver. Taking one more deep breath, Sandra slowly exits the cab.

Doug, looking at the woman who went through eight hours of labor and prepared his meals everyday for seven years, tries his best to push away the memories of the first night he noticed her on the dance floor. He cannot because he now realizes no matter how cold-hearted a man could be you never just erase seven years of events and memories from your life. "Snap out of it," Doug says softly to himself. Looking at her face, he can see that she is no longer the smiling and bubbly Virginian woman that knocked his socks off; no, this woman was emotionless and battered. She had now transformed into a wounded and scarred victim that he was fully responsible for creating. As her green scarf lowered as she walked, the white bandages that meant to heal her neck was clear for Doug to see. This strengthened his decision even more just to let her go.

Sandra, crossing the street and walking towards the garbage can where she had told Doug she would drop the discs, adjusts her scarf, to conceal the bandages. Getting closer to the garbage can, Sandra looks at the flashing red lights of the car that would take her home in a few moments. "Be cool, Sandra" she said softly as she is now a few yards away from the garbage bin. With her eyes, she quickly surveys the area because no matter how calm this Sunday afternoon seemed, Sandra obviously had her reasons to stay fully alert and not to ever underestimate Doug, who she could feel was watching every step she made. Now being able to see the contents of the garbage bin that consist of beer bottles, fast food wrappers and dirty snow, Sandra pulls the black case from under her arm and gently sets it on top of the metal-caged bin. With her eyes, circling the area at one hundred miles an hour, Sandra then makes a sharp right turn, walking towards the red Towncar that waits for her with the engine running. Now ten feet away from the car, Sandra never takes her eyes off Doug's vehicle that sits diagonally across from her direction. Reaching out, Sandra grabs the back door handle of the car, firmly pulling it open and quickly getting inside.

Looking at the grey-haired Sal, who smells like High Karate aftershave, Sandra calmly requests with a little quiver in her voice, "Excuse me, sir; can we go now, please?" Never looking back or saying a word to Sandra, the neatly dressed Sal puts the car in drive and proceeds to take Sandra home. Looking back through the smoked rearview window, Sandra stares at the red Navigator until she can see it no more. "Half way there," Sandra quietly says to herself as she sinks into the plush leather seating of the Towncar.

Realizing how easy this would be, Doug still makes sure that his guns are ready for use if needed. Putting on his shades, he unlocks his door and steps out into the bright sunshine that warms his baldhead. Looking around him as he slowly walks in the direction of the trash bin, Doug looks at every person that he passes with a little suspicion, trying not to get too comfortable. Jumping over a pile of water and slush landing on the sidewalk, Doug gets closer to his prized possession that will give him back the leverage he craves. Now a few feet away from the trash bin, he can spot the leather case sitting on garbage and snow. Letting a smile come to his face, Doug grabs the package admiring it for a few moments, then turns around to walk back to his vehicle. Walking with some bravado, Doug hits his remote switch that unlocks the door of his SUV. Stepping inside and taking a seat with little regards to where he just got the case, Doug gives it a long kiss as if it were a woman's lips.

Unknown to Doug, sitting directly behind him in a black sedan are Frankie, Vito and Johnny, who quickly check for their weapons. Johnny, removing a lead pipe from his shirt, slowly opens his door while Vito takes out his stun gun and gets out on his side of the car. Frankie, who is the driver, calmly starts up the car and waits inside. Without saying a word, they quickly walk to Doug's SUV.

Reaching for his keys that he laid on the passenger seat while he admired his case, Doug sticks the key into the ignition and begins to start his car up when from the drivers' side his window explodes causing what seems like millions of glass particles to hit Doug in the face and landing in his lap. Covering his face, Doug shouts, "Oh shit!" as he tries to regain focus. Able to see from his right eye, Doug notices a baseball bat coming towards his passenger side window. Covering his face, there is another loud smash that shatters that window. Reaching for his gun, Doug's left hand is struck with a pipe by Johnny:

"Oh shit, motherfucker!" Doug yells out in pain, feeling as if his hand is broken. Looking to his right he can see Vito pulling from his coat a funny-shaped gun. As Vito reaches inside the broken car window to open the door, Doug is able to raise his right leg and kick Vito's hand with such force that he smashes it on broken glass, cutting it open. Letting out a loud yell, Vito is able to pull his hand back: "Johnny, hit this fucking eggplant, come on!" yells Vito as he tries to point and aim the stun gun with his one good hand. Johnny, who is fat, is gasping for air as he tries to get another clean shot but is thwarted by Doug, who grabs the pipe. Johnny wrestles the pipe away from Doug, whose hand has swollen to the size of a grapefruit. Johnny hits Doug across the chest with the pipe but not as hard as the hit on the hand. Doug, still feeling the pain of the blow, is able to grab Johnny by his hair and smash his face into the steering wheel, causing the man's nose to split almost in half, shooting blood all over Doug's dashboard.

"Oh, fuck me!" Johnny yells as he grabs his now crimson-colored face, falling to the street in pain. With his good hand, Doug is able to turn the ignition, starting the SUV and now begins to put the gear in drive when Vito jumps through the passenger side window landing his upper body on top of the suitcase, which sits on the seat. Doug, with his right hand on the steering wheel, removes it to pound Vito as hard as he can on his neck and back:

"Get the fuck out, motherfucker!" Doug yells. Looking from his side view mirror, Doug spots another man, who is Frankie, getting out of the black sedan with a pistol. With all of his strength, Doug is able to lift Vito up by his coat pushing him back out of the window. Quickly putting his Navigator into drive, Doug slams down violently on his gas peddle, causing a loud screeching noise as his rear tires begin to smoke. Almost jumping the curb, Doug makes a quick left on Valentine Avenue, running through a red light as he heads towards Fordham road. Breathing hard and wiping glass particles away from his face, Doug looks in his rearview mirror and can faintly see the three men helping each other back into their car. Thinking that they are about to give chase, Doug pushes harder down on the gas, asking the SUV to release some of those three hundred horses. Looking again in his mirror, Doug does not see them behind him and quickly looks for his discs, which are lying on the floor. Feeling the throbbing of his hand returning, Doug looks at his left hand in total disgust, as it is no longer dark brown but red and blue. Sweating and wide-eyed, Doug looks at the passenger seat and instantly, he slams on his brakes, stopping at the corner of Fordham road:

"Oh shit! What the fuck!" Looking all throughout the SUV, Doug smashes his good hand four times on his bloody steering wheel as he now discovers the steel suitcase with the two million dollars is gone. Letting out a horrific scream that grabs the attention of some people, who stop and stare into the vehicle, Doug slowly shakes his head as he quickly turns on Fordham Road and drives in the direction of his apartment.

*   *   *

With less than two hours to go before Mr. X. expects the delivery of the two million dollars, a dejected and exhausted Doug sits on his couch with his hand covered with a Ziploc bag of ice. Looking around his large and quiet living room, Doug tries to put all of today's events together. Looking at his hideous left hand that resembles a club, Doug visualizes the men who assaulted him this afternoon and cannot figure out who they are or represent. One thing Doug is sure about though is they did not want him dead because they could have used their guns instead of their pipes.

Another thing that pounded at his head was why, minutes after Sandra dropped off the discs, did those cats show up at his truck? What could be the connection? Wiping sweat off his face, Doug could not find one simply because Sandra was a weak and stupid woman who had no guts or heart to attempt to plan something against anyone, especially him.

Looking at his diamond-studded movado watch, Doug says softly, "Just have to tell them the truth about getting robbed. Just tell them what happened." However, in his heart he knew that this could be suicide. He would have to explain why he was sitting in his truck on the corner with a little over two million dollars in his possession, instead of at home with the money hidden in a secure place until the delivery. He could not explain it, so Doug decided he would go to this meeting prepared not only to die but also to take some people with him. Looking to his right, he still, even through all of the madness, is able to smile because he had his precious discs.

Forgetting about his pain for a moment, Doug reaches over, picks up the leather bag and slowly unzips it, smiling as he does so. Not knowing it, Doug begins to hyperventilate, as his eyes get large as saucers. Slowly flipping through the book, Doug's eyes become very moist and misty as his head feels like someone is hitting him repeatedly with an aluminum baseball bat. Now flipping through the book faster, Doug unconsciously smashes his swollen hand on his wooden coffee table. Now sitting in front of him is the greatest collection of black films of all time from the 70's: *Foxy Brown, Across 110th Street, Abby, Uptown Saturday night, Three the hard way, Claudine, Cotton comes to Harlem, Hell up in Harlem* and *Blacula*. All for Doug to enjoy while he tried to figure out how some weak and dumb chick made him look like the biggest jackass in the world.

Reaching into his jacket, Doug removes his nickel-plated, semi-automatic magnum and holds the barrel of the gun to his face, rubbing it slowly across his nose and near his mouth. Beginning to weep, the man with the body made from granite, slowly moves the gun back and forth, letting it hit his teeth that make a tapping noise. Looking back at the assortment of movies, Doug slowly slides the shaft of the gun, looking at the one bullet that sits inside the chamber. Sitting all the way back on his couch, Doug slowly closes his eyes as he gently puts the barrel of the gun in his mouth and cocks it.

"There is no good reason" was the only thing that he could think of as he lets the taste of steel overtake his taste buds. Leaning his head back, Doug lets his mind think of a black chalkboard with him sitting in a chair looking straight at it. With his index finger, Doug begins to squeeze the trigger that would splatter his brains and skull all over the wall when his father, Fred Gunner, enters the empty room wearing his old bathrobe and his grey slippers that his wife bought him on Father's Day many moons ago. He is holding a piece of chalk in his hand.

Trying to push his father out of the room, Doug cannot because he never was able to push his father out of the way. With his finger still on the trigger, Doug listens to the deep baritone voice of his dad:

"Boy, what kind of man did I raise? I knew your ass was weak like your momma. Look at your stupid ass getting ready to let some bitch make you kill yourself like a goddamn coward. You pay all that damn money on that shrink because of all the shit I did to you and this is your answer for dealing with some country bitch?"

Fred, now letting out a loud hard laugh coming from the bottom of his gut, causes Doug to weep louder.

"Oh, shut the fuck up boy and take that goddamn gun out of your mouth!" Fred demands.

Doug, still sobbing, asks, "Why can't you love me and look out for me? I love you!"

Shaking his head and sucking his teeth, Fred answers, "Cause I ain't shit, that's why! You ain't shit, yo momma wasn't shit and I never got love from nobody, so how in the fuck could I give it to your dumb ass? Now I ain't got time for this shit, so if you want some revenge, you better pay attention and read, stupid."

Walking up to the chalkboard, Fred begins to write as Doug slowly removes the gun from his mouth. After a few seconds, Fred moves to the side so Doug can see what he has written. On the board in white chalk is the underlined word "Friends" and under that are three names "Carla," "Rose" and "Pamela." Doug, studying what is on the board, looks at his father whose eyes are now tomato red, just like someone living in hell.

"Take your ass to that meeting and do whatever you have to do to buy you some time and when you get that time, use it to flush Sandra out of her little hole before she leaves for the city with your discs. Everybody has a weakness stupid and hers is love for her friends. Use them to get her out and when she comes out you had better reopen that gash on her throat. Now get your ass up and be the fucking man that I raised."

Watching his father leave the room, Doug studies the chalkboard etching those names inside his head. Sitting up slowly from the couch, Doug looks at the movies one more time before picking them up and violently tossing them across the living room. Looking at his watch, Doug sees that he as about seventy-five minutes before his meeting. Getting up and walking over to his closet, he removes some fresh clothes along with a bulletproof vest. Looking in a mirror that sits inside his closet door, Doug looks at himself and says "Thanks, Dad."

D.J. Murray

Chapter Twenty-Eight
Meetings and Decisions

In Bensonhurst, Brooklyn, Tony sits in his social club office looking at an injured Johnny and Vito, who are pretty beaten up physically and somewhat bruised emotionally. Frankie, trying not to catch Tony's eye, stands off on the far side of the room next to a jukebox.

"Somebody please explain to me how one man could get away when both of you were practically inside his car?" asks Tony.

With everyone sitting in silence and their heads pointed to the ground, Johnny finally speaks, "Boss, on my son's eyes, we did everything the way you asked; I just feel he was expecting us."

Tony, looking at his soldier, replies, "Johnny, you are stupid, please sit down. Who could have tipped him off? The only people who knew of our plan are the ones standing in this room." Walking over from his desk and standing in the middle of the room, Tony picks up a baseball bat and begins to imitate a baseball player swinging in the "on deck" circle.

"You all understand he could be miles away now, don't you? The job was so simple and now I have to explain to my dead son's mother that her boy's killer is still on the loose. Do you understand how embarrassing that will be?"

Standing up from his chair, Vito looks somberly at his boss and says, "Tony, you have to know that Michael was like a son to all of us, and we would never do anything to screw up your plans on bringing that bastard to justice. We honestly tried everything in our power to bring him in as you asked us, unharmed and not dead. I understand your disappointment, but put us back out there and let us bring him in."

Calmly walking over to a table that sits near his desk, Tony violently begins smashing the large silver suitcase that was taken from Doug's truck. The three men look on nervously in silence, not daring to say a word to their furious leader. After about nine consecutive whacks, a sweating and heavy breathing Tony stops to look at the severely dented suitcase: "What the fuck is in this suitcase?" Tony asks.

Coming from the back of the room, Frankie answers, "We have no idea, Boss; during the fight, we were able to get our hands on it, so we grabbed it."

Looking quickly around the room, Tony walks over to his desk, opening the middle drawer, removing a hammer. Walking back over to the suitcase, Tony looks at his men, who are staring at him. Kneeling down and taking careful aim, Tony smacks the locks of the suitcase with the hammer until the latches pop open. With his men feeling a little more comfortable, they form a small circle around the suitcase and wait for their boss to open it. Looking at the anticipation on their faces, Tony slowly pulls up the top portion of the suitcase and is now looking at neatly stacked and wrapped one hundred dollar bills totaling more than two million dollars. Looking at his men, Tony lets a small smirk come across his face and says, "We still got a chance; Doug ain't leaving town yet.

*   *   *

With some minor scratches on his face and his left hand heavily wrapped, Doug rides the elevator to the presidential suite of the Westin Hotel in Manhattan. Feeling for his gun that sits in the back of his waistline and the bulletproof vest that covers his chest, Doug takes a deep dose of oxygen, while looking up at the red floor indicator inside the elevator. With the sound of the bell, Doug takes three steps forward as the doors open he begins to walk towards suite 3211 where he would do his best in explaining the situation at hand. Walking down the beautifully painted hallway decorated with pastel paintings on both sides of the walls and three-inch plush blue carpeting, he turns the corner and is about thirty feet away from the suite door. At the door are two guards who Doug has never met or seen. Stopping at the door, Doug looks at the guards, who are both wearing telephone headsets and long leather trench coats that, more than likely, conceal heavy artillery.

"Good afternoon. I am here for my three o'clock meeting with Mr. X."

One of the guards, looking at Doug and showing no expression, presses a button on his headset

"Sir, Mr. Gunner is here; may I send him in?"

Nodding to his partner, he opens the door for Doug using a magnetic card. As he walks past them and through the door, Doug is not surprised that they do not frisk him, being that he has yet given them any reason not to trust him. With the door closing behind him, a beautiful light-skinned female, looking to be in her early thirties, greets him: "Hello, Mr. Gunner. Would you like a drink?"

Doug, blinded by the woman's beauty, can only shake his head no.

"Well, ok, but if you change your mind, please do not hesitate to ask me. Now, if you would please follow me, I will take you to Mr. X." she says.

As Doug follows the woman through the suite, he is now facing two large mahogany doors with brass handles.

"Please, Mr. Gunner, go in; he is expecting you."

As the woman retreats to another section of the suite, Doug puts on a face of coolness and enters the room.

Sitting at a large desk, wearing a black pinstriped suit is Doug's boss, who has a smile on his face and a lit cigar in his hand. At his side are two more guards that he has never seen before. The first thing that comes to Doug's mind is "I have seventeen shots in my clip, so far I have seen four guards who are all probably armed and one female who I cannot underestimate because of her beauty. If this whole thing falls apart, I have to be prepared to fire first and ask questions later." Looking at his smiling boss, Doug manages to exhale unnoticed.

"Doug, how are you? Glad to see you are on time, but I just have one question for you: I see that your hands are empty, which means my two million dollars is somewhere else. Can you explain to me why it is not here on my desk?"

Looking at his boss, Doug knew the situation was intense. The only thing left to do was explain what happened, wait for Mr. X.'s reaction and do his best to respond. Mr. X. lighting a cigar and taking a few slow puffs does not offer Doug a seat, he just motions to him to answer his question.

* * *

It takes Doug twenty minutes to explain to his boss what happened to him this afternoon in full detail, not hiding or leaving out anything, except Sandra. Figuring no matter what should go down; at least he was honest to his boss about the money. Doug standing straight up faces Mr. X, waiting for his response. Taking another puff of the Cuban stogie, Mr. X turns away from Doug so that he is facing the window that overlooks the Manhattan skyline.

"Doug, I am in the business of transactions, and today you gave three men three different keys that will open trunks to three different cars. In each of those trunks sits fifty-six keys of pure Colombian cocaine that each one of those men you dealt with today gave you six hundred and sixty-six thousand dollars. Now using practical math that equals roughly two million dollars that you were suppose to deliver to me in what we call a transaction. According to you, though, there was a bump in the road that will not allow that transaction to take place today."

Standing and looking at the back of his boss's head, Doug has the urge to act first and blow the two guards standing at the sides of the desk away and then pump Mr. X. full of lead, but he holds his composure instead. Doug, not feeling nervous or anxious anymore is upset because of two reasons. First, he is upset because of the way his boss speaks to him as if he was a child. Secondly, who was this person to turn his back on him? The way Doug saw it, no matter what the situation; you always look another man in his eyes when dealing with him. It did not matter if you were going to kill him or hug him; you do it with respect by looking in his eyes. With his hands at his side, Doug kept alert and waited.

"Doug, I am going to be clear to you about this situation. Obviously, you did not take my advice when I told you to handle your business and personal affairs of your previous life when you became part of this organization. You did not take heed to my advice, so now a penalty must be paid," says Mr. X." Taking a quick glance at the guards, Doug figures he can get two shots off before they reach inside their jackets and just maybe get out of this suite alive. Turning around in his chair, Mr. X continues, "Doug, at this very moment, you will not be allowed to earn money from this organization until your debt is paid or our money is found and returned. How long this situation last depends on how good of a worker you are. You will have an unspecified amount of time to pay back your debt by working or simply finding our money. You must understand though that your time is unspecified and limited. As usual, we will notify you when to make your drop-off, but your fifteen percent commission now belongs to us. So without wasting any more of your precious time, this meeting is adjourned."

Reaching into his desk drawer, Doug's boss pulls out a package and tosses it to him, which infuriates Doug even more. Now knowing that he will leave the suite with his life, Doug swallows his pride and takes the insult.

"Doug we will stay in touch and you may now show yourself out," says Mr. X. Turning away slowly but doing so without showing them he was suspicious, Doug makes it out of the suite with his life. Walking past the guards posted outside the door, he heads for the elevators, still not feeling totally secure.

Sitting in his Navigator that still lacks side front windows, Doug looks at his work package thinking to himself, "I have no other options but to skim a little off the top and use that to survive until I can figure out how to get the money back. But first things first; I need to spread some of my pain and frustration on to others." Starting his truck, Doug begins to make his way to the West side highway to go home.

* * *

It is 5:00 p.m. and Sandra is watching the news or at least trying. With all that has happened today, she finds it very hard to focus. She has not received a phone call from Tony Marino informing her of what has become of Doug. Not feeling she has the right to call and ask him how everything went down, Sandra does the only thing possible, even though it scares the hell out of her and that is to assume that Doug is still alive, which meant she had to be alert and act fast in turning over the discs. She had the urge to call her friend Pamela, who she had not spoken to or seen in about a week, but she puts it off a little while longer because she knew other things had to be dealt with first. Picking up her cell phone while looking at Maria Copper report on a special investigation involving credit card frauds on the elderly, Sandra dials information for the telephone number for news channel four. After getting the number, Sandra turns off the television and looks at the discs that she has placed in a plastic bag.

"Ok, Sandra this is it, the moment you have worked and planned for. All you have to do is make the phone call and get the instructions on how you would go about getting the discs to Ms. Copper," Sandra says to herself. Sandra understands that if Doug were alive, he would know she had something to do with him being set up. On top of that, he would be twice as furious seeing what was inside that DVD case. Sandra knew she had to walk quietly as possible on the streets because Doug would have everyone he knew out there on the look out for her, and maybe a few of them were out there to kill her on Doug's command. Whatever the case, she knew the stakes were high. Looking at her cell phone, Sandra picks it up and dials Channel Four News. "Hello, I am a concerned citizen with a question: How would I go about getting information to special investigator Maria Copper involving murder and corruption?"

Chapter Twenty-Nine
Doug Strikes Back

Only getting three hours of sleep a night for the past two weeks, Doug has spent the other twenty-one hours putting together a plan to make things right while making twice the amount of money he was before to repay his debt. Thinking of Sandra for the majority of his waking days, Doug never reminisced about the days when they first met and shared many nights having fun enjoying each other's time. No, Doug spent the majority of his time picturing Sandra sitting wherever she was, laughing at him and gloating to herself how she made him look like a complete fool on that Sunday afternoon. Doug hated Sandra for rubbing it in his face that she was not as dumb as he thought she was. Doug also thought long and hard about how convenient it was for Sandra to enter a car that did not resemble a cab and leave the scene right before the ambush. Yes, Doug was beginning to put some things together while he labored his body and mind throughout most of the day. Make no mistake; he underestimated the feeble and dense woman from the south. Doug made a promise that from this point on he would make sure that he utilized every second to make things right. It was time to make Sandra suffer some more for taking his discs and Doug believed he knew just what to do. Therefore, Doug's plan was to have some of his old friends causally hang around that food pantry where Sandra has not been in some time, hoping she would feel comfortable and stupid enough to show her face. Doug also had a couple of his friends follow Pamela to the train station from a distance every morning so that he could learn her patterns and routes.

One night, with his old pal Bucky, Doug explained his plan and asked him to be ready on notice. He told Bucky it had to be fast and precise simply because time was of the essence. Always a loyal friend, Bucky assured Doug he would lend his assistance when needed.

As far as his debt went, Doug was spending a lot of his nightlife in the Wall Street area getting to know stock traders and executive wannabees who worked eighteen hours a day, always needing a jolt of energy to meet that deadline. Doug discovered that with all their college degrees, they knew nothing about the economics of the drug game. They only had one objective, which was to get high at almost any price. With him having the best quality cocaine, he charged them double compared to what he was getting on the streets in Harlem. That was something his mentor "Dollar Bill" told him: "The money is out there; you just have to sniff it out" and that is what he did. Doug wanted to kick himself in the ass for not finding these pinstripe boys years ago. It was so easy; all Doug had to do was hang by the nearby coffee shop, making sure to give the owner a little piece and like flies to shit, the zombies would come to him for nose candy. In repaying back the organization, Doug was able to pay twice as much, while at the same time keeping a little off the top for himself. Mr. X. respected Doug for never complaining about his punishment of paying back the two million dollars. Doug's goal was to get back into the good graces of the organization. Doug also hooked up with a blue-eyed blonde-haired woman, who admired his hustle and his penis, helping him invest five thousand a week into stocks and commodities. Yes, three hours a night sleep was just fine for Doug because he was accomplishing a lot with his time.

*   *   *

It is Friday morning, and Doug sits in the back of the coffee shop looking over the *Wall Street Journal* and drinking a cinnamon latte, checking on his new portfolio that is growing rapidly. Looking at his watch, Doug can see that it is time, so he dials a number on his cell phone: "Bucky it is now time to unleash hell; spare no one who gets in the way and make sure you call me when you deliver them to the spot." Hanging up the phone Doug watches the young server bring him an apple danish.

*   *   *

The pantry is three-quarters full this morning more than likely because of the seasonable weather outside. Ms. Carla is helping a new girl named April serve breakfast, which consists of oatmeal, milk, juice and fruit. The people are quiet, knowing that Ms. Carla does not take kindly to loud chatter. Also helping is Rose, who is pouring fresh water into glasses that sit on the tables. Looking around at the men and women who eat at her pantry every morning, she stops to admire the good work she has been allowed to do over the years: "Thank you Lord, for giving me the strength to help those in need," Carla quietly says to herself.

As Carla helps April evenly divide the fruit into the plastic cups, a thunderous noise causes Carla to turn holding her chest and April to let out a scream. With the people looking up at the main entry doors being violently kicked open, eight tall and muscular men walk into the pantry, led by Bucky. As three men cover the entrance door, five others make their way throughout the pantry, making sure no one escapes or gets up from their seat. A cold and quiet fear has come across the orange painted pantry where bright sunshine comes through the large windows. All of Bucky's men stand silently with hands at their side, each holding an automatic weapon. A few women, who bring their children to the pantry to eat, begin to shed tears as they shelter and comfort their children, who are all terrified. Standing in the center of the room, Bucky looks and smiles at the many faces that feared for their safety.

"Good morning ladies and gentlemen, please do be alarmed at the very men that stand before you holding guns. I do promise you that if anyone gets out of their seat and attempts to run, they will see their last bowl of oatmeal today. I give you my word, we will not be here for long and once we leave, you can carry on with your glamorous lives. So please just stay calm and this will be over in a moment."

A menacing but smiling Bucky, who stands about six feet four inches tall, is wearing a black leather vest with nothing underneath. His arms are huge and covered with tattoos of tigers and guns. As Bucky walks towards the large service table where fresh oatmeal and cereal sit, Carla, trying her best to hide her fear, while leading her second family through this ordeal, looks into Bucky's eyes not with defiance but with compassion. Bucky now inches in front of the grey-haired woman asks, "Are you Carla?"

Setting the large wooden spoon that is stained with oatmeal on the table while still giving comfort to a much shaken April, Carla answers, "Yes, I am, young man."

With a smile on his face, Bucky gently puts one of his large arms around Carla's shoulder. "Carla, this will not take long; I just need to ask you a few questions in private. Is there a place were we can chat?" asks Bucky.

At this point, Carla is feeling very nervous of the coldness in Bucky's touch but still continues to do her best in hiding it, as she answers, "There is a coat room right over there," pointing to a green colored room.

Slowly leading Carla to the room, April whimpers, "No, she did not do anything. Why does she have to go back there?" Carla smiles at April while holding her hand up in a gesture to show that everything will be fine, as she walks with Bucky to the coatroom. Meanwhile, sitting in the back of the pantry, Rose looks on in silence as one of the men stands directly to her left, holding a tech nine machine gun.

As Bucky slowly closes the door behind Carla and himself, he grabs a metal chair so he can sit down while Carla stands.

"Carla, the first thing I want you to understand is that I am not one of those old-school cats who believes in respecting someone based on age and gender, so because you are an old grey-haired woman, do not think for a fucking second I give a fuck about you. I am not here to learn how to bake cookies, I am here for one reason and that is to find out where your good friend Sandra Lyte is hiding. Now, you have to understand that I am not leaving here without some information, so whatever useful info you give me will go a long way in insuring not only your friends' safety but yours also."

Sitting with the chair turned around, Bucky removes a stick of gum from his vest and sticks it in his mouth, never removing it from the wrapper. "Sir, Sandra has not been here for a few months now and she never told me where she was going or staying so…"

Without letting her finish, Bucky quickly leaps out of his chair and pushes Carla violently into the coat rack, causing her to fall to the ground. Standing over her, Bucky spits the gum into Carla's face. Holding her chest, Carla is struggling to catch her breath.

"I hope your heart is still in good condition because right now lady, I am in a good mood, but you are not making this easy," says Bucky. Reaching down, he grabs Carla by one of her arms forcing her to her feet and sitting her in the chair. Still breathing hard and fast, Carla, for the first time, has the look of fear in her eyes and Bucky can see it. "Where is Sandra, old woman?" Bucky asks again.

Looking around the room with a face of confusion, Carla answers, "Sir, please have mercy on me; I am not lying when I tell you she just volunteered her time. We never discussed personal matters."

Kneeling down to Carla, a grinning Bucky slowly rubs his sausage-like fingers through her hair. "Is that your final answer?" he asks.

No longer able to hold back her tears, Carla begins to sob a little louder. Looking at the woman and twisting his head from side to side, Bucky, with the quickness of a rattlesnake, snaps his right fist on Carla's nose, breaking and causing blood to spill from it. With tears, swelling up in her eyes, Carla's head snaps back, and she almost falls from the chair, but Bucky prevents her from doing so.

"So, you really don't know anything, mama?" he asks. Carla is trying not to pass out as her once white apron has stains of her blood.

Staring up at Bucky and knowing her heart could give out at any moment, Carla looks up at the huge smiling man trying to regain her focus and says, "You are a piece of garbage, I promise you God will make your soul burn in hell for what you have done." Letting her head slump back down, Carla remains silent.

Bucky, who is no longer smiling, grabs Carla by her hair, yanking her head up so she is able to look in his eyes. "Fuck you old woman; my life is already hell and God can do no worse to me than I already done to myself." Knocking Carla out of the chair and onto the floor, Bucky proceeds to kick her in the ribs with his steel-toe boots.

* * *

After a few moments, Bucky reappears to the worried and frightened people, who still sit in silence. Upon seeing that he is alone and not with Carla, a few people start to cry. A man named Stanley, who is a retired veteran, slowly stands to his feet: "Where is Carla? What have you done to her?"

From behind one of the gunmen smacks Stanley over the head, knocking him out cold. Little children start to cry as panic starts to fill the pantry. Bucky, holding a small photograph in his hand starts to scan the faces of the people like a hawk. Slowly moving his head from side to side, Bucky brings it to a complete stop, looking directly into the eyes of Rose.

Now smiling, Bucky says, "Come on over here, Boo Boo." Rose, wearing a red hooded sweater and blue jeans, looks around for help but gets none from the frightened spectators. Slowly getting up from her table, Rose begins to cry as Bucky, who is holding a gun in his hand gently grabs Rose by the hand and caresses her face with the weapon.

"Don't cry, baby. Uncle Buck is going to take real good care of you; just don't upset me, Ok?" Looking at his watch, Bucky points to his men, who in turn harness their weapons.

"Ok everyone like I said earlier, if you all behaved, nobody would get hurt and as far as I can tell, only two people did not behave, that brother laying on the floor and your fearless fucking leader in the back. Therefore, without further ado, it is time for us to go. No one had better leave his or her seats. I will have a person right outside looking in and he will shoot anyone who does not follow those rules. So goodbye peasants and enjoy your lumpy oatmeal." Squeezing Rose tighter by her slender shoulder, Bucky takes the young woman out the pantry doors while his men follow.

People still sit at their tables with concerned looks on their faces wondering what to do next. April, looking towards the coatroom and at the entrance doors, looks at the others, who sit still.

"I have to go and check on Carla, so stay in your seats."

A woman holding her two-year-old son whispers, "Ms. April please; we do not know if that man was telling the truth about us being watched."

Shaking her head at the woman, April says, "You just stay in your seats; I will be ok" Looking at the door, April slowly makes her way to the other side of the serving tables. Keeping her eyes on the entrance doors, April walks at a brisk pace until she is standing at the entrance of the coatroom. As the people sit at their tables, the man struck on his head begins to regain consciousness. From the coatroom comes a faint scream because April has just discovered a bloodied and lifeless Carla on the floor.

*   *   *

Some time has passed and the police are questioning some of the people who were inside the pantry, the paramedics rush Carla, who is on a stretcher, into an ambulance with April joining her. With the sound of the blaring sirens, the ambulance speeds off with many people standing by the pantry crying loudly, wondering if their guardian angel will ever be the same again.

*   *   *

Pamela, leaving the neighborhood 99-cent store, walks to her building, which is about a block and a half away. Being careful as she walks on the snow-covered ice, Pamela stays close to the curb never taking notice to the grey sedan that has been slowly moving along side of her.

"Hi, Santiago," Pamela yells at the man who owns the corner bodega. Getting closer to her building, Pamela removes her keys with her sobriety-colored key holders from her pocket, when the grey sedan pulls quickly in front of her building, coming to a screeching halt. Looking around her surroundings cautiously, Pamela stops a few feet short of her courtyard looking at the car when the doors quickly open up and jumping out with guns waving in their hands are three large men all wearing sunglasses. One of the men whose name is "Sugar Bear" leads the charge towards Pamela, who drops her bags and tries to run in the opposite direction.

"Somebody help me!" screams Pamela when Sugar Bear runs up from behind her, grabbing her by her coat collar and sticking a nickel-plated gun in her face.

"Bitch, if you scream again, I will blow your fucking brains out."

Shaking and looking around frantically, Pamela is grabbed by two other men and thrown into the waiting car. Sugar Bear, looks around to see if they have been noticed. Not seeing any witnesses, he hurries into the driver's side of the car, takes off down the street and heads to the club where Bucky awaits him.

*   *   *

It is Friday evening, 6:00 p.m. to be exact and in the basement of Doug's club is a small, poorly lit room that stinks from the aroma of urine. The floor is made of concrete that is very cold and extremely damp. It is no bigger then a cheap motel bathroom and a person standing six feet tall would have to bend down to walk inside. The light bulb, which cannot be any stronger than thirty-five watts, flickers and is ready to burn out at any moment. Above the paint-chipped ceiling is a water pipe that drips hot, scalding water one drop at a time at the rate of a drip every five seconds. Inside this room is Rose Garden sitting in a puddle of urine mixed with dirty water. Her mouth is swollen and her left eye shut from the butt of Bucky's gun. Rose's hands are tied in front of her with duct tape and while her legs are free, she can barely walk on the count of her right ankle, badly bruised from Bucky stomping on it a few hours earlier. Rose is shaking like a leaf and her stomach has been making rumbling noises the moment they locked her inside the room. With her head slumped over into her chest, the young woman, just in her early twenties, makes whimpering noises. Sobbing, "Please, just kill me, God, just kill me now," Rose waits for her prayers to be answered, as she grimaces with pain as the drops of scalding water continue to hit her back creating a blister the size of a half a dollar.

Trying to erase the pain of her ankle from her mind, Rose using every ounce of strength in her body, is able to move a foot over to her right where the water no longer hits her back, but in the process, she badly scrapes her knee on a small piece of glass. With a stinging sensation now coming from her knee, Rose gladly accepts the trade off from the scalding water.

"Please God, just bring me to you. I can not take anymore," says a pleading Rose, who is now finding herself sitting up against the wall instead of on her knees. Closing her eyes, Rose begins to rock her body back and forth. The flickering light is no more as it has decided to quit and let darkness take over. Rose, holding her head up, sees nothing, so she continues to rock and cry, still hoping for the end to come. Shivering and shaking, Rose lets out a quick scream as she feels a cold sensation on her neck. The sensation is the breath of someone who smells of rotting and burning flesh, which gives Rose hives all over her body.

"Hi baby, how is Daddy's little girl?" The man who smells like death asks. Slowly opening her eyes, Rose tries to scream but nothing comes out. Knelling before Rose is her dad, Butch, who is smiling and is about three inches away from Rose's face.

Rubbing his daughter's face with his burnt and sticky skinless hands, he whispers, "Daddy misses his baby; do you miss Daddy? I miss all of my children, especially you, baby." Slowly standing to his feet Butch begins to remove his clothes, revealing his charcoaled, burnt body. As his clothes come off, his remaining skin does as well, exposing his ribs and pumping black heart. Now naked and standing over his daughter, who is unable to move, Butch smiles as he grabs on to his smoldering penis that falls from his body and into his hand.

"Daddy forgives you baby, just let daddy touch you one last time." Kneeling down to her, Butch opens his mouth and sticks out his black tongue, aiming it towards Rose's mouth. As he gets closer and closer, Rose lets out a loud scream, smacking her father in the face, knocking his laughing head off his shoulders as his hands still reach out to her. Waving and punching, a screaming Rose awakens to the still flickering light and the empty room that still smells like urine. Her entire body covered in sweat, the young woman can only continue to cry.

*   *   *

What feels like hours has only been thirty minutes as Rose is losing sensation in one of her legs as it begins to lose circulation. Her mouth completely dry and stomach aching tremendously from hunger, Rose's eyes widen as she can see a shadow from underneath the door while hearing the shuffling of feet getting closer to the room. Feeling frightened, a sick joy overtakes Rose's mind because she realizes this could be the end and she would be with her mother again. She sweats and shakes but never takes her eyes off the door as she can now hear the sounds of keys. Looking more intently at the door, Rose can hear the deadbolt lock turn as the door handle is pulled down. As the door opens, letting light from the hallway enter, Rose can only close her one good eye trying to adjust to the light. Trying to look through the opening of her squinting eyelid, Rose can only make out a tall figure, which is obviously a man and the other figure moves like a person just learning how to walk.

A thunderous voice breaks the silence of the tiny room, which almost bursts Roses' eardrums.

"Hey, bitch. I bought you some company!" Still not able to make out who the other person is Rose lets out a yell as Pamela falls forward landing on Roses' sleeping leg. Pamela not bound in any way, but badly beaten throughout her body probably for the same reason as Rose: they refused to give any information about Sandra. Straining her only good eye to gain focus, Rose can now see who lies on her sore leg.

"Pamela? Pamela!" Rose yells. Able to reach down, Rose gently feels for Pamela's swollen face, as she slowly begins to rub it. Aching and feeling weak, Rose painfully pulls Pamela up into her arms inch by inch until she is able to cuddle her head. Slowly rocking Pamela's head, Rose stops as she can faintly hear Pamela trying to say something.

Holding her ear as close as possible to Pamela's mouth, Rose listens carefully as Pamela slowly says, "Don't be afraid, Boo Boo. We ain't dead yet. Let's stay strong, Ok?"

Looking at the battered and weak woman, Rose answers, "Ok, I will be strong, I promise." Gently and slowly, Rose begins to rock Pamela in her arms.

* * *

Pulling up outside the club is Doug, who has gotten his windows of his truck repaired. Waiting for him in front of the club is Bucky. As the two men greet each other, Bucky says, "We got both of them baby, just like you asked."

A smiling Doug responds, "Very good partner; now it is time to use the bait to catch the big fish. Once I catch that fish I am going to fillet her ass for fucking with me." As the two men laugh, they both enter the club.

Chapter Thirty
Do You Play Chess, Sandra?

Monday morning finds Sandra putting on her coat and hiding the discs in the waistline of her pants. It took almost ten days, but Sandra finally got through to Maria Copper's assistant and convinced her that she had something that would interest them very much. Not totally disclosing what she had, Sandra, after about an hour on the phone, gathered some confidence from the assistant, who goes by the name of Gail. Sandra would meet the assistant at the loading dock of News Channel 4, be led up to an unspecified location and explain what she possessed to Gail. If what Sandra possessed had anything that warranted news coverage, then and only then would she receive a one-time opportunity to met Maria Copper. Sandra and Gail exchanged cell phone numbers and agreed only to speak again when Sandra was five minutes away from the agreed meeting place. Grabbing her keys, Sandra heads for her door when her cell phone begins to ring.

* * *

Inside Doug's office, a sweaty and trembling Pamela sits in a chair with a sawed-off shotgun held at her temple. Directly across from her, Rose with her feet and hands tied has her head tilted to the side by a man holding a brand new 36-inch machete to her throat. Standing on the other side of Pamela holding a cell phone to her mouth is Doug, who has instructed Pamela exactly on what she is to say to Sandra.

After the third ring, a sobbing Pamela says, "Hello, Sandra, this is Pamela; can you please hear me out?" Doug, now with his ear to the phone, can hear a hysterical Sandra on the other end asking Pamela what is going on. With her head nudged by the shotgun, Pamela, sobbing heavily, continues, "Sandra, they have Rose and me tied up with guns and knives to our heads, threatening to kill us if you do not return the discs. Please Sandra help us; they say if you return the discs, they will let us go unharmed, but if you do not return them in forty-eight hours, we are dead. Sandra, we are so scared; please help…"

Grabbing the phone from Pamela, Doug can hear, to his delight, Sandra crying on the other end. Looking at his two hostages, Doug speaks into his phone: "Ok bitch, you know who this is and you know what I want, right? You almost got me a few weeks back on that Sunday morning and those movies are classics; I had them sent to my father at his retirement home up in Westchester where he enjoys them with the rest of his elderly companions. However, I am not here to shoot the shit with you Sandra. I want my fucking discs back so let me explain the current scene to you. Your good friend and former neighbor who could not mind her fucking business is sitting in a puddle of piss with a shotgun pointed at her head by a friend of mine who shakes when he does not have his morning coffee. To my left, your little friend, Rose, the one I had gang-banged on film; she has a machete to her throat that, on my signal, my partner will take her head off like a hot knife slicing through butter. Finally, Boo Boo, there is your friend Carla; you know her, right? Well, I had her fucked up and now she is in the hospital, so let me ask you baby…do you still think I am bullshitting about what I want?

* * *

Sandra, sitting on her bed holding the discs in her hands, sits in silence as she listens to Doug as he describes the scene to her. Already ten minutes off her schedule to meet Gail, Sandra can only picture her friends brutally murdered if she does not do as told.

"Ok, Doug, you win alright? You just tell me when and where. But please promise me you…"

* * *

"No baby, you get no promises or guarantees from me, you understand? The only thing you had better hope for is that you have my discs Wednesday morning and I will call you with the location. Sandra, let me tell you something, Ok. If you do not put my discs in my hand on Wednesday guess what, Boo Boo? You can have them because I will send your two friends' heads to that fucking soup kitchen so that those animals who eat there can try something new and exotic. Therefore, Sandra, if you have any plans on contacting the police or going in another direction from what I tell you, then your friends will know just how much you cared about them the second before I kill them. I suggest your phone stay on and remain fully charged, Ms. Thickness, because I will be calling your ass very soon. Later."

* * *

Dropping her phone to the floor, Sandra holds her head, which now throbs with pain. Feeling anger, despair and confusion, Sandra can almost feel the end coming. Doug had her pinned in a corner in which she did not know how to escape. Feeling like a mouse in a maze that has no exit at the end, Sandra decides not to fool herself any longer; on Wednesday, the end would be here. In her mind, she put up a good battle, and she hoped her children could someday forgive her, but this monster was just too evil to overcome. Sandra also realized that the chances were slim that Doug would ever let Pamela and Rose really go once he had his discs and that ate at her mind since once again, because of her weakness, people she loved would die. "Just forget about it Sandra" she thought to herself.

Sitting on the floor and looking at the cloudy, dark day outside her window, Sandra could hear the door open as the footsteps walked from the back of her mind until it reached the front. Pounding her head in an attempt to send "The voice" back home, to Sandra's disappointment, it does not work.

"Don't you dare crumble Sandra, Doug is stupid and egotistical. Just take the time and use your mind to recall everything he said to you a few moments ago. You have two days before you must return the discs for the possibility of saving your friends, which at this point you know are slim. However, you have one day to think about his words that will possibly turn the tide back in your favor but you must focus. I am leaving you at this time to think alone, but remember I am always watching. Focus, Sandra; you can gain control of the board. You just have to focus."

Looking at the sweat that has transferred from her forehead on to her hands, Sandra listens as the footsteps in her mind fade away. Using her bed as support, Sandra lifts herself up and walks over to her window where she recalls every word spoken to her by Doug. Knowing that meeting with Gail is no longer an option, Sandra puts the thought out of her mind and focuses on regaining the upper hand, no matter how impossible that seemed. Walking over to her nightstand, Sandra goes inside the drawer removing a pencil and piece of paper to recite every word used in the phone conversation.

*　　*　　*

It has been two hours now and it is close to noon. Sandra continues to study her notes. As much as it hurts, Sandra has pushed the image of Pamela and Rose being terrified out of her mind, continuing to decipher Doug's speech. Feeling defeated and very frustrated, Sandra sighs, while letting the paper fall to the floor. Giving up all hope, she has yet to find anything with great significance. Looking at the paper, Sandra quickly sits up in her bed grabbing her phone and dialing "411" as the clue she has been looking for is staring her right in the face.

"Yes, can you locate the nearest car rental company in my area, please?" While on the phone with the operator, Sandra exchanges her address for the information that she needs. After calling in an attempt to rent a car, to Sandra's disappointment, she would need a driver's license and a credit card. With her credit card maxed out, no rental agency would help her. Through persistence, Sandra gets in touch with a car escort service that charges by the hour to drive someone to a distant location. Feeling energized, as she has not felt in a long time, Sandra stops in the middle of her kitchenette and recalls what she said to herself a few months ago: "Do not become like Doug," the statement echoed inside her head repeatedly. Doug is a monster who is beyond repair and Sandra had to think if she wanted to cross over to that side, because it would change her life forever. Then something popped up in her head; it was from a detective show she watched a while ago. A detective in search of a murderer said something that was a little strange but made a lot of sense: "If you want to catch a monster, sometimes you have to become a monster." Knowing that she wants desperately to put away Doug and the men responsible for her tragic loss, Sandra decided that only for this moment, would she become that monster.

* * *

On Tuesday evening at 7:00 p.m., Sandra gets inside a shinny black Cadillac CTS sedan that will cost her eighty-five dollars an hour. Reaching over to the driver, she hands him a one hundred dollar bill saying, "Besides, what I am paying your company for their services tonight; if you can turn your head to a few things that may happen, there will be another one of those for you when this is over." The driver, a white man in his late forties, turning around trying his best not look at Sandra's horrible looking scar on her neck says, "Ma'am, I cannot make any promises, but I have seen some crazy shit go on in that backseat. As long as you do not cross those lines, I do not see a problem in turning my head tonight." Giving the driver a smile, Sandra sits back in her seat enjoying the ride to the Shadybrook Retirement Home in Westchester, New York.

* * *

After a forty-five minute ride, the car comes to a stop at the visitor's parking lot.

"Sir, I should not be long, so if you like, you can keep the car running." Looking back at Sandra, the grey-haired driver just nods his head in acknowledgement. Gathering her belongings, Sandra exits the car.

Sandra remembers every wrinkle on Fred Gunner's face from the only time she ever saw him a few years ago when Doug had her and the kids wait in the car while he walked Fred to the corner store. She also remembered his walk and his dark hazel eyes that pierced her with evil glances. Walking towards the large oak doors Sandra enters.

* * *

Looking around in the large waiting area adorned with beautiful paintings and sculptures. Sandra's anger increases, because she cannot figure out why Doug showed so much love and care to a man that he claimed never loved him. At this point though, it did not matter anymore because the day of reckoning was about to begin. Letting a smile come across her face, Sandra walks up to the receptionist desk where a black woman in her fifties sits.

"Good evening, my name is Sandra Lyte and I know it is late, but I have been cleared for a visit with Fred Gunner. He is not expecting me, so I would really like to surprise him. If you like, you can confirm with a Ms. Celeste Davis; I believe she's the head supervisor."

Sandra, sitting in the cafeteria, looks at an orange-haired elderly woman sitting alone eating jello. The cafeteria immaculately cleaned and decorated with craftwork residents have created that is pleasing to the eye. Looking at her watch, Sandra knows she cannot waste time; she must act and speak precisely.

Admiring how the furniture and floors shine, Sandra's startled by a deep, hoarse voice: "Who is here to see me?" asks Fred Gunner, who is now sporting a grey sweat suit.

Regaining her composure, Sandra calmly turns to Fred with a smile on her face and responds, "Good evening, Mr. Gunner, that would be me; my name is Sandra Lyte."

Still standing at the entrance of the cafeteria, Fred looks at Sandra with curiosity on his face, trying to figure out who she is and why she is here to see him. "Why are you here and what do you want?" Fred asks in a nasty tone.

Knowing how crucial this opportunity is, Sandra remains cool and tries to ease the tension that is between them. "Mr. Gunner, I mean you no harm. I am your son's girlfriend and the mother of his children, Kareem and Chaka. I believe they visited you a short time before Christmas?"

Looking at her, Fred seems to be interested to listen as he enters the cafeteria and takes a seat next to her. "You are the one that my son had those damn kids with?" Fred asks. Starting from her toes, Sandra's anger and rage fills her body as she continues to smile at Fred.

"That is right Mr. Gunner. Those are my kids, but I am not here to discuss them. I am here to take you to see your son because he was injured and is home in bed. He sent me here because he wants to see you tonight, but we must make a stop at my place first before we go see him."

Fred pulling a pack of cigarettes from his pocket, lights up one and inhales, blowing the smoke in Sandra's face. Still smiling at the old man, Sandra maintains her cool: "Mr. Gunner, there is no need to become rude with me; I am just here to get you to your son. If you have no desire to see him, that's fine; I will just gather myself together and leave." Getting up from the table, Sandra begins to walk away.

"Hold on one damn minute, Ok?" Fred demands. Turning around and looking at the man, she perceives as Dr. Frankenstein, Sandra waits. "I got a lot of pull in this motherfucker. I could leave here whenever I wanted. Therefore, you know what, I will take your little trip to see my son and besides, that son of a bitch is back three payments with my allowance. So Sheila or whatever the fuck your name is, let's go" says Fred.

Shaking her head in agreement, Sandra calmly responds, "I will give you some time to gather a few things and clear things up with the supervisor, then we can leave. I have a car outside waiting for us as we speak."

Within the next thirty minutes, all is clear for Fred to leave with Sandra and as he said, he must have a lot of pull because no one asked questions as he and Sandra walked out of the front doors into the waiting car. Sandra, opening the door for Fred, gets in after him, telling the driver where they are going.

* * *

It is now 10:30 p.m. and looking at her cell phone, Sandra can see that she is down to her last bar on the battery indicator and still no phone call from Doug. Looking at Fred, who looks around her apartment as if he was standing in a garbage wasteland, she retrieves her charger and plugs her phone into a wall outlet, making sure her signal is strong and the phone is charging.

"Damn, you stay here in this hell hole? Where are your kids? Moreover, when are we going to see my son? I need my damn money."

Sandra, walking over to her stove, turns on a kettle and prepares to make two cups of tea. "My kids are with my mother until I can get a bigger place for us. Your son and I decided we needed to go our own ways but stay friends for the kids' sake. Mr. Gunner, I always have a cup of tea at about this time; will you please join me for a cup and I promise we will go see Doug."

Putting his foot on Sandra's dinette table while sitting in a chair, Fred grabs a magazine that sits on the table and answers, "Yeah, I don't give a shit; make me a cup and make sure you put honey in mine, you hear?"

With her back turned to Fred while clutching a spoon with all of her strength, Sandra responds, "No problem Mr. Gunner…tea with honey coming right up in one minute." Reaching up into her cabinet, Sandra grabs two tea bags, honey and a plastic bag that contains a yellow powder substance. Preparing the tea, Sandra quickly looks behind her making sure Fred is not looking at her. Opening the plastic bag, Sandra pours the contents in the cup that she will serve Fred.

"Damn woman, how long does it take for you to give somebody a damn cup of tea? I see why Doug kicked your ass to the curb." Walking over to the dinette table Sandra puts the cup of tea in front of Fred with a smile on her face. "You got any cookies or crackers?" Fred asks. Walking back to her cabinet, Sandra grabs a box of saltine crackers giving them to Fred, who is sipping on his cup of tea. As Sandra watches him enjoy his beverage, she takes a seat directly in front of him where she begins to sip on her tea. Noticing the small box that is on the dresser, Sandra smiles as Fred eats his crackers while rubbing his head. Looking again at the box Sandra envisions the two pair of handcuffs and duct tape that she purchased that morning.

"Damn, my head is killing me all of a sudden, shit," says Fred.

Sandra, putting on a face of concern asks, "Oh my goodness, Fred, would you like to lie across my bed? Come on, I will help you." Helping him to his feet and grabbing him by the waist, Sandra gently lays him onto the bed, taking off his shoes and positioning him face down with his head on the pillow.

It is now 11:47 p.m. and Sandra sits on her bed, totally exhausted from the twenty-five minute workout with Fred Gunner. While the old man slept like a log on her bed, Sandra got some old sheets and made him a bed inside her tub. Weighing close to one hundred and eighty pounds, it took Sandra every ounce of strength she could muster up to drag Fred from the bed to the bathroom putting him inside the tub. Once inside, she had to prop him up against the back of the tub and do her best to stabilize his head. Once done, Sandra gently handcuffed Fred's wrists and ankles then blindfolded him so he could not figure out were he was. Finally, for good measure, she duct-taped his mouth, making sure to cut a thin slit along the tape so that he could breath but not scream. Sandra also duct taped his thighs together to prevent him from walking. Before leaving the bathroom, Sandra checked her medicine cabinet and saw that she had more sleeping beauty powder and a needle because she knew that the next time would have to be by injection.

Sitting on her bed doing her best not to fall asleep, Sandra's arms ached like hell. She wanted to keep the phone near her in case it rings. Sandra was dead tired and hanging on by a thread. Then she said to herself, "Get up and help your friends! They have guns and knives held on them. Get up and wait for that call." Letting her feet hit the floor, she stands stretching her thick and firm body, when she almost jumps right out of her skin by the sound of her phone ringing. Looking over at the phone, Sandra can see the blue light illuminating after the second ring. Walking over to her nightstand, Sandra answers on the third ring, "Hello?"

*　*　*

Its midnight and Doug is sitting in his office inside his club, tossing cold French fries at an exhausted looking Pamela and Rose gagged and bound sitting in chairs. "Ok bitch, get a pencil and pad because I am only saying this once. On Tremont and Webster Ave. right across the street from Texas Fried Chicken there is the old club where I took you a couple of times called Paradise. At exactly six in the morning, you will walk through those doors and I mean not a minute later. You will go to the back where the bar is and meet me there with my discs. When you give me my discs, I will give you your two friends and allow you to leave in a cab. Sandra, if you play any games with me or I get the scent of cops or anyone else that should not be at this meeting, I am walking out of the club and you can watch your friends brains being blown from their heads. Do you understand me? Good. Fuck you very much and I hope you screw this up tomorrow because it has always been a pleasure killing people you love."

Slamming his phone down on the receiver, Doug looks at a now sobbing Pamela and Rose. "I want the both of you to think of a happy moment you spent with Sandra because it will be your last and when she is dead a few minutes after six this morning, by seven I will make you two watch each other get wasted, how is that?" asks Doug. As Rose still sobs and cries Pamela does not as she now stares at Doug with a cold look of hatred for which Doug can feel. Not liking the atmosphere, he calmly gets up and walks over to Pamela, quickly hitting her with the back of his hand, busting her lip open.

"Who the fuck you staring at?" he asks. Pamela obviously is unable to answer. "I thought so," says Doug as he exits his office to get a drink.   *   *   *

Sitting down and looking at the instructions that Doug has given her, Sandra tries to block the realization from her head that she could possibly die tomorrow. After a few days, the Landlord will come for his rent money and find Fred Gunner crying in the tub like a baby and after that, a very tainted picture will polarize about her. She died possibly a horrific death failing her children and friends.

"No, push that bullshit out of your head. You will think like a monster and more importantly you will think like Doug," Sandra said to herself. Getting up from the chair, Sandra goes to her bathroom to check on Fred and retrieve a bottle of rubbing alcohol.
                    *   *   *

It is 2:25 a.m. and Sandra has almost used the whole bottle of rubbing alcohol on her entire body. Because of it, she feels a whole lot better physically then she did earlier. Having checked on Fred, she is satisfied that he is doing well based on his breathing and the way he slowly moved his head when she stuck a feather in his ear. Sandra hoped Fred would sleep long enough, because the last thing she needed to hear was Fred hoopin and hollering. Looking at her window, Sandra could see how bright the sky was because of the full moon. For some reason, she felt compelled to do something that she had not done since her first week in New York almost eight years ago and that was to pray. She did not have the faith she once possessed many years ago, but Sandra figured this was the opportune time. So on her knees, Sandra prayed quietly to her God and asked not for revenge or justice but simply for strength.

Chapter Thirty-One
In Da Club

With the cold wind hitting her face, Sandra looks at her watch and sees that she is on time, just as Doug always liked. Looking out across the sky, the sun is beginning to send its rays of light across the borough of the Bronx. Looking around, Sandra can see that no other businesses are serving the public and only a few cars drive by in either direction. Looking up at the old club, Sandra cannot help but to remember the many times Doug had taken her there for nights of dancing and drinking. As the cold wind once again hits her face, causing it to freeze briefly, she snaps back into reality because beyond these doors could very possibly await her destiny. Holding onto her bag that Kareem and Chaka bought for her a year ago for Mother's Day, from the money they saved, is where the discs are located. Reaching out and grabbing on to a thick piece of cold chain that kept the doors of the club locked, have now have been unlocked for her convenience or demise, Sandra pulls the doors open and enters.

With the door slamming hard behind her, Sandra looks around in the club, which is dusty and full of spider webs. Many of the windows are missing panes, which explains why it is so cold inside. In front of Sandra are burnt tables and chairs that surround a bar that serves no more. Clutching her bag tightly, she has the urge to turn around and walk back out the door to save her own life, but that is not the plan today. The plan today is to take accountability for one's self and help those who need you. So putting her best foot forward, Sandra walks towards the back of the club, trying to see clearly through all of the dust that fills the room. Now in the back of the club where the women and men's bathrooms are, Sandra does not see or hear anything but her heart pounding inside her chest. Taking a deep breath, she breaks the silence: "Doug, I am here. Where are you?" she asks, as her echo asks two more times. Not getting an answer, Sandra speaks a little louder, "Is anybody here?" Still not getting an answer, she clutches her bag even tighter and begins slowly walking back towards the entrance doors.

Making sure, she does not bump into anything, Sandra stops suddenly, grabbing her chest so her heart will not jump out of it. There is a

tall figure that has emerged from behind one of the large columns and he is walking towards the doors. Sandra, watching in fear and silence, listens as the figure is grabbing and fondling the chains that weave through the doors. Still listening, Sandra hears a loud clicking sound and it is clear to her that whomever that may be at the door, is now locking her inside.
"Who is that?" Sandra asks with a quiver in her voice.

Backing up a little, she is unaware of the old beer bottle by her foot that causes Sandra to roll backwards, lose her balance and fall on her backside. Never taking her eyes off the dark figure that is now facing her, Sandra uses her sore arms to help her quickly get back on her feet. Brushing her pants and hands off, she now demands, "Listen Doug is that you? I am here like you asked, so why are you locking the doors?" However, deep down inside, she knew the answer to that question, but she figured she would ask anyway, hoping to invoke an answer in order to make out who was speaking. Still looking straight at her company, Sandra's chest expands larger and faster as the figure begins to take his first steps towards her.

Feeling like she could run and dive through one of the windows, Sandra can neither run nor jump because she is scared stiff as the figures footsteps are getting closer and louder. As the sun now sends more rays through the windows, Sandra has to shield her eyes with her free hand, as the light limits her vision. Lowering her hand, Sandra is now clear about one thing: Doug did not show. Standing in front of her is Doug's henchmen Bucky.

With her mouth, halfway open, Sandra dwarfed by this man, manages to squeak out of her mouth, "Where is Doug? He told me he would be here." Not saying a word, Bucky slowly starts to unbutton his long leather trench coat one button at a time, never taking his eyes off Sandra. Removing his coat from his body, Bucky is wearing nothing but a leather vest. Sandra, examining the large man from head to toe, can clearly see that on his left side of his waist, he is wearing a holster that contains an eight-inch bully club.

Reaching inside his vest pocket, he removes a stick of gum that he proceeds to put inside his mouth. Looking at her while feeling his club, Bucky asks, "Sandra, do you have that package for Doug?"

Looking down at her bag, Sandra looks back at Bucky. "Who are you and where is Doug? This was not part of the agreement and neither was locking me in here."

Blowing and popping a bubble, Bucky responds, "Bitch, I am only going to ask you one more time politely and if you do not answer my question, I will come over there and smash your fucking skull in, have sex with your dead corpse and just check for myself. Do you have Doug's package?"

For the second time in her life, Sandra smells the stench of death in the air and it was consuming her mentally as she begins to grasp the realness of the situation. When she turns the discs over to this sick bastard, not only will he kill her, but he will do only what a few sick minds in this world would. Before Sandra would just give up and let that happen, she knew a stand would have to be made.

Reaching down inside her bag, she removes the Ziploc bag of discs holding them above her head so Bucky can see them, "Yes, I have them right here" she answers. Looking through the rays of sun, Bucky sees the shiny discs above Sandra's head.

"Very good, now give them to me so we can get this over with," says Bucky. Looking past the large man and at the chained door, Sandra responds, "Listen, this is not right. Doug promised that my friends would be..."

Before Sandra can finish, an angry Bucky picks up an old bar stool and tosses it at Sandra, striking her on the left leg, causing her to scream in pain and almost fall to the ground.

"Bitch, enough with the pleading and questions; just give me the damn discs! I promise I will make this quick and painless as possible. Holding her leg while her eyes fill with fear, Sandra puts the plastic bag back inside her canvas bag and hops to a broken window in an attempt to yell for help. Because of the height of the window and the noise of the cars coming and going on Webster Avenue., her screams for help goes unheard. Quickly turning and facing a now approaching Bucky, Sandra limps over to a flight of stairs that lead to the upper level of the club. Letting out a loud and hearty laugh, Bucky slowly walks toward the stairs in pursuit of his prey:

"Go ahead baby; make it interesting...its cool. Your fate still remains the same; you will die and get screwed all within the same minute." Walking up the stairs Bucky removes his bully club from its holster.

Sandra is holding a piece of broken wood that she located on the floor and quietly hides behind what use to be the DJ booth. Hearing the loud footsteps of Bucky come up the final few steps, Sandra gently lays her duffel bag on the floor and grips her piece of wood tightly with both hands, hoping she will get a chance to strike Bucky somewhere on his body when he is not expecting it. Now on the second level, Bucky surveys the floor, taking notice to all of the possible hiding places Sandra could be.

"Come out; come out wherever you are Sandra!" Bucky yells. Picking up worn out chairs, he begins tossing them behind the bar and towards the jukebox. Sandra, sweating profusely, remains in her crouch waiting for her opportunity to strike. With dust stirring throughout the floor, Sandra is doing her best not to yell or make any sudden noises. Holding her head upward, Sandra wonders why she does not hear him because Bucky is a heavy man wearing boots. Trying to figure out where he could be, Sandra slowly and quietly begins to peep around the bottom of the booth. Pulling her braids from in front of her face, Sandra bites her lip, forcing herself not to scream because she is face to face with the back of Bucky's black combat boots. Not paying any attention to her now bleeding lip, Sandra slowly begins to lift her arms to strike him in the back of the leg when her face turns to pure red; there is no one in the boots. Shaking uncontrollably, she begins to crawl backwards when with her backside she bumps into Bucky, who quietly entered the booth from the opposite side bootless. Letting out what has to be the loudest scream Bucky has heard, Sandra tries to make it to her feet but is instead grabbed by her braids and violently yanked up off the floor.

"Where you going, baby? Were you going to stab me with that?" Bucky asks. Shaking and sweating, Sandra cannot get anything out of her mouth, so she just shakes her head no while letting go of the piece of wood. Still holding her tightly by the braids, Bucky is now inches away from Sandra's face when he begins to smell around her neck. Looking at her, he slowly releases her hair and smiles. Still shaking, Sandra somehow manages to take one-step away from Bucky, but that is all she manages because Bucky backslaps her so hard that he causes Sandra to fly over the DJ booth and crash onto the floor.

Looking over the booth at an agonizing Sandra, Bucky asks, "You ok, baby? I will come help you." Slowly walking out of the booth, Bucky reaches down and lifts a moaning Sandra off the ground by one of her arms. Looking at her with amusement, he slings her across the room, causing Sandra to crash into a bunch of stacked chairs. On the floor and barely moving, Sandra reaches for her back, which is throbbing with immense pain. Using her heels, she slowly tries to crawl away from an approaching Bucky, who is just toying with her.

"Come here baby and get some more pain before I screw your dead ass." Watching Sandra crawl, Bucky removes his bully club and hits her across her back, causing Sandra to scream without any sound leaving her mouth. Now face down on the floor, Sandra remains motionless, trying to take in little bits of oxygen. Satisfied that she is not going anywhere, Bucky calmly walks back over to the booth and retrieves his boots, putting them back on his feet. Looking behind the booth, he grabs Sandra's duffel bag and locates the Ziploc bag that contains the discs. Looking at Sandra, who is moving slightly but not enough to warrant any concern, Bucky grabs his cell phone and begins to call Doug.

Hearing Doug's voice after the third ring, Bucky begins, "Yo, dog; it is me. Listen, I got the package and I am watching her lie flat on her face as we speak. Yeah, ok. I will do her as soon as we get off the phone and then I will call you back to let you know that it is over. I will just put her body in the bathroom and chain the entrance back up when I am done. Do not worry about that; my cousin is the supervisor, so when this place is demolished, he will make sure all is cool. Ok, listen…let me get this over with and I will call you back in a few; that way you can take care of those two on your side. Ok, dog…later." Hanging up the phone and putting it back inside his vest pocket, Bucky slowly begins to walk over to Sandra, who now has painfully turned on her side. Looking down on Sandra with his hands on his side, Bucky shakes his head with a grin on his face as Sandra has now managed to sit up and stare him in the eye.

"You know what, Sandra? I will say this about you; you have a lot of heart baby. Too bad it has to end, though." Reaching down, Bucky grabs her by the collar of her coat and proceeds to drag Sandra to a wall. While pulling her along the floor, the knees of Sandra's pants tear from old broken bottles of glass. Sandra dragged to the wall like a cave woman; reaches out for something along the floor. Once at the wall, Bucky slams her against it, causing Sandra to bang her head. Still maintaining her consciousness, she looks over at the discs that Bucky left on the table. Grabbing her by the throat, Bucky lifts Sandra two feet off the ground so that her feet dangle in the air and her eyes meet with his. With his large black hands wrapped around her throat, Bucky begins to squeeze slowly, causing Sandra to grasp for air and kick her feet a little more frantically.

"Do not fight it baby, it will be over very soon." says Bucky. Feeling queasier, Sandra gags and spits into Bucky's face, as she begins to see Kareem and Chaka from a distance getting closer. With her eyes becoming blood-shot red, Sandra with her last ounce of strength, reaches up with her left hand and slices Bucky under his left arm between his armpit and his bicep with a very sharp piece of glass that she managed to pickup.

"Shit, what the fuck!" cries Bucky as he quickly drops Sandra to the floor. Sandra, who is coughing uncontrollably while trying to regain oxygen in her body, watches a now panic-stricken Bucky stagger on his feet:

"Bitch, where the fuck did you just cut me at?" he asks. As the blood increasingly pours from his body, Bucky begins to walk towards Sandra with bad intentions but falls about three feet short as he lands on his knees, still holding his arm.

Now kneeling in a pool of his own blood, Bucky is losing his wits and now begins to keel over mumbling, "Kill you bit…" when he falls flat on his face, taking three last grasps of air before dying on the floor. Leaning against a column, Sandra, who can barely move, wills herself to stand on her two feet while holding her aching back. Looking down on her victim, Sandra turns away and walks over to the table, grabbing the discs putting them back inside her duffel bag. Walking over to a cracked and dusty mirror that sits on the wall, Sandra looks at herself for a moment, running her hands through her braids when her friend, "the voice," returns from the back of her mind.

"You fought and you survived. Now you must hurry and get the hell out of here. You cannot go through the front, so check for a back entrance or as much as it will hurt, look for a bathroom window. Also, take his wallet and his bully club; these will be your trophies to remember this battle. Most importantly, take his cell phone; you will know why soon enough. Hurry Sandra, the rent is due and you do not want that nosey ass landlord possibly entering the apartment finding Fred, who more than likely is kicking and screaming like the bitch that he is. Pull yourself together and get out now!" says the voice.

Once again hearing the footsteps fade away into the back of her mind, Sandra more determined than ever pushes the pain out of her mind, walking over to Bucky checking his pockets; finding his keys, wallet, cell phone and the bully club. Standing over his body, Sandra stares at the large man for about three seconds before doing what her "voice" said. Putting everything in her canvas bag, Sandra hurries to the back of the club, looking for an exit. Turning to her right, she sees a stack of chairs in front of a wall. Looking up above the chairs, Sandra makes out a dirty sign that barely reads "EXIT." Sitting her bag on the floor, she steadily begins to remove the chairs one-by-one. With her children and two friends on her mind, Sandra begins to toss the chairs behind her with a little more gusto. With about fifteen more chairs in front of her, Sandra can see a metal bar that she hopes will open the door. Moving five more chairs, enough to give her a path, Sandra grabs her duffel bag, putting it on her bruised shoulder. Taking one deep breath, Sandra whispers, "please open" and with every ounce of strength she has left, Sandra opens the door allowing brisk air and sunshine to engulf her face. Now with the tears beginning to fall down her face, all Sandra can do is look up to the blue sky and say, "Thank you and please forgive me."

Letting the door close behind her, Sandra looks both ways and sees a gas station about thirty feet away. Looking at her pants and coat she, can see they are filthy and torn, but that does not faze her because she is alive. Quickly limping towards the gas station, Sandra can see a Spanish man filling up his cab.

Walking over to him, she manages to put a smile on her face when tapping him on the shoulder, "Good morning sir you working this morning?"

Looking at his watch, he responds, "Not right now; I am going to breakfast."

Removing a fifty-dollar bill from her pocket, Sandra flashes it in front of his face: "How about if I buy you breakfast?"

Looking at his watch and back at Sandra, the man returns the gasoline pump back inside the holder, nodding his head towards his car.

Sandra, smiling says, "Thank you," while painfully getting inside the vehicle. As the car starts to roll away from the station and goes north on Webster Avenue., Sandra manages to look at the club until it is out of her sight. Sandra leans her head back and thinks to herself, "No more tears," as she heads home.

* * *

Having paid her rent, Sandra walks down to her basement apartment. Sandra looks at her watch that reads 7:35 a.m., which to her seems almost impossible when she thinks about all she has been through this morning. Taking out her keys, Sandra following her instincts and takes out her new bully club just in case for some reason Fred miraculously escaped. Turning the keys inside the locks, Sandra slowly opens the door to her apartment, sticking her head inside and seeing everything is the same as she had left it, Sandra enters.

Standing in front of her bathroom, Sandra slowly opens the door and looks at her bathtub where the shower curtains are drawn. Slowly walking towards her tub, Sandra, while holding the bully club in her hand, slowly pulls back the shower curtains. There lays Fred Gunner, sweating, frightened and smelling like urine. Looking at Sandra, the elder Gunner begins thrashing about and mumbling under the duct tape that covers his mouth.

"Calm down Fred. This will be over soon, I promise." Sandra says. Walking out of the bathroom, Sandra returns with a glass of water and a steak knife. Closing the door behind her, she proceeds to cut the duct tape away from Fred's mouth, giving him some water.

Taking three large gulps, Fred looks at Sandra and spits the water in her face, yelling, "You fucking bitch; you better let me go or I'll…"

Putting the steak knife to his throat, Sandra responds, "You will what? You better shut your damn mouth because you do not have any idea what type of man you have spawned, so you better not upset me." Wiping the water from her face, Sandra can hear a phone ringing, but it is not hers. Leaving the bathroom, Sandra heads to her kitchen.

Looking inside her duffel bag, she removes Bucky's phone and cautiously answers it on the fourth ring: "Hello? No Doug you motherfucker, this is not Bucky. He will not be making it back to see you."

*   *   *

Doug, who looks as if he has just eaten year old cabbage, stands in his office with his mouth wide open looking at a tied up Pamela and Rose, who are secretly paying close attention to Doug's' every word. Trying to figure out what to say, Doug stumbling over his words angrily responds, "Fuck you Sandra. I have these two bitches right here and as soon as I hang up this phone, their asses are dead, you hear me!"

*   *   *

Sandra, never losing her cool, calmly listens to Doug as she walks back to her bathroom. Sitting on the toilet seat, Sandra puts the steak knife to Fred's throat and says, "Before you do that Doug, I want you to say hello to somebody first, ok?"

Putting the phone to Fred's mouth, Sandra motions with her head for Fred to speak: "Doug, come get me, son; she is crazy! She is gonna kill me!"

Pulling the phone away from Fred, a fierce looking Sandra says, "How much do you really love your punk ass daddy?"

"Daddy, please do not hurt my father!" pleads Doug. Shaking with the phone in his hand, he quickly looks over at Pamela and Rose, who are staring at him with a little less fear on their faces. "Sandra, please do not hurt my father!"

*   *   *

Listening as the mighty Doug pleads and whines as if a little baby only gives Sandra more hope: "Oh, fuck you and your daddy; you just shut the fuck up and listen. I mean listen closely because I am only saying this once and his life depends on it."

Chapter Thirty-Two
The End of a Relationship

It is noon and Sandra has done the best she could in replenishing her body and mind. Having washed her body over the kitchen sink, bandaged her knees and taken three extra strength Tylenols, she prepares to see Doug for the last time since Christmas Day to fight for her friends' freedom.

The meeting place Sandra has chosen is at a newly renovated housing complex on the south side of the Bronx. The rules are simple; when the three women enter a cab, Doug gets his father and the discs. Sandra has explained to him that if he shows up with anyone, she would destroy his discs and slash his father's throat just as he had attempted to be done to her. She also told him that over the years she has become quite friendly with two of the security guards who were once homeless and ate at the pantry, so they will be the ones to let them enter the complex. As far as the guards knew, they will just be meeting to get a look first-hand at the new apartments.

Having gone out, Sandra purchased a used wheelchair to transport Fred. Having given Fred another injection fifteen minutes ago, Sandra has removed his handcuffs and sat him in his wheelchair, rolling him by the door. She will ask the cab driver to assist her in getting him inside the cab. Once they arrive at the complex, she will put the handcuffs back on for safety reasons. Sandra has told Doug to meet her at three o'clock, but unknown to him; she will be there two hours earlier.

While putting on her coat and grabbing her bag, the only thing on Sandra's mind right now is not the dangerous meeting that could blow up in her face or the mere fact that today could be the last day of her life. No, those things did not enter her mind because Sandra would not let them. She felt in her mind and soul that there was nothing going to stop her from saving Pamela and Rose, including Doug.

What was on her mind at this moment, was how painful it was going to be wheeling Fred up the alleyway of her building, knowing how steep the walkway was and how bad her arms ached. Unlocking her door and wheeling an unconscious Fred into the hallway, Sandra begins to push the wheelchair to daylight as she can hear the sound of a car horn blowing.

* * *

It is now 1:00 p.m. and Sandra is pushing a sleeping Fred across the large courtyard that contains a playground. She cannot help to wonder how other kids would have had the chance to play with two of the happiest and lovable children in the world: Kareem and Chaka. Determined not to let her imagination overcome her, Sandra quickly pushes the thought out of her mind, as she is now about forty yards from building "D" where she will have a bird's eye view of Doug entering the complex hopefully with her friends in tow. Looking up at the tall newly constructed apartment buildings, Sandra figures the first floor will suit her just fine. Now at the front of the building, she painfully uses her arms to spin Fred around in the wheelchair and enters through the glass doors.

* * *

It is 1:30 p.m. and Sandra has not taken her eyes off the main entrance of the complex. For a brief moment, she turns her attention to Fred, who seems to be awakening as he slowly moves his hands and feet. Looking at this man, Sandra cannot help but wonder was he the main reason for Doug becoming the person he turned out to be or was he simply a father who did all he could for a son who was born to be evil? She could not answer this question, but she knew who could. Looking over at an open closet, Sandra sees a slop sink and decides to get some "wake-your-ass-up water", but before moving from her perch, she looks hard to make sure Doug has not arrived. Satisfied that she will not miss him, Sandra quickly walks over to the slop sink, finds an empty soda bottle and fills it up with cold water. Walking back over to the window, Sandra looks out again and sees nothing. Turning back to Fred, who is beginning to moan, Sandra slowly begins pouring the water all over his grey afro, causing the man to shake and rattle inside his chair. Shaking his head back and forth, Fred manages to open one of his eyes. Spitting water from his mouth, trying to gain some focus, Fred looks around with fear on his face trying to figure out where he is.

Frantically spinning his head around, Fred meets eye-to-eye with Sandra: "Let me go! You let me go! Where am I?" he yells. Now moving his feet and arms, Fred can see the handcuffs: "Get these motherfucking cuffs off me and I will kick your ass! You have no right doing this to me. What have I done to you, bitch, huh?" he asks. Calmly walking over and standing in front of him, Sandra removes a photo from her bag, a photo of Kareem and Chaka taken on their seventh birthday. Holding the picture in front of Fred's wet face, Sandra just stares at him.

"So, what the fuck does that suppose to mean to me? Why are you showing me a picture of these two fucking kids?" he asks.

Looking down on Fred with a face of fury, Sandra reaches back with all of her strength and smacks him across his face, snapping his head to one side. "The little boy's name is Kareem. He was a straight 'A' student who loved to play chess and dreamed of becoming an architect. He never let me carry a bag of groceries home and he promised me when he became an architect, the first house that he was going to build would be for me. This girl planned to become a lawyer, so that if her brother ever got in trouble, she would take care of him. She too was an 'A'student who loved to help the struggling kids in her class with their homework. She loved to watch her mommy cook and always asked me, when we were alone, why did her daddy not love us?"

Fred, staring at the photo, looks away and stares at a nearby wall. Sandra, still burning with rage, yanks the man by his hair, turning his head so that once again they are eye-to-eye.

"You see this scar? It took one hundred and forty-two stitches to close it up. My friend gave me two pints of her own blood and I was close to dying for two days. All thanks to your fucking son who loved money and power over his own family who was planning all along to have us killed. My children tossed out the fourth floor window. Yes these children; your grandchildren were murdered by your son."

Now looking towards the ground, Fred slowly begins to look up at Sandra, "So, you think you are totally innocent in all of this shit? What made you stay? You should have just left. You did know he was no shoe sales clerk, right? He was a fucking hustler and you loved the life. So, do not try to paint this picture of yourself as some innocent woman who did not know what she was getting into. When did he ever tell you that he loved you? Nobody deserved what happened to those kids and you, but just read a newspaper every now and then. Read how so many of you young girls are blinded by the fast money and the life. You have kids by these cats, thinking you can change them and make them settle down. They don't love you; you bitches are just trophies and when trophies start to tarnish, they get new ones."

Looking at the old man, Sandra wants to twist his head until it rips off his shoulders, but deep down inside, Fred said something that is troublesome and weighs on her mind. Why did she not try to walk away sooner? Turning back to Fred, who is now staring out of the large glass window, Sandra says, "I stayed because I loved him and thought over time I could change him. Simple as that, I just loved him. Judge me or call me stupid, but that is the only answer I have right now. My love for your son cost me what I loved most in this life: my children and today his monkey ass is going to pay." Reaching inside her bag, Sandra removes a red handkerchief and proceeds to tie it around Fred's mouth, deciding she has heard enough from Dr. Frankenstein. As both of them stare out at the courtyard and wait for "The Monster" to arrive, Fred does not move in his chair and Sandra never utters another word.

*   *   *

With a knife in her hand and her watch reading 3:00 p.m., Sandra now positions herself behind Fred, who, in a strange way, sits up straight inside his wheelchair almost with a sense of pride. It is almost as if he realizes the end has now arrived. Sandra's eyes get a little misty, but she makes them stop as she now can see Doug escorting a weak looking Pamela and Rose across the courtyard towards the building. Doug, wearing a brown leather coat and black pants, holds both women by their shirt collars as they walk without coats or sweaters on. Sandra can see their hands tied together as they limp across the dirt. Doug, who now stops in the middle of the courtyard, looks up at the glass and waves to his father mouthing the words "It's Ok" Not believing what she is seeing, an infuriated Sandra holds the 12-inch butcher knife to Fred's throat and silently mouths back, "No it is not." Looking up at the scene, fear comes across the face of Doug as he pushes the women to hurry inside the building. Sandra, hearing the sounds of the door closing and footsteps getting closer, she quickly rolls Fred to an apartment door marked 1A. With her back to the door, Sandra reaches with one of her hands and turns the doorknob, slightly pushing it open. As the footsteps get closer from around the corner, Sandra's eyes widen and her hands tighten around the handle of the knife. Turning the hallway corner is Doug holding a badly bruised Pamela and Rose. Instantly, their eyes meet and never leave each other as neither one of them say a word.

Sandra finally letting herself exhale speaks first: "Release them right now."

Looking at the two women, Doug violently pushes them to the side where they trip over each other falling to the cold building's floor. Sandra, watching her friends moan in pain, can see that Doug has used plastic tie-wraps to shackle them together. Looking at how Doug still manages to treat those close to her, Sandra decides to give him a taste of the feeling. Pressing the knife harder against Fred's throat, Doug looks at his father start to tremble as a trickle of blood now exits from his neck.

"No Sandra, please!" Doug begs. "Listen, all I want is my father and the discs. Like I said Sandra, I promise to let you and your friends go. I mean it this time." Looking at Doug with not a trace of trust in her eyes, Sandra slowly opens the apartment door and begins to roll Fred into the large empty apartment, never taking the knife away from his throat and her eyes off Doug, who watches as his father enters the apartment.

"Sandra, come on please. We do not have to do this; I promise to let..."

Watching the door close in his face, Doug looks back at Pamela and Rose, who still lay on the floor. "Doug, come get your father and the discs" Doug hears Sandra yell from the other side of the door. Now confused and sweating, Doug hesitantly begins to reach for the apartment door while, at the same time, looking back at Pamela and Rose as if they will give him some type of advice. Grabbing on to the doorknob, Doug slowly turns it while gently pushing the door open.

Cautiously sticking his head inside, Doug asks, "Sandra, where are you?" Not getting an answer, Doug removes his gun from the waistband of his pants. Doug standing inside the foyer area of the apartment feels the cell phone belonging to the organization vibrate and immediately, Doug knows what that means; Mr. X expects his payment today. Doug always answered the phone from the organization, but Doug knew he was in a precarious situation and needed to decide what was more important at this moment. He feels the vibration of his phone again and looks in the direction of where his father could be, not knowing if he was dead or alive. Doug ignores the vibration on his hip and walks towards the back of the apartment to find his father.

"Sandra, I am here and your friends are safe, now show me my fucking father," Doug demands.

Standing inside a large sunken living room with an entrance leading to a terrace, Doug listens carefully for an answer. "We are in here Doug, inside the bedroom," Sandra responds from behind a door. Walking cautiously in the direction of Sandra's voice, he locates the door and stands in front of it, with his mouth almost touching:

"Ok Sandra, I am coming in and my hands will be empty," says Doug, who puts his gun in the back of his pants. Turning the doorknob, Doug slowly opens the door and sitting in the middle of the room inside a wheelchair, is Fred wearing handcuffs and gagged. Running quickly to his father's aid, Doug is making an attempt to remove the handkerchief from around Fred's mouth when from behind him, Doug hears the bedroom door slam, causing him to quickly turn around facing Tony Marino and eight of his henchmen. Reaching for his gun, one of Tony's men reacts to Doug, smacking him in the face with a black object that busts his nose.

Tony, looking at Doug, sprawled out over the floor, motions for two of his men to get Doug on his feet. Pinning Doug to a wall, Tony walks over to Fred and removes the gag from his mouth: "Sir, I believe this is your son?" Tony asks. Fred, who is petrified, shakes his head up and down, looking over at his son, who is just regaining his sense of where he is. Walking inside the room is Sandra, who is holding her canvas bag and looking at Doug, who, for the first time since she has known him, has fear all over his face. Wearing a grey pinstriped suit, Tony calmly and coolly walks up to Doug and spits in his face, leaving a glob of thick yellow saliva rolling down the middle of his face.

"Doug, my name is Tony Marino and I am not big on speeches, so I will sum this up pretty quickly. A few nights before Christmas, you took away my wife's only son. He was no angel, but that does not matter because nobody is. You shot him three times, showing little or no mercy towards him causing us to have a closed casket funeral. Then you do the unthinkable to your own family and have your own children slaughtered for insurance money. You are beyond being a monster Doug and you are beyond reasoning to, so I am here to let you know for my son, Sandra, her innocent children and myself, you will die a horrible death today in front of your father and I will pass on to him what I had to carry." Doug holding his face just stares at his father, fully aware that his life will end.

Looking over at Sandra who is observing Doug intensely Tony asks, "Sandra, I need to get you out of here, but is there anything you would like to say to this man before he dies?" Not saying a word, Sandra walks over to a pile of iron radiator pipes picking up one about two feet long. Walking back over quickly towards a startled Doug, Tony and his men make a path for Sandra.

"Sandra, I am so sorry; please... looking at him with fire in her eyes, Sandra reaches back and swings the pipe forward hitting Doug across his face breaking his eye socket and nose all with one shot. Holding his face and backpedaling Doug hits a wall, falling to the floor. Standing over and looking at the only man she loved, Sandra gets a flashback of her children reaching out to her for help on Christmas Day. In a fit of rage, Sandra begins beating Doug unmercifully while his father looks on in disbelief and for the first time ever, Fred Gunner sheds tears for his son. Holding his arm up to protect his bloodied face, Sandra with two blows, breaks Doug's wrist and forearm. "Oh God Sandra please have mercy on me!" Now beating on Doug's legs, Sandra screams, "Fuck you motherfucker, you son of a bitch! Cracking Doug across his ribs Sandra is going berserk when Tony and one of his men grab hold of her. "Ok sweetheart, I understand but that is enough. That is not the person you are Sandra, let us do our jobs" says Tony.

"Make sure Doug and his father are allowed to speak to each other if they like. I will be back in a few minutes," Tony says to his remaining men inside the room as he removes a furious Sandra out of the apartment.

Fred looking at his bloodied and injured son sprawled out on the floor asks him "Son what did you get yourself into, you really had those kids murdered? Oh shit, Doug may God have mercy on our souls.

Inside the building hallway, Sandra runs over to Pamela and Rose, hugging and kissing them all over their faces and heads. Looking over at Tony she asks, "Tony, can you please help me get them loose?" Nodding to one of his guards, the man pulls out a knife and cuts Pamela and Rose free, helping them to their feet.

"Go get the package from the car," Tony says to the man. As he hurries out of the building, Tony walks over to Sandra and puts his hand around her shoulder and says, "You are a very brave woman Sandra; my wife and I would like to thank you for helping us bring closure to this situation. Your children would be very proud of you and I know these two women are." Running back inside the building holding a black suitcase is Tony's guard. Giving the suitcase to Tony, his soldier returns inside the apartment. "Sandra, in no type of way am I trying to tell you that this will bring your children back or make you forget them, but I am hoping that maybe it can provide a new beginning for you and your friends," says Tony, who opens the suitcase revealing two million dollars to Sandra. Looking up at Tony, she begins to speak when he places his finger across her lips: "Sweetheart, don't say a word ok? You just get your friends and yourself out of here and somewhere safe, like out of this city and start your new life. I will never forget you and you will always have a friend in me," says Tony. As they hug each other, Pamela puts her arms around

Rose, who is still a little shook up. Letting Tony go, Sandra carries her Duffel bag and her suitcase over to her friends, hugging them. Tony, watching the three women as they exit the building, returns inside the apartment where Doug awaits his fate.

* * *

Some time has passed, and Tony Marino stands at the entrance of the living room holding the wheelchair of a still handcuffed Fred, trying to turn his head away while one of Tony's men dissembles his son with a chainsaw. While Tony holds Fred's head, the old man witnesses his son's body parts tossed to the side as if they were chicken parts. The bedroom is crimson red with Doug's blood and guts splattered all over the walls. Walking out of the bedroom with Doug's head in his hand Tony's henchmen calmly sits the head, of what is the last of Fred's son, in the old man's lap. Fred, looking down, can see that his son never had the chance to close his eyes. As Tony's men all begin to exit the apartment, Tony bends down and whispers into Fred's ear, "Feel my pain." As Tony leaves the apartment, he can hear Fred screaming above the sound of a jumbo jet flying above in the sky.

* * *

To Doug's credit, he had prepared a document before his ill-fated meeting with Sandra. Doug instructed his Spanish mommy Jasmine to mail it express mail if she did not hear from him at a specific time. Crying as she exited the post office, Jasmine did her last favor for Doug.

* * *

Detective Tommy Davis sits alone in his office looking over open cases when he looks at the old wall clock that reads 8:37 p.m. Taking one last puff of his cigarette, he finds an express delivery package on his desk. Looking puzzled, the detective opens the envelope and removes a one-page letter.

Slowly scrolling over the letter, it reads, "Tommy, if you have received this letter, then it means I am more than likely dead and if you do not hurry, your precinct, including yourself, is fucked. From the time I met you, we have been involved in some shady shit, such as prostitution, bribery, drug use and murder. To your credit, you have always been on the up and up with me for these many years, but as you know, a brother can never be too sure. So, I am writing to let you know that during these wild times of ours, while you and your crew partied at my secret hideaway in the Bronx, I recorded all of the dirty shit onto DVD discs; just in case you ever tried to squeeze me, I had leverage. Well, possibly in death, I have to give you the bad news; those discs are in the hands of Sandra Lyte, the bitch that I paid you to kill along with her kids. Well brother Sandra is not as dumb and weak as we thought because she is still alive and has the discs. The chances are good that she watched those discs and at any moment, while you are possibly reading this letter, could be on her way to expose those involved. Tommy, I fucked up partner, by underestimating her. Therefore, I just want to say goodbye, hoping you find and kill her before she can find someone important to watch those discs, Good-bye...Doug."

Falling backwards into his chair, Tommy begins to tremble as his face turns beet red. Picking up his cell phone, he begins to dial all of those involved to meet up with him to find and kill Sandra at all cost.

Chapter Thirty-Three
A.P.B. On Sandra Lyte

Thursday evening, inside a nice motel, Sandra, Pamela and Rose are sitting on a carpeted floor between two queen-size beds listening to the sounds of the passing cars on I-95. The room smells of cinnamon and strawberries as each of the women have taken a long hot bath, doing their best to wash away the sins of Doug and very possibly their own.

As the three women sit, Sandra breaks the silence: "I am so sorry for what you all had to go through for me, I hope over time your wounds will heal."

Pamela, reaching across Rose, touches Sandra's badly bruised thigh and responds, "Please do not say sorry, Sandra; it is because of you that we all sit here right now. I just think at some point and time, we all need to thank God for keeping us alive and helping us cope with the horrors that we all have endured."

Sandra, looking over to the window where the neon sign is flashing, says, "Sometimes I feel so disconnected from God. It is almost as if I do not have the right to speak to Him about anything. My life at this moment compared to where it was ten years ago, I just feel so dirty and unworthy."

In a soft, clear voice, almost like a jazz vocalist from the fifties, Rose interjects, "Our righteousness is just filthy rags before the Lord and no matter how hard we try, we will always fall short of His glory. We must accept the gift that he has given us and not take it for granted. Let us not focus on the suffering we all have gone through, but believe God never left us and he is the one who kept us alive. We all have lost so much; we need to focus on the fact that even through all of the pain and sorrow we sit inside this room together for a reason. We are not sure for what reason, but it is according to His plan that we are together and safe."

As Sandra and Pamela look at Rose in silence as tears run down their faces, a now quiet Rose, wearing new pajamas that Sandra purchased for her, climbs inside the bed that feels much better than the hallway steps she usually slept on, falls fast asleep. Sandra and Pamela help each other up from the floor, sit on the other bed and watch Rose sleep for about an hour, never saying a word for the rest of the night.

*   *   *

Friday morning finds Pamela and Rose eating pancakes with beef sausages along with orange juice to wash it down. Pamela fondles through Rose's long silk like hair, trying to figure out what style of cornrows she will braid in her hair. Sitting on the bed with the discs by her side, Sandra is about to use her cell phone when she asks, "How does Phoenix sound to you two?"

With a fork full of pancakes ready to enter her mouth, Pamela responds, "Arizona? I heard its hot is hell all year round out there, Sandra."

"No big deal; we will just get us a big pool in our backyard of our house. Moreover, I will make sure we have an air conditioner in every room. So, I ask again how does Phoenix sound to you two?"

A smiling Pamela answers, "It sounds good to me" while an ecstatic looking Rose quickly answers, "Please, can we go now?" Sandra and Pamela let out a loud laugh.

Looking at the discs on the bed, Sandra says, "Sure, baby, we can leave here as soon as possible, but there is still one thing that must be put to rest before we leave."

Picking up her cell phone, Sandra dials the number of Gail, the assistant to Maria Copper at News Channel Four. On the fourth ring, Sandra gets an answer, "Hello, Ms. Smothers, you may not remember me, but my name is Sandra Lyte and not too long ago, I contacted you about some information pertaining to police corruption and murder?"

*   *   *

The newsroom is alive and kicking as people are running around like chickens without heads as they share information about a manhunt going on in the city. Looking for a place to find that is less noisy; Gail enters a supply room, closing the door behind her.

"This is Sandra Lyte? Yes, I remember our conversation, and I remember you not showing up that morning, as you said. Sandra, I understand that you want to speak to Maria Copper, but do you realize what is going on this morning? Sandra, are you near a television set? Sweetheart, you need to turn it on right now," Gail demands.

*   *   *

As Pamela and Rose stop talking a confused Sandra, walks over to the television. They all sit in silence as Sandra turns to channel four where a story runs relating to her. Looking at the screen, Pamela and Rose quickly jump out of their chairs and huddle next to a shocked looking Sandra. On the television screen is a picture of Sandra's face with the words wanted for the murder of Doug Gunner under her picture. Turning the sound up on the television, the women hear how Sandra is armed and dangerous with no regard for the law. With her phone still held to her mouth, a frightened Sandra can only whisper, "That is not true. I did not kill Doug. He was responsible for my babies being murdered, but I did not kill him; that is not true."

        *   *   *

Gail, who is listening to every word that Sandra is saying, is quickly running to Maria Copper's office where the special investigative reporter has just arrived. Maria, who is wearing a grey, shark-skinned, two-piece suit, is an olive-skinned Cuban woman with distinctive brown eyes and long, brown, curly hair that reaches all the way to the bottom of her back. Looking over her messages, Maria quickly looks up at her glass office door as she can see her wild-eyed assistant waving to get her attention

Looking somewhat amused by the excitement in Gail's eyes, Maria waves her in. Holding her hand over the receiver of the phone, Gail says, "You are not going to believe this, but I have Sandra Lyte on the other end right now and she claims she has that information concerning major corruption that she wants to bring in to only you."

Maria, looking at her assistant, gestures for the phone, "Hello, this is Maria Copper. Whom may I be speaking with?"

        *   *   *

Standing by the hotel window looking at the traffic and more importantly looking for police cars, Sandra answers, "Ms. Copper, my name is Sandra Lyte and I do not know if you have seen what is on the news right now, but I did not kill anyone and I can prove it if you give me the chance. Ms. Copper, I am not turning myself into police custody because honestly, I will not make it through the night. I have evidence that will shatter the foundation of the New York City Police Department. Certain officers, who have much to lose, would definitely kill me to keep things quiet. That is why they say I am armed and dangerous so that some trigger-happy cop can have an excuse to blow my damn head off as soon as I make a sudden move. Now Ms. Copper, I have great respect for all of the good you have done for the small people in this city. I know you have no reason whatsoever to believe me, but I am telling you I have major proof on video that will clear my name and bring those to justice responsible for murdering my children. You remember that story on Christmas Day, don't you Ms. Copper?"

        *   *   *

Sitting at her desk and twirling a fountain pen between her fingers, Maria, looking at her assistant, responds, "Yes Sandra, I know who you are and what happened to your children. I am so sorry, but you do understand that I cannot officially interfere in police matters. Sandra, this is a serious police matter that will come to head one way or another. Therefore, I will say this with no intention on hurting you or leaving you out there in the cold. At five o'clock this evening, for my Friday report, I am supposed to go on the air to report on fraudulent jewelry shop owners. If you somehow can make it to my assistant at a specified location that I will give you by five today, then Sandra, I promise I will look at what you have and if it is, as explosive as you claim, then I will lead in tonight's broadcast with your story. As I said, though, I will not help you elude the police that will be strictly up to you. Get a pen and paper because I am going to give you my personal cell phone number that will get you directly in contact with me, but you are to only use the number when you are near Rockefeller center in Manhattan."

*   *   *

Grabbing a piece of paper and pen, Sandra writes down all of the information that Maria gives her and says, "Yes Ms. Copper, I understand everything you have said and I appreciate you giving me this chance to tell my story. Well, I guess I better let you go now and I hope to see you later on today, Goodbye Ms. Copper." Hanging up the phone, Sandra turns to Pamela and Rose who have been sitting on the bed taking in the whole conversation.

*   *   *

Maria, hanging up the phone, looks silently at Gail for a moment when she says, "I want you to drop all you are doing right now, Ok? I need you to run a background check on this woman and tell me what comes up. Because if she is on the up and up on what she claims, this could blow us right past our other two rivals on the block and very possibly blow me up this stations chauvinistic ladder. So, Gail as always help me out."

Catching her phone from Maria, an excited looking Gail responds, "Yes, Ms. Copper, right away." As Gail exits her office, Maria plants her feet that are covered with seven hundred dollar crocodile shoes on her desk and quietly says, "Ok, Sandra, make me shine."

*   *   *

Sitting on the bed with her friends, Sandra grabs each one of them by the hand: "Ok, we all know the truth and we all know what that means to the police: nothing. I am a wanted woman, which means you two can not be seen with me at any time."

Jumping up from the bed and upset, Rose says, "No, we have to stick together and not let them scare us, Ms. Sandra."

Gently grabbing Rose by the arm and pulling her back down on the bed, Pamela says, "Sandra, I understand what must be done. You need to understand though, that these cops are nothing like the cops in Virginia. I have seen too many of us mistakenly gunned down, claiming a shiny object was seen in our hand. The only way baby you are going to make it is by staying low and buried in the cracks of the streets." Taking a deep breath, Sandra looks at Pamela shaking her head in agreement and says, "I have to get rid of these clothes and maybe do something different with my hair. Even though we used cash for this room, I still do not trust staying here much longer because who knows if the clerk at the desk remembered our faces."

Pamela looking Sandra over says, "Let me run out and get a few things that can help make you look a little different and then we can quickly decide what our plan is."

Grabbing Pamela by the arm, Sandra responds, "No Pamela, my plan, not ours, Ok? Once we leave this room, yes, we can agree to meet someplace and hopefully leave this city, but for any reason, sweetheart, I do not make it back…"

A now crying Rose jumps up from the bed and says, "Do not say that, Ms. Sandra. You have to make it back! Remember what we promised, the house, pool and us living with each other forever?"

Reaching out and pulling Rose close to her, Sandra says, "Yes, baby, I remember and I promise to do all that I can to make that happen for all of us. Pamela, when we leave, we will decide where you and Rose will stay. If by midnight tonight I do not return, in that suitcase is two million dollars that you; Pamela will take and start a new life with Rose, making sure she goes to college. While getting a house with a pool, you understand my sister?"

Pamela, fighting back the tears, shakes her head in agreement: "Yes sister, I understand. Listen time is not on our side right now; I better run out and get your things." As Pamela smiles and begins to walk out of the motel door, Sandra grabs her by the arm and pulls her towards her so that they share an embrace.

Chapter Thirty-Four
The Gauntlet

Inside a poorly lit room in the basement of police headquarters, Detective Tommy Davis stands in front of fellow comrades Sam Daniels, Joseph McCarthy and Tony Harris. All four men are putting on bulletproof vests and loading unregistered guns. Wearing dark shades and leather jackets, they are all very intimidating looking with emotionless stares on their faces. Walking in front of each man, Tommy hands out a photo of Sandra and i730's to communicate with one another.

"Very simple men, the situation as we know it has taken a turn for the worst. We all know what is at stake here. She must be disposed of immediately. Sam and Joe, you two will buddy up while Tony and I will work together. We will stay in constant contact, paying close attention to radios and scanners. Also, remember we have blues at our disposal and they are under strict orders to stay in contact with us if we need them. Finally, men, once caught, we shoot and plant immediately. Ok, everyone stay alert and be careful, let's go." As Tommy opens up the large black door leading to the stairs, he watches all his fellow officers leave with death in their eyes.

10:30 a.m. finds Sandra, Pamela and Rose all dressed, getting ready to leave the motel. Standing in front of a full-length mirror, Pamela admires the camouflage job she has performed on Sandra, whose long black braids are now cut down to the top of her shoulders and colored blonde. Wearing baggy carpenter jeans and a thick, blue-hooded sweatshirt, Sandra decides to go without a coat, simply because the weight could hamper her and the temperature; will rise to the mid fifties. On her head is a blue fitted baseball cap and on her face is a pair of black sunglasses. With Sandra's cell phone clipped securely to her belt and the discs taped to her back under her sweater, Pamela looking at her watch says, "It is time for us to go" at this time the three friends gather together.

Looking at each other, the three women hug and grab their possessions. Getting ready to exit the room Sandra says, "Remember what we agreed on, ok? A minute past midnight, you two go to the airport; no waiting, agreed?" Pamela and Rose, looking at each other, shake their heads slowly in agreement. Opening the door, they exit with Pamela holding the suitcase and Sandra holding Rose's hand.

The sun shines brightly on the street as Sandra, no longer looking at her friends, quickly enters a blue cab while Pamela and Rose enter a green one that sits right behind Sandra's. As the two cars pull off, Sandra goes towards the Henry Hudson while Pamela's takes her and Rose to a Holiday Inn, one hundred feet from JFK airport.

*   *   *

Riding down Broadway, Sandra's driver begins to merge with traffic at 254th and Broadway to get on the southbound side of exit 22. Looking at her watch, Sandra allows a small smile to come on her face because in about one hour, she will be at the news station bringing those to justice, while for the first time attempting to try to put her life back in order. Looking at the scenery overlooking the Hudson River, she can only imagine being with her new friends, with the hope of one day laughing again. More importantly though, Sandra imagines someday letting herself come to ease and allowing her two precious ones to rest in peace. Feeling her back, Sandra slides her hand across the plastic bag that would put the corrupt cops away for a very long time. If they have families, they too could also feel a little what Sandra felt: pain and suffering. As the driver continues to drive smoothly along, Sandra removes her shades and looks ahead at the traffic leading to the tollbooths ahead. Looking again at her watch, Sandra asks the driver, "Excuse me, sir; it is just a little past eleven. Is the traffic always backed up like this at this time?"

The driver, who is looking also at the scene ahead of him, answers, "Absolutely not. I come across this highway three or four times a week, and I have never seen it this backed up at this time before."

Taking a deep breath, Sandra's heart pumps a little, but she is able to calm herself down, not letting the scene upset her. With the traffic in all three lanes inching ahead, the driver can see the tunnel, which is now about 300 feet in front of him. "I cannot be sure because my vision is not that great, but it looks like I see police officers and for some reason, it looks as if they have created some type of check point." He says.

Rubbing her hands slowly but tightly together, Sandra takes a deep breath and stretches her head forward, trying to get a glimpse as they continue to inch forward. With her eyesight better than the driver's, Sandra's heart is racing much faster now and there is no way of slowing it down. Now about 150 feet from the tunnel, Sandra can clearly see flashing lights ahead and six police officers, from what she can tell, walking around near the tunnel with flash lights. She wonders how long have they been out here and why are they on this particular highway. Sandra asks her driver, "Excuse me sir, I am sorry for disturbing you again, but is there a way that we can get off this highway and maybe take the scenic route?"

Looking behind him, the driver points in the opposite direction to his right: "That was the last exit before the toll and there is no way I would ever try to back up. Besides, it has got to be at least three hundred cars behind us." As the cab gets closer to the tunnel leading to the tollbooths, Sandra now can clearly see police officers looking inside cars, while two officers have dogs.

With her anxiety building, Sandra takes forty dollars out of her pocket and makes a demand to the driver: "Sir, I know this is an inconvenience, but I need to get out of your cab, so can you please stop?"

Turning around slowly, the driver looks at Sandra as if she has lost her mind. "Lady, are you crazy? We are on the damn highway and if I let you out, I could lose my license. Besides, we are almost there and we have not done anything wrong; they will just look in the car then let us continue. Please just relax, Ok?"

While the driver was giving Sandra his rationale; she has gathered one hundred dollars, reaching over to the front seat and dropping it in his lap. "Sir, that is one hundred dollars for a ten-minute ride now let me out of this damn car, or when the cops get to us, I will tell them you are kidnapping me. I mean it now; open this fucking door," says Sandra. Bringing his car to a complete stop with only 40 feet separating them from the tunnel, the driver says, "You are sick; get the hell out of here. I hope you get run over."

Grabbing on to the handle, Sandra opens the door. Feeling her back and making sure her discs are still there, she gently steps one foot out on the highway. Adjusting her shades and hat, Sandra begins to walk quickly back to the previous exit, half crouched over. Ducking and weaving between slow moving cars, which are now honking at her, Sandra has now made it over to the left lane where the exit leading up to Riverdale Ave. is now 100 feet away. With sweat beginning to pour down her face, Sandra begins to remove her sunglasses then thinks better of it.

Huffing and trying to gather fresh air into her body to fight the fumes, Sandra hears a loud and long whistle. Knowing for a fact that it is in regards to some fool running in the opposite direction on a major highway, she does not bother to turn around when she hears, "Police, halt!"

Feeling cramps making an entrance inside her body, Sandra fights the tears and the pain, seeing the exit is now 20 feet away. Looking at the exit, packed with cars, Sandra is exhausted because the exit is on an incline. No longer running but limping along while holding her ribs, which feels as if someone has crushed them with a baseball bat, Sandra grits her teeth together and begins to lug her body up the incline. For some reason, she feels a need to look behind her and finds three officers, one holding a dog in pursuit gaining on her. Now on a walkway, Sandra is halfway up the ramp, but beginning to slow down and every step brings the urge to vomit. Taking a peep behind her, she can clearly see one of the officer's faces while he is saying something on his radio. Letting out grunts, Sandra stumbles and almost falls on her face but holds herself up by bracing on the trunk of a green Towncar. Removing her hand, she can barely read because of the sweat in her eyes.

"Flamingo cab#44 call 718-555-8989" is on the bumper sticker. Banging on the driver's window, which scares him half to death, the Dominican man rolls down his window and yells, "No working! Going home Mommy!"

Sandra, still unable to speak, looks back seeing the officers are now weaving through the cars, running towards her with their guns drawn. Quickly rambling through her pocket, Sandra removes a knot of hundred dollar bills, shoving them in the driver's face. Moving his head back to focus, he looks at the money and then at Sandra, saying, "Come now! Hurry now!"

Hearing the door locks pop open, Sandra quickly jumps inside the cab, slamming the door behind her. With her body running on empty for lack of oxygen, she is able to moan: "Trying...to kill...me...please go!"

Without hesitation, the cabby makes a sharp right, which causes the right front and rear tires to jump on the walkway. With half of the car on a tilt, the driver begins passing cars in front of him while blowing his horn. Still breathing very hard and feeling queasy, Sandra is able to lift her body up and look through the rear window where she can see the police standing and talking on their radios as they have stopped giving chase.

"Mommy, where you going?" the cabby asks.

Now coughing, Sandra is able to gather her senses to answer, "Rockefeller Center at Forty-Eighth Street in Manhattan, please. Here, take this one hundred dollar bill, just hurry."

Now clutching the money inside his stubby hands, the driver making a left, heads towards 230th Street and Broadway. Weaving through traffic, he makes a quick right heading towards the Grand Concourse and 205th Street. "Are you sure you know where you are going, mister?" asks Sandra.

Taking a quick look back at her, he answers confidently, "I know the city lady; you do not worry. What happened back there? Who is going to kill you?"

Wiping her face with her sweater, Sandra answers, "Some very bad people," as she lays her head back on the headrest.

* * *

Detectives Tommy Davis and Tony Harris are riding south on Broadway and 238th Street, paying close attention to their police scanner, which can pick up cab dispatcher frequencies. Hearing over their radio of the perp running on the Henry Hudson Parkway, Tommy goes with his gut and assumes that it is Sandra. Getting the color of the car, the company, and a partial plate number, Tony has radioed Sam and Joseph, telling them to play close attention. Turning up his scanner, Tommy listens carefully as he can hear the Flamingo dispatcher calling for car number 44. Pulling his car to the side and bringing it to a halt, Tommy listens closely, hoping to pick something up.

As the driver picks up the handle of his car radio, he answers his dispatcher, "Yes, I am on one nine five Grand Concourse going south to Rockefeller center. Come back Manny, you break up." Tapping the receiver of the radio on the dashboard, the driver cannot make out what his dispatcher is saying, so he tosses the receiver on the driver's seat of the cab. Looking back at Sandra, who is focusing on the numbered street signs descending with each passing block, the driver says, "Don't worry Mommy. We make on time, ok?"

Looking at him with a slight bit of confidence in her eyes, Sandra gives him a small smile while nodding her head. Looking up at the street sign as they come to a red light, Sandra reads that they are now on 188th street and the Grand Concourse, right next to the now closed Loews Paradise movie theater.

*   *   *

Tommy, breathing fast and hard, grabs his i730 and two-ways Detective Daniels: "Sam, listen up. What is your twenty?"

Getting two quick beeps on his phone, Tommy hears, "Right now where riding south on Webster Avenue and 202nd street and getting close to Fordham Road."

Pressing the button on his phone, Tommy says, "Listen, when you get to Fordham, make a left and blast your siren; they are on the Grand Concourse driving a green Towncar from the Flamingo Cab Company, car number forty-four. I know this bitch is heading to Manhattan to turn those discs over to someone in the media. We are heading that way also. Go, Sam, go!" Throwing his phone on the dashboard, Tommy hits his siren and takes off, heading south on Broadway.

*   *   *

With traffic picking up somewhat at 161st Street, the driver says, "Mommy, I take a short cut at one forty-nine street and go across one forty-five street Bridge that put us back near Broadway, Ok?"

Looking at her watch, which reads 11:25 a.m., Sandra responds, "Whatever mister. Just please hurry up." Shaking his head up and down, the cabby drives towards 149th Street.

*   *   *

Sitting inside a Holiday Inn room, Pamela sits on the bed, watching the television intently as the news at noon is going to begin. Rose stands silently looking out of the window, frightened but somewhat amazed at how close the airplanes are flying near their window. Turning her attention to Pamela, who has not spoken for the past fifteen minutes, Rose walks over and sits on the bed, tapping Pamela on the shoulder: "Do you think she will make it back to us? Because I do not think, it will be right if we go without her. We all promised that we would be a family."

Turning away from the television and looking deeply into Rose's eyes, Pamela strokes her gently across the head saying, "Yes, sweetheart. I do believe she will make it back. No matter what, Rose baby, Sandra will always love us and hold us dear to her heart until the bitter end, do you understand?" Shaking her head up and down, Rose lays her head on Pamela's shoulder, looking at the twelve o'clock news, which is getting ready to air.

*   *   *

As the traffic light turns green, Sandra's cab gradually picks up speed as they are now at the corner of 149th Street beginning to make their right turn. Riding down the bumpy street, Sandra exhales as she can see the 145th Street Bridge getting closer. With the static noise coming from his radio again, the driver picks up his receiver to announce, "Manny, I no hear nothing good, Ok? I am going on 145th Lenox Avenue I call when I coming back." Putting on his sunglasses the driver comes to the end of the bridge where he makes a left. As they drive down Lenox Avenue, flashbacks come to Sandra of when she rented a room not to far from the area. Now coming towards Harlem Hospital, the car slows down as the traffic light is at yellow when Sandra's body suddenly thrown against the back of the driver's seat because of a car smashing them from behind. The driver, who almost bangs his head on the steering wheel, looks behind him:

"Oh shit, what the hell!" Holding and rubbing her neck, Sandra is still able to look from the back of her window where she can see a black sedan with two white male occupants sitting inside. Looking closer, she can see one of them loading a gun. Sandra begins breathing harder and her heart starts to race as the man on the passenger side sticks half his body out of the window pointing his gun.

"Mister, go! Oh shit please mister they have guns, drive!" yells Sandra. Still rubbing his chest, the driver looks in his rearview mirror when shots ring out, smashing the rear window.

"Oh my God," he yells as he steps down hard on his gas peddle, causing a loud screeching noise from his tires.

Sandra, who has now dived on the floor of the car, can hear the screams of people who are witnessing what is going on. Holding her head between her elbows, Sandra yells to the driver, "Mister, please don't stop; they are going to kill me! Please just keep driving!" Feeling the car swerve from side to side, Sandra is squeezing her hands together, trying not to cry. "Mister, please do not let them catch us!" Four more shots ring out as Sandra can now hear the driver crying and saying a prayer in his native tongue. Two more shots are fired, totally shattering the rear window and showering Sandra with broken glass. Still not picking her head up, Sandra screams as she has just felt the car hit a bump. The car is swerving wildly now and she can hear the blasting of what sounds like one hundred different types of horns.

"Mister, are you Ok? Mister?" Sandra yells. Not getting an answer, she slowly tilts her head upward looking at the back of his headrest. Letting out a frantic yell, Sandra can now see that the driver's headrest has blood, brain and skull fragments all over it. With a look of shock all over her face, Sandra eases herself up from the floor and looks frantically around the car to see that not only is the driver dead but his foot is still on the accelerator as they speed down Lenox Ave. in the opposite direction, just missing oncoming cars.

"Oh shit!" Sandra yells as she dives over the top of the passenger seat, grabbing on to the steering wheel in an attempt to keep it straight. As cars swerve out of her way, Sandra, using one hand, attempts to move the drivers foot off of the peddle. Not being able to, Sandra focuses back on the street when a food vending truck comes towards her. She cannot turn quick enough, and it clips the right side of the cab, causing it to veer to the right jumping the curb, heading right towards a large pile of garbage.

"Oh God help me!" Sandra yells as she releases the steering wheel, burying her head in the passenger seat. Hearing screaming people who she hopes are running out of the way, the car hits the garbage and a fire hydrant coming to a stop, deploying the air bags. Looking for her sunglasses and hat, Sandra can hear the mulling of some people near her car. Opening her eyes and looking around, she covers her eyes with her wounded left hand because someone has just opened the passenger side door.

"Miss, are you Ok? Oh shit, this guy's head is blown open; somebody call the cops!" a black man yells. Reaching inside the car, the man who is tall and well built grabs Sandra by her waist and gently begins to pull her out.

"Stay calm lady, I got you," he says.

As a crowd of people begin to gather around the car, another man who is Spanish helps get Sandra to sit on steps of a nearby building. With her back aching, she reaches to feel for her discs and discovers that they are still there undamaged. Grabbing on the rail, Sandra winces in pain as she slowly lifts herself up. An old woman who is standing near Sandra says, "No, sweetheart. You stay still now; an ambulance is on its way and besides, Harlem hospital is only a few blocks away and the police are coming. Did you know there was a dead man in the car?"

Looking at the old woman while wrapping a handkerchief, someone had given her, around her injured hand, Sandra asks, "Where is the train station, miss?" a little Spanish boy looking at Sandra points up the block towards the 135th Street station. Stumbling down the steps, Sandra, to everyone's amazement, begins to slowly trot in that direction.

"Hey lady, where the hell are you going!" yells the man that got her out of the car. Sandra, determined to get to the train, ignores the yells of the bystanders, who are now looking in the opposite direction, hearing the ambulance siren getting closer to the scene.

Making a hard u-turn and coming to a screeching stop are Detectives Tommy Davis and Tony Harris, who quickly exit their car with badges around their necks and guns drawn. Running over to the crashed car, Tommy looks inside the vehicle to discover the dead driver, but the only thing he finds associated with Sandra is her sunglasses. Angrily looking at the crowd of people, Tommy loudly asks, "Where is the woman that was inside this car?"

With the crowd giving the officers the silent treatment, Tommy asks his partner, "Where is the nearest bus depot and train station?" Looking around his surroundings, Tony looks in the direction of the hospital and says, "The number two train is on one thirty-fifth street, three blocks that way." Grabbing his phone, Tommy pages Sam, "Daniels, listen to me, ok? You and McCarthy get over to the one twenty-fifth street Metro North Terminal and stay there just in case she shows her face. We are heading underground at one three five, you got me?"

Hearing the beep of his phone, Tommy listens at Sam's response: "That is a copy; we will be at Metro North Terminal until further notice, over." Taking one more look at the driver, Tommy and Tony run back over to their car and begin to enter when Tommy grabs his official radio sending out a call to the transit police to look out for Sandra at the Harlem hospital train station. Quickly getting inside their car, the two detectives drive off in that direction.

In the meantime, a police car and an EMS truck are now pulling up to the scene. The brother that pulled Sandra out of the car quietly says to himself, "Run sister, run."

*　　*　　*

Sandra, who is now standing at the front of the downtown platform, lowers her head in an attempt to conceal her face. Looking at her hand, she can now see that the bleeding has stopped and tosses the bloody handkerchief onto the tracks. Looking down the tracks, Sandra begins to get nervous when she sees no sign of a train approaching. Looking at her watch, it now reads 12:47 p.m.

Sandra almost jumps out of her skin when she hears from the uptown side of the platform, "Hey lady, why did you just litter on the tracks?" Slowly lifting her head up, Sandra peers in the direction of the voice and there standing on the uptown side of the platform are two unformed police officers. Deciding not to say a word, she turns her attention back to the platform floor when she can hear a transmission coming from one of their radios. Looking up again, Sandra and the officer on the radio catch each other's eyes. She can also see that he has whispered something to his partner, who is leaving the uptown side of the tracks to join Sandra on the downtown side. Sandra notices the officer that was on his radio unsnapping his gun holster as he slowly begins to walk down the platform so that he would be directly in front of her. Taking a quick glance down the tracks again, Sandra only notices people like herself frustrated with the delay of the downtown number two train. Looking back at the officer, as he slowly raises his hands saying, "Don't you fucking move lady. I mean it; don't you fucking move." Looking down the platform Sandra spots the other officer, who is walking towards her and right behind him by the turnstiles are Detectives Davis and Harris, who already have their weapons drawn. Some of the bystanders waiting for the train have just noticed what is taking place, causing some to hurry back outside while some remain in place looking at the scene unfold. Sandra breathing hard, takes a few steps backwards never taking her eyes off the two detectives especially Tony, who is slowly raising his weapon towards her direction.

"Lady, just fall to your knees with your hands up and all of this will be over," says the uniformed officer that is now 30 feet away from Sandra.

Looking at Tony, who has death in his eyes, Sandra says, "I did not do anything; if I do as you say, do you promise not to hurt me?"

The uniform officer has now stopped walking towards Sandra, raising his hands to signify that everything will be all right as he says, "I promise you, nobody will hurt you."

The officer looking over at his partner, who stands on the uptown platform, motions to him with his hand to relax, never seeing the two detectives behind him because of their plain clothes. Sandra, who begins to get on her knees with her hands in the air, starts to tremble because she sees the "Dragon" take aim. "No!" Sandra screams as she takes three steps towards the edge of the platform jumping onto the wet and dirty train tracks. Bang! Bang! Is the sound of bullets as they leave the gun of Detective Harris, both just missing Sandra's' head.

"What the fuck are you doing, Tony! Not here, you fucking idiot!" yells detective Davis, who is flashing his badge at the unformed officers who have turned towards them and are a split second away from returning fire.

"Officer, hold your fire! We are NYPD. Hold your fire!" he yells, holding his shield in the air as he weaves through screaming and running, panic-stricken people.

The officer on the uptown platform, who now has his gun drawn, yells, "She is in the tunnel! Pete, she is in the tunnel; radio in to command station to kill the third rail! I'm going in after her!" Officer Pete, who is looking at Tommy with a very pissed off stare, grabs his radio and does what his partner has requested.

*　*　*

Scared and nervous, Sandra holds her hands out in front of her as she runs in the middle of the downtown track with no idea of where she is going. Feeling her sneakers getting soak and wet with what smells like a combination of urine and sewage water, Sandra covers her mouth with one of her hands, pushing that morning's breakfast back down her throat. Breathing heavily, she begins to pick up her speed a little when after a few more steps; she trips over a loose bolt, causing her to fall on her hands and knees. Lying in brown, sewage water, Sandra is moaning in pain, trying to lift herself up when she hears "Lady, stop running; you are going to get yourself killed!"

Managing to turn her head in the direction of the voice, Sandra is able to make out a small beam of light that has to be a flashlight. Turning her head back around to see what is in front of her, Sandra lets out a blood-curdling scream, as standing on it's hind legs two feet from in front of her face is a 14-inch rat that has to weigh at least 4 pounds.

"Oh shit!" she yells while using every muscle in her body to lift herself up to her feet. As Sandra makes it to her feet, the monster rat scurries away from her and hides under the third rail. Now on her feet and knowing more than ever that she wants out of this dark sea of puss called a tunnel, Sandra ignores every ache and pain throughout her body, quickening her pace, hoping to see a ray of light.

Looking at his partner with disgust and anger, Tommy smacks Tony hard on the shoulder saying, "You stupid ass. I told you we do this my way. I am telling you asshole, if she gets away, we might as well put bullets in our fucking heads ourselves. Now come on let's go." Hurrying through the turnstiles, the detectives run upstairs to their car, leaving the lone uniformed officer on the platform.

As they enter their car, Tommy picks up his i730 and two-ways Sam, who is at the 125th street Metro North Station.

"Sam, listen partner, all hell has just broken loose down here. Sandra Lyte has just taken off into the one three five tunnel heading south. You two need to get to one two five and Lenox; I know she is going to come out from that side. You guys move your asses, fast"

Hearing the beep on his phone, Tommy listens to Sam respond, "That is a copy; we are moving over to said location right now, over." Throwing the phone back on the dash Tommy starts his car up and heads to 125th Street.

*   *   *

With the pain of her returning cramps, Sandra holds the left side of her rib cage as she continues to move, now only hearing low faints of the officers voice, which tells Sandra either he gave up on chasing her or he is assuming she is dead. Not caring what the officer is thinking, Sandra looks ahead about 20 feet and can see a blue light bulb that sits in a fixture to her right. Getting closer, Sandra begins to ignore the stench of the tunnel and lets a glimmer of hope enter her mind, as above the blue light is a sign that reads, "EXIT." Stopping and looking at the large read letters, Sandra listens in silence to hear if anyone or anything is near. With the reassurance that she is still alone, she looks up at an opening that looks like it contains stairs. Realizing now that she is about five feet down on the tracks, Sandra uses her hands to brace herself on the cold and dirty ledge trying to lift herself up, but she is unsuccessful in her first attempt. Breathing hard but feeling determined, she takes a couple of steps back and tiptoes quickly to the ledge. Jumping with all the springs that her thick but tired legs will give her, Sandra catches half her body on the ledge while her legs swing and dangle in the darkness.

"Please, please, please," Sandra squeals through her clenched teeth as she fights to get her whole body on the ledge when she feels a large hand touching her hip, pushing her up onto the ledge.

"Oh God, please don't hurt me!" she yells as she quickly turns around to see who is helping her. Grabbing her chest trying to control the fear that is running through her body, Sandra is looking into the eyes of a tall white man with a long dirty beard, who smells like garbage.

"Please don't be afraid; I won't hurt you. My name is Winthrop and I am cousins with the Duke of Earl. Are you looking for a place to sleep? I have many rooms in my mansion."

Sandra, looking straight into Winthrop's eyes, can only answer softly, "No, Winthrop. I do not need a place to sleep; I am just looking for a way to get back to the streets."

Looking at Sandra, he slowly stretches his hand out gently rubbing her head, saying, "Why do you want to get back to the streets? They will only hurt you out there. Why do you think...hey I know you? You are the woman that I saw on the TV before they kicked me out of the restaurant this morning. They say you killed some people, but I do not believe them because all they do is lie."

Standing up and bracing herself on the ledge and wall, Sandra is now looking down on Winthrop when she says, "That is right Winthrop; they are telling lies, but the only way that I can help myself is to get out of here. Do you think you can help me, please?"

Looking up and down the dimly dark tunnel, Winthrop looks at Sandra with pity in his eyes: "The younger ones try to set me on fire when I sleep and nobody cares anymore that all I have to eat is fur."

Sandra, who is now feeling antsy and frustrated, wants to get away from Winthrop in the worst way, but something is keeping her in that one spot: "What do you mean eating fur and people trying to set you on fire?"

Reaching into a dirty, half-ripped pocket of his jacket, the man pulls out a half-eaten rat, causing Sandra to turn her face in disgust. With her head still turned, Sandra says, "Winthrop, I promise that if you help me, I will help you so that you can eat and sleep somewhere nice, Ok?"

Looking at Sandra with skepticism, he answers, "The chief of the city always says that he will help us, but he never does. I just want to feel hot water again; I have the right to taste chicken soup again, right?"

Knowing the feeling of losing self-respect for oneself, Sandra says, "Help me Winthrop and then I can help you, but we have to hurry. Please, I beg you."

Grabbing the ledge, Winthrop pulls himself up on the concrete walkway, looking at Sandra, who is about one foot shorter then him.

"You really need my help?" Looking up at Winthrop, feeling that this man needs to feel wanted, Sandra answers, "Yes I do."

"Come this way; I know a way to the streets where the soldiers of this tunnel won't see you; just follow me." As the tall man walks into a doorway, Sandra cautiously follows behind him.

Looking at a set of metal steps that Winthrop has pointed out to her, Sandra looks up in the direction of where they will lead and lets a cautious smile come to her face as she can see a very small ray of light.

"You follow me up miss and I will open it for you so that you can tell them the truth." As the man begins to climb the steps, Sandra reaches out and grabs his dirty and bruised hand.

"I want you to have this Winthrop and I want to thank you for helping me. I want you to feel good, Ok?"

Stretching out her hand, Sandra gives the man ten fresh twenty-dollar bills.

Watching Winthrop close his hand around the money, Sandra says, "By the way, my name is Sandra." As Winthrop leads her up the steel steps, Sandra feels her back to make sure the discs are still in place. Now at the top of the steps, Winthrop positions himself so that he will be able to use his back as leverage when pushing up on the grating.

"You get ready Sandra, because I do not know how long I can hold this up." Shaking her head in agreement Sandra holds on to the guardrail and watches. Grunting and straining with his entire mite, the man pushes with all of his strength. Sandra, looking on, wonders if he will be successful because the grating seems so heavy when more light from outside begins to shine inside, letting Sandra see Winthrop's weather beaten face. Letting out a louder and heavier grunt, he now has the grating opened enough so that Sandra can make it through.

"Go, Sandra. I cannot hold it much longer. Looking at the redness overtake the dirt on his face, Sandra quickly squeezes her thick body past Winthrop and through the grating. Now standing on 129th Street and Lenox Ave. taking in all of the fresh air that she can at once, Sandra looks down at the grating where Winthrop stands underneath, looking up at her.

"Go tell the truth Sandra and be free," he says. Looking down on him, Sandra whispers, "I will and thank you." Looking around 129th street, then at her filthy clothes, Sandra looks back down towards the grating to say something to Winthrop, but just like that, he is gone. Brushing dirt from her hair, Sandra looks at her watch and sees that it is now 1:26 p.m.

Looking around hoping to find a store, she notices a few people who are in the area staring at her. Looking on the corner of 129th Street, she sees a bodega and lets out a sigh of relief as she is dying for a bottle of water. Walking slowly towards the bodega, Sandra hears a loud "WHOOP WHOOP" sound. Continuing to walk towards the store, Sandra acts as if she never heard the sound when a voice comes from a speaker, "You, lady with the blonde hair, come over here to the car right now." Taking a quick look at the car, Sandra turns and begins to walk in the other direction of the police car when from the speaker the officer says, "I said stop right there and do not move lady." As the police car stops and the officers begin to get out, Sandra makes a fast dash for it, running north on Lenox Ave.

With the two officers not far behind her, a dirty and exhausted Sandra looks across the street and spots a social club. Quickly dashing across the street, she swings the door open and walks to the back of the club, totally ignoring the forty men in motorcycle gear sitting at the bar and at a few tables. The men who were watching a DVD of a motorcycle exhibition are now staring at Sandra, who sits in a corner in the back of the club. The bartender, looking at a few of the "Black Nightfalcons," walks from behind his bar and proceeds to the back where Sandra sits.

A few of the men are pointing at Sandra and quietly talking among each other. One of these men, whose name is "Hawk," says to a fellow member, "Yo, I seen her around here a while back. My baby sister said her kids got thrown out of the window this past Christmas."

The other member named Eddie shakes his head from side to side: "Damn, Hawk you serious? She's probably fucked up in the head roaming the streets now and just wandered in here."

Sandra looking at her cell phone sees that she is down to two bars looks at her watch pounding her fist on her thigh.

"Running out of time, I have to keep going," she says not noticing the shadow that cast over her. Sandra wipes her face with some napkins that are lying on the table:

"Excuse me miss, but are you Ok?" asks Biscuit, the bartender who stands six feet five inches weighing about three hundred and twenty pounds.

Sandra, finally noticing her surroundings, looks up and scoots away from the giant of a man saying, "I'm sorry sir. Please don't hurt me; I am leaving right now, Ok?"

Holding his hands up, Biscuit says, "Whoa my sister, calm down. Nobody here is going to hurt you." Feeling a tap on his shoulder, Biscuit turns around and is face to face with Hawk, who whispers in Biscuits ear as Sandra, looks on. Looking at Sandra with a bit of compassion, Biscuit asks, "Miss, is someone after you? Is that the reason why you ran in here and hid in the corner?"

Looking at all of the men in the club, Sandra says to biscuit, "Some policemen are trying to kill me and right now I do not have time to explain my story to you. If you can be so kind just to let me wash my face in your restroom and then let me leave through the back exit, I promise you will never see me again."

Taking out his keys, Biscuit walks over to a closet, opens the door and turns on a light. Walking back out, he hands Sandra an extra large sweatshirt with the "Nighthawks" emblem on the front and a washcloth.

"It's a little big for you, but you can have it and there is a sink with some soap inside. Go clean yourself up and then you are free to leave" says, Biscuit.

Taking the sweatshirt, Sandra says, "Thank you very much" closing the door behind her.

Hawk, looking at the situation, begins to walk back to his seat when Detectives Davis, Harris, Daniels and McCarthy enter the club with their badges exposed around their necks. The club is completely silent except for the sound of bikes coming from the television.

"Good afternoon gentlemen. I am Detective Davis and I will make this short and sweet so that even you will understand. Over my radio a few moments ago, I heard a call about a female perp who goes by the name of Sandra Lyte. A brown skin woman about five foot four inches and weighing one hundred and forty pounds. She was last seen running down this block wearing a blue hooded sweatshirt and her hair is blonde. Can anyone help me?"

As the detectives look around the bar, all the club members remain silent until Biscuit speaks up: "No detective, I have been here all day, no one has entered my establishment fitting that description. If you would like to leave your card, I will be sure to contact you if anyone happens to see her."

Detective Davis, looking at Biscuit, looks over to Hawk who is opening the door where Sandra is: "Excuse me my man, but where are you going?" asks Davis.

Looking at Davis as if he is no one important, Hawk answers, "Detective, I am going to the men's room; there is no crime in that is there?"

Giving Hawk a long, dirty look, Detective Davis replies, "Not at this moment and watch you're fucking mouth, my friend." Turning away from Davis, Hawk enters the bathroom.

Entering the bathroom with his finger pressed against his lips, Hawk motions to a petrified Sandra to calm down. Gently grabbing Sandra by the arm and pulling her close to him, Hawk whispers, "We have three minutes to get you out of here before they wonder what is taking me so long, ok?"

Still shaking from the sound of Davis's voice, Sandra is able to whisper, "They killed my babies mister, please help me." Totally believing Sandra and with compassion in his eyes, Hawk leads Sandra to a window and proceeds to open it. Stepping on the toilet bowl, Hawk, who is thin but very muscular, quickly climbs out of the window, jumping to the ground that is three feet below.

Watching as Sandra now has half her body out of the window, Hawk reaches up and grabs her two hands, pulling her gently through the window, when Sandra screams, "He's got my legs, help me; he's pulling my legs!"

Quickly looking up Hawk can see somebody violently yanking at Sandra's leg. "Oh shit!" Hawk yells as he uses all of his muscles to pull Sandra as hard as he can through the window when he hears, "Tommy, help me! I got her, help me!"

Sandra, who is screaming in pain because of her stomach rubbing across the metal windowsill, uses her left leg to thrust back, kicking Detective Harris, also known to Sandra as the "Dragon," in his face, knocking him backwards onto Detective Davis, causing them both to fall to the bathroom floor.

"Pull me, please!" Sandra yells to Hawk, who does so, getting her out the window onto the ground.

"Come on Sandra, get up!" Hawk yells as he pulls her towards his grey Suzuki Hayabusa 1300 motorcycle. Grabbing his helmet, he quickly puts it on Sandra's head and jumps on his bike, starting it up. Grabbing her by the arm, Hawk gets her on and asks, "Where are we going?"

Holding on tight to his waist, Sandra yells through the helmet, "Rockefeller Center."

As Hawk gets ready to speed off, he comes face to face with the four detectives, who are yelling at him to halt as they start to remove their weapons. Quickly spinning the bike around on its front wheel, Hawk takes off in the opposite direction. Grabbing his radio, Detective Davis radios all cars in the area for back up, describing the bike and what direction they are heading.

The detectives, who are now running from the back of the club to their cars, are yelling at each other for letting Sandra get away.

"Listen, they are heading towards Broadway. You two get on Seventh because there is less traffic and we will continue down Broadway. They cannot get that far ahead with all of this fucking traffic," Tommy yells at Sam before entering his car.

As the detectives start their engines, getting ready to drive off, Sam looks at Joseph and says, "That dumb ass Tony cannot do anything right; if he would have cut her throat the right way, we would not be in this shit."

Joseph, shaking his head in agreement, responds, "He is a brain dead son of a bitch."

*   *   *

Sandra is holding onto Hawk's waist tightly as they swerve in and out of traffic heading south on 121st and 7th Avenue. Looking at the traffic ahead, Hawk begins to make a right on 120th street but quickly puts on his brakes, seeing a patrol car right in his pathway. Maneuvering the bike, he runs a red light and continues down 7th Avenue with the patrol car on his tail with sirens blasting. Looking back at Sandra, Hawk yells, "If they start shooting, you just hold on because things will get a little hairy on the back of this bike!"

With the helmet on her head, Sandra just nods up and down in agreement. Hawk, realizing that he will not be able to utilize the bike's speed in this traffic, begins to ride the lines of the street, dodging cars while briefly looking behind him to see how close the patrol car is behind him.

*   *   *

Maria, who is sitting in her office listening to the transmission of the police chase, turns on her computer and logs onto her GPS system to track the area where Sandra is. Looking up at her door because Gail has just entered, Maria says, "Come on in and sit down; I have something to ask you."

Sitting at Maria's desk, Gail pays close attention to her boss. "Gail, a few things bother me about this whole manhunt for this woman. First, they say she is the main suspect of a murder, why is Sandra running to me and not trying to flee the city? I mean, let's get serious; anybody with half a brain, knowing that they are going to prison is not sticking around, right? They are going to make a run for it. Something else puzzles me Gail; I was able to contact the detective that is covering Sandra's case. His name is Tommy Davis and every time I spoke to him about the case, I always got the same answer with a different level of hostility each time: 'We're working on it.' Finally and this has nothing to do with journalistic hunches just common sense. Sandra Lyte is one woman; tell me two things: why is the entire NYPD out chasing this one woman and why is it so difficult to catch her? Well as corny and stupid as this may sound, I will tell you why. Sandra has something very important that she wants to show me and it is destiny keeping her free. Gail what I am about to do will jeopardize my life and job. Can I continue to trust you as I have for the past nine years?"

Gail looking at her boss, who has never been so serious since they have known each other, says, "Yes, Ms. Copper you know you can trust me, but what are you about to do?

Picking up her cell phone and dialing a number, Maria answers, "Level the playing field."

Turning her attention back to her phone call, Maria says to someone on the other end, "Hello, this is Maria Copper. May I speak with my brother, Agent Ricky Copper? Yes I can hold."

* * *

It is now 2:23 p.m. Hawk and Sandra are riding on 86th street and Broadway with the same patrol car on their tail that is totally out of its jurisdiction. For some reason, the sirens on the car are not sounding off like they were in Harlem and though the car is keeping up at a steady pace; it has not attempted to run them off the street.

As the patrol cars' lights continue to flash inside the car, patrol officers Randy Thompson, a black man from Queens, and Stanley Combs, a white man from Staten Island, sit. Both men, listening for instructions from Detective Davis, are sweating profusely.

"Randy I just got on the force man, with a family and a new house. I am on those discs having sex with fucking prostitutes. If this shit leaks out man, I am done. I never should have listened to you."

Driving the car while angrily looking at his partner, Randy answers, "Oh, fuck you. Nobody twisted your arm to go with me to that damn party. You could not stop talking about it. Now act like you have a pair of balls and just get ready to smoke these two when Davis gives us the word."

As Hawk looks at the street sign, he sees that he is now on 74th Street, and the traffic is clearing up enough so that he may pick up a little speed. Doing so, Hawk comes to the corner of 72nd Street and pulling up right next to him are Detectives Davis and Harris. Both men have grimacing looks on their faces as they begin to steer closer to Hawk's bike. Hawk, looking in his side mirrors, can see that the patrol car is now speeding up on his left in an attempt to box him in. As people look on at the chase, which is now becoming more intense by the moment, Hawk fights to keep the bike steady as Detective Davis is now bumping him on his rear tire.

Looking ahead and seeing that all the lights are now turning green, Davis aware that Hawk will likely make a speed move tells Harris, "Tony, quickly take his tires out! Hurry up!"

Jumping from his seat into the back seat of the car, Tony quickly rolls down the left rear window and sticks half his body out, aiming his gun. Sandra, looking through the visor of the helmet, lets out a scream as she sees the tattoo on Tony's arm, pointing the gun in her direction. Hawk, looking to his right, sees this also and proceeds to put the bike in a faster gear, leaving the patrol car and the detectives behind when Tony lets off two rounds, causing people watching the scene to run in a panic. The first shot missed, but the second does not as it hits Hawk on the left side of his upper back.

"Shit, I'm hit!" He yells as he loses control of the bike, causing them to swerve to the right near the sidewalk on 66th Street and Broadway. Stopping the bike completely, Hawk is able to get Sandra and him off safely. Grimacing with pain, he falls to one knee as crowds of people gather around, some of them screaming for someone to call an ambulance. Still on one knee and barely able to breathe, Hawk can see that the two cars are only about a block and a half away. Reaching out to Sandra, he grabs the helmet, taking it off and looks her in the eyes: "Run sister! Hurry up and get out of here, go expose the truth!"

Looking back and seeing the cars getting closer, Sandra yells, "Come on get up. We can make it together! Get up; I can't leave you!"

Using all of his strength while falling to the ground, Hawk screams, "Run, Sandra. Damn it, run now!" Pushing Sandra away, Hawk collapses to the ground as Sandra begins running down Broadway, looking back one more time as she can now see the patrol car stopping and the two officers getting out and running towards Hawk with their guns drawn.

Because of the crowd gathering, Detective Davis and Harris are blocked and have to get out of their car, to pursue Sandra on foot now on 64th Street and Broadway.

As she dodges through the many people who are on the street, Sandra reaches for her cell phone, flipping the receiver up seeing that she is down to her last battery bar. Knowing that Maria has told her that she should not call until she was at their agreed location, Sandra feels she has no choice simply because she cannot run anymore. Holding her right side because of the extreme pain, Sandra presses the redial number, holding the phone to her ear while hopping across 62nd Street with Davis and Harris not far away on 63rd street.

*   *   *

Maria, who is standing by her desk along with Gail, quickly answers her cell phone: "Ok Sandra. Calm down and tell me where you are. I know where that is; how far are the men that are chasing you? My God, Sandra just keep going and do your best to blend in with the crowd, ok? Tell me what you are wearing...ok, get off the phone; I am going to do everything that I can, but you just keep going."

Hanging up from Sandra, Maria dials her brother directly: "Ricky, where are you? Ok, your people are going to have to hurry! She should be between 65th and 61st wearing..."

*   *   *

Detectives Harris and Davis are gaining on Sandra as they are now just a half a block away from her on 60th street when Davis two-ways Sam Daniels, "Sam, where the fuck are you guys? She is now running on the block of fifty-ninth street. I am still a half a block away from her; where are you? Forget it, I see you. She is the blonde woman running straight towards you. Grab her ass quickly and get her to your car!"

Sandra, now halfway in the middle of the block, slows down and wears a face of anguish, as she is 25 feet away from Detectives Daniels and McCarthy, who are holding out their badges and holding up their palms of their hands, motioning Sandra to halt.

Sandra can see a smiling Daniels silently mouth the words, "It's over, bitch," as he begins to walk slowly towards her. Looking behind her, Sandra sees Detectives Davis and Harris slowly approaching trying not to cause a scene that would alarm the shoppers around them. Detective Harris, looking hard into Sandra's eyes, takes his finger, slowly sliding it across his throat. As the four men now begin walking towards Sandra, she begins backing up towards the street, confused and not knowing where she can go. With a look of desperation on her face, Sandra yells, "Somebody help me! They are going to kill me!"

With people stopping and looking at the situation, the four detectives now realize they must move in quickly. Getting ready to pounce on Sandra, a black, unmarked van pulls up directly in front of Sandra, with the door sliding open; two agents dressed in black quickly grab Sandra pulling her inside. As the detectives look on in shock, Tommy Harris runs towards the van yelling, "Stop! No! Halt!" but to no avail as the speeding van heads down Broadway closing the door.

Looking around the dark but neat van, Sandra cannot say a word because of the fear running through her body when a tall, well-built Ricky Copper hands Sandra a bottle of water saying, "Just stay calm Ms. Lyte. Everything will be ok you are safe. I'm federal agent Ricky Copper and I'm taking you to my sister Maria." Slowly and cautiously taking the water, Sandra looks at the four agents that sit with her and says, "Thank you, you just saved my life" as she takes a long deserving drink of water.

Chapter Thirty-Five
Opening a Can of Worms

As Sandra, Maria, Ricky and Lou Peterson, the newsroom chief, sit and watch the DVD's, Gail enters the room, bringing Sandra a turkey sandwich and a bottle of ice tea. Rubbing Sandra on the shoulder and looking at her from the corner of her eye, Maria shakes her head slowly with admiration saying, "Sandra, are you sure you are Ok watching this again? I will never understand the pain you are feeling."

Taking a sip of the cold glass of ice tea that taste so good going down, Sandra answers, "I am fine, thank you and besides, I need to watch.

Looking at her watch, Maria says to her boss "Lou, we are leading with this in twenty minutes, right?"

Lou, staring at Maria as if she has lost her senses, answers, "Are you serious, Maria? You are damn right we are leading with this."

"Excuse me Agent Copper; I realize that I am going to have to answer some questions that could lead well into the night; do you think it would be ok if I call my two friends? I really need to let them know that I am ok."

Getting up from his chair, agent Copper answers, "Absolutely Sandra. Lets go to Maria's office where it is quiet."

*　　*　　*

Inside the hotel room by the cell phone are Pamela and Rose, who are sitting at the dining table working on a crossword puzzle. As the cell phone rings, both of them are startled as the blue light illuminates. Quickly flipping the receiver, Pamela answers, "Hello! Oh Sandra Please tell me you are ok!" asks Pamela.

Falling back into her chair, a crying Pamela looks at Rose and says, "Baby, Sandra made it, she is doing fine! She says to tell you that she misses you and very soon we will all be together."

Rose, biting her lower lip, cannot keep her emotions in check as she too begins to cry. "No Sandra its ok; we understand that you have much to do, you just please stay brave and stay in contact. Please call me so I can tell you where we are. Ok, Sandra we love you too, bye." As

Pamela puts down the receiver on the phone, Rose and she embrace.

* * *

As Maria gets her hair played with by the hairdresser, she looks over her notes as the producer lets her know with his fingers that they are going live in 10 seconds. Shuffling her papers one more time, the lights go on as the theme music plays. Sandra, who is backstage, watches intently as Maria leads in with the 5:00 evening news.

"Good evening, welcome to Channel Four News. I am Maria Copper and what we are about to show you tonight will involve extortion, sodomy, illegal drug use, attempted murder and the possible murder of two beautiful innocent children. My fellow New Yorker's, these crimes you must understand, were not committed by seasoned criminals but by different types of individuals that, when exposed, will rock the core of The New York City Police Department. That is right; the crimes committed all involve high-ranking officers who are detectives all the way down to uniformed officers. Viewers, this is not hear say or speculation. The crimes and criminal acts I speak of are caught on digital recorded discs and I must warn you that much of the footage you are about to see is graphic and strong. So, if you have children or easily offended, I advice you to please turn away because what is about to be shown will shock and anger you."

* * *

The whole hour has been dedicated to Sandra's discs as Maria has chronicled everything that has been shown on camera. Sandra, looking at everything, is relieved to see that the technicians were able to block out Rose's face as she performed sex acts in front of the cops. They were also able to enhance the sound and picture quality perfectly so that the whole city was able to watch all of the officers doing the evil things that would send them away for a very long time. Every officer, clearly seen and identified by Sandra, also includes a laughing and smiling Doug. Wondering what came of him and his father, Sandra only lets the thought last for a split second.

* * *

Standing around with his many aids inside, Gracie Mansion, the Mayor of New York City is beet red in the face as he watches and listens to the story of his police force spread like wildfire. Picking up a telephone as his staff looks on in silence and shame, the Mayor says, "Chief Brown, I want Captain Clarke, Lieutenant Jackson and yourself standing in my office in thirty minutes. Do I make myself clear?"

Getting his answer, the mayor calmly hangs up his phone and looks to his press aide, Yvette Jackson, asking, "Ok, Yvette, how do we handle this with the press?"

It is Friday 7:35 p.m. and Sandra is sitting inside a room along with a court-appointed attorney, four detectives and a criminal reporter. A detective Frank Zeigler is recording the session.

"Sandra, I want you to take your time and ask for anything you may need--a beverage, some food or just rest time and we will be glad to give it to you. We just want you to relax and answer our questions to the best of your ability because I am here to let you know that you are not on trial here. No ma'am; in my opinion, you are a hero." Taking a long and deep breath, Sandra begins her five-hour long session.

*   *   *

The mayor has ordered a special task force of the best decorated police officers to be put together to make major sweeps of all officers that were seen and involved on the discs. The unit consists of 50 highly trained men, who at exactly 8:00 p.m. under the command of the Mayor and Chief of Police are to swoop down like avenging angels bringing in all nine officers by nights end.

*   *   *

8:20 p.m. in Bensonhurst, Brooklyn a Detective Joseph McCarthy is being led out of his single-family brick home in handcuffs as his neighbors look on. His wife Judy, holding their six-month-old daughter, is screaming at the officers while being restrained by her father. While being lead to the police car, McCarthy silently words, "I am sorry," before being taken away.

*   *   *

8:45pm in the Bronx, Detective Sam Daniels is being handcuffed in the living room of his two-bedroom apartment while his wife of 24 years, Kim, looks on in tears as she hugs their crying daughter, Wendy age 19, who one hour ago surprised her parents by coming home from college for the weekend. While being led out the door, Wendy falls to her knees grabbing her father's leg to keep him home. Three officers gently take Wendy to another room.

*   *   *

8:50 p.m. in Elmhurst, Queens's five police officers being led by their sergeant, stand at the door of Detective Tony Harris. As they knock on the door announcing themselves as police officers, Tony commands them from the other side of his door to "Come on in". With the instructions of their sergeant the officers enter cautiously, wearing riot gear and their weapons exposed. Entering the apartment, infested with flies and roaches, the officers lower their weapons as they observe Tony Harris sitting on his couch with nothing on but a pair of boxers. Holding in his hand a half empty quart of Jack Daniels, Tony looks up at the officers saying, "Before you take me in, brother, let me first say this: I'm a fucking warrior that has been dealing with the scum of this city for twelve years now. You, my brothers in arms are taking me away because some fucking whore claims that we are bad people. No, my friends; I am not bad! I was trying to do all of us a favor by getting rid of that bitch before; she could hurt us and stop us from doing the job! So, take me in. I do not give a damn because I am not ashamed of who I am or what I have done because I was doing it for us, my brothers."

Staring at the drunken and disorientated Tony, the sergeant says, "Detective, please put some clothes on so we may take you in."

Tossing his bottle of whisky to the side, Tony holds out his hands and says, "Fuck that, take me in just like this in all my glory."

Handcuffing the detective, the officers lead him out of the apartment.

*   *   *

9:05 p.m., Detective Tommy Davis is sitting in a small rental fishing boat in the waters of City Island that is about 100 feet from shore. As a smiling Tommy sits inside the 9-foot rowboat, he stops paddling and lets the currents take over. Reaching inside a small black shaving bag, he removes three detective badges, setting them neatly on the floor of the boat. The badges belong to his father Jack Davis, his grandfather Benny Davis, and finally himself. He also removes from the bag a blue rosary that he lays across all three badges.

Looking up at the half moon, Tommy says, "On this night, I want to apologize for the dishonor and disgrace I have bestowed on you two. You taught me the rules, and I swore that I would always honor them. I have disgraced the force that I represent, while ruining fifty years of our name on the force. For that, I accept punishment. I love you both, and I am sorry. Please forgive me." After completing the sign of the cross, Tommy removes from his bag a revolver and gently puts the barrel in his mouth. Taking one more look at the badges, he closes his eyes and pulls the trigger, breaking the silence of the night for a split second. As the current continues to control the boat, Tommy lays motionless looking up at the heavens.

*   *   *

Saturday 1:35 a.m. finds Pamela and Rose waiting anxiously by the main entrance of the Holiday Inn in Queens. Holding Rose by her shoulder, Pamela's eyes widen as she spots a police car coming towards them. As the car comes to a stop, an officer exits and open the back door where an exhausted but jubilated Sandra exits, walking very slowly towards Pamela and Rose, Sandra's body is in pain and she is exhausted. As the police officer looks for a moment, he returns to his car, leaving the scene. Sandra, Pamela and Rose engage in a loving embrace. For the first time in a while, they all feel safe.

Chapter Thirty-Six
The Jury of Your Peers

On April 24th, four weeks into the explosive trial that rocked the city, Sandra is sitting inside a packed Bronx courtroom listening and watching the defense make their last stance for the dirty cops, consisting of Detectives Sam Daniels, Joseph McCarthy and Tony Harris, who sits handcuffed in an orange jump suit because he could not make bail. For the past four weeks, Sandra and the officers have not taken their eyes off each other. Sandra looks for closure and justice while they look for their attorney Alvin Peachtree to pull off a miracle, while proving Sandra is no angel. As Sandra, sits next to her attorney, Dorothy White, a black woman in her late forties who dresses out of Vogue magazine. They listen closely to Peachtree, a tall lanky man in his mid fifties who specializes in defending drug dealers and organized crime members. "Ladies and gentlemen of the jury, before I close out my questioning and defense of my clients, I would like to make one last crucial point if I may. The same people that are supposed to protect and serve us may have committed a horrible crime and you can only decide if that is true in this court of law. But ladies and gentlemen, another crime is being overlooked here today: The crime committed by Sandra Lyte."

With the hisses and mumblings coming from the packed courtroom, the judge banged his gavel: "Order! I said order in this courtroom!"

Quickly standing up from her chair, attorney White says, "Objection! Your honor, my client is not on trial here and furthermore, she has not been accused of any wrong doing, including murder and I request, judge, that Mr. Peachtree please close his argument so that we may hand the decision to the jury."

Looking at Peachtree, the judge takes a long, deep breath saying, "Mr. Peachtree, I am getting quite tired of your antics; what is your point here?"

Standing up from his chair, the attorney answers, "Yes your honor; I do and it may prove that it should not just be my clients being charged for murder but also Ms. Lyte for kidnapping and accessory to the murder of Doug Gunner. Your honor, I would like to call to the stand Fred Gunner."

The courtroom doors swing open and a tall Fred Gunner enters the courtroom walking with a cane and wearing a black two-piece polyester suit. Walking up to the stand, Fred puts his hand on the bible and takes his oath while Sandra, shivering inside her body, does her very best to hide the fear she is feeling at this very moment. Setting his cane by his side, Fred looks at the desk where Sandra is sitting and strangely gives her a quick grin. Sandra, who can feel her head spinning by the second, can also see the walls crashing down around her.

Attorney Peachtree, smiling at Fred, says, "Mr. Gunner, I understand the anguish you must be going through right now and I promise that this will not take long."

People in the courtroom begin sucking their teeth and letting out sighs. Pamela, looking on quietly, mumbles, "Fuck him and Doug," as she looks at Rose, who angrily stares at Fred.

"Mr. Gunner, please tell the court the same exact account you explained to me that happened to you on the evening of February twenty-first at approximately seven o'clock that evening, and sir, it's Ok; we understand if you speak a little slowly."

Looking at the judge and then out into the crowd, Fred leans into the microphone, clearing his throat to answer, "Just like I explained to you sir, when I was watching television that night...I saw a large bright light come through my window and it hit my body, not allowing me to move or call for help."

Attorney Peachtree, stares at Fred with a perplexed look on his face, then looks over at the judge, who is staring at Fred as if he has lost his mind. Sandra is looking at her attorney while Ms. White is doing her best not to bust out in laughter. The jury is looking at each other while laughter comes from the crowd in attendance.

"Order! I said order right now!" Walking over to the bench where Fred sits, Mr. Peachtree angrily says, "Mr. Gunner, that is not what you told me, and must I remind you sir that you are under oath!"

Fred, looking out in the crowd again, catches the glance of an Italian woman sitting to his right in the middle of the crowd. The woman wearing all white gives Fred a gentle wink of her eye. Fred cannot take his eyes off the woman, who paid him a little visit a week ago while he sat in a coffee shop. Connie Marino, wife of Tony, had a little sit down with Fred, explaining to him why it would be to his best interest if he forgot about the encounter between Sandra and himself because she now considered Sandra a friend of the family.

"Mr. Gunner, please complete your statement," asks the judge, knocking Fred back into reality.

"Like I told him, judge, I woke up and a room where the aliens held me and made me watch while they chopped up my son in little pieces. Then they put me back on my own private ship, sending away..."

Banging his gavel once again to quiet the crowd, the judge looks at attorney Peachtree with little respect, asking, "Mr. Peachtree, do you have anymore case-blowing witnesses for us today?"

Looking at Fred and never taking his eyes off of him, he answers, "No, your honor, I have no further questions,"

Looking over at Fred, the judge says, "You may step down, Mr. Gunner."

With the assistance of his cane, Fred does so, walking out of the courtroom, never once looking at Sandra.

"Ladies and gentlemen of the Jury, you have heard testimonies from both sides and now the fates of these defendants are now in your hands. I ask that you carefully review all of the evidence before you and return with a decision that is fair and just. We will proceed on Monday at nine o'clock in the morning," says the judge.

*   *   *

It is now 2:22 p.m. on April 27th; outside the courtroom are news trucks and news reporters waiting anxiously because the rumor spreading like wildfire is that the jury has reached a verdict. About twenty police cars line the street as seventy police officers wearing their uniforms line the courtroom steps in solidarity.

Sandra, sitting with her attorney, shivers as the jury enters the room being lead by the jury foreman while the courtroom is full to its capacity. Reaching across the railing are Pamela and Rose, who are grabbing Sandra's shoulders.

"Ladies and gentlemen of the jury have you reached a verdict?" asks the judge.

As the male foreman stands, he answers, "Yes your honor, we have."

"What is your verdict?" asks the judge.

Reading the letter in his hand, the juror answers "We the jury finds defendants Anthony J. Harris, Samuel D. Daniels and Joseph P. McCarthy on the charges of murder in the first degree...guilty."

The courtroom explodes with screams of joy as the judge is now banging aggressively on his gavel.

"One more outburst and I will hold this courtroom in contempt. Juror, you may continue," says the judge.

"In the charge of attempted murder, we find the defendants...guilty"

With the other charges announced, Sandra's attorney and her two friends were ecstatic. As the other police officers, who were involved in lesser but still career-ending acts await their fate, the guilty detectives are being led out of the courtroom and stare at Sandra, who stares right back at them. Opening up her collar, Sandra reveals the lifelong scar inflicted on her, while at the same time, Sandra pulls from underneath her shirt a necklace that contains two wallet-size pictures of Kareem and Chaka.

Sticking them forward so that Tony Harris especially may see them, Sandra watches until they disappear behind the courtroom doors.

Rose, turning to Sandra, asks with tears in her eyes, "Can we go away now and start over?"

Sandra, putting her arms around Rose's shoulder, smiles and says, "As soon as we get out of here sweetheart." As Sandra's attorney leads them out of the courtroom, hordes of reporters and supporters begin screaming questions at her.

Final Chapter
A New Start to A New Beginning

It is July 15th and Tempe, Arizona is like an egg in a hot skillet. Sandra, Pamela and Rose are now parking their blue Lexus GS430 in front of the bookstore of Arizona State University. As the women exit the car, Rose holds a list that she looks over nervously.

"I am so afraid it has been so long since I have been in a classroom." As Sandra and Pamela smile at Rose, Sandra says, "Rose, we have complete faith in you and we know you will do well. With all that we have been through, I know this will be a piece of cake for you. Now, get inside and buy those books and we will be right here when you come out."

Rose, smiling and shaking her head confidently, happily jogs inside the crowded bookstore with her list in her hand.

As Sandra and Pamela lean against their car, Pamela says, "Sandra, I am really happy that you have decided to attend those counseling sessions. I know it has only been two weeks, but I really see a difference in the way you are carrying yourself, and I am happy for you. In addition, I think what you did concerning Kareem and Chaka was nothing short of incredible. I know they are happy you did."

Looking at Pamela with pure happiness, something she has not felt in a while Sandra replies, "Well, I would have never been able to find my mental and spiritual wellbeing if it was not for God, Rose and you, so I want to thank you for everything. As far as my babies go, it was the least I could possibly give back to them as their mother."

"Sandra, I also meant to ask you yesterday; for the past couple of days, you've been spending a lot of time at the Big Top supermarket; what is up with that?

Looking down at the ground, Sandra looks up at Pamela and says, "Just wanted to take care of someone who took care of me and taught me so much when I was lost, that is all. Hey, when she comes out, how about we drive over to the mall for some shopping, banana crunch ice cream and then we can head on home to take a swim in our real big pool?"

"Sounds like a plan to me," Pamela says laughing.

It is 3:30 p.m. in the Bronx and Ms. Carla with her cane by her side is instructing her new three volunteers, Angela, Christine and Esther, where to set the food and beverages for the patrons. A tall and large man enters the pantry sweating and holding an invoice.

"Excuse me, but I am looking for a Carla Smith."

Looking at the man while opening a very large can of fruit cocktail, Carla answers, "Good afternoon, sir, I am Carla. Can I do something for you?"

Inspecting his invoice, the man answers, "Ma'am, I am with The Big Top Food Corporation and I really think you need to come outside because someone has sent you something that you need to see."

Looking at her volunteers, Carla says, "Ladies, you keep preparing the food Ok? I will be right back." Following the man outside, Carla steps into the hot and humid street where men, women and children are already gathering for dinner.

"Ma'am, this is for you and it comes with a note." The driver leads Carla to two eighteen-wheel trailers. The driver waves at another man who walks to the back of his truck. Simultaneously, both men open the back of the trailers, revealing to a shocked and confused Carla two trailers filled to their maximum capacities with nothing but food. There is so much food that Carla will not have to worry about how she will feed her friends for a very long time. The driver who cannot help but to smile gives Carla a letter and says, "Someone must really like you."

Taking the letter, Carla slowly unfolds it and reads silently to herself "By the time you have this letter in your hands; I hope God has blessed you with good health and your loving heart. There is no way I can ever put into words how much I love you and what you will always mean to me. When I did not have a mother or a place to hide, you became that mother for me and that I will never forget. I just want you to know that I am doing much better and have learned to take life one day at a time. In addition, Rose is doing great and she speaks about you all the time. She has just started college and the first thing she said was as soon as she got her classes together, she would mail you a picture. You have brought so much love and joy to so many people. I hope this food helps at the pantry. Maybe one day real soon we can talk, but right now I am just getting myself settled and I need a little time before I can pick up a phone again, but you be sure that when I do get the courage to call someone, that someone will be you, Ms. Carla. With love and blessings for you always, I love you and will never forget you…your daughter, Sandra."

Holding the letter at her waist side, Carla cannot stop the tears from falling from her eyes as the two truckers look on. Carla, still crying, looks over at four of her regular friends who come to eat everyday "Excuse me fellas, do you think you can give me a hand unloading this into the pantry?"

In an instant, not only do the four men run over and begin to empty the trailers but so do the women and children. Within minutes, more than forty people are unloading the trailers, taking the boxes of food inside the pantry. Standing back and looking how the people help her while laughing and smiling with one another, Carla looks up to the sky and quietly says to herself, "I love you too Sandra and no matter what, we will see each other again, either in this life or in the next. God bless you baby.

*   *   *

Now three o'clock in the morning and the Arizona temperature at around fifty degrees, Sandra is standing sixty feet from the back of her home. In front of her sits, two handcrafted marble tombstones, one pink and the other blue. Before Sandra left New York, she had her children's bodies dug up and removed from the one hundred dollar pine boxes Doug had them buried into previously. Paying top dollar to have their bodies restored the best they could, Sandra made sure Kareem and Chaka had the proper burial they deserved.

Getting on her knees, Sandra looks at the tombstones that have an eight-inch square cut out with each child's picture encased within six-inch thick glass. In the middle of the tombstones, a constant blue flame burns in their memory. "Hey boo boo's mommy could not sleep so I figured I would come out here and pay my babies a visit. As always, I miss you and love you. I hope that you two are doing well and are getting ready for the day when mommy will be able to see you again. You will never leave my heart or my soul simply because we are one and no one will ever separate us."

Getting up and beginning to return inside, Sandra bends down so that she may kiss the top of each tombstone. Walking back towards her house Sandra can see Rose who has watched the whole scene. Sliding the patio doors open, Sandra hugs her around the neck giving her a kiss on her forehead, as Rose reveals a deck of cards so that Sandra and she can play the memory game.

To all the readers who purchased my book, I want to thank you for your support.

Before you put this book down, let's have some fun!

If *The Mouse that Roared* was ever made into a motion picture here are my picks:

Sandra Lyte	Taraji P. Henson from *Hustle and Flow*
Doug Gunner	Michael Jai White from *Spawn*
Pamela Brown	Tichina Arnold from the sitcom *Martin*
Fred Gunner	Danny Glover from *The Color Purple*
Rose Garden	Camille Winbush from the sitcom *The Bernie Mac Show*
Tommy Davis	Kevin Bacon from *Stir of Echoes*
Tony Harris	Christopher Meloni from series *Oz* and *Homicide*
Ms. Carla	Della Reese from *Touched by an Angel*
Bucky	Stu "Large" Riley from *Shaft*
Tony Marino	Chazz Palminteri from *A Bronx Tale*

For more information and upcoming publications, or to tell me what your picks are for the "motion picture", you can contact me at

Dwayne Murray, Sr.
Madbo Enterprises
1444 East Gunhill Road, Suite 32
Bronx, New York 10469

Or visit my website at:

WWW.MADBOENTERPRISES.COM

Click on either my guestbook or email address, I would love to read you opinions about the book.